ROOSEVELT and Hattie

DYANN WEBB

Bloomington, IN Milton Keynes, UK

AuthorHouse™
1663 Liberty Drive, Suite 200
Bloomington, IN 47403
www.authorhouse.com
Phone: 1-800-839-8640

AuthorHouse™ UK Ltd.
500 Avebury Boulevard
Central Milton Keynes, MK9 2BE
www.authorhouse.co.uk
Phone: 08001974150

This book is a work of fiction. People, places, events, and situations are the product of the author's imagination. Any resemblance to actual persons, living or dead, or historical events, is purely coincidental.

© 2006 DYANN WEBB. All rights reserved.

No part of this book may be reproduced, stored in a retrieval system, or transmitted by any means without the written permission of the author.

First published by AuthorHouse 5/3/2006

ISBN: 1-4259-3097-2 (sc)

Library of Congress Control Number: 2006903750

Printed in the United States of America
Bloomington, Indiana

This book is printed on acid-free paper.

CHAPTER 1

The room was dimly lit and the young girl Trilly grasped the center post of the old brass bed. The pain was excruciating. She rolled her head on the sweat soaked pillow and looked at her mother with the silent question, would the child ever come? Dorie read the tortured expression. Her throat became tight and her voice silent, she was at a loss for an answer. Her daughter had been in labor for many hours and the last three were extremely hard labor. Having been mid-wife to several births she realized the delivery was taking much too long and made the quiet decision to wait another half-hour, if by then the baby hadn't arrived she would seek help. Once more she lovingly applied a cool rag to her daughter's face, gazing at her worriedly.

Dorie remembered the night her Trilly had been born. She, like the unborn child they were awaiting was also the offspring of a white father. Her thoughts then drifted to Trent, her husband. Unlike her daughter, she and Trent never hid their love for each other. They were too much in love, trying to conceal it would have been impossible. Therefore, they had lived with constant scorn and in jeopardy. Once more the loss of him weighed heavily upon her as she visualized him. Her eyes remained dry, the tears long spent. Trilly was only a year old when he was run over by a carriage, killing him instantly. To this day it was questionable in Dorie's mind as to whether it was truly an accident or intentional. Their love was a forbidden one. Trent had made the decision to take her and Trilly from Georgia, West to San Francisco hoping to escape the harshness of the Southerners, only to discover it was of no avail, a white man preferring a black woman to a white one was unthinkable, anywhere.

Trilly's shriek interrupted her thoughts. She looked up at the clock. It had only been a few minutes since the last pain ripped through her daughter's body. Again, she instructed her to bear down. Finally it happened, she could see the baby and cried with relief, "Praise the Lord Trilly, your child is on the way." Dorie grasped the tiny head that emerged and instructed her daughter to bear down once more. Exhausted, Trilly bore down, her scream momentarily drowning out the cries of the newborn boy. Dorie held the infant in her hands and was surprised by his size. He was small for taking so long to arrive. She announced, "You have a son Trilly." Weakened, Trilly gave her mother a half smile. Dorie cut the cord, counted fingers and toes, thanked the Lord and swaddled him in a blanket that had been warmed by the fireplace. She then placed him into the frayed wicker laundry basket that several days before with anticipation had been converted into a bed. Returning her attention to Trilly, she wearily looked at the clock. It had been ten minutes since the birth and she still appeared to be in labor. After birth pains didn't come this soon. Once again, her concern returned, something was wrong. Dorie made the decision to seek help but was detained by another scream. She rushed to her daughter and was shocked to witness another birth in progress. With-in minutes, a tiny girl emerged, totally enraged by the inconvenience. Amazed and in awe, Dorie stared at the second infant and exclaimed, "My Lord, Trilly, you have twins, this ones a girl." Trilly was silent. Hurriedly, Dorie cut the cord and wrapped the infant into a towel and placed her next to her brother.

Trilly was now unconscious and bleeding heavily. The door to the room opened and Elise from the flat next door stood there. "I just got home and heard a scream. Is Trilly in labor?" Dorie glanced up at the perfectly moon-shaped face of her friend and cried, "No, it's over she just had the babies and needs a doctor."

"Babies, Elise questioned with shock?"

"Yes, she's had twins and I just know she's going to die if we don't get her help, please see if you can find a doctor." Elise hurriedly left the room hoping to fulfill Dorie's request.

Watching her leave, Dorie wondered where she would find a doctor. There were no black physicians in the community right now. Old Doc Jackson died over a year ago and they were still waiting for a replacement, leaving them dependant on the doctors from the white community. Most of whom performed their services begrudgingly, never rushing to attend the calls for help from what they referred to as Nigger Town.

Almost two hours later, Elise returned with a doctor. He was a short, stubby little man sporting a thick gray handlebar moustache that resembled his eyebrows.

Trilly had only regained consciousness once while awaiting his arrival, just long enough to see her babies. After a weakened glance, she whispered, "I did good, didn't I, they're beautiful, aren't they, Mama?" Dorie took her daughter's limp hand and was shocked at how cold it had become, she gently squeezed it. "Yes, baby you did real good. Now you just have to get well and strong for them." Trilly's tired face saddened as she replied, "I'm sorry Mama, I don't think I can." Dorie pleaded, "You have to baby, were going to need you and you gotta see these babies grow." Once again the word sorry spilled slowly from Trillys mouth before she slipped back into unconsciousness.

Dorie and Elise watched with concern as the doctor examined her. After a moment, he went over to the two infants in the basket. He picked each one up and gave a quick glance. With eyes void of compassion he turned to the two women standing there worriedly and commented matter of factually, "The mother is not going to make it. Her pulse is weak and she's lost too much blood. There's nothing that can be done for her. The babies are small but appear to be healthy enough. I suggest you find a wet nurse." He motioned towards the window with his hand, "I'm sure there are plenty of them around here." With that statement, he requested his two-dollar fee.

Numbly, Dorie went to the cupboard and removed the small tin that held her meager savings. Through her tears she carefully counted out the sum he had asked for, two dollars. That was it, two dollars, to hear that her daughter was dying, she had to accept his diagnosis; there was no one else to turn to for help. Holding out the money, he eagerly removed it from her small hand. Counting the coins and assured that he had received the correct amount, the man left the room as coldly as he had entered it.

Elise held Dorie closely, crying with her, exclaiming, "I'm sorry I couldn't find a doctor anywhere Dorie, Sam Jacobs suggested I get that man since he had just delivered a colt at the livery stable. An animal doctor was all I could find." Dorie's heart sank as she tried to reassure her friend she had done the best she possibly could have.

There were no longer any screams coming from her daughter, just small whimpers. Dorie went to her side. She had begged Trilly to ask the person responsible for her pregnancy to help financially so they could afford a doctor but she refused, fearing it would cause him trouble. She accepted her daughter's decision, knowing how much she loved the man. Had her Trent wanted to keep their love a secret, she would have. Just knowing he loved her would have been enough. . Dorie removed a tear with a silk hanky Trilly had given her one Mother's day. She had assumed it would be an easy birth. After all, Trilly was a healthy eighteen- year old. She glanced across the room to the wicker basket containing the two infants, thankful for their silence and wondering if they sensed their inevitable loss.

Elise watched helplessly, her heart felt like a brick. Dorie held her daughter's hand. It was becoming colder and she rubbed it briskly, hoping to warm it and draw back the life that was slowly slipping away. The life that she had worried and cared for over these last eighteen years, the only thing Trent had left her. She moaned, "My baby, my beautiful Trilly, please don't leave me" She prayed silently, asking God to transfer the warmth and life from her body to her daughters. Several hours passed when once more the clock told her the time. It was one fifteen in the morning when Trilly left her and the twins.

Three weeks had passed since the birth of the babies and Trilly's death. Even with the help of Elise, Dorie knew she could not take care of the infants, physically or financially. She prayed for her daughter's forgiveness but for twin's sake, now named Roosevelt and Hattie, she would have to call James Marshall, their father.

Trilly had told her James Marshall was a very wealthy man. He owned several silver and copper mines. His home sat on the peninsula along with the other mansions of San Francisco's wealthy industrialists, stockbrokers and bankers. She had met James on the beach one afternoon while returning from work. Having been standing all morning at the cannery, the cool bay water soothed her feet. She wandered out further than she should have to soothe her legs as well, when a man on shore yelled to her. She couldn't tell what he was saying so she moved closer to hear what he wanted and tripped on some debris, causing her to fall underwater. He rushed to her rescue and that was the beginning of their affair. From that day on, she told Dorie they had met at least twice a week. Once she realized she was pregnant and began showing the signs, she quit seeing James, knowing it would create a problem for him. She knew he loved her and never expected him to give up his lifestyle with San Francisco's elite for her. She explained to Dorie that she had no desire to put him in harms way because of their love. She planned to raise the baby secretly and continue to see James as much as possible after the birth.

Dorie sighed wearily, shaking her thoughts. Too much work had been missed since the twin's arrival. She needed to get back to the cannery, where both she and Trilly had worked these past few years. Tomorrow, she would meet Mr. James Marshall and ask for help in raising the twins. Tomorrow, would tell her just how much her Trilly really meant to the man.

James Marshall sat at the long, oval; linen covered table, reading the newspaper, while sipping coffee from a gold rimmed, white porcelain cup, which he felt, was much too delicate for him. He momentarily looked up and peered at Lillian his wife, as she buttered her toast. As far as he was concerned this was a simple task, but for Lillian, each piece was done daintily, slowly making sure both slices were covered completely. She wasn't a beautiful woman, but she was a good woman. He had come to the conclusion that he had fallen in love with her because of her love for him. She made him feel important, something he strove for. There had been years of hard work before his mines hit the lode. Lillian's father was one of San Francisco's leading bankers. Even though he was successful himself, marrying into the Sheldrick family reinforced his credibility with the circle of elite people he desired to be apart of. He had a special love for this woman but nothing like the love he had for Trilly. Strange, he thought, how many types of love there are. Trying to return his attention to the newspaper was unsuccessful. The minute Trilly entered his mind; he could think of nothing else. It had been too long since he had seen her. She informed him that she had to go away for awhile, promising to let him know when she returned but refusing to tell him where she was going. He silently questioned, what had happened? Where did she go? Why did she just disappear from his life? She promised to let him know of her return but it had been almost three months. He sighed, folded the paper, looked at the watch that dangled from a gold chain on his gray cashmere vest and exclaimed to Lillian that it was time to go to the office. She smiled, knowing that every week-day morning at precisely eight o'clock he made the same announcement.

Dorie put on her best attire, which included her favorite black straw hat and waited for the trolley that would take her uptown to the white community, hoping to meet with Mr. James Marshall. It would be a long ride and she would receive many curious glances. Entering the white mans world made her extremely nervous.

James sat behind the rich mahogany desk, peering out the window, which offered a view of the bay. Pride and satisfaction surged through him. He owned the beautiful two-story structure; a sigh escaped him, the Marshall Building. Thus far, all his goals had been achieved. A tap on the door interrupted his thoughts. His secretary entered the room announcing, "There's a Mrs. Patterson here to see you. Lowering her voice, she whispered, "She's a Negro."

He was surprised, as he knew Trilly would never have come there to see him and a person would not describe her as a Negro. Had she not mentioned her heritage, he would never have guessed. He decided it could only be her mother, but what would cause her to seek him out? He found it hard to believe that Trilly would send her to let him know of her return.

Had she told her of their relationship? Anxious and curious he replied, "Send her in Mrs. Hansen."

Dorie trembled as she entered the rich wood paneled room. Hopefully, what she had to say would come out of her mouth correctly, she had been silently praying for verbal assistance from the Lord while nearing the tall building and his office. She crossed the room on weak knees, feeling uneasy walking on the thick jewel toned oriental carpet that caressed the heels of her shoes. James stood to greet her. Even though she was darker than Trilly, he immediately recognized the apparent likeness, which shortened his breath.

"Mrs. Patterson, pleased to meet you." He offered her a chair and once seated, questioned, "Now, what brings you to me?"

Dorie hesitated before replying in a lower than normal voice, "Mr. Marshall, I'm Trilly's mother and she told me all about you. She loved you very much. The words Trilly loved him warmed him momentarily until he realized it was said in a past tense. His heart now felt as though it was beating from inside his stomach and he questioned with fear, "What do you mean, loved?" Tears welled up in Dorie's eyes as they always did when she had to hear herself say that Trilly was dead. "She died birthing. She didn't want to tell you of her pregnancy, fearing it would cause trouble. I pray my daughter will forgive me for coming to you but the twins are yours Mr. Marshall and I just can't take care of them. I have to return to work at the cannery. They are beautiful and healthy, a boy and a girl."

James returned to his chair in silent shock. He had heard her talking about the babies, but the words "Trilly died," were all he could think about at the moment, his beautiful, Trilly. She had been so full of life. My God, what had he done to her? Was he responsible for her death? The thought of never being able to hold her again and confess his love for her was more than he thought he could bear. Why didn't she tell him? He could have gotten her the best doctors? Did she think he didn't love her enough, that he would worry about only himself and not her? Slowly, the babies came to his mind.

After what seemed forever to Dorie, he finally spoke, asking her where the twins were and if he could see them.

"They're at my place Mr. Marshall and yes, of course you can see them. He walked to her, helping her out of the chair and putting his arm around her. "I would like to see them now." Dorie looked at him with concern. "I will take you if you don't mind having to go to Nigger Town!" "Not at all, he replied, let's go."

James had to convince Dorie that it was quite safe to ride in his new horseless carriage. She sat on the soft, brown leather seat praying that once he cranked the frightening machine; it wouldn't take off without him. Her heart quickened, as she heard and felt it come to life. "Please hurry and get in here with me Mr. Marshall."

Pulling himself onto the seat, he apologized for scaring her. As they drove from town, he told Dorie how much he loved Trilly and was ashamed for not taking better care of her. He would have helped her had he known of her condition. Dorie knew that many times he had tried to give Trilly money but she wouldn't accept it, stating "I don't want to be paid for being in love. It would be wrong." She tried to assure the gentleman next to her that she believed him and that her daughter had told her of his generous offers.

As they reached their destination, his heart sank. This was where his beloved Trilly had lived, in run-down buildings, spaced only a few feet apart, their exteriors showing the ravages of time. Cracked and peeling paint appeared to be trying to escape from the worn boards beneath it. He followed her up concrete steps that sported large cracks from previous earthquakes. Trilly had endured this while he sat in his big house enjoying all his wealth? Shame overwhelmed him as they entered the small flat. It was clean and orderly, defiant of the exterior surroundings.

Elise stood to greet them, smiling sadly as Dorie introduced her. James remembered Trilly telling him of her fondness for the woman. His heart quickened at the sound of a baby's cry and his eyes followed the sound to a basket sitting next to an old brass bed. Slowly he walked towards it. The planks on the floor creaked under his weight. He looked down with amazement on the two little figures snuggled so closely together that they appeared to be joined. He didn't think he could have children. Twelve years of marriage with Lillian had left them childless. Dorie informed him, "Their names are Roosevelt and Hattie if that's alright with you Mr. Marshall?"

He smiled and told her they were good names. He leaned down and picked up his son, tenderly kissing him on the head. He studied him for a moment and exclaimed, "He's a fine boy," and returned him to the basket. He proceeded to pick up Hattie. Her cry had turned into a whimper. Once more he studied the face. They were both equally beautiful, perfect, just like their mother. With unashamed tears in his eyes, he turned to Dorie, once more asking forgiveness. He set Hattie down. Reaching into his pocket he pulled out a handkerchief and wiped his eyes. He replaced it and questioned, "How old are they?" Dori replied, "Three weeks."

"Did Trilly have a decent burial"? Dori sadly informed him that she was buried without a marker. James exclaimed, that will be corrected. Choose the marker you want for her, money is no object, she deserves the best. Tell the stone maker to send me the bill, here's my card. He then removed his wallet, placing several large bills in Dorie's hand. "Take this as care money for the twins until I can make arrangements to have them brought to me. I'll be back for them as soon as I can. Please trust me." Excusing himself, he left the room leaving Elise and Dorie staring at the more than generous donation.

He barely remembered the ride back to the office. He was too bereft with all that had happened. He remembered the first time he met Trilly. The minute he retrieved her from the water, he knew he wanted more than just directions from her, he wanted her. Never once had he strayed from his wife, but this was uncontrollable. His heart skipped a beat as he relived that meeting. A carriage swerved, and a man yelled, cursing his horseless vehicle. Startled, James drew himself from his stupor and concentrated on the twins. The challenge was going to be getting Lillian to accept them. Like he had always said, "She is a good woman," but this would be a lot to ask of her. Having mistresses were quietly accepted in their circles and she had never questioned if he had taken one. Would she be horrified and disappointed in him? He truly didn't know how she would react. All he knew for sure was that he owed it to Trilly to take care of their children, no matter what the consequences.

Dorie was pleased with the outcome of her visit with James Marshall. She could understand how Trilly had fallen love with him. There was something about him that made you feel you were in the presence of a gentle power. She guessed him to be in his early forties. He stood tall. His chestnut brown hair showed a small amount of graying around the temples, giving him a distinguished look. She gazed at the money that had been placed in her hand and took a deep sigh of relief. Everything was going to be okay. She would do as he asked. She would trust him.

As he had done these past few nights, James lay next to Lillian wondering how to admit his affair with Trilly. Having to ask her to accept the fact that he had taken a mistress, much less suggesting they care for the offspring's of that union seemed more and more unlikely. He had never lied to her in their twelve years of marriage but for Roosevelt and Hatties sake he made the decision not to confess. It would be better for both Lillian and the twins. He would think of something else, something that would hopefully get her to accept them. Once more, his thoughts drifted to Trilly. The beautiful cameo shaped face and sensitive hazel eyes that had looked at him so lovingly. She was so young to have been taken away. How he longed to hold her again.

Lillian awoke, once more being disturbed by James restlessness. He had interfered with her sleep these last few nights leaving her to wonder what was upsetting him. After a few moments of wondering, she asked, "James, why are you so restless?"

"I'm sorry, he replied, unaware of the fact that he might be disturbing her as he sorted through his memories and problem. "It's just the copper mine."

"Anything serious," she asked with concern, moving closer to him.

"Yes, an equipment problem but I think I have it solved." The beginning of the lies, he thought sadly. Content with his answer, she nestled to him and returned to sleep, leaving him once again alone with his thoughts.

CHAPTER 2

True to his words, James kept in touch with Dorie, assuring her that he was making arrangements for Roosevelt and Hattie to be welcomed into their new home. Dorie pondered as she prepared the twins bottles. How was he going to explain them? With a sigh, she reminded herself to have confidence in him. All she could do was try to be patient and wait. Hopefully, her long absence at the cannery hadn't caused the loss of her job. The money she received from James Marshall had been more than sufficient thus far, but what would she do once the twins were gone. Once more she decided not to worry about it. Roosevelt and Hattie were her main concern. She was sure James Marshall would take care of everything. He seemed a good and sincere man. After all, Trilly loved him and that was good enough for her.

Elliott Donlan sat behind his desk fascinated with the story his client was telling him. Actually, James was more than just a client; he was his best friend. They met in Nevada when James was still working his mine. As a young overly eager lawyer he had gone there not to dig for silver, but dig up business from the miners. His goal was to convince the miners they needed his assistance to legally protect their claims. He remembered the day he was sitting in the claims office when James came to declare his stake. Unlike so many others that entered the room loud and drunk from celebrating, James was very quiet and reserved. Immediately, Elliott knew the man was special.

He approached James and introduced himself. "I'm Elliott Donlan, here to legally protect you and that claim you just staked." James stared at him momentarily as if convincing himself whether he would need such a service, then held out his calloused hand and replied, "You're hired. I'm James Marshall, and I do believe I can use you. I've worked hard and for a long time Mr. Donlan and I don't want to lose one cent of that hard earned money due to ignorance. I have to admit; at this point I'm nothing more than a toiling miner but I intend to learn what I need to know and how to handle my newly acquired wealth myself. Until then, I will need your help." Fourteen years later, he was still under James employment and not because James hadn't learned to handle his wealth, in fact, he had more than tripled it playing the stock market. It had just become too time consuming to control it himself.

Completing his story, Elliott was silently surprised that his friend had taken a mistress. He just hadn't seemed the type. Even more shocking was the fact she was Negro. As an attorney he hoped that his training over the years to hide his thoughts and remain expressionless no matter how shocked hadn't deceived him. He agreed with James that the best way to get the twins accepted by Lillian was not to confess his affair. The plan James had devised would be put into action. A telegram would be delivered to his home, informing him that his long lost younger sister had died giving birth to twins. Her husband had died several months before, leaving the twins orphans. The death bed note would read, "Please James, I beg of you, take care of my babies, there is no one else."

James felt secure with his plan. He really did have a sister, Maureen. He hadn't seen or heard from her since she left the country sixteen years ago. She spent three years with him at the mining camps, cooking and doing some digging of her own until she met and fell in love with a Frenchman. The man became homesick, sold his mine and took her with him.

Elliott assured James that he could make arrangements for a telegram to be delivered from Europe and he would handle all the details. The two friends shook hands. "Thank you Elliott, James said as he tightened his grip. I knew I could depend on you!"

"After all these years you should know that," Elliot exclaimed. James patted him on the shoulder. "You're a good friend."

The cry shattered the night's silence, first Roosevelt, and then Hattie. Dorie looked at the old clock, resenting the hour, it was eleven p.m. Being so small and incapable of drinking much milk at one time, feedings were often. Slowly she made her way towards the icebox and removed two bottles. After heating them, came the decision as to which child would be held for the feeding and which would receive a propped bottle. This feeding she decided it would be the one that was crying the hardest, Hattie. She picked up her grand daughter and looked over at Roosevelt. He seemed quite content not being held through his feeding

Hattie nestled close to Dorie's ample breast as she drank vigorously from the bottle. Dorie whispered, "How small you are my little Hattie, just like your mama was." Dorie watched the lids that covered the infant's eyes flutter as if to show off the already long, dark lashes. She was light skinned, even more so than Trilly had been. As for Roosevelt, he was the larger of the two and bigger boned. Even though he was as fair as Hattie, his facial characteristics if looked at closely would show signs of Negro blood, but only if for some reason it was suspected. Once more, the feeding was short and Dorie placed Hattie in the basket next to her brother, smiling as she observed the way she instinctively snuggled herself next to Roosevelt. She tucked a blanket around them, hoping her Trilly was able to observe them from heaven.

While lying in bed, trying to get back to sleep, her thoughts drifted to the Marshall's. James continued to keep in close touch with her and there had been more than enough money received to support her and the twins. She was overwhelmed by his kindness, remembering him asking her if she would consider becoming the twin's nanny. He explained it would be a way for her to remain with her grandchildren. She readily accepted. No more cannery and to remain with the twins was more than she could have ever hoped for. Once again she understood Trilly's love for him. He was a good man, but what about Mrs. Marshall? What kind of person was she? A yawn escaped her and eventually the darkness and still of the night enabled her to return to sleep.

As James stared out his office window he noticed how calm the bay was, which in turn calmed him. He marveled at how often the bay created his mood. If it was rough and stormy he became restless. Silently, he was thankful for the calmness being that this was the day the telegram was to be delivered at his home around dinner time announcing the twins and Maureen's death bed wish. It had taken over a month to set everything up and he figured it would take equally as long to have the twins supposedly arrive from Europe. He pulled out his pocket watch and realized that quite some time had slipped by while he was lost in thought. It was time to go home, dinner would be ready shortly.

He watched Lillian as he awaited the letters arrival. She was sorting through her dinner with her fork as if trying to determine what was worth eating.

He questioned, "Lillian, what's wrong? You seem disappointed in the food. Should we find a new cook?"

"No, the cook is wonderful." Her gaze left the plate and met his. It's not the food. I just can't seem to get excited over much of anything lately, food, home, or even the woman's club." James couldn't have been more pleased. With her feeling that way, what better time to have the letter arrive? As he consoled her he heard the front door bell ring. Tullah, the head servant answered it. A moment later the young black girl entered the room announcing, "There's a man at the door with a telegram for you Mr. Marshall." He took a deep breath and replied, "Thank you Tullah, I'll take care of it."

"A telegram, Lillian exclaimed, suddenly coming to life. Who would send us one of those?" James gave her a concerned look before replying, "I don't know but we will soon find out."

Lillian felt the excitement of suspense as he left the room and anxiously awaited his return. James entered the room with the yellow page in his had. "What is it James? What does it say?" He passed the message to her and watched closely as she read, hoping to detect what effect it was having on her. He was becoming nervous, unaware that she was reading it for a second time. Her heart ached as she read the words, "Mr. Marshall, I regretfully inform you that your sister Maureen Dushay has died from childbirth. She delivered twins, a boy and a girl. Unfortunately, her husband is also deceased, leaving the children orphans. As requested we are forwarding her last wishes. "My dear James, I pray this letter finds you after so long. I regret my lack of communication and I beg of you, take care of my babies. There is no one else." Love, your sister, Maureen.

Lillian set the letter down and looked at him sympathetically for a moment before exclaiming, "I remember you telling me you had a sister. She married a Frenchman, a miner and went to France with him. Poor thing, she lost her husband and then her own life. Those babies will never know their mother or father." James agreed it was a sad situation, exclaiming that he of course, could not honor Maureen's request. It would be too much to ask of her to take on two infant children. He held his breath, waiting for a reply.

"Nonsense, James," Lillian was shocked at his comment. We have to honor a deathbed wish, she was family. I just got through telling you how empty I've been feeling. We can't seem to have children of our own. It will be good for us to have more than just each other."

More than just each other! The statement sent a sickening guilt rushing through his body. He fought the feeling, once more telling himself there are so many kinds of love and he did love Lillian. She was very special to him and right now he loved her more than ever.

"If you think you're ready for something like this Lillian, I will be forever grateful on behalf of my sister." She smiled and took hold of his hand. "Yes, James, I'm more than willing. In fact I will be anxiously looking forward to their arrival." James hoped she hadn't detected his sigh of relief.

"I'll contact the person responsible for the telegram and make arrangements for the twin's passage to the states first thing in the morning. Thank you Lillian." He kissed her gently. That night he was finally able to sleep soundly, he would have his children with him.

Dorie heard from James. He informed her it would be another month before she and the twins could join him, explaining to her that there was a very important time element involved with the transition. He would brief her when the time was near as to what she should know and do, pleading with her to remain patient.

At the breakfast table several days later, James told Lillian that he had secured a nanny for the children. "Wonderful, she replied, everything is working out nicely. I have only a short time to ready a room for them but it's going to be a fun project." James was beginning to feel he had done her a favor. He hadn't seen her excited as this in a long time.

She continued, "I'm going shopping this afternoon. There are so many things they are going to need." He smiled, noticing that she was hurriedly buttering her toast, proving she was anxious to get started with her day.

Elliott sat at his desk, carefully going over everything that had been planned for the twin's arrival at the Marshall household. As far as he was concerned, everything was going well. He realized the success of the procedure depended on the people involved. The grandmother for one and her friend Elise, whom he had been assured, was a close friend of Dorie's and would do nothing to expose them. The only thing that could go wrong would be Maureen's reappearance. Sadly, he had to inform James their story was almost true. His sister died several years ago of tuberculosis. She was childless.

Lillian spent the afternoon at Berkfield's Department Store, carefully selecting items for the twins. It didn't take long before the clerks became excited after realizing two of everything would be her standard order. Their training had taught them not to question customers. This quieted their curiosity but did nothing to quench it. After all, this was one of San Francisco's elite, buying doubles of baby clothing, furniture and accessories with no apparent signs of a pregnancy. Even if she were pregnant and shopping early, why would she be buying everything in pairs? How would she know she was going to have a double birth, much less a boy and a girl?

Satisfied she had accomplished her mission, Lillian requested everything be delivered to her home as soon as possible, magnifying the clerks curiosity and leaving them whispering to each other as she departed.

Dorie packed her meager belongings into a small worn, brown leather suitcase as she prepared herself to be picked up by Mr. Marshall. This was the day she was to be taken to his home and introduced as the twin's nanny. She was scheduled to arrive several days before Roosevelt and Hattie. Elise would care for them until James returned to claim his children. She observed the tiny, helpless infants once more. Oh, how she had grown to love them in such a short time. As always they were nestled as close as they possibly could get to each other. She reached down and patted each of their silken heads, "Goodbye, my little ones, I will see you soon.

James arrived as planned and once more she had to endure the horseless carriage. Even though she had ridden in it once before, she still feared it. Sensing her fear, James exclaimed, "Relax Dorie, it's just like a horse, but easier to command. A horse can be startled but not this. I can stop it much faster than a horse if I see a dangerous situation."

Dorie wasn't convinced in the least but replied, "If you say so Mr. Marshall. I'll try to remember those things." On the way James briefed her on the plan he and Elliott had devised. He informed her that Lillian had been told that she had cared for a pair of twins for thirteen years. They out grew the need for a nanny when they were sent to finishing school. "I know our having to lie is uncomfortable for both of us Dorie but it had to be done for the twin's sake. You understand that don't you?" "Yes, Mr. Marshall, I know." She silently worried if they would be able to carry it through.

They arrived at the house and Dorie took a deep breath as she stared at the mansion, which would now be her and the twin's new home. "My, how the whites live," she said silently to herself. The magnificent structure was three stories high and flaunted two turrets. The beveled glass windows and doors glittered in the sunlight. A dozen stairs led up to a porch that surrounded the exterior, decorated with wicker tables and chairs. The gardens were the most beautiful thing she had ever seen. A multitude of rose bushes showed off large blossoms in shades of red, pink, yellow and white. Purple wisteria climbed the ornate wrought iron fence and flowers she couldn't identify bordered the pathways.

James held her arm as he helped her out of the automobile. He couldn't help but notice the look of amazement on her face. He understood after witnessing where her and Trilly had lived, leaving him once again feeling guilty for his lifestyle. He was anxious to make it up to Trilly by sharing what he had with Dorie and the twins. As they climbed the stairs, Dorie marveled at one rose bush in particular. It had smaller blossoms than the other roses. The petals were two different colors and the mixture made it more beautiful, much like her Roosevelt and Hattie

Tullah, the housemaid greeted them at the door. After the introduction, James requested that she show Dorie to her new quarters. Dorie followed, relieved to see that she would not be the only black woman in the household. They climbed the lush carpeted staircase to the second story. Tullah opened the door for her and stood aside with a pleased look. She was happy for Dorie as to be so fortunate to have a room on the second floor. It was a small room carefully decorated. A canopied mahogany bed and matching chest of drawers sat on a floral carpet. Next to the fireplace a winged back chair invited you to share promise of warmth during the winter months

"Look Dorie, Tullah's voice drew her attention, "Here's the children's room." She led her through an adjoining door leading to the nursery. Dorie felt a lump grow in her throat as she observed the room. It was filled with doubles of everything, two chests of drawers, two cribs, two rocking chairs, and music box for each child. A doll and tiny toy train made it apparent that both a boy and girl shared the room. Truly, the Marshall's had gone all out for the twins.

"You'll like it here, Tullah exclaimed, Mr. and Mrs. Marshall, they are good people. I guess Mr. Marshall's sister went and died after giving birth to those two babies."

"Yes, that's what I was told, that's very sad," Dorie replied.

"Well, I think it's a good thing for them babies to be here. Mrs. Marshall will be a fine mother." Dorie momentarily begrudged the statement feeling that her Trilly should be there to mother them. Observing Tullah, she guessed her to be in her early teens. She questioned, "How long have you worked for the Marshall's Tullah?"

Tullah smiled, exposing a set of dimples and perfect teeth. "Five years. My uncle got me a position here after my aunt died. She had been with Mrs. Marshall for most of Mrs. Marshall's life. My uncle works the stables. For awhile he feared he might lose his job when Mr. Marshall bought that horseless carriage but was told not to worry, they would still have the horses for pleasure riding. Well, I better get back downstairs. When you get hungry, the kitchen is just down the stairs and through the door to the right of the dining room. The cook's name is Angie. Just introduce yourself and she will get you something to eat." Dorie thanked her and watched Tullah's exit, then she proceeded to unpack her suitcase. Her small stack of possessions existed of her wedding photo, a picture of Trilly, two changes of clothing, a nightgown, her favorite black straw hat, the old clock and her Bible. She placed the Bible on the nightstand next to her bed, wishing Trilly's picture and her wedding photo could be placed along side of it as they always had been but knew better. Instead, they were lovingly tucked away in the chest of drawers. An hour later, she was summoned to meet Mrs. Marshall.

Nervously, she entered the parlor. James stood to greet her, taking her hand he introduced her, "Lillian, this is Dorie."

Dorie studied the woman before her. She wasn't a pretty woman. She appeared frail and was small in stature. Her long dark brown hair was pinned up and covered with a net. Lillian greeted Dorie with a smile that instantly reflected an inner beauty. She stated "I understand you are familiar with the raising of twins Dorie, it must have been difficult after all those years with the Delaney family to no longer be needed. I assume you suffered much like a parent would when the children outgrow them." Dorie managed a nervous smile and replied, "Yes, ma'am but now I am looking forward to meeting my new wards." "Good, Lillian exclaimed, because I'm going to need a lot of help being that I have never had children of my own." James stepped forward and questioned, "I hope you are pleased with the nursery and your quarters Dorie. "Yes sir, I'm very pleased. "Well, James announced, the twins are due to arrive in a couple of days, so rest up. If you feel we have neglected something that you or the children might need, please take it up with Lillian." Dorie nodded, "I'll do that Mr. Marshall, thank you." She left the room, hopeful that she had pleased them both. Like Mr. Marshall, she didn't enjoy the lies but knew it was their only choice.

Once more Elise looked out the window, waiting for James Marshall. She would be thankful for his arrival. It would relieve her of the responsibility of the twins. Returning to her chair she sighed, wondering how all of this was going to turn out.

She worried for her friend. Were they really going to be able to pass the twins off as white and if they should ever be discovered, what then? Another sigh escaped as she glanced towards the basket containing the infants.

James pulled out his watch as he climbed the stairs, upset that he was late.

Today he would finally have his children. Anxiously he knocked on the door.

Elise stood and hand pressed her clothes, realizing that she must have dozed off.

She opened the door, admiring the distinguished man standing there. "Please come in, Mr.

Marshall, the twins are ready to join their grandma."

James entered the room. The aroma of a stew simmering on the stove made him realize he hadn't eaten since breakfast. He bent down and placed his arms around the full figured woman, "Thank you Elise for all that you have done, please accept this payment your efforts. He placed several large bills in her hand which she graciously accepted, then walked to the basket and momentarily admired his son and daughter before whispering, "Let's go home."

Lillian paced the floor. James should have returned by now. He was almost an hour late. Hadn't the twins arrived as scheduled? Finally she heard Tullah's excited greeting. "My goodness Mr. Marshall, they're so tiny!"

She wanted to run and meet him but suddenly found herself frightened at the thought of seeing the twins and becoming a mother. Standing there frozen, she waited for James to come into the parlor. He entered carrying the basket and smiled as he set it down beside her. Lillian thought her heart would burst as she observed the tiny twosome. "Oh, James, they're so small."

"Yes, I know, he replied but they're very healthy." Roosevelt let out a cry, and

James suggested she pick him up. Unsure of herself, she carefully picked up the small unfamiliar person and felt proud of the fact he quit crying. She held him close. Hattie appeared unconcerned with the episode. Meanwhile, Tullah had gone upstairs to inform Dorie of the twins arrival. Dorie anxiously entered the parlor eager to see her grandchildren.

"Lillian exclaimed, "Look Dorie, aren't they wonderful?" Dorie answered with pride, "Yes, Mrs. Marshall, they sure are beautiful babies." Lillian returned Roosevelt to the basket and James handed it to Dorie. She anxiously accepted her wards, thankful for the reunion. Tullah followed closely as Dorie headed for the nursery.

Lillian asked James as to whether or not the twins had been named. He informed her that the people he received them from referred to them as Roosevelt and Hattie.

"Well, those are strange names, she replied, certainly not French. Obviously your sister didn't have time to name them. After a moments thought she exclaimed, "That can be changed."

Change their names," James questioned?

"Yes, she continued. I'm assuming that we will be adopting them, so we should have the right to name them. Surely your sister would want us to." He shook his head in agreement, wondering how Dorie would feel about it.

CHAPTER 3

Dorie lovingly changed the twins and put aside the two small gowns she had made, being the Marshall's had bought them so much fine clothing. She requested two bottles of milk to be brought up from the kitchen and Tullah eagerly returned with the order before questioning, "Why are they both in the same crib?" Disliking still another lie, Dorie explained, "The twins I raised were almost a year old before we could separate them. I have a feeling these two little ones will put up a fight if we try separating them this soon. See how they cling to each other?" Tullah nodded and Dorie continued, "I'll know when the time is right."

Tullah handed her the bottles, and asked, "Do you suppose that since Mrs. Marshall isn't here I could help with the feeding?" Dorie was pleased with her eagerness to participate. "Thank you Tullah, I would appreciate it." They both took their wards to the rocking chairs and Dorie inquired, do you have children Tullah?"

"No, but I wish I did, but I'm not even married yet. Sometimes I fear I'm going to die before I get any of the pleasures of life, like falling in love"

"Why would you say such a thing?" Dorie asked with concern.

"Well, first you have to meet a man and I'm almost always here, tending to the Marshall household. I met someone at church once. That's about the only place I go other than the marketplace. He was so handsome. He talked me into joining the choir. The problem was, I had to attend practice once a week and to do that I had to go across town in the evening. As you well know, it's not safe for a Negro to travel at night in the white man's community. I got frightened and Willie, that's what his name was, volunteered to take me back home that first night. We were stopped several times by whites, wanting to know what we were doing in town after dark. That was my only trip to choir practice. Willie decided we were both in harms way and I agreed. Oh, Dorie, if you could have seen the look on those white men's faces. All we wanted to do was to sing in the church choir and be together." She looked down. Hattie had fallen asleep.

"Well, whatever happened to Willie," Dorie asked anxiously?

Tullah continued, "You can't get nowhere going with a man if you only see him for a few hours after church, one day a week. He asked me to move back to our community and get work there but I was too frightened to walk away from what I have here. I feel safe and secure with the Marshall's. Willie ended up marrying the Deacon's niece. Sometimes I feel I made a bad mistake and should have gone with him but security was something I never had until I found it here. I was just too scared."

Dorie was saddened by the story and once again thought of her beloved Trent. The two women rocked as they silently mourned their losses.

James sat and watched Lillian with her toast. This morning she only had it half buttered and stopped. She was in deep thought. He decided it was her first day of motherhood and she was more than likely overwhelmed. "Are you alright this morning Lillian?"

She jumped slightly at the sound of his voice before answering. "Aaron and Allison Marshall, what do you think of those names, she asked as she came out of her trance?"

"Aaron and Allison." James repeated the names several times as if to digest them along with his meal. "Yes, I like them."

"Good, she said with pride. As of today, they will no longer be Roosevelt and Hattie."

"Will you be tending the children with Dorie this morning," he asked? A smile covered her face as she daintily set down her teacup. "Yes, I'm looking forward to it. Although I have to admit, it scares me just a little." James reassured her, "Nothing to worry about my dear, I'm sure your motherly instincts will take over. If not, you have Dorie." He gulped down the last of his morning coffee, made his usual announcement, kissed her and left for the office.

Dorie sent a message with Tullah to inform Mrs. Marshall that if she wished to participate, it was time to bathe the twins. Lillian climbed the stairs, becoming nervous as she approached the nursery. Never having children of her own, or even a sibling, she wondered, if she would be capable enough to be of any kind of help.

Dorie was pleased to see her enter the room and greeted her, "Good morning Mrs. Marshall, their baths are ready." Lillian was warmed by her smile and questioned, "What would you like me to do Dorie?" She pointed to Roosevelt and replied, "You take him and I'll take Hattie, if that's alright with you?" "Yes, that will be just fine."

She watched as Dorie merged Hattie into the tub. Carefully mimicking her, she picked up Roosevelt and brought him to join his sister in the warm sudsy water. The two women smiled at each other as they performed their act of love. With baths completed, they sat and chatted as the twins drank their bottles.

Lillian exclaimed, "Dorie I have come up with names for the twins. I detest the names those people gave them. James and I decided on Aaron and Allison. Dorie's heart sank heavily and it took a moment to answer. She also knew Lillian was innocent of the hurt she had just inflicted on her. She cleared her throat and answered, "Those are fine names." Silently, Dorie wondered how easy it was going to be to call them Aaron and Allison, after all she had been calling them Roosevelt and Hattie for two months now. It had been the last thing she could do for her daughter, naming her children for her, and now that was taken away. She looked at her grandchildren and told herself, "In my heart, you will always be Roosevelt and Hattie.

Lillian was pleased with the way the morning had gone. She was already very fond of Dorie. The dark woman's confidence with the children and her friendly nature had set her immediately at ease. She looked forward to returning to the nursery for the noon feeding.

James sat behind his desk in deep thought. He felt everything was going to be alright. Elliott called anxious to hear how the twin's arrival went and was equally as pleased with the outcome. James shrugged his shoulders, forcing himself to concentrate on business at hand, the stock market. "You're a father now. You have more than Lillian to provide for." The silent statement and a mental picture of the twins caused a smile to spread across his face.

It was Lillian's turn to host the Women's Club. Despite Dories help, the twins had taken much of her time, leaving her ill prepared. Tullah entered the room announcing Mrs. Thomas had arrived. She came to discuss the details for the next meeting. Lillian sighed, instructing Tullah to show her into the parlor. She wished she could refuse the responsibility of the meeting but knew she must not, it was her social obligation.

Vera Thomas stood in front of the large leaded glass window. Her medium nicely shaped frame silhouetted by the sun. As Lillian approached her, she once again marveled to herself how someone could be that pale. The large brown eyes and dark hair were such a contrast next to the chalk white face. Still, it was a pretty face. The day dress she wore was gray and tailored.

"Lillian, what's going on? You're the talk of the town?" She kissed Lillian softly on the cheek and continued, "It's been said that you have been purchasing baby goods. Are you pregnant and if so why didn't you tell me? I've always considered myself your best friend."

Lillian listened to the barrage of questions. She considered Vera a good friend, they grew up together and both were from successful families. They had attended finishing school together and she was the maid of honor at her wedding. "I'm sorry Vera, but there has been so little time. I'm not pregnant, but I am a mother now. James sister died giving birth to twins, leaving them orphans. Her death wish was that James and I raise them. They are here with us now and they are wonderful."

Vera stared at her friend in disbelief, waving her gloved hand in front of her face dramatically, as if trying to prevent herself from fainting. (An act they learned in finishing school, if one was shocked.) "You mean to tell me they are here, right now?" Lillian replied "Yes."

Vera continued the questioning. "Are they boys or girls? Are they identical? How old are they?" Lillian replied, "A boy and a girl, not identical and they are three months old, come, let me show them to you."

Walking to the nursery, Vera inquired if she had help with the children. "Yes, of course, James secured a nanny for them almost immediately. As they entered the nursery, Vera immediately noticed the outcome of Lillian's shopping spree at Berkshires that had been the talk of the woman's club.

Dorie stood to greet them as they entered the room. Lillian introduced the two women and Vera scanned Dorie for a moment before acknowledging the introduction, making her uneasy. The twins were awake which pleased Lillian. Observing them, Vera exclaimed, "They're so small."

"Yes, but they are perfect," Lillian replied as she picked up Allison to show her off. Vera admired the child and exclaimed, "Oh, she is a beauty isn't she, and look at those eye lashes! Well, you're right, they may not be identical but both are beautiful." After several minutes with the twins they returned to the parlor to discuss the upcoming meeting. Before the discussion began, Vera questioned, "Just out of curiosity Lillian, why do they have a Negro nanny instead of an English one?"

Lillian exclaimed, "James found her for us. She has had experience raising twins. Do you realize that twins are quite different from children born of a single birth?" Vera sighed, and replied, "I guess so," and dropped the subject.

The upcoming meeting was discussed over tea and biscuits. An hour later Vera left, feeling confident Lillian would be prepared, despite her now demanding schedule.

Dorie leaned over the crib, admiring her grandchildren. She was concerned with the lady whom she had just met. Vera left her uneasy even though she showed no signs of suspicion regarding the twin's heritage. There was just something about her she didn't like. Softly, she spoke to the twins. "My little ones, Good Lord willing, you are going to grow up in the white man's world, but I must teach you to be compassionate to blacks. The day might come when you have to return to their world." She squeezed Roosevelt's miniature hand and made the decision to keep a diary, suddenly feeling the need to leave records. "If you should ever be discovered, you should know of your mother Trilly and your grandfather." Two innocent faces stared up at her, leaving her to wonder what the future held for them.

CHAPTER 4

Tullah was eager to return to the nursery. It had been two years since the twin's arrival and she considered herself a very important person in their lives. They always squealed with delight when she entered the room. She and Dorie were their companions. Lillian participated as much as possible but her social life limited her. Aaron and Allison had bonded with the two colored women that tended to their needs. As for James Marshall, he would stop by the nursery every morning on his way to breakfast, never ceasing to marvel at the twosome, seeing Trilly in Allison and a small part of himself in Aaron and always hoping it would go undetected. They would run to him the minute he stepped into the room, always as fascinated with him as he was with them. He realized their fascination was due to the fact he was the only male they had contact with. After all, they were around women ninety per-cent of the time.

Tullah rushed into the room. "Sorry I'm late Dorie."

Dorie looked up from the novel she was reading, "That's alright it gave me time to finish the last pages of this book. This was the day of the week that Tullah was to care for the twins so that Dorie had a free day. Sometimes when she didn't feel the need to leave the premises, Mrs. Marshall had granted her permission to work in the gardens, if so desired. She loved being there with the beautiful aromatic flowers, watching the butterflies and listening to the variety of songs coming from the many birds that dwelled in the large trees surrounding the Marshall estate. She was at peace tending the roses, especially the ones that bore the two different colors, the one she had silently named the Roosevelt and Hattie bush. But today, she chose to visit her friend Elise. It had been sometime since they had seen each other. Traveling across town on the trolley took away a large per cent of the day and a trip she would only attempt if the weather was warm and clear. Because of this time element she no longer attended church on Sunday's there just wasn't enough time. She had to be content with just reading her Bible.

"I love that hat" Tullah stated as Dorie pinned on her favorite black straw cap. "Thank you, I do too. Take good care of my babies while I'm gone."

Tullah exclaimed, "You know I will. They are like my own." Dorie smiled, "Yes, I know they are. I'll be home in time to prepare them for bed."

James stared across the room at Lillian in disbelief, "Are you positive, he questioned?"

"Yes, according to Dr. Eastman, I'm three months into the pregnancy." James had noticed lately that she ate very little at breakfast. When he mentioned it she would just say she wasn't hungry. He walked to her and put his arms around her, reassuring her that he was happy that they were going to have a child of their own.

Tears, filled Lillian's eyes as she confessed, "James, I don't feel I'm able to do enough for the twins and now there is going to be one more child to care for. Even with Dorie and Tullah's help, I find myself drained."

He held her close and stated, "Everything is going to be just fine. I'll get you more help. Just let me know what your needs are and I'll take care of it. The important thing is that you take care of yourself."

The drive to work that morning was a blank as he wondered how Aaron and Allison would accept a sibling. Would it come about after the birth of their child that Lillian would feel the twins should be told of their adoption? If that should happen, eventually the twins would want to inquire about their real parents. "Well, he told himself, now is not the time to worry about it. Hopefully, Lillian would never feel the need to mention the fact the twins were not their own."

Dorie returned from her visit with Elise, warm from summer heat, exhausted and anxious to get off of the trolley. It had been a long day, but enjoyable. She had taken a photo of the twins to show Elise. She hadn't seen them since they left that day with Mr. Marshall. Her friend refused to go anywhere outside the black community. She would simply state, "I know where I belong, and this is it. Everything I need is here, ceptin a doctor. We still don't have one, she exclaimed with disbelief. It's goin over three years since Doc Wilson died." Once more Dorie felt sickened and wondered if her Trilly would have lived, had they had a doctor of their own. Sadly, she felt she would have. The trolley came to a halt, and she prepared herself for the walk back to the peninsula.

Tullah, excitedly greeted her return, stating in a louder than normal voice, "You're never going to guess what has happened!" Dorie couldn't begin to imagine what might have happened to excite her so. "For heavens sake Tullah, what is it?" A grin spread over her face, exposing the familiar dimples. "Mrs. Marshall is going to have a baby." Dorie was left speechless.

"Dorie, did you hear what I just said?"

"Yes, I guess I'm just shocked. I didn't think she could bear children."

"That's what makes it all so wonderful, she didn't think she could either."

Like James, Dorie's immediate concerned was for the twins. What effect would it have on them? She smiled at Tullah, trying to conceal her thoughts as she looked towards her grandchildren playing peacefully in the corner of the room. "Well, Tullah stated, "I better get back downstairs."

"Yes, Dorie replied as she removed the pin from her hat that had been delayed by the news.

The next few months passed quickly for Dorie, even though she knew they were dragging for Lillian Marshall. She felt sorry for the fragile lady. Her body was not adjusting to pregnancy. Nausea seemed to remain throughout the ordeal as well as severe backaches. Dr. Eastman was at the house frequently, pampering Mrs. Marshall and giving proper instructions for her care. Dorie fought her feelings of resentment over the fact that rich white women were not neglected when pregnant. Lillian would never have to suffer like her Trilly had. Not that she wanted Lillian to suffer. She had become very fond of her. It wasn't her fault that Trilly refused to ask James for help. Only a few more weeks and it would be over for the delicate lady.

Lillian shifted, trying to get herself comfortable. She had been instructed to remain in bed for the final few weeks of her pregnancy. Sighing, she remembered how much easier it was to adopt and prayed that when this was all over, she would have feelings for the child inside of her, after all the misery she had been through. The thought of the delivery terrified her. Because of the twins, she knew women could actually die during childbirth. She wasn't a strong person. Would it be too much for her? Dr. Eastman didn't appear to be too concerned.

James entering the room with Aaron and Allison interrupted her thoughts. She hadn't seen the children in several days. James instructed them to be very quiet and not to crawl up on the bed. Aaron was the first to greet her, "Hi, Mommy." She leaned over and kissed his forehead, running her fingers through his soft golden brown curls. A moment later Allison had her turn, leaving Lillian wondering how she could love any child more than them. "I have missed you both, she stated softly. "Have you been good for Dorie and Tullah?" She held back a chuckle, as they looked at each other, unsure of themselves. Breaking the silence, she exclaimed, "Well, I'm sure if you haven't, they would have informed me. Therefore, that means you have been very good." They smiled in agreement.

As James observed, he noticed how very tired Lillian appeared. He knew the pregnancy had been difficult for her and he was also worried how well the delivery would go. He informed the twins, "Back to your rooms now, Mommy needs to rest." He took their hands, leading them away, promising Lillian that he would return later, after her nap.

Another week had gone by with no signs of the impending birth. James sat in his den trying to concentrate on business. Once more the decision was to be made. Should he take the proceeds from the mines and purchase stock? It was a lucrative market and thus far seemed to be the best investment. Tullah startled him by entering the room without knocking. Excitedly, she announced, "Mr. Marshall, nurse Albright says Mrs. Marshall's time has come." James heart skipped several beats as he exited his chair and ran upstairs, hearing her moans as he neared the room. The nurse met him at the door and informed him that Dr. Eastman needed to be notified immediately.

Hours passed, and as feared, the delivery was as difficult as the pregnancy had been. It took Jonathon Marshall, thirteen hours to come into the world, leaving Lillian sure that through the ordeal, she would die as Maureen had. When it was over, she thanked God and prayed she would never suffer such a horrendous thing again.

Dorie and Tullah admired the new arrival as the nurse handed the small bundle over to his nanny. "Another beautiful child in the house Mr. Marshall," Dorie exclaimed as she held the infant closely.

James smiled with pride, "Yes, there is Dorie. Would you please take him up to the nursery and introduce him to the twins? I'll be up shortly"

Dorie exited the room with Tullah following close behind. They entered the nursery and the twins came running, anxious to see the baby that had been anticipated for so long. Dorie sat down in the rocker and pulled the blanket away from her new ward. "This is your new brother, Jonathon." Aaron and Allison squealed with delight. Dorie exclaimed, "From now on, the three of you will be sharing your lives together. They smiled at each other before returning their gaze to Jonathon. Dorie silently worried about this new responsibility. Could she raise them to love and care for each other and could she be equally devoted to this child? Knowing the Marshall's apparent love of the twins, she should not fear favoritism towards Jonathon. She sighed deeply, telling herself that only time would tell. Tullah sensed that something was bothering Dori and concluded that she might be overwhelmed by the added burden. She placed a hand on her friends shoulder. "I will help you as much as I can Dorie. You know how much I love children."

Dorie realized that fact. Tullah had been totally dedicated to spending as much time as she could with the twins. Suddenly a feeling of confidence came over her. This was a house filled with enough love for everyone.

CHAPTER 5
FIFTEEN YEARS LATER

The bay was unusually calm today. How many times had he stared out the window at it? Since the twin's arrival, the days had turned into years. Was it possible they were seventeen and Jonathon almost fifteen? Aaron, despite his size at birth was now a tall, muscular, handsome man. Allison, he admitted to himself, was even more beautiful than his Trilly had been. Jonathon was still developing into manhood and would be smaller than Aaron. He had inherited his looks and stature from the Sheldrick's His fair complexion a contrast compared to the twins, soft, beige skin. His hazel eyes and light brown hair created a fine looking young man. James was proud of his children. Between Lillian, Dorie and Tullah, the women had been successful in their raising. He appreciated Lilly for never having felt it necessary to inform the twins they were adopted, Dorie for loving all three equally and Tullah just for being there, so willing to help. Pulling out his pocket watch he was surprised at the hour. It was time to go home. Tonight was an important occasion at the Marshall household, Allison's coming out party.

Dorie watched proudly as Allison posed in front of the mirror. She was home from finishing school and ready to be introduced to the young, sophisticated, men of San Francisco. She marveled at what a beauty Allison had become. The image in the mirror reflected a young woman adorned in a silk peach colored chemise, covered with an intricate, floral beaded design, the fashionable straight lines concealing the voluptuous body hidden underneath it. Her breasts were tightly bound causing Dorie to sigh, telling herself it was the style of the times. Several years ago it took three times the fabric to make a dress. A matching beaded headband complimented the soft, dark auburn waves of her bobbed hair. Peach colored tee strap shoes drew attention to the perfectly shaped legs and exposed rouged knees. It was the cameo face with the large brown eyes so like her mothers that held her attention. Another sigh was released. She was thankful Allison hadn't followed the fashion fad of shaving off her brows for the painted look. Holding back tears, her thoughts drifted to Trilly, and she silently spoke with her as she had done often through the years, "You would be so proud. She resembles you, only fairer which enabled her and Aaron both to be accepted into the white's world. I pray by now, you have forgiven me for bringing them to their father but it has given them opportunities I never could have."

Allison interrupted her thoughts, asking anxiously, "How do I look Dorie? She cleared her throat, "You look beautiful child."

Indignantly, Allison exclaimed, "Child!" As of tonight Dorie, I'm to be considered a woman."

"True, Dorie answered, to all those young men downstairs you are, but to me you'll always be my child."

Allison put her arms around the woman that had always been there for her. "Oh, Dorie, I know, but I'm ready to become a woman. I suffered through finishing school and now it's time to reap the rewards. Where's Tullah? I want her to see me."

"She's busy attending to what's going on downstairs. I promise you, she won't miss your entrance." Allison turned from the mirror once more and hugged her beloved nanny, exclaiming, "I'm so nervous." Dorie reassured her, "Don't be (she caught herself to keep from using the word, child) you'll be just fine."

Allison exclaimed, "I'm so glad Aaron is home. I miss him terribly when were separated."

"I know Dorie replied, remembering the day Aaron went off to college and wondering if the separation had been as difficult for him as it had been for Allison. She smiled to herself. Even after all these years, she still considered Allison, Hattie and Aaron, Roosevelt, the names she secretly kept in her heart and her diary.

Tullah was busy replenishing the table. As she set down a plate of petite sandwiches Aaron approached her, putting his arms around her. "Oh, how I wish I could ask the most beautiful woman here to dance with me!"

"Aaron, she reprimanded him, trying to appear angry. "How many times must Dorie and me tell you that you're not to talk with the servants during social occasions? "Now mind me and get goin."

Aaron gave her a quick peck on the cheek, causing her to give him a swat. She smiled as she watched him walk away, thinking she couldn't love him more than if he were her own son. Both she and Dorie were concerned for him, feeling he had no goals. They came to the conclusion that if you have everything, what is there to strive for? James Marshall had made sure there was nothing the twins or Jonathon shouldn't have if they wanted it. Returning her attention back to her duties, she convinced herself he would be all right.

There was a knock on Allison's door and Jonathon entered. He inspected her for a moment before exclaiming, "You look beautiful. Every man in San Francisco will be crawling at your feet. "You're the cats meow."

Silently, Dorie wondered if Jonathon's statement, "The cats meow," was a repeat of "You look beautiful." She felt the youth of the twenties seemed to be trying to develop a new language of their own.

"Enough Jonathon," Allison replied, you know you can wrap me around you're fingers with that kind of talk."

He grinned. "True, but I really do mean it." Allison put her arms around him. "Thank you little brother. Now, please go downstairs and tell mother, father and Aaron that I'm ready to be introduced." He gave a slight bow and they both smiled as they watched him leave the room. Dorie, despite her earlier fears, loved Jonathon and had been the greatest participant in his up-bringing. Many affectionate hours were spent rocking him and telling him stories of her ancestors, just as she had done with the twins. She never once put the twins before him. A few minutes later, Aaron arrived to escort his sister to her presentation. He took a moment to appreciate the exquisite young woman standing in front of him before offering his arm and stating, "You will capture a multitude of hearts this evening, my dear sister." She thanked him and accepted the strong arm that would lead her to the reception. Dories heart swelled with pride as she watched him guide his sister down the staircase.

Allison took a deep breath as they descended the stairs, surveying the crowded room until her eyes met the person she was searching for, Gerald Thomas, son of Vera Thomas, her mother's best friend. How handsome he looked in his tuxedo. Allison had been infatuated with him since childhood. He was everything she desired in a man, leaving her to care less about any of the other males in attendance.

Vera edged Gerald forward wanting him to be the first to greet Allison at the end of her descent. Gerald responded to the nudge and Allison's heart quickened as he approached, holding out his hand.

"Allison, may I escort you to the ballroom and have the first dance?" Her face became flushed as she accepted his offer. Aaron surrendered his sister reluctantly. He didn't particularly like Gerald, considering him arrogant and on the wild side. Silently he hoped that with all the young men in attendance, Allison would find someone of interest. Someone, who could distract her attention away from Gerald Thomas.

Vera admired the pair as they danced, hopeful the two would eventually become engaged. It was obvious they were fond of each other. What could be better than to have Gerald wed into the Marshall family? Granted, their family was equally as wealthy but two fortunes merging would make things even better. Lillian had mentioned at the last Women's Club meeting how nice it would be if Gerald and Allison became serious. Yes, even the Marshall's approved. Now, hopefully Gerald wouldn't ruin his chances with her. She scanned the room evaluating all the other young men that might be of some competition. As far as she was concerned, Aaron Marshall was the best looking and most eligible bachelor there but of course he was no rival. Possibly Anthony Babcock, his father owned several canneries. Then there was Arlo Hansen, no, she told herself, no matter how much money his family had he was not the least bit appealing. There was one man that stood out as far as she was concerned and she had no idea who he might be. Whoever he was, the man was extremely handsome and watching Allison and Gerald intently as they danced. She decided to find out his identity, he could be a problem if he had money and appealed to Allison, not that she didn't have faith in Gerald's ability to charm women. In fact that was his problem. He was charming and women loved him and in return, he loved women. She knew he would never be a faithful husband but most men were not. That was of course for her husband Edward, he wouldn't dare.

Aaron stood quietly observing the attention being shown Allison. He was proud as he watched her dance gracefully to the slow music, so prim and proper and then completely let herself go as she did the Charleston, the new dance craze. A grin covered his face as the elders in the room gasped when the dance began. He appreciated his mother's willingness to shock them for Allison's sake. His parent's even chose to ignore the young people drinking what they referred to as "Giggle Juice," from their fashionable ornate, silver flasks. Silently, he wondered how many of the young men attending this event had goals for themselves. He had no idea as to what he wanted to do with his life. His father had asked many times but he just didn't know.

As James approached Lilly to ask for a dance, he came to the decision that she had become beautiful with age. She maintained her shape and her face remained free of the wrinkles so many of the other women her age had received. The only real signs of aging showed in her hair as small streaks of silver wove their way through it. He felt a great love for her as he spoke. "May I have this dance, my dear?"

"Of course," she replied with her usual warm smile. He led her to the dance floor exclaiming, "It's a wonderful occasion Lilly. You've done a magnificent job as always." She looked towards Allison and exclaimed, "Thank you James. Isn't she beautiful? You're sister would have been so proud."

The usual twang of guilt he had experienced so many times through the years tugged at his heart once more. "Yes, Lilly she would have been, thanks to you Allison's not only beautiful she's a good person."

"Don't make me cry James. I could have done more. Dorie and Tullah have been the ones responsible for her upbringing. I'm sorry I didn't participate more with the children." James made her face him. "You underestimate yourself Lillian, if it hadn't of been for your acceptance of Aaron and Allison, where would they be now?"

She wiped away a tear with her silk handkerchief and replied, "Thank you James. It's nice to be able to feel I had a small part in their lives."

"You don't realize how important you are to all of us." He held her close as they continued their dance. After all these years, he still loved her. Not as he had Trilly, but he knew there were many types of love.

As Dorie sat in her room, she re-lived Allison's descent down the staircase. The sounds of music floated through her closed door. She went to the closet and removed the old suitcase that held her diary. She purchased the little book and started filling the empty pages soon after the day her and Vera Thomas had been introduced. She still disliked the woman. She didn't record in it daily but faithfully entered important occasions as well as anything she felt of importance to Roosevelt or Hattie, always fearing their true identity might be discovered. If that should happen, they would know their roots. Tonight, she would write for Hattie.

> *My dear Hattie,*
> *It is June 24th and this is your night. It's an important occasion in the social world of wealthy whites, you're coming out party. This evening, you descended the staircase as radiant and elegant as any queen, I watched from a distance. There are many young men down there hoping to gain your interest. Your mother and I never knew such a thing as a coming out party. I just pray to the Lord above that you find a love as great as your mother Trilly and I both found.*

She laid the book on her lap, closed her eyes and tried to anticipate what was happening downstairs.

Begrudgingly, Allison had to sacrifice part of her evening with Gerald to dance with the other men in attendance. One in particular disturbed her. He approached her, arrogantly stating, "If you can take your mind off that young man, his eyes directed towards Gerald, I would appreciate a dance." He was older and she felt he was obviously not part of the male lineup her mother had chosen to invite on her behalf. Still, he was a guest and recalling her training, she was obligated to accept the dance. As they approached the floor she questioned, "Who are you?"

He smiled, "I apologize for the lack of introduction Miss Marshall. I am Blake Donlan."

"Well, Mr. Donlan, hopefully I won't offend you, but it's obvious you're too old to have been on my mother's list of eligible suitors. What is your relationship with my parents?" Another smile appeared as he replied, "Miss Marshall you truly have offended me. Do I not dance around the floor as agile as the other men, and do I not have a full head of hair? Allison became speechless. He continued, piercing her with his blue eyes. Perhaps I lack the look of lust for you that all the young men in this room have written on their faces. We older men can disguise our emotions."

She blushed, the word lust, flustered her. She was a girl of the twenties. Women were more brazen and it upset her to be shaken by such a comment. Always after returning from school she would try acting out what her peers were doing but between her three keepers, especially Dorie she was set straight in no time. Dorie would scold, "Child, you can bring back from school all that fancy French language and etiquette you learned but don't try talking any of that women's liberation or whatever it is to me." This evening, she was probably the only young lady in the room not sporting a silver flask of "Giggle Juice." As the word lust hung over her and not knowing quite how to handle herself with this man she broke the rules of etiquette, "I believe we have both offended each other Mr. Donlan, this dance is over as far as I'm concerned."

Blake smiled with fascination as she walked away. He was attending the party with his parents. Even though his father was James Marshall's attorney, this was the first time Blake had met the prominent young lady of the evening and she was breathtaking. He silently figured he was about eight years older than her and that was a big gap to someone her age. He continued to watch her throughout the evening promising that this would not be the last time he would see Allison Marshall.

As Allison exited the dance floor escaping the obnoxious man she carried a vision of him. He was very tall and quite muscular. Even though dressed formally he had a rugged look about him and yes, he had a full head of hair. In fact, it was unusually thick, dark brown, almost black. He ignored the shiny, slicked back style that was popular; instead, it was loose and free of oils. The one thing that stood out the most in her encounter with him was a pair of deep blue eyes and he was right, she hadn't seen lust in them, so why was she so intimidated by him? Gerald returned to her, erasing the upsetting vision. The rest of the evening she made it a point not to encounter the disturbing Blake Donlan.

Dorie sat in the rocker reminiscing. There were no longer any babies to attend to. She still maintained her room that was once adjoined to the nursery, which was now Allison's room. The Marshall's had kept her on and to make her feel worthwhile, she now tended to the garden's full time. Other than raising children, it was her next love. Tullah was still needed to help with the household and thankfully they both still remained part of the family. Her thoughts of Tullah came to life as her friend entered the room announcing that Allison and her coming out party were a success and going to be the talk of San Francisco. Dorie thanked her for the information even though she had no doubt of the outcome.

"Our babies are all grown up Dorie," Tullah exclaimed.

"Yes, Dorie sighed, they sure are."

Tullah's eyes wandered to the book on Dorie's lap. "Did you write in that little book of yours tonight?"

"Yes," she replied as she protectively wrapped her hand around it. Tullah inquired, "What do you write in it?"

"Important events that happen in my life, it's like a diary."

"Did you write about Allison's party?"

"Yes."

Tullah shrugged, "Well, I better get back downstairs. The guests should be gone by now and it will be time to clean up, goodnight Dorie." After her exit, Dorie returned the book to its hiding place in the old suitcase.

The party was ending. James and Lillian thanked their guests as they departed. James was especially pleased that Elliott and his wife had come and brought their son with them. He met Blake several times while playing golf and was very impressed with the handsome young man. Not only did he play a good game of golf, he was intelligent.

"Your Allison has grown into a beautiful young lady," Elliott exclaimed as he shook James hand and kissed Lillian on the cheek. Blake and his mother Molly reinforced the statement. They said their farewells, with the men making promises of meeting for a round of golf.

Aaron returned upstairs with Allison. "You were sensational, little sister."

"Why thank you Aaron. I couldn't help but notice a few of my girlfriends going out of their way to get your attention."

Aaron tried to conceal a smile before replying, "Just a couple." Allison, please tell me you found someone other than Gerald Thomas this evening to hold your interest." She became defensive.

"Why don't you like him Aaron?"

"I don't know. I just feel you could do so much better. I don't think he's for you. She questioned, "Who could be better for me than Gerald?

"I don't know right now, but trust me Allison, I just have a feeling. You know I want nothing but happiness for you and I don't think Gerald can give it to you."

"You wouldn't say that Aaron, if you could feel my heart whenever he's near. How about you, haven't you met anyone yet that effects you?"

"No, not yet," he replied with a boyish grin.

"Well, Allison stated in a superior tone, when you do, you'll understand how I feel." He rolled his eyes and kissed her goodnight.

On their return home, the Donlan's discussed the evening's events, agreeing it was a splendid party and obviously no expense had been spared. Blake questioned his father in regards to Allison. He appeared agitated by the questions, surprising Blake and suggesting that he forget any interest in her, stating, "Besides, she's much too young for you."

Blake exclaimed, "That's the second time tonight I've been made to feel ancient at twenty-five!"

"How's that?," Elliott asked curiously.

"The young Miss Marshall informed me I was much too old to be on her mother's list of suitors." Elliott laughed, "Well, that should tell you not to bother." Blake felt his father's reaction was strange. He had dated younger women before and he never seemed to think it was out of line. No matter, he was determined to pursue Allison, despite his father's suggestion to forget her.

The next day, Allison started receiving bouquets from hopeful suitors. She couldn't help but be flattered by the response. "Goodness, Allison, if I have to answer that door and except one more bouquet, I think I'll scream, Tullah exclaimed with exasperation. Lillian smiled at her daughter. "You have a lot of eligible men begging for your attention, did anyone in particular impress you?" Allison sighed, "Yes, Gerald."

"Gerald Thomas? My goodness Allison, I'm not saying he's unworthy of you, but surely with all the other gentlemen there, didn't someone else spark you a little." Allison became defiant. "No mother, no one." Lillian sighed as she observed a strange bouquet exclaiming, "My, this is quite unusual, I've never seen this combination of flowers before. Allison eyes followed her mother's gaze. It was odd, a mixture of wildflowers combined with a single rose bud. Lillian handed her the card. It read, "Please observe your bouquet carefully. The wildflowers were cut much sooner than the rose, but they are hearty and will wait for the rose to bloom." It was signed Blake Donlan. The vision of him returned and she became irate. Did that mean what it seemed? Was he actually saying he was waiting for her to grow up? How could he presume that even for a moment she would ever be with him? That half of a dance would be all that he would ever receive from her.

Vera prompted Gerald once more. "Don't you think you should propose to Allison? Gerald was fond of Allison and felt he might love her but didn't feel ready to commit himself. He adored women and there were so many out there. He answered, "Mother, I wish you didn't feel the need to push me into marriage."

"Well, your nineteen now and certainly old enough to be considering marriage and starting a family. If you don't act soon you may lose her to someone else. She's the best catch in San Francisco and I don't think you should take any chances. Gerald sighed and promised her he would think on it, as he hurriedly left the room.

Vera loved her son but was aware of his shortcomings. He partied too much and was a womanizer. The fact that he had been expelled from college and as of yet showed little incentive as to what he intended to do with his life, left her despaired. Carefully she set down the small silver frame she had unconsciously picked up. It held his baby picture. She had always felt he would be successful, like his father. Perhaps she was wrong. Disappointment welled through her as the chances of marriage between Allison and him were looking more and more unlikely. Her thoughts drifted back to the party. She discovered that the handsome man she had admired was Elliott Donlan's son Blake. Trudi Cartland informed her that Blake Donlan was becoming very wealthy, investing in real estate. "Both he and his father are buying any property that becomes available around here Trudi exclaimed." Vera came to the conclusion that Blake would definitely be a threat, especially after observing the way he stood there watching Allison as she danced.

James put the paper aside just as Lillian was preparing to butter her toast. This morning he was paying less attention to the procedure. The stock market was making him extremely nervous lately. Last night, after dinner at his in-laws, Robert Sheldrick asked him to join him in the den for brandy and a cigar. He remembered the discussion. It was the stock market.

Robert exclaimed, "The market is declining as you well know, and not at a slow pace. If stock values continue depreciating at this rate, I'm going to have to start believing what Roger Babson (a highly regarded financial statistician.) has been saying. "He has predicted a crash is coming and it's going to be a horrific one."

James tried to console his father-in-law while hiding his own fears, stating that the economists are saying Babson's an alarmist. Robert continued to tell of news articles he had read by the man. "He warned, too much stock into too many unquestionable companies had been sold and unwise bank loans had been made." Robert sighed, "If this keeps up, my bank will go under. We've invested our depositor's money in the market, most banks have."

The memory of that conversation was upsetting him. Abruptly, he excused himself from the breakfast table, startling Lilly. He needed to get to the office and check the ticker tape.

CHAPTER 6

The music was loud and the dance floor was crowded, cigar and cigarette smoke veiled the patrons. Blake was at his favorite speakeasy with his friends. While nursing his illegal gin and tonic he observed the group at the table across from him. It took a moment, but he was finally able to place the tall, good looking young man that was indulging with overly boisterous and inebriated companions. He was James Marshall's oldest son. Another, now recognizable face appeared. It was the man Allison was so taken with at her party. As he assessed the young man, he wondered what was it about him that attracted Allison. He was of average height with a weak build. Maybe, it was the blond hair. He was definitely enjoying the females at his table, which fascinated Blake. Why would he be spending time with them, when he could be with Allison? Suddenly his thoughts were broken as someone yelled, "It's a raid."

Whistles blew and women screamed. Once again, Blake looked back to the table Allison's brother and friends occupied. The group was so drunk they appeared oblivious as to what was happening. Running across the room he startled Aaron by grabbing him by the arm, stating, "Trust me, I'm a friend of your families and you don't want to get caught in this place, follow me."

Even though he was drunk, Aaron understood the stranger. No, he wouldn't want his parents to discover he had patronized a speakeasy. He shook his head in agreement and followed the stranger. They entered the kitchen. The staff, as well as several distinguished people dressed in elegant evening attire, calmly but quickly were exiting through the pantry. Aaron was fascinated as he noticed a wall of canned goods was actually an escape route. The distinguished group nodded to the man he was following. After all had passed through the opening it was put back into place. They walked a short distance down a dimly lit hallway and entered through another door leading them into what appeared to be a storage room. Another wall rotated and they were suddenly entering an elaborate apartment. A large man announced in a whiskey rasped voice, "Macky say's "Stay and have fun." Most the group chose to remain there and continue on with the party. Aaron silently followed his leader out of the apartment, down some stairs and into the street, before questioning," How did you know that escape route was there?"

Blake smiled, "A friend of mine, Macky, owns the place"

Concerned, Aaron asked, "What is he going to do now?"

"Raids don't slow Macky down. He'll just find another location. This is nothing new to him as you can tell by that escape passage."

Aaron shook his head and then held out his hand. "I want to thank you Mister???"

Blake received the hand, "Donlan, Blake Donlan, I know you're a Marshall, what's the rest your name?"

"I'm Aaron. You said you know my parents!" Blake explained that his father was their family attorney.

"Of course, Aaron replied. I know your father. No wonder the name sounded familiar. How come we've never met?"

"I guess it's because I was in military school most the time and then college." Blake released him from the handshake. He liked Aaron. Maybe his resemblance to his sister had something to do with it. He asked, "Do you need a ride home?"

"Yes, as a matter of fact I do, if it's not too much of an inconvenience." Blake assured him that it was not out of his way. On the drive to the Marshall house Blake commented. "I'm rather amazed that fellow you were with chooses to be with those women instead of your sister." Surprised, Aaron responded. "You know my sister?"

"Yes, I met her the night of her coming out party. She's a beautiful lady. I was fortunate enough to share a short dance with her. I got the strong impression she's quite taken with that man."

Aaron groaned. "Yes, unfortunately she's taken with Gerald." Blake commented, "Obviously he's not as serious as she is." Aaron replied, "The trouble with Gerald is that he wants Allison but he doesn't want to give up other women for her. I've tried to discourage her feelings towards him but she just won't listen. She's very opinionated when it comes to Gerald, they say, "Love is blind."

Continuing their ride Aaron asked Blake what it was he did for a living.

"I'm an investor"

"Oh, Aaron questioned, the stock market?" Blake pulled up in front of the Marshall estate and turned off the car's engine. "No, I don't like the market, don't trust it. I like something more solid like real estate."

Aaron sighed, "I wish I had a goal. I envy those that know what they want from life. My father keeps asking me what I want to do and I just don't have an answer for him." Blake felt fortunate that he knew what his goal was. In fact it was to one day own a large per cent of San Francisco. He laughed to himself. He literally worshiped the ground he walked on," and so why not own as much of it as possible? He loved the city. Wanting to console Aaron he replied, "I know how frustrating that can be. My father had hopes I would become an attorney like him, but it wasn't for me and it took me sometime to figure out what it was I wanted."

Aaron stated, "I read once the every man is born with a gift for survival. I guess I'll find out what mine is someday."

Blake reassured him, "It will come to you and when it does, you'll know its right for you." Aaron opened the car door and exclaimed, I hope so, "Thanks again, and hopefully we will meet again soon, under better circumstances." Blake acknowledged the statement before nodding and driving off.

Allison heard Aaron enter. The rest of the family had long retired. She was up only because of the new Scott Fitzgerald book she started reading much earlier, (This Side of Paradise) she couldn't put it down. Seeing the light in the library, Aaron became curious as to who would be up this late, he peeked in. Seeing it was Allison, he entered. "Good morning Allison. What are you doing up?"

"She laid the book on her lap and replied. "I'm hooked on this book." Arching a brow, she asked, "What about you? Where have you been?"

Though dreary, a spark of life returned as he exclaimed, "I've had quite an experience." He went on to explain the evening's events. Hearing that Gerald was there with several girls upset Allison but Aaron felt the need to let her know. She questioned, "The man that rescued you was at my coming out party?"

"Yes, He said he danced with you. Aaron went on to describe him. A picture of Blake came to her and once more she became agitated. "Yes, now I remember, and we only shared half a dance. I found him very arrogant and offensive."

"Strange," I liked him, Aaron replied, wondering how she could have possibly found the man he had spent the last couple of hours with, fitting into such categories.

"Well, my dear brother, you can like him if you wish, but I don't."

Aaron exclaimed, "I rather see you with someone like him than Gerald." Once more Allison became defensive.

"You must be kidding," she said in disbelief. "He's an old man. I think it's time we both retire, you've had a long evening and it's affected your brain."

Allison was right, it had been a long evening but Aaron was sure there was nothing wrong with his way of thinking. Blake would be a much better catch than Gerald. They walked to their rooms and he kissed her goodnight.

James heard the grandfather clock chime twice. He knew what it was that interrupted his sleep, the stock market. He was thankful that Lillian and the children were oblivious to what was going on. Their only concerns now were what the next social event would be. Hopefully nothing would happen to change that, although it wasn't looking good. Lillian and her mother had left for Europe to visit with relatives, so he didn't need to worry about disturbing her with his restlessness. Once more he questioned himself. "What if the market does crash? What would become of them?" Everything that supported his family was invested in stocks. He sold the mines several years ago. "Dear God," he sighed, for the first time in his life he knew fear. Sleep had been his only escape these last few weeks, but it appeared tonight there would be none. Helplessness had created a fear that would rob him of a peaceful slumber.

Elliott Donlan was proud of the way his only child Blake had grown not only into a handsome man but an intelligent one. He remembered his disappointment when Blake informed him he had no desire to become an attorney and asked for the money it would take to send him to law school to invest in real estate. His proposition had been, they would be partners and share any profits from the original loan. Anything he purchased after that, the profits would be his alone. Overcoming his disappointment, Elliott agreed and in the last seven years he had been paid back and still making money from Blake's original investments. In fact the profits were so good he started investing in properties himself, rather than the stock market. Between the two of them, they were accumulating a healthy percent of San Francisco's real estate. The way the stock market was roller coasting these days, he was even more grateful than ever that Blake had swayed him away from it. Now it appeared to be on a downward ride with little promise of ever rising to the top again. He pulled out his pocket watch and silently questioned, "Where was Blake? He was already ten minutes late for their luncheon date. Looking towards the door once again, he noticed his son enter.

"Sorry I'm late. I went to see about purchasing some property down by the bay and to my surprise it turned out to be the Marshall Building."

Elliott's heart sank and he questioned in disbelief. "Marshall building?"

"Yes, sadly his stock investments have dropped too low to sell without losing everything and he needs some cash flow until it rises again."

"Can't he borrow on it? After all, his father-in-law owns a bank."

"Blake replied, "I asked why he wasn't taking out a loan. His answer was that the bank was in the same predicament. Most the banks deposits were also invested into the market."

"Didn't he try another bank other than Sheldrick's?"

"Yes, but the solvent ones are refusing loans right now. They're protecting their depositors in case there is a crash. Fortunately, our bank is one of them. Only a small amount of money was invested into the market."

Anxiously Elliott asked, "Should we be withdrawing our money just to be safe?"

"No, Blake replied, I think we should pull out half our savings just for a little protection. We don't want to help start a panic by withdrawing it all. Hopefully the bank will survive a crash if there really is one. If not, we'll be a lot better off than most. We will still have our properties."

"My God, What about James," Elliott asked with concern for his friend?

"I offered to loan him the money myself. I told him I rather not buy property from a friend due to hardship, he flatly refused. You know him as well as anyone, he's a proud man. Hopefully, he wasn't offended by the suggestion. Anyway, I need you to write up the papers. He said he was much happier knowing the building was going to me rather than a stranger."

Elliott sighed, stating "The Marshall Building was James pride and joy." A waiter arrived to take their order. The two men had lost their appetites, leaving both wishing they could order an alcoholic drink to take the edge off of what they feared may happen to most their acquaintances, James Marshall was going to be just the beginning. Blake was quietly concerned for Allison and Aaron, especially Allison. It appeared difficult times were ahead for the twins, leaving him wondering, how would they handle it?

Allison accompanied her friend Beatrice as she searched for an apartment. The bay area had become quite popular and good apartments were hard to come by. Bea, as Allison called her, rang the doorbell of the apartment marked Manager. A plump woman with red hair and a face full of freckles answered the door and stood there silently observing them. Breaking the silence, Bea announced, "We have come to see the apartment you advertised!"

With a small groan and as if overworked, the woman replied, "I'll get the key." She returned a moment later commanding, "Follow me." The two young girls withheld a giggle as they obeyed the command and followed the wobbling woman to the second floor of the three-story building. As they entered, they were both impressed with the cleanliness and tasteful furnishings, leaving them silently hopeful it was affordable and secretly nudging each other with approval.

Bea questioned, "The ad only stated apartment for rent, how much is it?" The plump, slow moving woman replied, "Fifteen dollars a month." Beatrice exhaled, disappointed that it was out of her price range.

"Allison commented, "Fifteen dollars a month, don't you think that's a little much?"

Redness muted the freckles on the landlady's face and she replied, "I'm just the landlady for Mr. Donlan and I just ask what he requests. I don't own the building." The name Donlan rushed through Allison's mind, as she wondered to herself, was it the same man who danced with her at her party and rescued Aaron? She convinced herself no, it couldn't be.

The twosome left the building discouraged. Bea was Allison's best friend. Even though for several years Allison went away to finishing school and Bea had to remain behind, due to the fact her parents couldn't afford such an elite school, the two always anxiously awaited their reunion.

Allison encouraged Bea as they continued their search for an apartment. Bea had the option of remaining at home with her parents. She loved them but felt at the age of eighteen, she should move on and become more than Mr. and Mrs. Lawton's daughter. Allison related to her friend's feelings, telling herself she should consider doing the same. She figured silently that between the two of them, they could afford the much wanted apartment. It had room enough for two. First, she had to decide, was she ready to leave her beloved home.

James stood and stared out of the office window at the bay for the last time. Standing allowed him the view where he had first met his Trilly so many years ago. He never quit loving or missing her. That morning he signed over the Marshall Building to Blake. As far as he was concerned, Blake was a fine young man and he appreciated his offer of a loan even though refusing it. Hopefully the money from the sale would tide his family over until the market rose again. The sound of the ticker tape had been non-stop for days now. Sometimes, he felt the noise would drive him crazy. The phone rang, breaking the agonizing sound. It was his father-in-law Arnold.

"My God, James, it's happened. The market has totally collapsed. The bank's doors are locked. People are demanding their money. We don't have it. I'm broke and penniless, just like them."

James heart sank. Babson's prediction had become a reality. Between his own bank loss and his savings at the Sheldrick bank gone, he too was left destitute except for the money he would receive from Blake, for the sale of the Marshall Building.

Arnold's anguished voice returned him to the moment. "I'm so sorry James." James tried to speak but lost his voice. Once more Arnold apologized and requested, "Please tell Annie and Lillian I'm sorry." A moment later, James was startled out of his trance by the sound of a gunshot. He yelled through the phone, "Arnold, Arnold." There was no answer, just the sound of a woman screaming. He came to the sickening conclusion that Arnold Sheldrick had shot himself. Numbly, he hung up the phone and fought the urge to do the same. How was he going to explain this to his family? Their lives would be changed forever. He questioned himself, could he be stronger than Arnold? Could he face the horrible reality of what has happened? He wasn't sure. Another feeling overcame him. One he had never experienced before. He didn't want to go home.

Chapter 7

Gerald Thomas stood there in disbelief watching his father Edward pulling at the heavily starched throat collar, trying to enable himself to breath as he announced they had lost almost everything that morning with the collapse of the stock market. He tried to comprehend what was happening. Money had always been there for his sister Karen and himself. Were they being told there was no more? That just couldn't be.

Vera had never seen her husband this distraught. She spoke, "Surely things will straighten out Edward. The market dropped several times before and we made it through."

Edward shook his head negatively, "It's happened before but not to this degree. In a day one of our stocks went from a hundred a share to fifty. Most of us sold out of fear that the next day it would be down to twenty dollars or possibly less, the plunge is incredible. This time I don't see a rebound. Three quarters of our fortune is gone. It's hard to believe, but were luckier than most, were just going to have to accept a much more modest, life style."

Vera wondered to herself! How do you live modestly?

Gerald was also trying to interpret the statement. Karen seemed to be the only one to understand they were going to have to give up certain things and questioned hopefully, "Does that mean I no longer have to attend Mrs. Bard's finishing school?"

Edward removed a handkerchief from his pocket and blew his nose, hopeful he had hidden the fact that he wiped tears from his eyes in the process, and replied, "Yes."

Karen smiled and stated, "Then today is not all bad. I hate it there." He realized that being only thirteen, the transition would be easiest for her. His main concern was Vera, often wondering if she really loved him or had married him for his wealth. He knew he would be receiving the answer to that question soon.

Gerald found his voice and asked fearfully, "What about my allowance?"

"Gone," his father answered.

"What am I going to do for money?"

Edward sighed, "You'll have to find a job." He watched horror spread over his son's face as he questioned, "A job, what kind of job?"

"Whatever, you can find. Hopefully there will be something out there you can do with the small amount of college education you received." I suggest you start looking soon. I don't know how long what little we have left is going to last. I'll be looking for work as well. Gerald left the room in a silent trance.

Vera was aghast. Karen no longer enrolled at finishing school, Gerald having to get a job, what was she going to have to give up? She instructed Karen to leave the room, "Your father and I need to talk." Anger was overcoming her fears but she didn't speak until her daughter exited and closed the door behind her.

"Edward, exactly how much are all of us going to be expected to give up?" He looked directly at her and stated, "If it will make you feel any better my dear, about the same as most our friends. We will have one car instead of two. The chauffeur and rest of the servants will have to go. We can no longer provide for them. We will need what we have for ourselves. Parties and social functions I'm afraid will be a thing of the past. Vera felt her knee's becoming weak, he was serious.

"What about the cook, she asked fearfully?"

"We will keep Pearl as long as we possibly can." He fought the previous urge to go to her and try to give comfort, due to the fact he now noticed the anger that had build up with-in her.

"How could you let this happen, she moaned?" He sighed and stated, "Like so many others, I put too much faith in the market and why not? For so many years it provided very well for us. You even stated it had fallen before and come back. I had no reason to believe any different. I'm sorry Vera. Do you think this has been easy on me?" He continued, I didn't want to say anything in front of the children, but you should know that Arnold Sheldrick committed suicide this morning after the crash, he shot himself, the bank's doors are locked. Not only did he lose his money, the banks depositors lost theirs, leaving hundreds poverty stricken."

The statement shook Vera to the core. Surely, the world had come to an end. Not just her world, but everyone's. There was going to be hell on earth. Despite inner warnings, Edward went to her and embraced her. She pushed him away demanding "Leave me alone, I need to think." A sinking feeling came over him. Granting her request he left the room and entered his den. Reaching into the desk drawer he pulled out his bottle of illegal bourbon and poured a drink. It had become obvious it was the only thing in his home to console him.

Wearily, James looked at the faces of his three children. They were looking back at him with curious expressions. Never had they been summoned to a family meeting without their mother. Even though she was in Europe, he would normally await her return to make any family decisions. Aaron was the first to speak.

"What's wrong father, is mother alright?" Allison and Gerald held their breath as they awaited an answer.

James replied, "Your mother is fine. Up until now, I felt I had endured hardships in my life but never has anything been harder for me than what I've experienced over these last few days and what I'm about to tell you. He cleared his throat and explained the events that had taken place with the stock market. He knew it would be a day that not only his family but millions would never forget. As he spoke, he witnessed their expected look of shock and disbelief. Silence followed his speech while each one of them became lost in thought. After what seemed an eternity to James, his children rushed to comfort him. Aaron stated, "Don't blame yourself dad." Allison confirmed her love and Jonathon exclaimed, "I'm going to take care of all of us when I become a professional golfer, I'll earn lots of money."

"Well, James replied, holding back tears of relief. It appears I haven't lost the important things. I'll always be rich as long as I have your mother and the three of you." The word mother tore Allison from her father's embrace and she questioned, "What about mother, does she know?"

James answered. "I sent her a telegram but there's still some more bad news. He dreaded telling them, but knew they had to eventually hear it. "Your grandfather is dead." he committed suicide this morning. The crash of the market was more than he could bear. Once again disbelief engulfed them. Allison wept openly while Aaron and Gerald looked at each other and then back at their father hoping they misunderstood the statement. The expression on James face confirmed, they had not. Aside from Allison's weeping the room was silent as all four grieved their losses and wondered what the future held.

Lillian and her mother returned to aunt Rebecca's house after a day of lunch and souvenir shopping in Paris. Rebecca greeted them at the door excited, flashing an envelope in her hand exclaiming, "You have a telegram Lilly, I've been delirious waiting your return. Lillian was immediately concerned. All day she had been plagued with a feeling of uneasiness. She received the envelope from her sister and reluctantly opened it.

"My dear Lilly, you must return home sooner than expected. Your father has died. I'm sorry you have to be the one to tell your mother. I will explain when you arrive home. Love, James."

Ashen, she read it once more. Her reaction alerted both her mother and Rebecca. "What is it, they asked in unison?" With tears in her eyes, she replied that she needed to sit down and they should also. They followed her to the parlor and seated themselves. Lillian had a difficult time believing her words as she exclaimed, "Mother, father has died," Both women gasped. Annie Sheldrick felt the darkness of a faint closing in on her, shaking her head, she asked, "What happened?"

Lillian hated to admit her lack of knowledge as she exclaimed, "James didn't say."

Annie cried, "How could this happen? I wasn't there for him and we are so far away. We must leave as soon as possible."

"Yes, mama," we will." She held her mother close. Their sobs intermingled as Rebecca sat silently stunned.

The funeral service could not be held off. Due to the length of the ocean voyage Arnold's wife and daughter were absent. It was a dark, wet day as James, the twins and Jonathon stood graveside. There were a small amount of mourners. Most acquaintances were still reeling from Black Thursday and too distraught to depress themselves even further by attending a funeral, especially one that would remind them the reason Arnold Sheldrick took his life. James would miss his father-in law, he was a good man. His thoughts drifted back to the day he had asked Arnold for his daughter's hand in marriage.

"Young man, you're asking for more than just her hand. You're asking me to turn her life over to you. Can you be responsible for my daughter's life?" The magnitude of the question momentarily overwhelmed him. He cleared his throat and replied with a determined promise "I will care for and cherish her life, as my own." Now looking down upon the casket and the large hole in the earth that in a few minutes would consume Arnold Sheldrick, he renewed his promise. "I will do everything in my power to take care of Lilly and I will always cherish her."

Dorie hugged Tullah as she stated, "This won't be the same place without you. You make sure that man of yours takes good care of you."

Tullah replied, "Grange is good to me Dorie. I'll be okay and I'm so glad that you are able to remain here. I feel strange having to leave this place. This has been home to me for so long. She shook her head, "I can still see that sad look on Mr. Marshall's face when he informed us they could no longer afford servants. I will remember that look to my dying day. Poor man still has to tell Mrs. Marshall when she returns."

"I know, Dorie replied. He felt it would be easier on her if she didn't have to witness your departure."

"Well, they're good people and have always treated me kindly. I pray they will be all right, I better go now, Grange is waiting." Once more they hugged and kissed. Dorie watched sadly as her friend walked away and silently prayed, "God be with them." She went to the closet and retrieved her diary from the suitcase. She felt the need to write.

> *"My dear Roosevelt and Hattie, by now you have learned of the terrible thing that has happened to your father and Lillian. I'm thankful that your father is still able to maintain our home. I know that as long as he is alive, he will do everything in his power to provide for us.*
>
> *I often wonder if you should have been told of your true identities. How many times I wanted to tell you I was your Grandmother and talk to you about your mother. I realize this diary is more for me than you. It has enabled me to speak to you as my grandchildren and feel closer to Trilly. It's almost full now and the decision I have to eventually make is to keep it or destroy it.*

Slowly, she closed the little book and returned it to its dark hiding place in the old suitcase.

Lillian pleaded, "James, will you please tell us what is wrong, you're behaving strangely?" He had refused to tell her and Annie how her father died and insisted her mother come home with them rather than return to her house.

"Trust me Lilly, it's best for me to explain everything when we get home." The silence was weighing on her. Annie Sheldrick sat quietly, trying to understand what was going on. What could he have to say that would be worse than losing Arnold and why couldn't he at least tell them how he died? Another thing bothered her, why couldn't she go home? The ride from the pier seemed to last forever. Approaching the house, James tensed as he waited for Lilly to question why Tullah wasn't there as usual to greet them.

"James, is Tullah ill? She has always greeted me at the door after a lengthy trip?"

"She's fine, James replied. I'll explain everything soon." The sound of Jonathon and the twins momentarily dissolved her concern.

"Mother, grandmother, we're so glad your back," they all exclaimed in unison. After a few hugs and kisses, Lillian exclaimed, "I brought you all gifts from Europe." The threesome stood there with artificial smiles, knowing that in a few minutes their father was about to tell the two frail women they loved so much, something that could or would destroy them. James interrupted the welcome. "Please excuse yourselves now. I have to talk to your mother and grandmother in private." Once more, Lillian felt uneasy. Outside the closed parlor door Aaron, Allison and Jonathon were grateful they were not included in the heartbreaking statements their father had to deliver. They paced and it seemed to be taking forever to break the devastating news. Then it happened, they stood there staring at each other as terrible moans leaked out from under the door that separated them from the sad scene with-in. Tears rolled down Allison's cheeks as she listened.

"No, no, my dear God, no, why would he kill himself?" Then there was nothing left to hear but the sounds of the two women, sobbing. Knowing that their grandmother still hadn't discovered she didn't have a home to return to they looked at each other sadly and went to their rooms to sort out their feelings. Allison went directly to Dorie. After losing Tullah, she feared losing her also, even though her father reassured her that Dorie would be the last to go.

She knocked on her beloved nanny's door. Dorie answered the knock. "Come in Allison." She knew it was Allison even though she hadn't announced herself. She took pride in the fact she could recognize each of her wards knocks. They were like their personalities. Allison's was one dainty knock with a pause before the next (conservative.) Aaron s, were two strong, ones (out-going). Jonathon's was continuous (aggressive). Allison approached her like the child she once was when frightened.

"Dorie, I'm so worried about my parent's and grandmother." Dorie was proud of her grand daughters concern for someone other than herself. In fact, she was proud of all three children and the way they were reacting to the inevitable change in their lifestyles. She pointed to a chair and instructed her "Sit down Allison. It's a terrible thing that has happened to not just this family but so many others. Those who loved each other for more than just the material things will be the ones to survive and rebuild their lives. This family is one of them. I know, you, Aaron and Jonathon will do everything you can to help your parents through this, I believe in you."

Allison put her arms around Dorie and exclaimed, "We will do what we can for them and that includes you, I love you Dorie." She replied, "I love you too child." This time being referred to as a child didn't upset Allison. Right now she felt like one again, needing comfort and reassurance from her nanny.

Aaron lay on the bed wondering where all this would take them. He had just left Jonathon, who stated he would never give up his dream of becoming a professional golfer despite what has happened. Even if they lost their membership at the club, he could get a job as a caddy. Aaron envied him for knowing his goal in life. His thoughts reverted back to the night with Blake Donlan. Blake had told him the time would come when he would know what his gift was. It better come soon," he told himself as the realization came to him that he no longer had the luxury of money enabling him to do anything he decided upon

Lillian lay next to James that night trying to absorb everything she had been told. Her father killed himself and her mother couldn't return home for several reasons. The servants were no longer there and she couldn't survive without them. Besides that, the creditors had ceased the house and furnishings, leaving Annie with only her clothing. As for them, everything was gone but their home. Sighing, she told herself she would do whatever she must to help James, her mother and the children through this. She must be strong for them.

James lay next to Lillian wondering what she was thinking. So much had been thrown upon her. A flash of insecurity rushed through him as it had Edward Thomas. "Does she love me enough? He remembered their vows, for richer or for poorer. Lillian snuggled up closer to him, innocently giving him the reassurance he so badly needed. Once again, he felt the familiar twinge of guilt he had endured through the years. He kissed the top of her head and enjoyed the sweet aroma of her hair, then drifted off into the first sleep he had in many of nights.

CHAPTER 8

Blake sat uneasy in the chair as he overlooked the bay, hopeful that one day he could truly enjoy the view. He fought the feeling that he had done something wrong by purchasing the Marshall Building, but why should he feel this way, after all, he offered James a loan and was refused. What more could he have done? Allison and Aaron kept creeping into his thoughts. It had been several months since the big crash and he wondered how they were coping with the life changing events. He closed his eyes and visualized Allison. His heart felt heavy as the image reminded him how much he desired her. He still intended to pursue her but knew he must be patient.

Lillian held her mother's hand as the Sheldrick house possessions were auctioned off to cover the bank's debts. The decision was made that Annie would return to Europe and stay with Rebecca, San Francisco only reminded her of the happiness she once had and lost.

As Lillian listened to the auctioneer she still could not understand why her mother would want to witness the sale of her home and belongings. When questioned, Annie explained to her that each item held a story and being able to see them once more as they came up for bid, would allow her to relive the memories for one last time. Silently, Lillian wondered if she would meet the same fate and one day lose her own home, so many others had. The only thing her and her family were living on now was the money from the sale of James beloved building, again her heart was saddened by his loss.

"Oh, look Lillian, Annie cried, "That's the beautiful Ming vase that held the flowers your father brought me the day you were born." Lillian had seen the vase as far back as she could remember, filled with flowers, adorning the table in their parlor. Until now, she hadn't known the story behind it. Sighing, she squeezed her mother's hand silently wishing she had the means to bid on it.

Tullah and Grange returned to the black community. Thanks to James Marshall, Grange had a job. Mr. Marshall had talked with his friend Elliott and Elliot offered both Grange and Tullah's uncle a job as maintenance men for several buildings he and Blake owned.

Tullah observed her surroundings. It was a far cry from the luxuries she had known at the Marshall's. Not unlike most the dwellings in the neighborhood, the walls were thin, leaving you feeling they were an optical illusion, as the neighbor's voices leaked through. The faucets and toilet dripped non-stop and no matter how clean she kept the place, roaches remained roommates. She hadn't had to deal with insects at the Marshall's. A man would come once a month and drive them from their hiding places and destroy them. She couldn't bear to step on or crush them when they appeared, so she would simply capture them buy putting a cup over the obnoxious insects until Grange returned home to perform their execution. It was a custom that Grange had become accustomed too. As she sat in her chair staring at the traps, she rubbed her belly. She was four months pregnant and at thirty-six years old, anticipating the child she never thought she would have. She relived her first meeting with Grange. He had only been employed at the Marshall's a week before they met. It was on her one free day a week that she always made time to go to the stables and visit with her Uncle Jake. As they were conversing, she noticed a horseman in the distance and became intrigued with the way he mastered the mare. It was Allison's horse and well known for not liking riders other than Allison. "Who is that" she asked her uncle?

"That's Grange. He got himself hired on as a handyman. She couldn't see his face from that distance and hoped disappointment wouldn't come to her as he came closer into view.

Jake continued, "Mrs. Marshall informed him she didn't need him today so he's exercising the horses. Poor things don't get much riding these days, not since Mr. Marshall brought home that horseless carriage. Miss Allison rides the most. She's loved to ride every since she was old enough to sit in the saddle."

A few minutes later, Grange entered the stables leading the beautiful sorrel. Tullah gasped. Seeing him up close was not a disappointment. All six foot three of him seemed too perfect. After being introduced, he spoke with a deep voice, "Well, Miss Tullah, all the beauty and fine things in that big house you live in have obviously rubbed off on you," Remembering that statement made her blush once again. From that day on she managed to get to the stables as much as possible. It really was love at first sight. Two months later they were married. A feeling of warmth spread over her as she remembered how wonderful the Marshall's had been to celebrate their wedding day. They were her only family other than her Uncle, who gave her away. Dori was the matron of honor and the wedding party consisted of James, Lillian, Aaron, Allison and Jonathon. Even with the loss of her job at the Marshall's she marveled at her good fortune and felt sorrow for the family who had lost all their wealth and given her so much love and respect through the years. She glanced down at an overturned cup that housed a roach, anxious for Granges return home.

Vera and her son were already tired of and resenting their new lifestyle. Her daughter Karen and Edward seemed to be adjusting with few problems. Gerald had turned to romancing older, still rich women and making illegal gin in the basement rather than seek employment. He purchased a still known as an Alky Cooker. It could produce a quart of gin a day at a good profit. The pungent smell of distilled alcohol and oil of juniper reeked throughout the basement. Vera figured if he could make money doing this, why not? She was upset with her daughter. How could Karen so easily accept their conditions after all they had known? Hadn't she appreciated their previous lifestyle? Edward entered the room receiving Vera's usual disgusted glare. He obtained a job at the surviving Bank of San Francisco which she considered humiliating.

"Look what you have become," she commented as he handed over his paycheck. "Do you realize we live on less than we used to pay our servants?"

Edward sighed. He had become used to her stabbing comments. "Yes, Vera, I'm very aware of it, but consider myself fortunate to even have a job, when so many are without work." The conversation was interrupted by the cook announcing dinner was ready. Much like the rest of the previously wealthy victims of the stock market, the cook was the only remaining servant. Pearl had accepted her pay cut and even at that, Edward silently hoped with what little money was left from the last stock he had sold and as Vera called it, "His meager pay check," he would be able to keep her. His hopes were not just for Vera's sake, no one in the family had ever cooked a meal. Vera continued her verbal lashing as they entered the dining room. Gerald and Karen were awaiting them. "Do you realize our daughter has worn out the soles of her best shoes, looking for work?"

Edward seated himself and directed his reply to his daughter, "Good for you Karen, I'm proud of you." They exchanged smiles. Vera stared at them in disbelief as he continued. "At least someone in this family has gumption and is willing to seek honest employment." The statement was directed at Gerald, which went ignored. Edward loved his son but didn't like him. Gerald's affairs with older women disgusted him. It was just an added hurt that the son he had so much hope for was nothing more than a gigolo and bootlegger.

"She's only sixteen," Vera exclaimed.

"Correct me if I'm wrong my dear, but were you not sixteen when I married you?"

Humph, she returned, "I guess our children will have to pay for my mistake." Karen cried, "Mother, I can't believe you said that!" Edward disregarded the comment. The only consoling factor in realizing that Vera never really loved him was that he had begun to lose his love for her, so the hurt wasn't as deep as it had been. The remainder of dinner was completed in silence.

Jonathon rushed into the Marshall dining room late for dinner, exclaiming, "I have an announcement to make." He immediately gained their attention as they wondered what was causing his excitement. With pride, he informed them, "I am now an official caddy at the club." The family cheered "Congratulations." They knew how important it was for him to be at the golf course. James silently wondered who amongst his friends could still afford to remain a member. After going through a mental list of associates, he decided, "Oh, yes, the Donlan's for one." He was thankful his dear friend had not been affected by the crash.

Aaron asked, "Will you be allowed to use the course to practice?"

"Yes, I can golf the early morning hours before the club opens. Everything is working out just great." Lillian smiled with pride at her son.

Aaron was happy for his brother but shamed by the fact that he hadn't come up with any kind of work even though he had been trying, but so few jobs were available. After the market crashed, the competition for a job anywhere, doing anything thing, was horrendous, several hundred people would apply for one available opening. He and Allison both filled out an application for a job at the sugar refinery. Four jobs were offered and a thousand hopefuls applied. His frustrated thoughts were interrupted as Jonathon predicted, "I just know I can be a professional golfer and make lots of money." No one doubted him.

Allison lay in bed that night thinking of Gerald. She realized that their worlds would never again be as they once knew it but that didn't change her love for him, nothing could. Her mother mentioned how Vera had become very distant at the Women's Club meetings. Those meetings were really all that was left of their social world. The Mah Jong games and tea had continued, despite the depression. She decided that tomorrow, she would pay the Thomas's a visit. Envisioning Gerald she drifted off to sleep.

It was a sunny day when she arrived at the Thomas's house. Memories of the past saddened her as she remembered the wonderful garden parties and dances she had attended at the beautiful Spanish style mansion just a short time ago. Now, the once beautiful grounds showed signs of neglect which surprised her. Their family had done the best they could to maintain their gardens, especially Aaron and Jonathon, while Dorie faithfully attended the roses. She followed the terra cotta tiles up to the porch and knocked. After what seemed a lengthy time, Vera answered the door.

"Oh, my dear Allison, what brings you here? She raised her arms and smoothed her hair. I feel I look a fright for this unexpected call." Allison couldn't help but notice the dark circles under Vera's eyes and the one time perfect hair appeared as unkempt as the gardens.

Allison replied in a quieter than normal voice, "I was just in the area and I thought I would stop by and see Gerald, if he's here."

Vera took her hand and exclaimed, "Yes, as a matter of fact, he is. Do come in but please excuse the house if it appears a bit untidy. Things haven't been the same since we lost the servants, Karen and I do the best we can."

Allison replied sympathetically, while being led to the parlor, "I understand Mrs. Thomas." Allison felt the loss of gaiety she had always experienced when she was at the Thomas's. Empty vases that one time held beautiful flowers from the gardens stood on dust neglected furniture, looking abandoned. Unopened curtains concealed the stained and leaded windows she had always admired. Suddenly she was regretting her decision to visit Gerald. Vera instructed her to sit.

"I'll inform Gerald your here. I'm sure he will be delighted." Vera walked through the large vacant kitchen that was once filled and bustling with servants to retrieve her son from the basement. Depression flooded her as she remembered that just a short time ago she had hopes that Gerald and Allison would marry and the two families' wealth would merge. Now, the Marshall's were just about as broke as they were.

It seemed forever to Allison before Vera returned with Gerald following. Her heart quickened as it always did when he was near. He greeted her with a large smile, leaving her relieved that he appeared the same.

"Allison, it's good to see you, these months haven't changed you. You're as beautiful as ever." She blushed and thanked him. He took her hand, and her heart quickened. "Follow me," he led her outside. They walked along the overgrown garden path to an iron scrolled bench and sat down. Allison was the first to speak.

"I've missed you Gerald. It seems everything and everyone has changed so much. Tell me you haven't changed." She watched as the expression on his face saddened.

"I'm sorry Allison, I have changed. Everyday I mourn my previous life. I want it back and I will do anything I have to, too regain it." As he spoke, he admired her beauty and innocence. She now appeared child-like compared to the much older women he had been with, the ones that provided him with some of the luxuries he was used to. Allison questioned, "What if you never get it back?" Gerald stood and looked down at her and she witnessed the previously sad look turn bitter.

"I said I would regain my world back and I will." She saw the determination set in his face and her heart froze with his next words.

"Forget me Allison. I have nothing to offer you." We can't afford each other. She stood and put her arms around him stating, "How can you tell me to forget you? I have loved you every since we were children." He pulled away.

"Well, were not children any more and the parties over. When I said I had nothing to offer, the same goes for you. You have nothing to offer me. You're as poor as I am." Allison began to feel physically ill and tried to deny what she just heard. Gerald was the first boy to kiss her, she was twelve. He even whispered in her ear that wonderful moment that he loved her. She believed him and loved him from that day on. This just couldn't be. Her own voice was strange to her as she pleaded, "You don't mean that Gerald. I can't believe you won't let yourself love me because my family no longer has money. What about your heart, doesn't it tell you anything?" His eyes grew steely cold, frightening her.

"What heart, he replied? I have to go now. There's something in the basement that requires my attention." She watched numbly as he walked away, leaving her standing there feeling as wilted and dead as the once beautiful gardens.

Walking away, Gerald cursed the situation. He too remembered that fist kiss and realized that he actually had loved Allison, but he also knew he loved himself more and had no desire to live poorly.

Driving home, Allison had difficulty seeing through her tears. She tried to convince herself Gerald couldn't really be that shallow. He was just bitter and resentful right now, eventually he would return to the man she loved, it would just take a little time. Feeling the need for consolation she decided to stop by her father's office. He would reassure her that Gerald would come to his senses. She parked her car and walked up the marbled staircase to the second floor. Reaching the door to his office, she became confused. The gold print on the door read San Francisco Bay Real Estate

Brokers. She entered and the aged Dorothy Hansen greeted her. Dorothy had been her father's secretary as far back as Allison could remember.

Surprised to see Allison, Dorothy welcomed her, "Miss Marshall, so nice to see you." Allison smiled and thanked her before stating, "I'm here to see my father." The elder lady's smile faded and she became perplexed.

"I'm sorry Miss Marshall. Didn't you're father tell you he sold the building?" Mr. Donlan purchased it a several months ago." Seeing Allison's face pale confirmed to her that she hadn't been told. "I'm sorry dear, it was a sad day for me too when I found out. I was with your father for twenty years."

Allison questioned, "Elliott bought it?"

"No, his son Blake," Dorothy answered. Numbed, Allison thanked her and turned to leave. Blake walked out of his office just as she was exiting. He would not have known it was Allison, had she not turned to ask Dorothy another question. Stunned by her sudden appearance, he froze, staring at her from across the room. Allison returned a stare as coldly as the one she had previously received from Gerald. Blake spoke, "Miss Marshall, what brings you here?"

"I came to see my father but have been informed that he no longer owns this building, Tell me Mr. Donlan, What's it like to be a vulture and pick the bones of a broken man?" Dorothy was shocked as she witnessed the confrontation. The loathing look Blake received from Allison silenced him momentarily before he replied, "I regret you have such a low opinion of me Miss Marshall and it appears I have offended you once again, I apologize."

"Enjoy your purchase Mr. Donlan," Allison stated as she turned and walked away. He stood there gazing at the closed door until Dorothy exclaimed, "I don't understand her behaving like that. Mr. Marshall sold the building voluntarily. I have known Allison since she was a little girl. She's always been so sweet. I can't believe she said that to you."

Blake sighed, "The depression has changed a lot of people Dorothy. Let's hope that it hasn't changed her and this was just a temporary outburst." He excused himself and returned to his office. He tried to concentrate on his work but visions of Allison kept interfering. She was more beautiful than he remembered. It seemed that each time they met he managed to push her further away. Once more he reminded himself to be patient. The rose would bloom. He grinned to himself and called the florist. Afterwards, he looked at his watch. He was scheduled to meet with Kathryn at Macky's new place for dinner. They were what he considered intimate friends although he knew she wanted much more than that. She was the proprietor of DeLeons, a very successful woman's clothing salon, despite the depression her business was flourishing due to the continued patronage of the old rich who were only slightly affected by the crash. Putting on his coat and hat, he informed Dorothy he would be gone the rest of the day.

Allison ran to the den in search of her father. He wasn't there either. She found her mother in the parlor and asked anxiously, "Mother where is father if he's not at home and no longer has an office to go to? I went to The Marshall Building to see him and was informed by Dorothy it had been sold."

Lillian sighed and put aside her mending. "We didn't want to have to share another loss with you children. The money from the sale of the building is what we are living on. As to where your father is and has been during the day, he's out looking for work." Allison moaned and left the room in tears. The day had been too much for her.

CHAPTER 9

James wandered aimlessly. He had left home early that morning, searching for work. "Where is there to look, he asked himself?" All he ever knew was mining and the stock market and he was certainly too old to start mining again. Just as Aaron and Allison had experienced, for each available job, hundreds were applying and most much younger than he. Defeat overwhelmed him as he witnessed the lines outside the employment agency. Around the corner was a breadline with equally as many people in it. His eyes fell on a distinguished looking man in an expensive suit, which made it obvious that at one time he had been successful. He was selling apples for a nickel each. James remembered reading in the paper that a vessel was docked in the bay, bringing with it a large shipment of apples and offering to share the sales profit with anyone willing to hawk them. James arrived too late. Already, they were being sold on every corner. Discouraged, he headed back home.

Aaron smiled at Robert Cunningham as the overly large man behind the desk sweated without obvious reason. He felt that he should be the one sweating after having endured the lengthy interview. The man was telling him to report for work, first thing in the morning. Aaron couldn't believe it. He was now assistant editor of The Bayside News. Maybe this was his gift for survival. At college he wrote for the campus newspaper and enjoyed it. His father obtained him the interview after reading an ad in the paper. Cunningham and James had known each other for many years. Aaron remembered his father's statement. "I got you the interview, the rest is up to you. If you get the job, it's because he believes you're capable of it."

Aaron stood and accepted the pudgy hand extended to him and thanked the man.

"You're welcome Aaron, but don't think I've done you a favor, its hard work. The job is stressful. We have to meet all the deadlines. See you in the morning."

Aaron replied, "Yes, and I promise you, I will give it my best."

"I know you will, that's why I hired you." Aaron left the newspaper exhilarated.

Flowers arrived for Allison, causing excitement in the family. What a short time ago would have been considered a simple jester was now a luxury and display of wealth. She read the small card, even though without reading it she knew they were from Blake, wildflowers and a single rose bud. She remembered the first one she received. He had told her to observe her bouquet. She hadn't wanted to, but became intrigued with it and as predicted, the wildflowers lasted and once the rose bloomed, they wilted and faded away together. His card simply read, Blake. She felt a slight remorse for her behavior towards him the previous day.

"There's that unusual bouquet again, who sent them, Lillian asked?" Setting the card down, Allison replied, Blake."

James was surprised and questioned, "Elliott's son. Why is he sending flowers?"

"I don't know Allison exclaimed, ashamed to mention her actions towards him the previous day. We merely shared half a dance at my coming out party.

"Well, Lillian replied, he's a fine looking man and he's wealthy."

Allison screeched, "Money! Money! Is that all Gerald and everyone else thinks about anymore, is that all that's important. Lillian was distraught over her daughter's outburst. She knew Allison had gone to visit Gerald and wondered what could have happened to cause such a reaction to such a simple statement. She thought silently to herself, regarding Allison's question. "Yes, of course money was important, it represented the carefree lifestyle they lost so abruptly, but no, it wasn't everything. She put her arms around her daughter.

"Allison, she replied, "It is very difficult for us who have known prosperity to adjust, be patient, most of us are trying, you mentioned Gerald."

"Yes, as a matter of fact I did, she answered while trying to hide her tears. In a choked voice, she continued. The Edward's house and gardens have been neglected. It was so beautiful mother, I can't believe how different it is, and Mrs. Edward's was like a stranger. She was almost as un-kept as the house and grounds. She was not herself! Then Gerald informed me that since we no longer have money there could never be a serious relationship between us.

Lillian gasped while James shook his head sorrowfully before stating, "Maybe you're lucky to find out his true character." Allison became even more disturbed. Her father hadn't said what she wanted to hear, that Gerald would eventually change his attitude. She cried, "I just can't believe he meant it."

"Time will tell my dear," James replied sadly. Like Aaron, he was not fond of Gerald. He considered him a loser but knew better than to mention those feelings to his daughter. Allison wondered how much time it would take before Gerald might return to the boy and man she had fallen in love with. Frustrated, she handed the bouquet of flowers to her mother, exclaiming, "I'm going to take Charmer for a ride and groom her."

James became uneasy. It was getting close to the time he would have to explain to Allison that they could no longer afford to keep the horses. It was difficult enough just to feed and shelter the family. Some of their friends had taken to having their horses slaughtered to put meat on the table, which was something he refused to do. He dreaded the thought of his sweet Allison having to give up the mare and wondered how much more she could take. Once again the feeling of helplessness overcame him. What was he going to do? The funds from the Marshall Building wouldn't last forever.

The wind felt good on her face as they raced along the beach. Riding Charmer was always invigorating too her. Already it seemed to help clear her head. She convinced herself that Gerald would loose his bitterness once he adjusted to the new life they all were experiencing. "He's just not himself right now." Confidant that she was right, she returned to the stables to groom Charmer. Never once had it occurred to her that she may also lose her beloved horse.

Kathryn watched admiringly as Blake approached the table at Macky's. The quote, "God created all men equal" would be impossible to believe in reference to the tall, dark-haired man now standing in front of her. His appearance never ceased to arouse her. He apologized. "I'm sorry I kept you waiting." She smiled and replied, "Believe me Blake, you're worth waiting for. He thanked her for the compliment as he seated himself across from her.

"Don't thank me Blake, just feed me, I'm starved."

Shortly after ordering dinner, Macky arrived at the table exclaiming, "Blake, Kathryn, my two favorite people and might I add, my best customers. You grace my establishment. It's good to see the depression hasn't hampered you from enjoying illegal booze and good food."

Blake teased, "Macky, "You old fox, I quit counting, how many locations have you had now?"

Proudly, Macky confessed, "About eight. He continued, I have to admit though, it's getting expensive. That's why my prices keep going up. I'm about ready to give in and pay for protection, but enough of this talk, the next drink is on the house." They thanked him as he excused himself to welcome other guests. Macky was well liked and most patrons would follow him to a dozen different locations if need be.

Even though he was laughing, Macky was experiencing a lot of heat from the so-called protection committee. He had already made the decision to pay. They had won, although he prided himself for holding out so long.

While eating, Kathryn mentioned she needed a sales clerk. Her friend who had been with her for so long got married and was going to move to Los Angeles.

On a hunch, Blake figured Allison might be searching for a job and asked Kathryn, "Do me a favor, there's a young girl I know that could possibly use a job, would you consider her?"

Kathryn noticed an unusual look on his face as he mentioned the girl. There was something about her that affected him. "Please excuse me, I'm suddenly feeling jealous. What's this girl to you?"

Taken by surprise with her detection of his feelings, he replied, "She's the daughter of a longtime friend of my fathers. The family was hurt badly when the stock market crashed." Realizing she would do anything he asked of her, Kathryn replied, "Okay, if that's what you want, what's her name?" With a smile that expressed thanks, he answered, "Allison Marshall."

Surprised, Kathryn repeated the name. "Allison Marshall, Allison and her mother are two of my best customers. I missed them coming into the shop but didn't realize they were victims of the market, I'll get in touch with her first thing tomorrow." Blake thanked her, leaving her still feeling uneasy regarding his concern. She remembered admiring the young girl's beauty each time she appeared from a dressing room questioning if a certain dress was flattering or appropriate. There was no such thing as an unflattering dress when it came to Allison Marshall, she would look good in anything. Already she was beginning to regret her promise to Blake.

Gerald adjusted his tie. Tonight he would be with Annabelle Gilder. She was old and so was her money. In fact, she hardly noticed the crash. He found security with her despite the fact she was twenty years his senior. Her body was pretty good for a woman of her age, which helped. If he kept himself drunk enough he could endure their sexual encounters, she wasn't overly demanding. The evening would consist of dinner, drinks and dancing at Macky's. Then she would take him to her home on Knob Hill and seduce him. His reward would come the next day when he would play a polo match, riding the horse she purchased for him and held in her stables. One last look in the mirror assured him of his handsome outer image while ignoring the condition of his inner self.

It was a full house at Macky's as Blake escorted Kathryn from the dance floor. He recognized Gerald the moment he and the older woman entered the room and silently observed them for sometime. Kathryn followed his gaze, and questioned, "Do you know them?"

Blake answered, "Not personally. The man is a friend of Allison Marshall's."

"Well, she replied, "I know the woman he's with, they don't come any richer and as you can see, she likes her men young. I guess money can buy you anything." The comment struck him, Allison was no longer rich, perhaps now Gerald would lose complete interest in her. Then again, she may lose interest in Gerald, he silently wondered, "How much does money mean to her?"

Dorie observed the activity at the Marshall household. She was extremely proud of all of them, especially James and Lillian. Despite their misfortune, they remained very close and supportive of each other. She knew the young could draw from their youth to help carry them through, but for the elderly, it took courage and faith. She went to her room and retrieved her book from the suitcase. As she turned the pages, she noticed they were becoming tattered on the edges. Once again she wondered, were the words she had so carefully written through the years merely for herself. The fear of the twin's true identity being discovered still haunted her even though Mr. Marshall had tried to convince her it would never happen. He always stated, "They're more white than black." Lovingly she held the book close, telling herself, she would have to destroy it. Sadly her babies would never know the truth about her or their mother Trilly. The phone rang and Dorie heard Jonathon inform Allison, "It's for you."

Allison assumed it was Beatrice calling her and was surprised by an unfamiliar voice.

"Allison, this is Kathryn DeLeon. I heard you might be looking for work and I am in need of a sales clerk, if you're interested." Allison was awe struck. How could she be having such luck? She replied enthusiastically, "Yes, Miss De Leon I am seeking work and would truly appreciate a position at your store."

"Good, then come in Thursday morning and I will start training you." Allison thanked her and hung up the phone. Screeching with joy, she ran into the parlor to inform her mother.

Lillian immediately noticed the excitement on Allison's face as she entered the room. "Can you believe it, she exclaimed, I have a job. I start tomorrow morning as a sales clerk at DeLeons." Lillian shared her excitement and then sighed as she remembered their shopping trips to the elegant salon. That too was a thing of the past. She questioned, "How did you manage to get a job there?" Allison stood before her with a blank look. How did she get the job? She hadn't applied. Answering honestly, she exclaimed, "I don't know."

Lillian stated, "Well, someone is watching over you!" Allison could not imagine who it could be.

It was Aaron's first day at the newspaper and he found himself anxious to become apart of the activity that was going on around him. The phones were ringing, newsmen anxiously answered them hoping for a headline story. Typewriters sat awaiting the return of reporters out on assignment. The room was filled with an air of anticipation. The city was waiting for the news and there was a deadline to meet. "Yes, he told himself. I'm going to like this." He went to the office assigned to him and settled down behind his desk. A timid knock on the door drew his attention. It opened halfway before a young woman spoke as she entered. "Mr. Marshall, I'm your secretary Melissa Barnum. He had been informed that he would have a secretary but dared not hope she would look like this. Aaron stood and greeted her. "Nice to meet you Miss Barnum, is Miss correct?"

"That's correct," she answered with a smile. He was pleased with the reply.

She questioned, may I get you a cup of coffee or is there something else you need me to do?"

Aaron hoped she hadn't detected the effect she had on him as he replied, "A cup of coffee would be nice." He watched closely as the petite redhead exited, telling himself that she could become a real distraction.

As Melissa poured his cup of coffee, she reminded herself that he was her boss and she must try to ignore the physical attraction she felt the moment she saw him. Aaron was a far cry from old Mr. Edgar's, who finally came to the conclusion to retire after thirty-five years. She was his secretary for two of those years, and was relieved to hear his decision to quit. He had become a grumpy, old man. She returned with the aromatic brew. "Here's your coffee Mr. Marshall."

As Aaron thanked her, he gazed into the greenest eyes he had ever seen.

"Is there anything else I can get you?"

Pulling away from her eyes he answered, "Yes, as a matter of fact there is. Would you bring me copies of the last two weeks newspapers?"

"Yes, I will get them for you right away," she replied eager to please him." As she turned to leave, Aaron questioned, "Miss Barnum, do I detect an accent?"

She blushed and exclaimed, "Yes, I haven't been able to conceal it even after all this time. My family moved here from Georgia about fifteen years ago.

"Well, he stated, I find it quite pleasant. She thanked him and left the room. Once more he watched her exit. Yes, she was definitely a distraction.

"Help me, Tullah pleaded to Grange." She had started labor two weeks early. He tried to get a doctor. There were now two in the community but they were unable to attend Tullah due to the more life threatening demands of others. I'll get you a doctor from the white community, he exclaimed."

"No, she pleaded, get me Dorie. She can help me," Having no other choice, Grange agreed. He feared leaving her alone but had to get to a telephone. It was a foggy, rainy day as he called for help from a pay phone in a restaurant a block away from their apartment. Lillian answered and could tell whoever it was on the other end of the line was extremely distressed, he asked for Dori. Hurriedly, she went to her room, "Dori, you have a phone call." Dorie couldn't imagine who would be calling her. She answered the phone in Allison's room.

"Dorie, it's me Grange." Immediately she detected the desperate sound in his voice and knew it had something to do with Tullah.

"Tell me what has happened," she asked worriedly.

"I'm scared Dorie. Tullah is in labor too early and we can't get a doctor here, she's asking for you." Her heart sank and she became silent, remembering Trilly. The voice on the other end of the line cried, "Are you there," Dorie?

"Yes, she answered. I'll be there as fast as I can. Hopefully Mr. Marshall or one of and tell her I'm coming." Grange thanked her and eagerly rushed back to his wife to tell her Dorie was on the way. the twins can bring me. The trolley will take too long. You get back to Tullah right now

Dorie entered the parlor. "Mr. Marshall, Mrs. Marshall, I hate to disturb you but there's an emergency and I'm hoping you can give me a ride." They both looked at her with concern. James questioned, "What's the emergency Dorie?"

"It's Tullah. The baby is coming early and the doctor's are too busy to attend to her. I have been a midwife before and she's asking for me."

Lillian exclaimed, "Heavens, I didn't recognize Grange's voice, of course James will take you. As a matter of fact I'll go too, maybe I can be of some help, Tullah has always been special to me."

"Thank you Mrs. Marshall. I'm sure she'll appreciate it."

James informed them he would get the car, as he ran to the hall tree for his coat and hat. With-in minutes the three of them were on their way. As they rode, both Dorie and James remembered a similar situation over eighteen years ago. The fog slowed them down causing it to take much longer than anticipated in reaching their destination. Arriving, James recognized the same type buildings he had rescued the twins and Dorie from and a surge of sorrow ran through him as he felt he had let Tullah and Grange down, subjecting them to these conditions. It was a first experience for Lillian and she remained silently appalled by the sight of the dilapidated structures lining the street. Grange was pacing curbside frantically awaiting their appearance. A look of relief covered his face as he greeted them. "Thank God you're here, he exclaimed. I'm so worried. She looks so tired and weak." They climbed the wooden stairs that moaned even under Lillian's small stature. Grange opened the door to a small one-bedroom apartment. Tullah, not surprising had it spotless despite, poor conditions.

Dorie and Lillian quickly entered the bedroom announcing their presence. "Were here Tullah and were going to help you through this. Tullah peered at them through eyes blinded with pain and questioned, Dorie, Mrs. Marshall?" They both answered, "Yes."

The two men sat helplessly in the next room trying to ignore Tullah's agonizing screams. Retrieving a pot of boiling water Dorie tried to conquer the fear she was feeling. Surely a double birth wouldn't happen again. She looked at her watch. It had been two minutes since Tullah's last contraction, the time was close. She passed by the two men quickly and returned to the bedroom with the water. She grabbed the hand Lillian wasn't holding and was surprised by the strength of Tullah's grip. Dorie looked to see if Lillian could handle the painful grasp. Understanding the silent question, she smiled at Dorie and nodded her head. Between contractions, Tullah expressed her love for them. They assured her the feeling was mutual. Once more a pain hit and Dorie instructed her to bear down. "Bear down hard with this one Tullah and your baby should come into the world. Lillian's heart raced as she remembered her last pain before Jonathon had been born. An experience she was still thankful for only to have endured once.

Grange and James leaped from their chairs as a scream surpassed all the others. James felt a weakness in his legs. They held their breath and silently stared at the closed door. Suddenly it was quiet; leaving them feeling the silence was worse than the screams. After what seemed forever, an infant's cry released them from their trance. Lillian opened the door and proudly announced, "Grange you're the father of a handsome, healthy son."

The two men exhaled and embraced each other before Grange rushed into the room to his wife and new son.

James put his arms around Lillian and expressed his love for her. Dorie entered the room holding the infant and was warmed by the sight. James peered at the baby and exclaimed, "Well, little fellow, thanks to you, I feel like I did years ago working the mines, totally exhausted. You sure took long enough getting here." Dorie and Lillian shared a grin. They had only been there for an hour.

Returning the baby to his mother, the two women and James said their goodbye to the happy parents. Dorie wanted to stay but there were no accommodations for her so she promised to return the next day.

On their return home, each of them, were quietly lost in their own thoughts. Suddenly the fog thickened. From the back seat Dorie overheard Lillian questioning James regarding the conditions. He assured her it was just a small bank of fog and they would be out of it shortly.

The headlights of the other vehicle seemed to appear from the fog like a phantom with large glaring eyes. A shout from Lillian, the grinding of metal and breaking glass were the last things Dorie remembered.

CHAPTER 10

The twins and Jonathon sat huddled together, numb with shock. They were in the waiting room of the black community's hospital awaiting word on Dorie's condition. Allison stared into the distance with sad, swollen eyes. Aaron relived the horror of the call, informing him that their parents had been involved in a head on collision with a truck and killed instantly. The feeling of loss was so great for Jonathon he had to fight to keep from moaning out loud. The black patron's observed them curiously, wondering who could be important enough to bring them to Nigger town. After and hour or so a doctor entered the room and advised them if they wanted to see Dorie once more they best go in, her internal injuries were severe.

With dread and knowing it would be their last goodbye to their beloved nanny, they approached her bed. Allison took one of Dorie's hands in hers and Aaron held the other. Jonathon stood at the foot of the bed still trying to fight the painful moan with-in him. Allison whispered her name and Dorie responded. She saw Jonathon in front of her and weakly called his name. He forced a smile for her. Then she realized that someone was holding her hands. She looked at the twins and a smiled crossed her face as she exclaimed, "Roosevelt and Hattie." Confused, the three looked at each other and Jonathon replied, "No Dorie, its Allison and Aaron." She sighed, "Oh, yes, that's right." She then asked what had happened. Aaron explained to her that she had been in a car accident. She questioned, "Are your parent's alright?" Never having lied to Dorie, he told her of their deaths. Tears rolled down her cheeks as she remembered her first ride with James Marshall in a horseless carriage and how fearful she had been. Through all these years she still had gained little faith in automobiles. Allison squeezed her hand and pleaded, "Please don't you leave us too Dorie."

With effort, she replied, "My babies, I don't want to leave you but I'm afraid the time has come for you to take care of yourselves. I must leave you now and join my Trent and Trilly." Taking a final breath, a look of fear came over her as she realized she had neglected to destroy her diary. Her last words came, "My book." The three remained silent; not understanding anything Dorie had said. Names of people they were unfamiliar with and what book? Suddenly they realized she was no longer with them. "Dorie, Dorie," Allison cried, as she felt the now limp hand in hers. The hand, that comforted her so many times, brushed her hair, wiped away tears, held hers after a nightmare until she fell back to sleep. What would she do without Dori? Aaron came to her and put his arms around her as tears unashamedly fell from own his eyes. Jonathon ran from the room to find a place where he could finally let out the moan that he had held prisoner in his throat for so long.

The day of the Marshall's funeral was as miserable as the night they had been killed. Fog hung over the city and rained dripped off black umbrellas as if imitating the tears of the people grasping them. Blake stood motionless as he observed Allison in a black dress and veil. A far cry from the lively peach colored creation she wore the night he met the debutante. He couldn't see the sorrow on her face due to the veil but he felt it for her. How badly he wanted to comfort her. As the services came to a conclusion, he watched as Gerald Edwards approached Allison and put his arms around her. Jealousy surged through him. His father distracted him and they followed the procession back to the Marshall house to express their condolences.

The crowd was large and Allison was tired. Each expression of sorrow just reminded her of her own but she knew these were friends only trying to console her and her brothers. Gerald was there and that was important to her. He remained beside her most the day, leaving Blake experiencing a continued jealousy, which was temporarily erased by his father's next statement.

"I'm afraid the problems for the Marshall children are really just beginning."

"What do you mean," Blake questioned?"

"James let his insurance lapse. Without insurance it will be impossible for them to maintain it. Between payments, taxes and upkeep it will be unaffordable for them." Blake was deeply concerned by what he was hearing.

Elliott continued, "You know as well as I, that because of the depression if they try to sell now, they will only receive half of what it's worth, if they're lucky, and luck doesn't appear to be on their side. If they did sell, between the three of them there wouldn't be enough profit to afford any of them a year's worth of average income. There is still a mortgage owing. James believed there were better places to invest his money and borrowed against the house to invest in the market." After his statement Elliott recognized Blake's concern and he knew it was directed towards Allison. He also noticed the way he watched her during the services. "Son, please get your mind off that girl, she's not right for you."

"How do you know that," Blake questioned in an extremely annoyed voice? Elliott flinched. Due to his friendship with James through the years and his trust, he felt the obligation to keep the secret of the twin's true heritage, but feared the thought of Blake possibly uniting with Allison and introducing Negro blood into their pure Irish lineage. He answered his son's question the best he could without betraying James trust. "I know this doesn't sound like a good reason, but I just feel it."

Blake replied, "You're right, it's not a good enough reason. Besides at this point you need not worry. She wants nothing to do with me. Maybe she never will, so relax." Elliott detected the annoyance in his son's voice and excused himself to give his condolences to James and Lillian's children.

After the crowd around Allison and her brothers subsided, Blake decided it was time to express his sympathy.

Allison was the first to notice him approach. Immediately she became intimidated and told herself too not over react. He was merely there out of respect for her parents. Aaron greeted him, he was pleased to see Blake again and extended his hand, "Blake, thanks for coming. You've met Allison, and this is my brother Jonathon." Allison smiled demurely at him for an instant before turning her attention back to Gerald who seemed overly attentive. Blake accepted the response and held out a hand to Jonathon. "It's good to meet another member of the Marshall's. All of you have my deepest sympathy." As he spoke, Allison couldn't help but appreciate the soft spoken but masculine voice. The word he had used at her party came to her, "lust." He had said all the men there were looking at her with lust on their faces. True to his word, if Blake had any for her it was well hidden. Besides, the only one she wanted to see that look on would be Gerald. After giving his condolences, Blake and his father headed home. It was a quiet ride. Elliott didn't want to say anything that would bring up the subject of Allison. The car pulled up to the house and his father exited the gray sedan. Blake bid him goodnight and asked him to tell his mother that he was sorry she wasn't feeling well and unable to attend the services.

Elliott assured him she would get the message. As his father disappeared into the house, Blake continued the drive home. It had been a long day and the renewed vision of Allison lingered in his mind. Suddenly it was blurred by another vision, Gerald Thomas. He lay in bed that night once again trying to understand Allison's fixation with Gerald and why, was his father was so adamant that he should ignore his feelings for Allison.

Dorie's funeral was two days after their parents. Thankfully the sun was finally shining. The services were short and consisted of Aaron, Allison, Jonathon, Tullah, Grange, Jake and the baby. Sadly, they realized they were all she had. Each stood graveside remembering their beloved nanny and friend. Allison was thankful that the roses were in bloom and made sure each one that had blossomed in Dorie's garden, decorated her grave. Especially the two-toned ones she had referred to as her favorite. After the services, Allison returned Tullah, Grange and the baby back home.

Tullah had decided after all the family had done for them, Marshall would be a fine name for their boy. Allison held the child close to her as she rocked him and conversed with his mother. Tullah wiped a tear away while expressing her guilt for having called Dorie for help that evening. "You're parents and Dorie would be alive if I hadn't."

Allison consoled her. "You can't blame yourself. You had no idea of the weather conditions. For heaven's sake, you were busy trying to have a baby."

Tullah cried, "I miss them so much. Your parents were so good to me and Dorie was like having a big sister. I can still see her writing in that little book of hers."

Allison exclaimed, Dories last words were, "My book." She seemed confused and disoriented. She mentioned "Roosevelt and Hattie. Do those names mean anything to you?" Out of respect for the Marshall's and knowing they never felt it necessary to tell the twins they were adopted, Tullah declined from telling Allison that her and Aaron were originally called Roosevelt and Hattie. She lied. "No, perhaps those were the names of the twins she cared for before you and your brother."

"That's probably it," Allison replied. She stayed a little longer and they sipped tea, reminiscing tales of their missing loved ones. On the way home Allison became curious about the book Dorie and Tullah had spoken of. She would look for it and hopefully learn more about her dear nanny and who the people were she spoke of for the first time on her deathbed, Trent, Trilly, Roosevelt and Hattie? Why hadn't she ever mentioned them before?

Arriving home, Aaron informed her that Elliott called and requested them to be at his office in the morning. "He needs to go over the will with us." Allison sighed and asked where Jonathon was.

"He had to work right after the funeral." Aaron felt his sister's depression and made a suggestion. "Hey, I just got a paycheck, so let's splurge and go have some Chinese food. We need something to cheer us up."

"That sounds like a great idea," Allison answered with enthusiasm.

During dinner at The Pagoda, Aaron expressed his surprise at enjoying his new job and how taken he was with his secretary. This pleased Allison since until now he hadn't shown interest in any of the women he had dated. She observed her brother for the first time as a man. A handsome man any women would be proud to be seen with. Aaron caught her stare and questioned "Why are you looking at me that way?"

Allison smiled and exclaimed "You're not going to believe this but for the first time I realize that you're a grown man, not just my brother."

Aaron dwelled on her words for a moment before laughing and replying, "I'm so glad I have become a man in your eyes and someday I may look at you as a grown woman."

Allison threw her napkin at him. "Darn you Aaron, I'm a woman now."

"Okay, if you say so," he replied still laughing. Allison joined in and after a moment stated, "I honestly didn't think I had a laugh left in me after all that has happened." Aaron took her hand in his and said, "I know, but it's good to laugh. They would want it."

On the way home, Allison told Aaron that Kathryn DeLeon, was understanding in regards to her absence from the employment she had offered her. "She told me the job was there for me as soon as I felt up to it. I think I'll start the first of next week." Aaron stated that it would be good for her. "It will help to keep your mind off of all the terrible things that have happened lately."

They returned home. Entering the house, it felt empty, so many voices missing. They would never again hear their parents at breakfast or in the parlor discussing the day's events. Nor would they hear Dorie humming peacefully while attending to her garden. Allison always loved her home, but now, more than ever, she cherished it and its memories. It was the only thing left of her past.

Elliott sat in his office waiting to hear from his secretary that the Marshall's had arrived. He dreaded telling them even more bad news and wondered how much more they would have to endure. He sighed when informed they were there.

He, stood to greet them as they entered, then instructed them to sit. They sat in silence waiting for him to speak. Nervously he cleared his throat a couple of times before he began. "Aaron, Allison, Jonathon, I have been your father's attorney for many years and have considered myself his friend as well, therefore what I have to say is not easy for me." He hesitated. In all his years he never had a more difficult time getting words out.

"What is it Mr. Donlan," Aaron questioned?"

"Your father had little left other than the money from the sale of the Marshall Building. The entire fortune he gained from stock was lost when the market crashed. The house was never paid off. He felt there were better places to invest his money. It all went into stock. At the time it seemed right."

"What about insurance, Aaron questioned?"

"None, after the collapse of the market he quit paying it, probably hoping there would be a come- back, and he could re-activate the policy. None of us plan on dying." The threesome sat quietly for a moment trying to digest the words they had just been fed. Aaron was again the first to speak. "You're saying there is nothing left. Not even our home?"

"No, you still have some money coming from the sale of the Marshall Building, plus your equity in the house and its belongings. You have your cars and the horses in the stables." Instantly Allison thought of Charmer and cried inwardly. "No, no, she couldn't lose her too, but how would she be able to keep her?" Elliott observed them as they tried to absorb their situation. He especially watched Allison and could understand his son's attraction to her, she was beautiful, and marveled that there were no visual signs of her Negro heritage. It was undetectable in both her and Aaron.

Aaron stood and thanked him. "On behalf of my father Mr. Donlan, I know he considered you a good friend and we thank you for all you've done. We will keep in touch." Allison and Jonathon then stood and thanked him before leaving the room as quietly as they had entered.

Elliott sighed with relief that the ordeal was over. His thoughts drifted to James and he spoke silently. "I don't know if you can hear me James, but you have children to be proud of. They didn't whine, protest or blame anyone. They just accepted what is. I know they will make it. After all, they did inherit something valuable, your fortitude." He picked up the phone to call Blake, as promised.

Dorothy informed Blake, "Your father is on the phone." He thanked her and picked up the receiver, anxious to find out the results of the meeting. "How did it go?"

"As good as could be expected for three people learning they have almost nothing after having almost everything. I have to admit I was very impressed with them."

The statement didn't surprise Blake. After what little time he had spent with them he had been impressed. He questioned, "Did they say what their plans are?"

"No, they just said they would keep in touch." Blake thanked his father for the call and hung up. He turned to look out at the bay. He had developed the habit of swimming in it as well as observing it. "Why not today," he asked himself?" I need to release some stress. He knew the beach would be quiet. Sixty degrees discouraged most people from getting into the water.

On their way home the three Marshall's discussed their futures. The house would be sold for whatever they could get for it. Next came the dreaded subject of the horses, they would have to be sold also. For the first time, Allison cried over a material loss. Jonathon tried to console her by assuring her that when he became rich from the game of golf he would buy Charmer back for her. "I believe you will," she replied as she tried to stop the tears.

The minute they arrived home Allison went to the stables, she needed to ride. As always, Charmer greeted her at the stall door, anxious to be released from her confinement. Allison opened the door and ran her hand down the mare's neck, enjoying the smooth feel of it. Two pairs of deep brown eyes stared lovingly at each other. Eager to get going she decided to eliminate a saddle and ride bareback. She mounted Charmer and headed for the beach.

Just as Blake figured, the beach was deserted. He jumped into the bay, shrugging off the initial shock of the cold water that surrounded him. He swam out several yards before noticing a horse and rider in the distance, traveling at a fast pace. He swam out a little further and then stopped to admire the horsemanship as they passed. It appeared to be a young woman. He watched until they were about a quarter mile down the beach and then continued his swim.

Allison just wanted to keep riding as fast as she could. She knew she was really running from all the things that were happening to her. Once more she urged Charmer on.

Completing his brisk swim, Blake was in the process of drying himself off when he noticed the horse and rider returning up the beach at a continued fast pace. They were about fifty feet away when suddenly the horse tripped. The rider lay on the sand motionless. While rushing to help he noticed the horse limp to its rider and nudge the lifeless form. His heart was racing by the time he arrived at the scene and began to race even faster when he turned the small form over and realized it was Allison.

"My God Allison, he said out loud as he shook her lightly several times hoping she would regain consciousness. Her thick lashes fluttered for a moment and then the lids opened, revealing the troubled look in her eyes. He questioned, "Allison, can you move?"

She was confused. What was she doing lying on the beach and what was Blake doing there? Why was he asking her if she could move? Now he was asking if she felt any pain, he looked worried. Suddenly she became aware of Charmer and the fall came back to her. But how did Blake get involved? She took a deep breath and exclaimed, "I'm fine and I don't feel any pain. At least not physical and yes I can move. If you'll just help me up I'll continue my ride."

Blake was amazed how quickly the troubled look in her eyes changed to a look of stubborn determination. With his help she stood and started wiping the sand from her. "Allison, Blake exclaimed, you're more than a mile from home. I'm taking you both back. You're not getting on that horse. You've had a terrible fall, and if you don't care about yourself, consider your horse. He questioned, "What is its name?"

Shocked by the tone of his voice, she answered, "Charmer."

He turned her around to face her mare. "Charmer is limping Allison and you should walk her back home, not ride her." Allison looked at her mare with concern. Until Blake informed her, she hadn't questioned Charmer's condition. She felt ashamed of herself and the feeling of guilt overtook her defiance. She exclaimed, "Your right, Mr. Donlan but I believe we can make it without your help, thank you anyway."

The comment maddened him and he replied, "You can't quit thinking of me as the enemy, can you?" Before she could answer, her legs buckled as the impact of the fall settled on her. Blake grabbed her before she hit the ground. Swooping, her into his arms he tensed at the feel of her body next to his. It was a feeling he had no desire to relinquish, her warmth, her smell, and the feeling of being responsible for her.

Allison regained consciousness almost immediately and became embarrassed. Not for just the fact she had fainted but by the feeling of security he was providing her while in his arms. Security was something she had been deprived of for some time. Flustered, she informed him he could put her down. Blake smiled and answered, "Not until you tell me you'll let me walk you and Charmer home."

"Oh, alright, she agreed as she looked into a pair of eyes that dared her to say no. The walk was quiet. Most the conversation revolved around her and the joy of riding. She informed him that her father had given Charmer to her on her thirteenth birthday. He listened to her intently and wanted to tell her how bad he felt about everything that had happened to her but figured it would only remind her of things she rather forget. He also wondered what she would do with Charmer once the house was sold. His heart ached for her at the thought of her might having to lose another thing she loved.

As they approached the stables, Aaron was saddling up his horse to go looking for Allison. He had worried about her since the meeting that morning and how the discussion regarding selling the horses had left her so distraught. It had been a couple of hours since she left for her ride, which was much longer than normal. Glancing up, he noticed Allison approaching and breathed a sigh of relief. She was with a stranger and Aaron smiled when he recognized it was Blake. He walked to the stable door to greet them.

Blake held out a hand to Aaron as he exclaimed, "The horse tripped and Allison had a bad fall. When I reached her she was confused. It's possible she might have a slight concussion, you should call a doctor."

Aaron answered with concern, "I will, and thanks for escorting her home."

Allison didn't appreciate the way Blake was explaining everything as if she were a child and exclaimed with aggravation, "I'm fine Aaron. It's Mr. Donlan that's confused."

Blake couldn't understand the sudden outburst. Aaron looked at him and rolled his eyes also wondering what had sparked her temper. He stated, "Blake doesn't appear to be the type to confuse easily Allison, so I think we should call the doctor just in case." Tired and exasperated, she removed Charmers reins from Blake's hand and led her to the stall. Aaron thanked Blake once more and offered him a ride to his car.

Blake turned him down, exclaiming, "The walk will be good for me and it's a nice day. Take care of Allison."

Allison listened from the stall and mumbled to herself, "Just because he's so much older than me, he doesn't have to treat me like a child." She had no idea how wrong that statement was. To Blake, she was every bit a woman.

CHAPTER 11

Vera Thomas paced the floor. That's what she figured she did best these days. Once more she moaned to herself. The death of the Marshall's was just a sign of the times. As far as she was concerned, nothing good was ever going to happen again. She detested being subjected to this new lifestyle. It was Edward's fault and now she detested him as well. He still maintained his job at the bank, Gerald had his bootlegging business and Karen seemed completely content, referring to their new life as an adventure. It appeared she was the only one who hadn't adjusted.

Gerald interrupted her pacing as he entered the room to inform her that he was going out for the evening. She was used to his evenings out and knew exactly what he was doing most the time, sleeping with older women who had lots of money to spend on him. She would have never guessed that it was Allison he was going to spend the evening with.

Gerald gave her a peck on the cheek and recommended, "I would quit pacing if I were you mother, you'll wear out the carpet and we can't afford to replace it." Laughing at his suggestion, he left the room. Vera didn't think it was the least bit funny. She looked at the mantle clock. It was time to go to the Women's Club and play Mah Jong. "At least, she told herself, I have something to look forward to once a week."

Gerald was anxious to be with Allison. He knew she wasn't rich anymore but since the deaths of her parents, maybe there was some kind of inheritance. There would be her portion of the house, the horses, which were all superb and he vaguely remembered that the Marshall's owned some mines. Even if they weren't producing, the land would still be worth something. If so, he would apologize for his actions in the garden that day and tell her he loved her. The thought of her young, firm body was already arousing him.

Allison sorted through her clothes trying to decide what to wear for the evening. Gerald refused to tell her where they were going. It was to be a surprise. She didn't know for sure why he was suddenly being attentive, but happily accepted his invitation. While dressing, she noticed the new bouquet of flowers she received from Blake sitting on her bedroom table, reflected in the mirror. As always it consisted of wildflowers and a rose bud. They now arrived once a week. She felt a rush of anger at herself for accepting them but she was curious to see if just once, the wildflowers would wilt before the rose bloomed. The notes simply read, Blake. Something else was annoying her. Since that day on the beach he had entered her mind too much. She remembered waking up in his arms and feeling their strength, the concerned look that covered his tanned face as he whispered her name and the fresh smell of sea water that still lingered on the black hair that covered his chest. The doorbell interrupted her thoughts. Realizing it was Gerald; she chose a dress and quickly prepared herself.

Aaron was downstairs when Gerald arrived. He opened the door to see him standing there looking dapper in the latest fashion. He also noticed the gold watch on his wrist and wondered where it came from.

Gerald spoke first, "Aaron how goes it? I hear you're the new assistant editor for the newspaper."

"That's right," Aaron replied, dryly, as he led him to the parlor.

"Well good for you. Some people know how to find work. As for me, I have my own little business going. If you ever need a good bottle of gin, just let me know."

"Thanks Gerald," I'll remember that, Aaron replied with an edge of sarcasm.

Allison entered the room. She had chosen to wear her favorite dress, yellow silk, with a floral print. She purchased it at DeLeons just before the market crash. That was the last time she had been shopping. Gerald gave a whistle of approval and exclaimed, Allison, you look great." Allison smiled, pleased that she made the right decision and returned the compliment.

Aaron questioned, "Where are you going?" Gerald helped Allison with her coat and replied, "It's a surprise. Somewhere she's never been before." Aaron didn't care for the answer and preferred to know where his sister would be. He also knew better than to pursue the conversation, knowing it would upset Allison. Lately she had been very defensive in regards to the fact she was now a woman, not a child. He knew it was true but old habits were hard to break. They bid him goodnight and left with Gerald's arm wrapped around Allison, reminding Aaron of an animal flaunting its prey.

Aaron still mistrusted and disliked Gerald. He especially didn't like Allison becoming part of his harem but knew the more he objected to her being with him the more determined she would be to continue the relationship. He also wondered why all of a sudden Gerald was coming around. It was well known by now that he had become a gigolo, at least to everyone but Allison. He dare not tell her, she would only defend him. Lighting a cigarette, a habit he acquired with his new job, Aaron turned on the radio deciding a quiet evening at home sounded good. The music was soothing and took his mind off of Allison. Now his thoughts were directed towards Melissa. He was right about her becoming a distraction. He couldn't keep his mind off of her, never had he felt this way before but something deep with-in him kept warning him to ignore the feeling, but why? He lit another cigarette.

Allison wasn't sure of what Gerald was doing as they passed through the heavy mahogany door after being scrutinized by a pair of eyes staring out of a small peek hole. Then an extremely large, burly man greeted them at the second door with a smile. It was becoming obvious Gerald was known here. He held the door as she entered. Allison controlled a cough that threatened her from the smoke filled room. The place was loud and crowded. They were led to one of the linen covered tables that surrounded the dance floor. Bud vases were placed on each table, containing a rose, which momentarily irritated her.

"Well, what do you think, Gerald asked, announcing, it's a speakeasy?"

Allison smiled, "I always wondered what one would be like. This is so exciting Gerald, thank you." He ordered a bottle of Champagne. Tonight he was going all out. After all the evening was a business investment.

Allison anxiously awaited having her first taste of Champagne but questioned, "Gerald, are you sure you can afford it?"

He exclaimed, "Don't worry. We wouldn't be here if I couldn't." The band played a slow song and Gerald brought her to the dance floor. They danced and her heart raced as usual when she was near him. She silently questioned his new clothes, buying her dinner and ordering champagne, had he come into money? For both their sakes, she hoped so. His, for simply knowing he couldn't live without it and hers for knowing she couldn't bear to live without him. Money would make a difference. They returned to the table and the bottle of champagne was awaiting them. Gerald poured the bubbly liquid into the glasses and made a toast, "To the most beautiful woman in the room." Blushing, their glasses met and she silently added, "I love you Gerald

"Blake, isn't that Allison Marshall over there?" Blake followed Kathryn's eyes. She continued, "I believe that's the same young man that was here with Annabelle Gilder." A quiet rage welled up inside him as he observed Gerald with his arm around Allison, nibbling on her neck. What angered him most was that she was enjoying it. Kathryn was beginning to realize by the look on his face that she had been right to be jealous the first time that he mentioned Allison to her. She exclaimed, "I guess he's tired of older women." Blake didn't reply. They sat quietly for a moment until Blake broke the silence. "The son of a bitch is getting her drunk."

"Appears that way, Kathryn replied, and then questioned, why are you concerning yourself with it?"

Blake replied, "She has enough problems and doesn't need to get involved with someone like him right now." Kathryn felt there would never be a good time for Allison to be involved with Gerald as far as Blake was concerned. Suddenly Blake stood and she questioned him, "What are you going to do?"

"Talk to Macky, I'll be right back." She watched, as he walked away in search of his friend then returned her attention to Allison. She admired how great the young girl looked in the yellow dress and wondered if the dress was flattering her or was she flattering the dress. She also remembered the day Allison and her mother came into DeLeons and chose it. At that time, Allison had everything and now she had nothing. Then Kathryn's heart sank, except for possibly Blake." His actions were confirming the fact that she had a right to fear not having him for, herself.

"Blake, what the hell is wrong with you?" Macky exclaimed, noticing a look of rage distorting the handsome face he always envied.

"That couple over there," Blake pointed his finger. Macky followed its direction and remarked, "You mean Gerald Thomas?" Blake answered bitterly, "Yes."

"What has he done?"

It's a matter of what I think he's going to try and do, not what he's done. The young girl with him is a friend of my families and she's only eighteen. Do me a favor, cut them off before they get drunker than they are.

Macky nodded his head and replied, "If that's what you want me to do, I will, but I don't think Gerald is going like it. It's the first time I've seen him with a young woman in a long time, usually they're much older." Blake patted him on the shoulders and thanked him. Macky smiled, "Hey, you're a friend. I'll just tell him she's too young to be here."

Blake returned to Kathryn, anxious to witness Macky inform Gerald the evening was over.

Kathryn questioned, "What have you done?"

"I just asked Macky to cut them off before Gerald gets Allison drunker than she already is." They watched as Macky approached the table and whispered into Gerald's ear. Gerald started to argue with Macky and Allison appeared oblivious to the confrontation as she watched the dance floor. The conversation lasted for just a few moments more with Macky ending it by shaking hands with Gerald. Allison appeared confused as Gerald led her away.

Kathryn sighed and asked, "Now can we concentrate on ourselves for the rest the evening?"

Blake apologized. "No, I'm sorry Kate, but come with me. I have to follow them, I'm sure he's up to no good." Kathryn stood and stated sarcastically, "It's quite obvious you're with the wrong woman this evening Blake, I'll take a cab home." He reached into his pocket, handed her some bills, apologized and made a quick exit. Kathryn stood there for a moment staring at the money he had pushed into her hand, leaving her with regrets of her own, the promise to hire Allison.

Allison was half-asleep, when Gerald drove up the circular driveway and parked in front of the house. Turning off the car, he gazed at her for a moment. She had aroused him all evening while they danced and was anxious to feel her close to him again. Reaching across the seat, he pulled her into his arms. Allison in her drunken state felt limp and her body tingled. "Oh, Gerald," she murmured as he held her tightly against him. He kissed her gently at first, then suddenly the kiss began hurting her lips and his hands were touching places she wasn't prepared for. Trying to catch her breath, she asked him to stop as he forced her hand onto his hardened manhood. He moaned, "Tell me you still want me Allison."

"Yes, I do, she answered but not like this." He was at the point of no return as he pushed her down on the seat of the car. The feel of the firm, warm flesh under him caused him to prematurely climax. The moment was suddenly interrupted, as he felt himself being pulled from the car. Someone was attacking him. He hit the ground and heard Allison scream. Once more he was picked up and found himself staring into the face of a stranger, informing him he was lucky to be alive and to get in his car and leave before he changed his mind and finished him off. Through an already swollen lip, Gerald asked, "Who the hell are you?"

The stranger introduced himself. His breath hit him in the face as he peered at a pair of piercing eyes. "I'm Blake Donlan, remember that name, so if you ever decide to try forcing yourself on Allison again, it will be the name of your killer and you can take it to hell with you." The sincerity in the statement sobered Gerald as he once again wondered who this person was.

Allison stood there trying to make sense out of the situation. She wasn't sure what had caused her to scream until she noticed Gerald bleeding. She ran to him crying, "Are you alright Gerald?" Her scream had brought Aaron out of the house just as Blake was pulling Gerald from the car. He sensed what the problem was but wondered how Blake fit into the picture. He looked at his sister and instructed her to get into the house. Allison was shocked by his demand. Suddenly she realized the man threatening Gerald was no other than Blake. He was the cause of all this commotion.

She confronted him. "What have you done to Gerald and why are you here? Blake had become used to Allison looking at him hatefully and replied, "You should do as your brother requested and go into the house." She began to argue until Aaron interrupted and commanded her once more to do as he said. Glaring at Blake, she obeyed.

The two men turned their attention back to Gerald. "I don't know why everyone is so upset, Gerald exclaimed. Allison is all right. I didn't hurt her."

"I'm sure you didn't, thanks to Blake, Aaron replied with disgust as observed the stain on the front of Gerald's pants. Now, as the man said, get out of here."

Gerald cursed but did as he was told. They watched as he drove away.

Thanking Blake, Aaron exclaimed, "It appears between myself and my sister, you're not going to get much rest." Blake straightened his suit and tie. He smiled and replied, "I'm beginning to believe that."

Aaron returned the smile and asked, "May I pour you a drink from my father's stash?" Blake accepted, stating, "I'll take you up on that, a night cap will be appreciated." They entered the house only to be greeted by Allison.

"Well, I hope you two are pleased with yourselves," she shouted angrily. They looked at each other, smiled in agreement and replied, "Yes." Now she was totally infuriated and stomped out of the room, leaving them both grinning. Aaron motioned Blake to follow him. They entered the den and Aaron removed a key from the desk drawer. Blake watched as he went to the mahogany cabinet in the corner of the room and unlocked the doors, revealing several bottles of bourbon. He poured two glasses and handed one to Blake before stating, "I'll never understand why my sister is so taken with Gerald. She has been every since we've been children." Blake didn't comment as he sipped the appreciated drink that was beginning to calm him. That was until Aaron questioned, "You're a real estate broker, aren't you Blake?" Sadly, he knew what was coming next and answered, "Yes."

Aaron continued, "We just found out from your father that our parent's home is not paid for. Would you be interested in selling it for us?" Blake knew he could get them the best possible price, but he also knew Allison would more than likely resent him even more for being involved in the sale of her home. He knew that he would have to take his chances, he couldn't refuse Aaron. He agreed.

Jonathon entered the room in his bathrobe exclaiming, "I was asleep until Allison slammed her bedroom door. What's going on?" He noticed Blake and held out his hand to greet him. Aaron answered. "Blake had a run in with Gerald, seems he was taking advantage of our sister."

Jonathon yawned and said, "Somehow that doesn't surprise me, he's capable of anything lately. So, it was Gerald she was mad at?"

"No, Blake stated, as a matter of fact, I'm the one who got her mad, I guess she didn't appreciate my interfering." Jonathon shook his head and replied, "She's crazy for Gerald. Blake was tired of hearing about Allison's obsession with Gerald.

Aaron asked, "Are you working tomorrow Jonathon?"

Another yawn escaped Jonathon before answering. "Yeah, that's why I better excuse myself. There's a tournament in the morning."

Aaron informed Blake, "Jonathon caddies at the country club but someday he'll have his own caddy. He's going to become a professional golfer."

Blake replied, "Is that right? He shook his head and exclaimed, Golf is a great game but unfortunately it doesn't like me as much as I like it."

Jonathon smiled and informed him as he was leaving the room, "Actually, you're not alone. Golf, doesn't like anyone, good night."

Blake finished his drink and affirmed with Aaron, "I'll discuss the sale of the house tomorrow with you if that's convenient!"

Aaron agreed, "Sure, the sooner we get things taken care of the sooner we can get on with our lives. At least we'll each know how much we have to work with."

"Okay, I'll see you tomorrow," Aaron led him to the door.

Allison felt that if she raised her head from the pillow, it would surely explode. The chirping of the birds outside her open window echoed inside her brain. She had heard friends speak of hangovers. Now, she knew what one was, which left her to wonder why anyone would ever drink again. Slowly she raised herself from the bed. A pair of shaky legs carried her to the bathroom. She put a wash rag under a cold faucet and applied the coolness to her face. She admitted to herself that last evening was somewhat of a blur and still questioned why Blake was there and why had Jonathon defended him after he hurt Gerald? She returned to her bed, thankful that she wasn't to start work at De Leons., until the next day.

Aaron was eating breakfast when Allison entered the room eager for some juice to quench her thirst. He chuckled to himself, knowing just how she was feeling. "How is my little sister this morning?" he questioned as she rubbed her temples.

She looked at him and replied, "Just fine."

"Well then, perhaps you would like to join me and have some potatoes and eggs smothered in ketchup." He laughed inwardly knowing she was fighting nausea and wondered if she felt the evening had been worth it. Trying to blot out the image of food, she downed a glass of orange juice and then a glass of water. As he observed her he remembered having to tell Angie, their cook that after all these years they would have to let her go, they were selling the house. She had cried, stating, "This is the only home I've known for twenty-six years!" He tried to console her, telling her they would give her the best of references. If he listened close enough he could still hear her crying in the adjoining room.

Allison stared into space as he informed her that the house was going up for sale. She sat expressionless while he spoke, leaving him to wonder if she was grasping any of his words. He continued, "Jonathon has been offered a place to stay at the golf club in exchange to help maintain the grounds. You and I can stay together or you can be on your own, it's your choice."

Allison suddenly showed signs of renewed life and exclaimed, "Oh, this morning I have a choice of taking care of myself!" He ignored the statement. She sighed and continued. "I will probably call my friend Bea and see if she still wants to get a place. Besides that, you don't need to be burdened with your sister. It's time for me to take care of myself." His watch told him he didn't have time right now to further the conversation. He didn't mention that he had an appointment with Blake. He kissed her, telling her they would continue the discussion later.

"What happened to you," Vera questioned as she reached to touch one of the cuts on her sons face?"

"Ouch, he cried. Don't touch me."

"Who did this to you?" He groaned and replied, a friend of Allison's."

Confused she asked, "A friend of Allison's, why. When were you with her?"

"Last night. The guy seemed to think I was taking advantage of her." Gerald observed his wounds in the mirror, as his mother continued her questioning, "Where you taking advantage of her?" He dabbed at a cut and answered lazily, "She didn't seem to be putting up a fight."

Exasperated, Vera exclaimed, "Gerald don't you get enough favors from the women you've been with, without having to push yourself on Allison?"

He answered. "I rather have a young rich girl than old wealthy women any day." His statement surprised Vera and she questioned, "What makes you think Allison is rich?"

He looked up from the mirror. "I assume that since her parent's deaths, there must be some money. Such as insurance, the house, horses and some mines." Vera let out a small laugh. "My dear son, there is probably nothing more than the house left for Allison to share with her two brothers. The mines were sold a long time ago and I heard through the Women's Club that the Marshall's had no insurance. Allison will never have enough money to satisfy your needs. I'm afraid you're going to have to revert back to your older ladies."

Gerald's stomach turned at the thought. Last night had been a lost cause, the expense, the beating and he didn't even get to seduce Allison. "My God, he cried inwardly as he envisioned another night with Annabelle Gilder. Vera interrupted the disturbing picture.

"Who was the man that hit you?"

"I don't know, probably one of Jonathon's friends. He seemed quite interested in Allison, but I saw the way she looked at him and he doesn't have a chance with her. It was me she defended. I'm still not sure how he got into the picture but I know one thing for sure. I don't want another encounter with him."

The word encounter reminded Vera that Edward informed her at the breakfast table he needed to talk with her after work. There was something important to tell her. She assumed he got a promotion at the bank and wanted to make a big announcement about it. She watched Gerald leave the room.

Gerald headed to the basement to check his liquor. In a couple of more days he would have a good supply to sell.

Vera awaited Edward's arrival home. She had hopes that he did get promoted and hopefully be released from the bars he had to stand behind all day looking like a caged animal. Once more, she became embarrassed at the thought of her friends witnessing him like that.

He entered the room looking weary rather than excited which surprised her. Impatiently she asked, "Well, what is it you have to tell me?"

Edward sat in a chair across from hers in the parlor and stated, "I'm going to divorce you Vera! I'm willing to give what little support I can!"

He watched as the color drained from her face and reappeared again, blood red.

Vera couldn't believe what she was hearing. "You can't leave me. I won't let you divorce me," she screamed.

"You can't stop me Vera. Besides that, why do you want me here? You don't love me. You made it quite obvious that my money was what you loved, not me. At first realizing it hurt, but it doesn't anymore. I don't even like looking at you with all that disgust for me written all over your face. I dread coming home from work everyday."

"What about the children," she cried?

"They're not children anymore. Gerald obviously can find women to care for him and Karen can come with me if she wishes."

Vera couldn't believe what she was hearing. All these years she thought he loved her, forgetting that once, he had.

Edward felt the room was as cold as the woman in it. He left her alone in silence and went to his den. Tomorrow morning he would leave.

Vera sat in shock. Edward, the man she had always been so sure of, was leaving her. What would she do without him? Suddenly, the small amount of money he had been providing her seemed much more important. Now there would be even less. "Good God, what next, she questioned?" "The woman's club, that's what." The silent answer to her questioned filled her with panic. "What would they say?" How could he do this to her and the children?

Chapter 12

    Allison had been at DeLeons for over a week now and was enjoying her new job, but was uneasy around Kathryn. For some reason she felt the woman disliked her. A smile from her was rare. She put aside the feeling she was doing something wrong and was thankful to be around beautiful clothes once more and assisting the elite clientele with their selections.

    Kathryn couldn't find a reason to show displeasure in Allison's performance. The customers had taken to her and trusted her opinion as to what best suited them and she was a natural at sales. Blake crossed her mind. She hadn't spoken to him since that night at Macky's, and he made no attempt to get in touch, leaving her to wonder if it was his way of letting her know a serious relationship between them would never happen. She observed Allison with a customer and tried to decide what there was about her that captured Blake. Kathryn considered herself attractive. True, she was several years older than Allison, but she had a body to be proud of. Her hair was golden blond with soft natural waves. Her complexion was lighter, the desired color of peaches and cream, not the look of someone that spent time trying to obtain a tan. Was it her personality? Whatever it was, she wished she had it. She tried to convince herself it wasn't Allison's fault that Blake was enthralled with her. In fact, she didn't show the least bit of interest when she brought up his name, while mentioning that he was the landlord of DeLeons.

    The Marshall house was sold in less than a week. Sadly reminiscing, Aaron and Allison walked through the rooms. Tears streamed down Allison cheeks as she remembered the good days, Christmas's, her coming out party, their parents and Dorie. Both were surprised how fast it sold.

Including the furnishings, they received a generous price. The buyer even purchased the horses, relieving Allison of the burden of having to sell Charmer on the auction block. The difficult part was still to come, the time to start packing not just their belongings but their parents and Dories. Jonathon had already moved out and Aaron located a small apartment close to the newspaper. Allison and Beatrice would be roommates. They lost the apartment they desired and settled for one in the same building that had a single bedroom with a Murphy bed. It was on the first floor and like the other, clean and tastefully decorated. Aaron led her to the kitchen, now void of the cook, poured them a cup of coffee and discussed packing. He would tend to their parent's belongings and Allison could take care of Dories.

Gerald sat mourning the fact that Allison was still as destitute as he was. He couldn't get her off his mind. She came to see him after the incident at her place, apologizing for Blake and Aaron's actions. Once more he remembered the effect she had on him when she leaned over and gently kissed the bruise on his face. Again, he had pulled her close to him craving her body and wanting her. Between passionate kisses he confessed he loved her, exclaiming, "God Allison, why don't you have money so we can be together?" She informed him that love could carry them through life. He replied, breathlessly, "Your young and naïve, quit kidding yourself." She kept repeating, "You love me." He cringed, remembering the look on her face when he pushed her from him, telling her he loved money more and stating, "If I had money Allison, it would afford me the luxury of having you, but I don't." In a defeated voice she replied, "I suppose I should wish you success Gerald and I guess I should be honored to be considered a luxury."

A nudge from Annabelle broke his trance. "Gerald, get your racket there's an open court." Allison's image disappeared with the command.

While packing, Allison wiped away a tear that was brought on as she remembered her last meeting with Gerald. She was becoming mad at herself for loving him and wondered how to combat something as powerful as love. The feeling of helplessness overwhelmed her as she headed to Dories room. Entering the room, she could picture Dorie sitting contentedly in the old rocker, the one she had rocked all three of them as infants. With a sigh she walked to the chest of drawers. Opening it, she had to fight the feeling of invading Dories privacy. In the first drawer she found an old broken clock, leaving her to wonder why she would keep such a thing; a couple of bars of rose scented soap and perfume that she had given her, a brush and comb. The next one contained her under garments and strangely, two infant gowns. Why baby clothes, she questioned silently? Underneath them, there was a decorated box that at one time held chocolates. She opened it. Several photos lay inside. The first was Dorie, in her youth. There was a man standing next to her, a white man. Taken by surprise, she gasped, realizing it was a wedding picture. There was another photo of her holding a child. Allison was getting confused. As far as she had known, Dorie had never been married and only cared for a pair of twins before she became their nanny, never a single child. The next photo revealed a beautiful young woman. At the bottom was the hand written name, Trilly. Allison recognized Dories handwriting. She returned to the first photo and attempted to piece the puzzle. The young woman resembled the man with Dorie. Was the photo of the infant and the girl named Trilly the same person? Was she Dories child? If so, what happened to her and the man? Dorie never mentioned either of them. She put the photos back into the box and carried it to her parent's room to find Aaron.

Allison's entrance distracted him from his depressing task. She appeared excited. Glancing down at her, he noticed the box she was holding and questioned, "What have you got?"

"Pictures," she replied as she handed them to him. She watched while he went through the photo's wondering if he would come to the same conclusion. After a moment he looked at her and exclaimed, "I can't believe it. Dorie was married, to a white man! Do you think the child is hers?" Allison looked at the photo's once more and replied, "Yes, and I think the picture of the young girl Trilly is the infant Dorie is holding, it must be their child." Aaron let out a small whistle before exclaiming, "What do you suppose happened and why Dorie never mentioned them?" Allison shook her head, "I don't know but I think we both knew Dorie well enough to know they must be dead or she would have been with them. She placed the photos back into the box and exclaimed, "Maybe Tullah can tell us something. I'll bring them with me when I deliver Dories belongings to her tomorrow. They both decided that since Dorie had no living relatives, at least as far as they knew, Dorie would want Tullah to have her few possessions. Allison exclaimed, "I hope she knows something, I'm really curious now."

Returning to her chore, Allison opened the drawer to the nightstand next to the bed. It contained Dorie's bible. She opened it hoping that there might be dates recorded and was pleased to discover there were. Yes, there it was. Her husband's name was Trent. As she counted the years between his birth and death, she felt a pang of sorrow, realizing how very young he was and wondered what took his life. The same feeling overcame her again when she discovered how young the girl Trilly was when she died. Disturbed, she set the bible next to the box of photos and went to the closet. On the shelf were Dorie's two hats. The black straw, for going to town and the one she always wore in the garden. Allison smiled sadly, as she pictured her wearing them. A total of three dresses hung in the closet next to a pair of nanny uniforms leaving her to believe that Dorie had hopes of renewing her job someday when grandchildren arrived at the Marshall household. Allison ran her hand down the bathrobe and nightgown that hung on a hook and whispered, "I miss you Dorie." Her eye caught glimpse of an old leather suitcase. "Perfect," she told herself, I'll pack her things in there." She removed it and set it on the bed, wondering how old it was as she worked the latch. Raising the lid, she looked in and to her surprise, there was a book. Suddenly, Dorie's words came to her, "My book!" and she wondered if this was the one Tullah had told her about. Eager to read it and hopeful to find out more about the people in the photos and Dories past, she went to the rocker and opened it. Once more, Allison recognized Dorie's handwriting and experienced a feeling of guilt for invading her privacy but curiosity prompted her to continue.

My dear Roosevelt and Hattie, now having been re-named by the Marshall's, Aaron and Allison, (Allison felt as though the wind had been knocked out of her and tried to catch her breath while staring at the statement. That's what Dorie had called her and Aaron the night she died. She gasped a breath of air before continuing), you were brought to the Marshall household August of 1911 at almost three months old. I arrived a week before. As I fill the first page in this book you are now five months old. I made the decision to write, as to allow myself an outlet to express my feelings, but also felt you should someday know your real ancestors. It is going to be difficult for me to raise you as your nanny, instead of as your grandmother, but I understand, for both your sakes, it must be done.

Allison slammed the book shut, hoping the impact would destroy what she had just read. Nanny, instead of grandmother! Roosevelt and Hattie! Her heart raced as she tried to comprehend what the perfect penmanship had just informed her. After a few moments, she reopened it with shaking hands and continued.

"Still, I'm very thankful that Mr. Marshall, you're father, arranged for us to be together. He's a good man and loved your mother, my Trilly, very much, (Allison gasped, the girl in the picture.) Numb, she continued reading. Tragically, she died giving birth to you."

Aaron entered the room and became frightened for his sister. She was staring into space and visually shaken. "Allison, are you all right?" There was no response. Once more he questioned her. She looked down at the book on her lap, unable to find the strength to pick it up. Aaron reached for it and opened the cover. He read for a moment, and then sat on the bed. Dear God, could it be true. Both sat speechless for sometime, staring at each other. Allison broke the silence with a whisper, "Roosevelt?" He replied, "Hattie?" On weakened legs, Allison got out of the rocker and sat next to her brother on the bed, exclaiming, "We need to finish reading it." They continued. It was there, every important event in their lives and Dories. She told of the love she had for their grandfather Trent and his untimely as well as questionable death. How their mother and father met and how badly James felt having to deceive Lillian but knew it was best for all concerned. She pleaded with them not to be ashamed of their Negro blood, that they were actually descendents of African royalty. When they reached the last written page, Dorie stated that she had made the decision to destroy the book once she completed the last few pages and was thankful for the outlet it had given her to express herself. The book allowed her to talk to her grandchildren not as a nanny, but as a grandmother.

Allison broke the silence again, stating, "Our mother was beautiful, wasn't she Aaron?" He shook his head in agreement, finding speech difficult. She continued, "Are we going to tell Jonathon what we discovered?"

The gruffness in Aaron's voice startled her. "No, were not going to tell anyone. Nobody needs to know. Do you realize what would become of us if people find out we have Negro blood? Our lives have already changed. But it's nothing compared to what will happen if this gets discovered. As much as I loved Dorie, I would have been much happier not knowing my heritage. I feel, no shame in it, I just fear it. Too bad she didn't get around to destroying her diary. We would have been better off." We have passed as white all these years and we will remain white. He put his arm around Allison as they both quietly tried to digest all that they had learned. After a short time they continued with the packing, each deeply lost in their own thoughts.

Aaron wondered if they were discovered, would he lose his job. The only blacks at the newspaper were janitors and message carriers. Suddenly, he felt extremely vulnerable. He tried to reinforce to himself with what he had told Allison, they have passed for white this long, why should anything change? He went to the mirror and studied his features carefully. "Yes, he told himself, now I see it." He turned away, suddenly fearing the image that had pleased him through the years, trying to convince himself that it was his imagination, there were no Negro characteristics.

Allison was also standing in front of a mirror in the next room. She held the picture of Trilly and compared herself. The resemblance was there. The eyes were similar and the same cameo face stared back at her. Her nose was sharper and her lips, not quite as full as her mothers were.

She felt a loss as she looked at the photo and wondered what she was like. The fact she had died giving her and Aaron life saddened her. Suddenly it struck her. What would Gerald think if he discovered she had Negro blood? What would any man think? She returned to the photo of Dorie and her grandfather. He was white and loved Dorie, despite her color and the same with her father and Trilly. Maybe it wouldn't make a difference. Besides, she told herself, Aaron said they were not going to tell anyone, not even Jonathon.

Aaron helped Allison move into the apartment with Beatrice. He liked the spunky girl and felt she would be a good roommate for his sister. Kissing Allison, he returned to the Marshall house one more time, to collect his belongings.

The toss of a coin won Bea the bedroom. Allison pulled the Murphy bed out from the wall, and crawled in, looking forward to a nights sleep. The strain of the last few days weighed heavily on her and had taken its toll. She drifted off to sleep, dreaming of riding Charmer along the beach with the sea breeze once again on her face, enjoying the exhilarating effect it had on her. Suddenly, Blake appeared, interrupting her dream, holding a single rose and staring at her with those intimidating eyes. She awoke abruptly, cursing him for invading her dreams. Was there no where to go to escape the man? She went to the kitchen and heated a glass of milk, something Dorie always did for her when she couldn't sleep.

Curtis Kemper, the clubs golf pro had been observing the young man's early morning practice for some time and was impressed with his game. He was a natural and showed professional potential. If he was this good at such a young age, with a little guidance he could have a great future in golf. He made the decision to talk the clubs owners into sponsoring Jonathon for tournament play.

Jonathon wondered if he would ever tire of golf. It was a damp morning as he once again executed a perfect distance putt. Not only was the early morning his practice time, it was his thinking time. He missed his sister and brother. It had been several weeks since they had been together and was looking forward to being with them in a couple of days for dinner. He was content with his life at the club and still determined to make golf his profession. He knew he was good enough, even the pro at the club told him so. Swinging his club, he performed flawless drive. Looking at his watch he realized it was time for work. There were caddie jobs awaiting him this morning and afternoon. The tips were good and his advice was becoming something the patrons of the club depended on for their game.

Melissa Barnum delivered Aaron's coffee the same time she had every morning for the last few weeks, receiving the usual smile and thank you.

She couldn't understand what was wrong. She felt he was attracted to her but did nothing to reinforce the feeling. Setting the coffee down, she returned the smile and left the room.

Aaron looked forward to work everyday and wasn't sure if it was because of Melissa or the job itself. The only thing that held him back from asking her out was a comment she had made that cinched the fact they never would get together. One afternoon a Negro messenger delivered a note. Aaron looked at his watch after the man left and mentioned he wished he had received it earlier. Melissa exclaimed, "Henry is the slowest Nigger messenger we've ever had at the newspaper. I always thought natives were supposed to be fast on their feet. If this were Macon Georgia, he wouldn't have a job." Right then he regretfully knew a relationship between them would be impossible because of her southern upbringing, but it still did nothing to curb his desire for her. He questioned himself, as Allison had. If he were to enter into a serious relationship, would he confess their heritage? He tried to adjust the best he could since reading Dorie's diary, but was finding it difficult. Work was his salvation. He buried himself in it, loving the constant activity and excitement of breaking news and the adrenaline rush he would receive making the deadline. The newspaper was not only the heartbeat of the city, it had become his. As he previously predicted, Melissa was the only distraction. The face, the body, the soft southern drawl, that served as a constant warning and the smell of her perfume. He ached to be with her. Shaking the thought, he forced his concentration back to his work.

Blake smiled as Charmer nudged him for another carrot. Once more he had accumulated something that was dear to Allison, not through want but circumstance. He had hopes that someday she would give up on Gerald and he might have the chance to create a relationship with her and hopefully return all this to her through wedlock. Deep with-in, he sensed it could happen. He felt little guilt in purchasing the house after giving a more than fair price for it. The place needed repair and carpentry was something he enjoyed. The feel of a tool in his hand and the smell of sawdust, like swimming, relaxed him. He returned from the stable up to the house and continued his project, repairing the porch. The steps needed reinforcement and he also decided it was in need of painting. A car pulling into the driveway drew his attention. It was Kathryn. He hadn't seen her since the night at Macky's. She got out of the car exclaiming, "Blake, this place is wonderful."

Surprised at seeing her he questioned, "How did you find it?"

"Your secretary told me how to get here." She grabbed his arm and requested he show her the rest of the house. Blake was glad to see her and still felt guilty for his actions that night, he truly had been rude. As he escorted her through the house he wondered if she knew it was once the Marshall's. If so, she made no comment about it.

"Well tell me Blake. Are you going to keep this one or just fix it up to sell?"

Blake smiled, "No sale, this one is for me. I have enough income property and I'm comfortable here." Kathryn silently wondered if it was because he truly liked the place or because Allison once lived there. His secretary Dorothy informed her, "Now he owns both the Marshall Building and the Marshall house, leaving Kathryn guessing how much longer before he'd own Allison as well. Still, she was determined to continue pursuing him until there was absolutely, no hope for her. "She, exclaimed, "I see your renovating the place. As soon as you're through, you should have a house warming party. How does that sound? I'll help with it."

Blake hesitated before replying, "It's going to be awhile. There's a lot of work to be done."

"Well, whenever, I'll be ready. How about going to Macky's for dinner this evening, I've forgiven you for the last time we were there?" Blake put his arms around her and replied, "Sure, I owe you a dinner." Kathryn smiled and gave him a friendly kiss. "Thanks, I'll see you at eight." As she drove away, Blake wondered if Allison had begun working at DeLeon's, but refrained from asking Kathryn. Maybe she would mention something at dinner. Looking at his watch, he decided he could get in a couple more hours of work in before he had to clean up.

Edward carried his bags down the stairs as Vera pleaded, I'm sorry Edward. I really do love you. I've just been so confused, so much has happened. Please don't leave. What will I tell the women at the club?" He couldn't help but feel somewhat sorry for her. After all, it was his business decisions that had caused their problems. He almost weakened and gave in. She looked so pathetic, but too much hurt had been inflicted upon him. He could never erase the disgust that she had shown towards him.

He exclaimed, "You may be sorry Vera but it's too late. You don't really love me and you never have. You'll be all right." He set his suitcase down and went to her. "The house is paid for and yours to keep or sell. If you keep it, I fear it will become a burden with what little money I'm going to be able to give you, there is a lot of expenses involved with maintaining it. If you decide to stay, you might consider renting out some of the rooms for extra income." He handed her a piece of paper stating, "This is my address and phone number in case Karen or Gerald wish to get in touch, Goodbye Vera."

She made no further attempts to stop him as he picked up his luggage, turned and walked away. She stood there stunned, staring at the heavy oak door. He really had left her! What was she going to do? The humiliation was going to be unbearable. First, she would have to inform the women at the club that Edward had left her and then inform them that she was leasing out rooms in her home. She shuddered as she pictured her home a boarding house. She knew Edward was right. If she wanted to keep it she would need money to maintain it, so what else could she do? Gerald would be of no help. The proceeds from his business merely took care of his needs. The job Karen obtained at the diner paid poorly and tips were scarce. She pounded on the closed door, "Damn you Edward, for your stupidity."

As usual Macky's was crowded. Kathryn gazed at Blake from across the candle lit table and wondered if he could sense the desire building up inside her. They had been intimate several times. Blake was good at everything but excelled in lovemaking. She had been to bed with more than a few men and none could compare. He caught her stare.

"What are you thinking about?"

"I'm thinking it's been a long time since you and I shared a bed together. I miss that. She reached under the table and put her hand on his knee and continued, How about we finish dinner, skip desert and go to my place and discover each other again?"

Blake was ready. She was right, it had been too long. Not necessarily too long without Kathryn but too long without sexual satisfaction. He cupped her soft, well manicured hand in his and replied, "Sounds like a very good idea."

They arrived at Kathryn's with-in the hour. The house was small and tastefully decorated. The furnishings reflected Kathryn's personality. Bold but softened by feminine accessories. Without further conversation she led him directly to the bedroom and began undressing him. She unbuttoned his shirt, eager to caress his chest. She ran her fingers through the light covering of hair that failed to conceal the muscles that lay beneath. The aroma of his cologne stimulated her.

Blake caressed her as she unbuckled and removed his trousers. Aroused, he picked her up, carried her to the bed and skillfully removed her clothing, making it obvious he was well practiced. Breathing became difficult for Kathryn as he fondled her breasts, leaving a tingling path on them with his tongue while teasing the erect nipples. She felt the hardness of his manhood against her. Slowly his kisses and caresses covered the entire length of her impassioned body. Unable to bear the anticipation any longer she guided his entry into her. His manhood filled the void as they became one. Small moans escaped them both. They were rhythmic in their motions as their bodies strove for fulfillment. Riding the waves of passion, they clung tightly to each other, both wanting it to last as long as possible. After having reached satisfaction, they rested in a quiet embrace. Later, in the dark, Kathryn's head lay on his chest. He was fond of her in many ways and truly wished she could be the one he thought of constantly instead of Allison. They were close in age, sexually compatible, he enjoyed being with her and she was a nice looking woman, one any man would be proud to be seen with. What more could he ask? Allison was the only answer he could come up with, but why? It was a question he asked himself many times. What was it about her that had captivated him? Was it just the challenge she provided? If he gained her love would this feeling leave him? "No," he told himself. It's much deeper than that. He just simply knew he loved her. Why, was still unanswered.

CHAPTER 13

"C'mon Allison, come with me and have some fun," Bea pleaded. We've been invited to this great party. There's going to be live Jazz, food and drinks." Allison answered hesitantly, "I just don't feel very sociable right now."

"That's the whole idea Bea exclaimed, you need to get out and remember what it's like to have fun, you've forgotten, "Please." Allison observed the look on her friend's face and reluctantly agreed.

The party was in an old warehouse. The sound of jazz echoed through the building and illegal booze was plentiful. Allison questioned Bea, "How are they able to get away with this?"

"Simple, she explained with a grin, it's the mayor's son's birthday party. There's been an official raiding ban put on it. Paul and I are going to dance, mingle Allison; there are some prominent people out there." Bea left her standing alone, feeling very uncomfortable, as several men inspected her. Suddenly, out of nowhere, Gerald appeared, exclaiming, "Allison, what a surprise to see you here." The shock of seeing him momentarily stunned her into silence. When she retrieved her voice, she replied coldly, "I'm surprised to see you too Gerald." The moment was interrupted by a woman's voice calling for him from out in the crowd. Allison traced the voice to a woman she figured had to be twice his age. Gerald appeared slightly embarrassed as he shrugged his shoulders and stated as he walked away, "I do what I have to do Allison, enjoy the party." For the first time, she felt pity for him and wondered to herself, if Black Thursday had never happened, how different their lives might have been. She remembered the vow she made to herself, never to let him make her cry again. He would be buried with the rest of her past. The Gerald she loved no longer existed.

It was midnight before the party broke up and Allison was more than ready to return home. Bea and Paul dropped her off at the apartment. They excused themselves, stating that they were hungry and going to get something to eat, since they neglected doing so at the party. Allison bid them goodnight, anxious to crawl into the Murphy bed and get some sleep.

It was five thirty a.m. when the first tremor hit. Aaron was shaving, preparing himself for work. He had grown up like most the inhabitants of San Francisco, experiencing earthquakes, but this one was different. It was much stronger than others he had felt. Holding onto the sink, he watched the walls shimmy. Coffee spilled from the cup sitting on the counter top before tipping over. The roar of the quake was mingled with the screams of fear coming from the building's occupants. He made the decision, due to the chaos outside his door, to stay where he was, praying that the structure would endure nature's wrath that so many times had tested San Francisco.

It was still dark when Blake was awakened from a sound sleep by the motion of his bed. It took several seconds before he realized just what was happening. Having faith in the construction of the Marshall house he rode out the quake without fear for himself. It was others he concerned himself with, especially Allison. He was aware that her and her friend Beatrice had rented one of his apartments. It was a well kept, but older building. Would it withstand a quake of this magnitude?

Allison was awakened abruptly. Pain reeled through her body, darkness surrounded her and she blinked her eyes to assure herself if they were open. Yes, they were, but it was still dark, a deep darkness, like none she had ever experienced. She felt a crushing weight on her legs, pinning her down. It wasn't a dream, it was real. The pain reinforced the fact. What happened," she asked herself. She screamed for Bea and received only silence. Suddenly, another tremor hit. "My God, she told herself, "This, is the apartment that's on top of me, there's been an earthquake!" The continued tremor settled the boards even more heavily upon her. The air was filled with dirt, causing her difficulty in breathing. The darkness and pain were frightening to her as her moans mingled with those of other victims. She cried her friend's name, "Bea, please answer me, talk to me." Was she there, buried alive also? She closed her eyes to prevent more dirt from invading them. Pain overcame her and she lost consciousness.

Blake arrived at the scene and his heart sank as he gazed through horror filled eyes at the skeleton of what was once a three- story building and wondered if Allison was in there. A group of men were already attempting to rescue victims from the rubble. He joined in immediately and frantically started removing debris and calling Allison's name. Suddenly Aaron was beside him. He had sensed his sister was in trouble. Blake greeted him without letting it interfere with his digging. Aaron put on the pair of gloves he brought with him, knowing he would more than likely need them, but noticed Blake had none. His hands were bleeding and filled with large splinters. "My God Blake, Aaron exclaimed, stop until you get your hands taken care of and some gloves to wear!" Blake, in his frenzy hadn't noticed or felt his hands being violated by the debris. He stopped for a second and replied, "No, there's no time to waste," and continued on with his project, causing Aaron to cringe at the sight. Slowly they extracted occupants from the fallen building. Thankfully, so far none had perished. Allison and the rest the people occupying the first floor were still among the missing. It had been two hours since the quake. One of the rescue teams yelled, "Over here!" Blake and Aaron rushed to the scene. It was the muffled voice of a woman. Aaron recognized it as his sister's. She was calling for Charmer. "It's Allison. His voice was filled with anxiety. Blake's heart quickened at the news.

Semi-conscious, Allison called for her horse to release her from the darkness and take her to the beach where they could ride with the wind and breathe the fresh sea air.

After removing boards and remnants of furniture, they finally reached her. Horror struck them as they noticed a huge beam lying across her legs, a beam that would require several men to remove. Fifteen minutes seemed forever to Aaron and Blake, until they were finally able to release Allison. For a moment, she regained consciousness, only to be once again, facing Blake Donlan. Drifting off, she ordered Charmer too flee. She needed to escape the image that seemed to haunt her, even though it appeared impossible, he seemed to be everywhere.

Beatrice screamed for her friend as she observed the remains of their apartment building. Her boyfriend, Paul held her close trying to comfort her. She was not prepared for what they found. The three- story building was now one level. "My God, she asked herself, "Is Allison underneath all of that?" Paul drew her attention exclaiming, "There's a Red Cross worker, let's go see if he can tell us anything!"

The tall, lanky, dirt covered man shook his head apologetically and explained, "Right now, none of the victims have names. Sorry I can't help you. I can tell you they have taken the injured to Memorial Hospital and as far as I know, none were dead." They thanked the man. Beatrice suddenly noticed Aaron. Running to him, she attacked him with questions. He was relieved to see her, after fearing she was also in the rubble. He informed her that Allison had been removed. She was taken to the hospital and that her legs were badly injured. That was all he could tell her at this point. Bea, sighed with relief, her friend was alive.

There was pandemonium at the hospital due to the amount of injuries arriving. Blake had gone onto the hospital due to Aaron's insistence, demanding, "Get those hands taken care of." Allison was on a gurney in the corridor, still unconscious. He was standing protectively beside her, when Aaron arrived with Bea and her friend.

It was two frantic hours before a young intern approached and introduced himself, "I'm Gary Franks, and I apologize for the delay." Aaron gave him the information he requested and the intern exclaimed, "We'll be taking her to the examination room and I promise to let you know the outcome as soon as possible." They thanked him and watched with anxiety as she was wheeled away. Blake knew her legs were badly damaged and silently prayed that someday, he might finish the dance they never completed.

A member of the Red Cross observed Blake as he paced. She also noticed his bleeding and swollen hands. Muriel had witnessed him at the rescue scene and had found it difficult to keep her eyes off of him, as he struggled with the debris. His muscles, being strained, had become more emphasized from under the sweat soaked shirt. Torn trousers exposed a masculine leg as he repeatedly called out the name Allison. She asked for God's forgiveness, as she watched, after wishing it was she under the debris he was searching for. Muriel took a deep breath and approached him. "Excuse me, but your hands need attention."

She startled him. Blake was still so engrossed with his concern for Allison he was trying to ignore the pain. Aaron spoke, "Go with her Blake, she's right, they need to be taken care of." She gently took one of his injured hands and he didn't pull away. "My name is Muriel; may I please tend to them for you?" He smiled at her and replied, "Yes, Muriel, I would appreciate it."

Her heart fluttered at the sound of her name coming from his mouth and the warmth of his hand in hers. She led him into a small room and proceeded to clean the cuts and remove splinters. She grimaced as she extracted pieces of wood, some measuring almost half an inch long and marveled at his silence during the tedious, painful procedure. Holding the large tanned hands, she couldn't help but notice the lack of calluses, making it obvious that he was a man that used his head not his brawn. Muriel wished now, more than ever that she had been born one of the beautiful people, but she hadn't and that was all there was too it. She had a shapeless body, straight mousy brown hair that she was unable to style or control, and to top all that off, she was condemned to wear thick glasses. As far as she was concerned, even her name was ugly.

After he was bandaged, Blake thanked her, promising a donation to the Red Cross. Muriel expressed her appreciation, while still dwelling on her pathetic image.

Panic set in as Blake looked down at his bandaged hands. How in the world was he going to be able to function? Both hands were wrapped to the wrist and the fingers were individually covered. Admitting the pain was finally getting to him, he reached into his pocket and retrieved the pills Muriel gave him. It had been an hour by the time he returned to the waiting room. Blake gazed at Bea, thankful that she hadn't been in the apartment at the time of the quake. Guilt flooded him. He had always maintained his buildings but wondered if there was something he could have done to prevent its collapse. A nurse entered the room, drawing their attention. "Are there any relatives of Allison Marshall in here?" Aaron stepped forward. "I'm her brother."

She approached him stating, "Mr. Marshall, you're sister is stable. As far as the conditions of her legs, we still don't know. The x-rays, due to the large amount of injuries, won't be read until tomorrow some time. The doctor will talk with you after the results. If you want to see her, you may, she's in room 103."

The four of them stood there staring at the small body occupying the bed. Her face was swollen and bruised. Aaron choked back tears. Suddenly, his stomach flipped. Was Melissa all right? Knowing that Allison was safe and with Blake, he excused himself and headed to the newspaper. Because of the quake he was sure that the staff would all be there, trying to make the deadline. It suddenly hit him, as assistant editor he should have been there hours ago. "My God, was he going to lose his job? The elevator wasn't functioning when he arrived, so he ran up the stairs to the fourth floor and entered the newsroom. The phones were ringing non-stop and the reporters were struggling to hear, due to the deafening, hammering sounds of the typewriters. His arrival went un-noticed to everyone accept Cunningham, as he questioned, "Where in the hell have you been? Did you forget you're an editor for a newspaper?"

Aaron explained his involvement in the rescue and watched as his boss dabbed a hanky to his sweaty forehead before replying, "You're young in the business. What you did was understandable but not acceptable. The Red Cross has their job and you have yours. There are thousands of people out there right now waiting for news regarding the quake and it's your job to help make sure they get it. You've done well until now, so I'm giving you another chance but remember, there's nothing more important than the news if you want to succeed in this business. Now, get to work and I'm glad your sister is okay."

Aaron thanked him and went directly to his office hoping to find Melissa there. She greeted him, throwing her arms around him, stating how worried she had been. The display of affection took him by surprise. The feel of her body pressed so close to his made it difficult, but he forced himself to push her away. She felt him stiffen as he exclaimed, "I'm glad your safe Melissa, we have work to do." Hurt by his cold reaction, she held back tears and replied, "Yes," Mr. Marshall, and left the room. Aaron set to work, drowning out all thoughts of Melissa. It was time to concentrate on the news.

Allison awoke and immediately regretted it. The pain in her legs was excruciating. Where was she? It was a dreary place, with gray walls. Suddenly she remembered the earthquake. The tremors she had felt returned to her and she silently cried, "My legs." There was the desire to examine them but fear stopped her. She tried moving them but the pain was too excruciating. Suddenly it dawned on her, were Aaron and Jonathon all right and what about Bea? Noticing a small buzzer on the bed, she pushed it. With-in moments, a woman as drab as the room itself, entered.

"My name is Muriel, Miss Marshall. What do you need?"

Allison pleaded, "Please can you find out if my brothers and friend are alright?"

Muriel smiled and assured her, "They are all okay. I'm with the Red Cross and we are helping the staff here. I made it a point to check up on your family for you. Both your brothers are just fine. In fact Aaron was right beside Mr. Donlan when they dug you out of the rubble. Your friend Beatrice was here when you were admitted. She wasn't in the building when it collapsed."

Allison sighed with relief and thanked her. She vaguely remembered Blake being somewhere in her dream and trying to escape him by coaxing Charmer to run. She grimaced from the pain in her legs and Muriel informed her, "The doctor is due to arrive on this corridor anytime now and I'm sure he'll prescribe something for your pain Miss Marshall." With that statement, she left the room and soon after, the doctor entered. It was obvious he had been without sleep. With a weary voice, he introduced himself, informing her that he studied her x-rays and as far as he was concerned, the damage could be repaired through surgery and rehabilitation. A sigh of relief escaped her. He continued, "It could take several months if all goes well after the surgery. First a wheelchair and then crutches, to a cane and eventually to walking on your own."

The word months sent fear through her. How could she work? How could she afford to keep an apartment with Bea? How much more could go wrong? She started crying uncontrollably as the doctor tried to reassure her that she would walk again. Muriel entered the room with the pill that would not only help kill the pain it would allow her to sleep. Allison gratefully accepted it, eager to escape the throbbing in her legs as well as in her heart.

Muriel checked in on her. It had been half an hour since Allison had been sedated. She stared with envy at the young lady in the bed. Even though her face was swollen and badly bruised, she knew she was one of the beautiful people. In fact, she told herself, "Even in this condition, she's prettier than me." Blake Donlan came to her mind and she knew how much he loved this woman as she remembered him calling her name and digging in the ruins, ignoring his hands which would forever carry scars. Muriel continued the silent conversation with herself. Did this Allison know how fortunate she was? She should try living this hell on earth I'm living, born so ugly that there was little hope of anyone ever falling in love with her, therefore eliminating any chances of having children. Her destiny was loneliness. She was thankful for the Red Cross. At least there she was needed if not loved. Being needed was the most she could hope for. As she was leaving the room, a nurse brought in a bouquet of flowers and set them bedside the bed. Muriel had never seen such an unusual combination, wild flowers with a single rose bud.

"I don't know what I'm going to do about Allison," Aaron confided in Blake. "She's going to need care and both Jonathon and I have to work. Her rehabilitation will take months.

Blake was very fond of Aaron and due to circumstances he decided to tell him that it was he who had purchased the Marshall house. Right now it seemed the only answer to the problem. Aaron listened without a word and then sighed. Now he knew why they received such a generous price for their home. "What can I say Blake other than thank you for your generosity?"

"I'm not generous Aaron. That's what the house would be worth under different circumstances. It's a fine house and the value will return. The reason I told you is because I would like to help. I know Allison doesn't approve of me and I always seem to offend her in one way or another, but if she agrees, they, Bea and her, can stay at the house until she is rehabilitated and the apartment building is restored. That's the least I can do, after all it was my building that collapsed on her."

Aaron had total admiration for the man in front of him who now sat behind the desk his father had occupied for so many years. He was glad it was Blake. He came to see him looking for a solution after realizing the man loved his sister, but this was much more than he hoped for. He took notice of the bandages on Blake's hands and wondered if Allison would ever appreciate the man.

Blake's voice drew back his attention, "It's a large house as you well know. I can arrange it so that we don't encounter each other if that's what she wishes." Aaron detected sadness in his voice. "If you can persuade her to accept my offer, it will be in her best interest. I have asked Tullah to return. I need a housekeeper and I'm sure she will be more than eager to help Allison with her rehabilitation."

"Tullah," Aaron repeated with a smile of delight.

"Yes, Blake smiled back at him. She can take care of Allison while were all busy working."

Aaron let out a sigh of relief. "I just can't thank you enough Blake but the hard part is going to be convincing Allison it's for the best. I really don't think she dislikes you, she just dislikes everything that has happened to her and unfortunately, through no fault of your own, she connects you with all that has gone wrong."

Blake replied, "Well, I hope your right about her not really disliking me. Aaron shook his hand and replied, "I'm sure of it." Blake watched as he disappeared out the door, then, turned his chair around to look out at the bay. It was as restless as he was. Mesmerized, he watched as the water struggled to get closer to shore, reaching out for something it could only hope to conquer for a short time. Like the bay, he had struggled to get close to Allison and if he should eventually reach her, could he keep her?

Vera Thomas inspected her home. It appeared to have survived the quake with little damage. She remembered thinking at the time it was rumbling and shaking, "What now God? Are you going to take my house from me, the only thing I have left?"

The decision had been made. She would not turn her home into a rooming house, it would be a hotel. That had a much better sound to it. The location by the bay would be desirable to tourists. From the terrace you could view the water and it was a short distance to the beach. Edward managed to get her a loan, using the equity in the house as collateral. She resented how happy and well he looked as he handed her the check. She also remembered the woman that delivered the check to him in his office and the way she looked at him, leaving little doubt regarding her feelings. Bitterness returned and caused her to flush as she remembered informing the women, while playing Mah Jong, that she had tired of her marriage with Edward and was seeking a divorce. "Vera they all exclaimed, doesn't divorce frighten you?" She smiled to herself. Instead of the shame of

Edward leaving her, with one small lie, she was admired for having the courage to terminate an unworthy marriage. Next, she was going to have to inform them she was becoming a businesswoman and turning her home into The Cypress Lane Hotel. Hopefully they would admire her for that also. Yes, hotel sounded so much better than a rooming house. The renovation was almost complete. They would keep their cook and Karen would wait tables. As for Gerald, she expected little help. She sighed in dismay as he appeared from the basement with a box of his homemade gin.

Gerald greeted his mother with a weary hello. Due to the fact that real booze was becoming so expensive through the bootleggers, Macky decided to give Gerald's gin a try after testing the concoction, he ordered a case. Supplying Macky would help him financially but not enough to satisfy his needs. Annabelle was starting to drop hints of marriage. He shuddered at the thought of having to spend the rest of his life trying to sexually please the old lady. He could no longer fool himself into believing there was a young, firm, curvaceous body lying under him while having sex with her. Still, he had to consider the beautiful clothes she provided him, as well as jewelry, a polo pony and entrance to the country club. Deep down, he knew he would have to eventually marry her. There really were no other options, since there was a complete lack of young, rich women. The offspring's of San Francisco's old rich were all taken and the new rich vanished with the depression. A picture of Allison raced through his mind and he quickly erased it. Thankful the bottles survived the quake, he headed for Macky's.

Bea and Aaron sat next to Allison's hospital bed. It had been two weeks since the quake. The outcome of her surgery pleased the surgeon. The doctor informed her that morning she would be released, leaving her to wonder, what was to become of her? Where would she be going? With Aaron seemed to be the only answer but who would help her while he was at work? Already she detested her dependency.

Aaron took her hand in his and asked, "Allison, how would you like to be able to go back home?" Confused by the question, she repeated, "Home?"

"Yes, back to our parent's house." She was even more confused now. Excitedly, Bea exclaimed, "Oh, Allison, it's so exciting. Mr. Donlan invited us to stay there until you get well and the apartment is rebuilt. Allison's thoughts froze on the words, invited to stay, stay at her house. She remained silent as the realization that Blake Donlan had bought their home. Evidently, The Marshall Building wasn't enough.

"Allison, Bea shouted, what's wrong," as she witnessed the look of rage that was overtaking her friends face. Aaron also witnessed the expression and exclaimed, "Allison, Blake's a fine gentleman. I don't understand why you react towards him the way you do. He's been a friend to us. He didn't force our father to sell the Marshall Building and we received much more money for the house than we should of, thanks to him. It wasn't his fault the market crashed. He was smart enough not to have invested in it. Besides that, I don't know if you realize it, but it was Blake that pulled you from the rubble. He wouldn't give up." Allison listened as he continued. "I went to him explaining my dilemma, that Jonathon and I had to work and you needed care. His offer was more than I could have hoped for."

Numbly, she exclaimed, "You don't really mean that he's to care for me. That will never happen."

"No," Aaron replied elatedly, Tullah will."

"Tullah," she echoed back to him.

"Yes, Blake needed a housekeeper and he hired her. Grange, Tullah and little Marshall will all be living there."

Bea spoke, "Blake explained that he feels he owes us something since it was his building that collapsed and created the problem." Aaron and Bea watched as Allison tried to come to terms with the situation. After a minute, Aaron spoke, "Allison, it's the only answer. Unless you can come up with something better, you must resign yourself to it and quit being childish."

Allison wondered what there was about Blake that frustrated her so. Aaron was right. He had done nothing wrong and had been good to them. What was it? Deciding Aaron was right about having no other choices; she decided to accept the offer. Besides that, the thought of being home again with Tullah pleased her. "Your right Aaron, please tell Mr. Donlan I accept his generosity." Aaron sighed with relief and Bea squealed with delight, exclaiming, "It will only be for a short time Allison."

Allison looked over at the flowers sitting on the bed stand and replied, "Yes, hopefully it will be a short stay."

CHAPTER 14

Tullah couldn't remember being this happy for a long time. She would be back at the Marshall house. Oh, how she had missed it. "God Bless Mr. Donlan!" she shouted as Grange entered the room. "Amen," he replied. It was good to see his Tullah this joyous.

"I tell you Grange, I could just get down and kiss those roaches goodbye." He chuckled, "I'm sure they're going to miss you chasing them around the room." They packed the rest of their belongings, bundled up little Marshall and returned home.

The house looked wonderful to Allison. She immediately noticed that the porch had been repaired and painted. They stood there to greet her just as they had done so many times before. Tullah held Marshall and Grange stood ready to take the luggage. Their hearts saddened at the sight of Aaron carrying her up the stairs. He brought her to the parlor and set her down on a tapestry covered chair.

Tullah exclaimed, "Oh, Miss Allison, isn't it good to be back home and together again?"

"Yes, Tullah it is. Allison reached for Marshall. "Please let me hold him for a moment. I swear he's grown a couple of inches since I last saw him." Tullah sat him on her lap and exclaimed, "I think your right Miss Allison. He's a big boy, just like his daddy." As she held and admired him, she couldn't help but notice the fact that Blake was not there to welcome her. In fact she had heard nothing from him since accepting his generous offer. It was probably just as well, being she was uncomfortable with the thought of him looking down on her as she sat in the dreaded wheelchair. She was determined to do whatever it would take to get out of it as soon as possible. At least with crutches, she could stand tall. Even though she only stood a little over five foot two, it seemed tall to her now. After a few moments, Tullah removed Marshall from Allison's lap and Aaron picked her up once again and delivered her upstairs to her room. Grange followed closely behind with the wheelchair.

She had only been gone from the house a short time but it seemed much longer, although nothing had changed, her bed, the rugs and the lace curtains were still there. She sighed, reminding herself she was only there for a short time. Blake owned the house now and she was merely a guest.

Aaron left Allison feeling secure she would be well cared for. Between Blake and Tullah, he had nothing to worry about, at least when it came to his sister. He did have other worries to deal with. His Negro blood haunted him. The fear of it being discovered burned like a fire in the pit of his stomach. So many times he had wished Dorie hadn't written the little book, innocence was bliss. It didn't seem to be affecting Allison, which he was thankful for.

The day of Allison's arrival, Blake purposely left for the office rather than greet her. He had told Aaron the house was large enough that Allison need not encounter him and he was sure that was relayed to her. Therefore, unless Allison requested to see him, he would remain distant. He sat at his desk and threw his thoughts into the reconstruction of the apartment building. He vowed to spend whatever it would take to make it earthquake safe, thankful that there had been no casualties. If all went well, it would be done by the time Allison's rehabilitation was completed.

Tullah was happy in her old room on the third floor, which held her family comfortably. It was a large room that at one time she shared with two other servants. The first week of Allison's return went by swiftly. She had done her best to help her with her exercises but between the household chores and little Marshall it was difficult. Trying to hold back tears, fearing his disappointment in her, she went to Blake and explained, "Mr. Donlan, I'm so sorry but I'm concerned for Miss Allison. The statement, immediately caught Blake' attention, "What is it Tullah?" Wiping away a tear, she replied, "I try to be with her as much as I can but there's just too much to do, and she's not getting the attention she needs."

Staying in the background, he hadn't noticed that Tullah had been overloaded with work. He handed her his handkerchief and consoled her. "I'm sorry. I should have paid more attention. I'll see about getting some more help."

"Thank you Mr. Donlan. I sure appreciate it. Miss Allison is very fortunate to have you for a friend." She left the room, still crying into his hanky.

"A friend," Blake silently repeated her words. "Yes, he told himself, he was Allison's friend whether she accepted him or not. After a moments thought, he decided to look up the kind woman from the Red Cross that had attended to them both after the quake and offer her temporary employment. She would be perfect for Allison's therapy.

Muriel's heart skipped several beats after being informed a Mr. Donlan was there to see her. Puzzled, she wondered what brought him to her. She entered the room flushed, which on a natural beauty, would be appreciated by the observer, but on her she felt the glow merely enhanced her homeliness.

Blake stood and greeted her, asking if she remembered him. She had to hold back not a chuckle, but a downright laugh. How could she or any other woman once seeing him, not remember? Calmly as possible, she answered "Yes, of course Mr. Donlan. What can I do for you?"

"It's not for me Muriel. Please excuse my familiarity, but I don't believe I've ever heard your last name."

"Schuster, she replied, but please, Muriel's just fine. Blake liked the little woman standing before him and hoped she would accept his offer. "Thank you Muriel. I'm here to seek your employment for several weeks. Do you remember Allison Marshall? She had her legs damaged during the quake and needs help with rehabilitation."

Once again Muriel marveled how he could question her memory in regards to the two of them, the beautiful people. Her mind whirled, yes she could get a leave of absence from the Red Cross but did she want to subject herself to witnessing the love this man had for the young woman, making her face the reality every day that it was something she would never experience? "No," she thought out loud, the unexpected sound of her voice startling her.

"I beg you to reconsider Muriel," Blake replied. Once more the sound of her name coming from him thrilled her. It sounded almost beautiful. He continued, "It will only be for a few weeks and I promise you a healthy payment for your time."

Muriel thought how innocent he is. He had no idea what she was thinking. Money couldn't buy what she needed. He was looking at her so pleadingly. How could she refuse him? At least, she was needed. She gave him a timid smile and replied, "Okay, Mr. Donlan, I guess I can do it." Without thinking, Blake put his arms around her and gave her a hug, thanking her. Muriel thought she would surely faint from the display. Her heart raced and once again she became flushed. He asked how soon she could start. "I can be there tomorrow, unless, God forbid, there's a disaster."

"Great, he replied, and please drop the Mr. Donlan, we need not be formal Muriel." The statement left her with nothing more than a shy smile to give him as he walked away. "Tomorrow, she told herself would be a day to look forward to, even though she had mixed emotions.

It was opening day of the Cypress Lane Hotel. With the conversion, it housed eight rental rooms. Out of the eight, there were two reservations. Vera told herself not to panic; it wasn't the tourist season. Putting on a smile, she greeted her first guests. They were a young, giddy couple, she assumed as newly weds, which was confirmed after another round of giggling from the girl. The second couple was from Washington State, he was in the lumber business. "Well, that's a good start, she sarcastically told herself, a lumberjack and honeymooners, where's the oil barons? Gerald came to mind. He had not been the least bit interested in the reconstruction going on, nor questioned anything about the hotel. His only comment being, "Keep everyone out of the basement." Once again, she faced her disappointment in her son as she led the guests to their rooms.

DeLeons had survived the quake with little damage. It was a busy day at the boutique and Kathryn had to admit to herself, Allison's absence was felt. She observed the new girl. She was too quiet and shy. The clients didn't have confidence in her. She lacked Allison's assuredness in their selections. "I'll have to let her go," she told herself. Her thoughts drifted to Blake. They had gone to dinner the other night and he informed her that Allison was staying at his place with her friend until she recovered. She remembered fighting back her anger. Why should he feel guilty the apartment collapsed, many had? As far as she was concerned it was nothing more than a reason to get closer to Allison. Her reply was "Well, you certainly have dedicated yourself to caring for her." He didn't respond. All she could do at this point was wait and see what happened next, telling herself not to hope for more than a sexual, platonic relationship with Blake, unless Allison should reject him.

Allison wheeled over to the window and pulled the lace curtain aside. She could see the stables and wondered if Blake had kept the horses or gotten rid of them. Was Charmer in there? Oh, how she would love to go for a ride. A car drew her attention as it pulled into the circular driveway. Blake got out and opened the passenger door. She was surprised that for an instant, her heart fluttered at the sight of him. A woman got out and Allison recognized her as the lady who attended her at the hospital. What was she doing with Blake and what was she doing there? Blake looked upwards towards the window and their eyes momentarily locked before she let the curtain fall aside. Now, her heart was racing. Why was he having this effect on her?

Muriel was introduced to Tullah who led her to her room while expressing how happy she was to have her there. She opened the door to a pleasant room, exclaiming, "This used to be Allison's nanny's room. This door here, leads to Allison's room."

"How nice and convenient," she replied.

"C'mon, I'll take you to her." Tullah tapped lightly on the door, leaving Allison confused as to why someone was knocking from Dorie's room. She answered the knock, "Come in." They entered and Tullah announced, "This is Muriel Schuster, she's here to help you with your therapy." Immediately Allison became concerned, she couldn't afford a nurse, and replied, "I remember you Miss Schuster and I think it's very nice of you to come, but I am unable to afford you assistance."

"That's quite alright Miss Marshall; Mr. Donlan has taken care of that." Muriel was becoming confused over what the relationship was between the two of them. The young woman appeared to be even more confused than she was. After a moments silence, Allison merely said, "I see." Muriel looked at her pendant watch and questioned, "Shall we start your exercise routine after lunch?"

"Yes, Miss Schuster that will be just fine." Muriel requested, "Please just call me Muriel." Still appearing confused, Allison agreed. Tullah bent down and kissed her on the cheek before they left the room. Once they were gone, she sat in deep thought. Why was Blake doing this for her? She should have told Muriel to leave, that she couldn't accept her services but realized she needed her if she wanted to get well and continue on with her life. Tullah couldn't give her the time she needed and at this point she couldn't exercise alone. She needed to talk with Blake and find out what he expected to gain from this. Meantime, she would let Muriel help her and eventually she would get her answers. It had become obvious by the lack of his presence; he didn't want to be around her.

Elliott knocked on the door and Tullah answered. "I'm here to see my son, Blake, is he home?"

"Yes, sir, he's staying down in the guest house." Noticing the curious look on his face, she stated, "It's only till Miss Allison leaves."

"Allison Marshall," he questioned?

"Yes sir." Now she witnessed the man's face redden. Without another word, he turned and headed to the guesthouse, leaving her wondering what had upset him so.

Elliott couldn't locate his son until he heard the sound of a hammer and followed it to the stables. Blake was busy repairing a hinge on the stable door when he approached. He was always curious why his son enjoyed working with tools so much. He definitely hadn't inherited it from him. Approaching his son, he questioned, "What the hell is going on here Blake?"

Blake looked up to see his father standing there with an angry look on his face and questioned, "What's wrong?"

"I find it very strange that my son lives in the guest house while Allison Marshall lives in the home he just purchased. What is she doing here?"

Blake still had a hard time understanding his father's reaction to Allison, and replied, "She and her friend are staying here until she recovers from the injuries she obtained when my apartment building collapsed on her during the quake. It's the least I can do for her since she has nowhere else to go. Are you forgetting that she was your good friend's daughter?"

"No, but I don't understand why she's up there and your in the guest house." Blake replied, "I like the guest house."

"You like it?" Elliott knew his son well enough to know that this would be the only answer he would receive. He wanted to question his son's intentions regarding Allison but knew this was not the time. If Blake should ever admit he was in love with her, he would have to break his vow to James Marshall and tell him the truth about the twins.

"What brings you here dad?"

"I couldn't get a hold of you at the office, so I thought I would stop by here to let you know there's a nice chunk of land going up for sale."

"What land," Blake asked eagerly?

"The land, next to the cannery, Halladay's letting go of it before he loses it to back taxes."

"How much does he want?"

"A thousand for the land, plus the back taxes, twenty-five hundred dollars total. "Twenty-five hundred," Blake murmured as he visualized the property. Ahh, yes, it was a beautiful piece of real estate. He looked at his father and said, "Partners?" Elliott smiled and replied, "You bet, let's get it." They embraced and Elliott exclaimed, "I'll see you at my office in the morning to close the deal."

As he drove away from the Marshall house, Elliott dreaded the thought of possibly breaking his son's heart, should he admit being in love with Allison. A picture of her came to him, leaving him more than understanding how his son could fall for her, but hopefully once he learned the truth, Blake would feel as he did, the importance of protecting their pure Irish bloodline.

The pain was excruciating and Allison wondered at times if the exercises Muriel was putting her through were not creating more damage.

"Allison, I know it hurts, Muriel would acknowledge sympathetically, but it has to be done. The muscles would rather stay still but we can't let them, they will deteriorate if you don't use them." The first week was the worst. By the second week she could notice the difference which excited her. Muriel informed her she would be ready to advance to crutches with-in a month. To exercise her arms, Allison made it a habit to travel in her wheelchair up and down the hallway at least half a dozen times a day. Many times she stopped in front of the door that had been her parent's room, but always refrained from opening it, fearing the sadness it would cause her. After several weeks, she felt the need to enter and opened the door. What she saw shocked her. It was the only room in the house that had been changed. A huge mahogany, four poster bed, replaced her parent's bed. Oriental rugs covered the now refurbished wood floors. A winged back, leather chair sat next to the fireplace and the small table next to it sported an empty crystal glass and decanter, as if waiting patiently for the end of prohibition to be filled with fine brandy. A large oriental carved chest sat at the foot of the bed and its wood filled the room with an exotic aroma. "Blake's room," she told herself. She could almost feel his presence. She had been told that he resided at the guest house and once again questioned his absence, still unaware of his conversation with Aaron, promising to remain distant. Did he find the thought of seeing her in a wheelchair repugnant? She backed out of the room, closed the door, both thankful, and angered by his absence.

Blake stepped out of the bay. The brisk water rejuvenated him. He wiped himself down with a towel and slipped his riding pants on over his bathing suit. Charmer was tethered to a large piece of driftwood anxious to run again. Blake received a soft nuzzle from her, before mounting and heading back home. As he rode, his thoughts were on Kathryn. He had spent the night with her, enjoying sex until the morning hours. Why she continued to put up with him, he couldn't understand. He had no desire to hurt her and she seemed willing to accept the fact that there could be nothing more than a platonic relationship between them. He was pleases that Allison's name never entered their conversations. His pulse quickened, Allison wanted to speak with him. Tullah delivered the message to him that morning. He wondered what she had to say. She was to meet him at the guesthouse. It had been two months since her arrival and as of yet they had not encountered each other. Muriel was keeping him updated on her recovery. He had become very fond of the drab little woman who was so eager to please, and reminded himself to get her something special when her services were completed. As anxious as he was to see Allison, he caught himself running late for the appointment. Time had escaped him. With a nudge, Charmer happily ran faster.

For Allison, it was the longest walk she had made on crutches. Slowly she worked her way towards the little bungalow that had been built for guests, feeling that she was the one that should be there. Noticing the door had been freshly painted; she knocked and waited nervously for an answer. When there was none, the disappointment she felt shocked her. She was so sure he would be waiting for her. She knocked once more and still, no answer. Turning to leave, she noticed a horseman in the distance and realized it was Blake and Charmer. She was elated, Charmer was there, Blake hadn't sold her. Hurriedly, she wiped away a tear as the two of them raced towards her.

Blake came to a halt and slid from the saddle, apologizing for being late. While he apologized, Allison found it difficult to ignore the tanned, bare chest exposed by an unbuttoned chambray shirt. It was lightly covered with dark silken hair and she watched, mesmerized as his muscles flexed while removing the saddle. She thought of Gerald and his body. It was so different than what she was observing. Gerald was pale and much leaner and lanky. She told herself it was only because he was younger than Blake, and eventually his body would mature, then she became silently angry with herself for comparing or even thinking of either one of them.

"Please don't apologize, Mr. Donlan. After all, time is something of which I have more than enough, your delay interrupted nothing. Charmer is a wonderful horse, isn't she?" Blake, patted the mare and replied, "Yes, she is." Charmer looked at Allison and whinnied. She approached her horse and once more enjoyed the feel of the long, velvet neck as she ran her hand down it. She whispered in her ear, "How's my girl?" Suddenly she started to lose her balance, causing Blake to reach out to steady her. Immediately she regained her balance and pulled away.

Once again, Blake witnessed her stubborn independence and questioned, "What did you want to talk to me about Allison?"

"I just felt it was time to thank you for your hospitality of which I accepted and appreciate. I also want you to know I will reimburse you for Muriel's services as soon as I possibly can." Blake's heart ached watching her standing there on crutches, proudly trying to overcome another obstacle in her life. His voice stammered slightly as he replied, "That's not necessary."

"Yes it is," she insisted. Blake stared her straight in the face with his piercing blue eyes, causing her to wince, and stated, "The building and its tenants were insured. The insurance company is taking care of the debt, not me." He hoped his lie went undetected. The building was insured, but not the tenants.

Relief swept over Allison at the realization she owed him nothing, at least as far as Muriel's debt was concerned. "Well, she replied, Now that we settled that, I want to thank you for allowing Bea and I to stay here."

"You are quite welcome Allison," he replied with a pleased grin that exposed teeth, shockingly white next to his tanned face, leaving her to wonder what had caused the smile. "Well, Mr. Donlan, Muriel is waiting for me. Once more, I thank you." He acknowledged the statement with a slight bow of his head. She adjusted her crutches and returned up the path. Blake watched her for a moment until Charmer distracted him. He whispered in the mare's ear," Don't worry, she'll be riding you again, soon."

Another month had gone by and according to Muriel, Allison was close to full recovery. Blake sat behind his desk reading the newspaper. The article on the society page jumped out at him. Heiress, Annabelle Gilder, to wed Gerald Thomas. "My God," he told himself, Gerald is going to marry Annabelle. It could only be for her money." He wondered if Allison had read the article yet, if so, how was she taking it? "You're a damn fool Gerald Thomas," Blake said to himself as he folded the paper.

"No, no, it can't be," Allison cried from behind the paper. Muriel was sitting across from her at the breakfast table. "What's wrong," she questioned with concern?" Allison had become very dear to her.

"Oh, Muriel, Allison moaned, Gerald is getting married. He's marrying Annabelle Gilder, a woman old enough to be his mother!"

Muriel asked, "Who is Gerald and why would he marry a woman that old?"

"Money," Allison replied bitterly. Muriel silently laughed, telling herself, "I would marry someone for nothing." She detected the hurt as well as bitterness in Allison's statement and asked, "You care for this man, don't you?"

"I have loved him since I was a child," she answered, trying to hold back the tears she swore she would never shed again, because of him.

"Has he ever told you he loves you Allison?"

"Yes, once he informed me he loved me but couldn't afford me."

"Couldn't afford you?" Muriel asked, confused by the statement.

"Yes, he was raised with wealth, like I was. When the stock market crashed, both our families lost everything. He told me he loved me but due to the fact we were both now poor, we had nothing to offer each other, and he's right, I have nothing."

The words," I have nothing," ripped through Muriel like a searing knife. She had nothing? Muriel couldn't contain herself. "You have nothing Allison? You have everything, look at me. Would you trade places with me? She continued, I would, without flinching, give my soul to be you!"

Allison was shocked by Muriel's outburst and questioned, "Why would you trade places with me?"

Muriel continued, "Do you have any idea what it would be like to be me? Look at me Allison. What are my chances of anyone ever telling me they couldn't afford me, or even telling me they love me, much less having a man like Blake Donlan, want me. You have the most handsome, generous, kind and wealthy man I have ever known, in love with you,"

Allison gasped in disbelief, "Blake Donlan doesn't love me. I've given him no reason to feel that way towards me. Muriel laughed and just shook her head. Love doesn't need a reason, it just happens. I was there after the quake and watched as he was digging you out of the rubble with his bare hands. If you look closely you'll see the scars that he will bear forever. He was screaming your name over and over. I remember wishing it was me under that building instead of you."

Allison couldn't believe what she was hearing. Blake loved her, impossible. The thought made her heart skip. She observed Muriel. True, she wasn't a pretty woman, all her beauty was locked up inside. If a man could see that, he couldn't help but love her. Suddenly, she felt ashamed of herself and exclaimed, "I'm sorry Muriel.

"Don't you understand Allison that you can have anything you want except maybe for Gerald." Muriel witnessed the confusion on her friend's face and continued. "A word of advice Allison, Wake up and forget Gerald. Let him have his rich wife. You have everything a woman could want, right here."

What Muriel said was true. Blake had bought everything that was dear to her, even Charmer. She blushed at the thought of thinking of him as anything other than annoying. She never once considered that he might love her. She just assumed he enjoyed frustrating her since rejecting him at her coming out party and informing him that he was much too old for her. The strange bouquets he sent came to mind. The wild flowers and single rose bud. Was she blooming, as he predicted? She must be, suddenly Blake Donlan didn't seem that old. She smiled, telling herself, "Yes, wildflowers are hearty, and they can survive while awaiting the rose. Muriel questioned, "Well, are you going to waste your life waiting for Gerald or are you going to give Blake a chance to give you everything you need, not just wealth, but love?" Allison looked up at Muriel and replied, "I'm not sure what you say is true about Blake loving me. If so, why is he staying in the guest house and not here? Why is he ignoring me? Muriel sighed, "I have no idea, I just know what I witnessed the night of the quake and how he pleaded with me to come and help rehabilitate you."

Allison knew that Muriel had given her much to consider, but she needed to know for sure Blake's feelings before she dare open herself to him. Gerald came to mind, maddening her. Yes, she thought, Gerald you will marry for money and so might I. An image of Blake flashed before her and she realized loving him was not impossible. There had always been something about him, deep with-in her but until now she had no idea what it was. She had been too consumed with Gerald. She also knew that unlike Gerald, she would not marry just for money. Her heart fell. The thought occurred to her once more. What if Muriel was wrong? She broke the silence. "If your sure Blake Donlan is in love with me, tell me what I should do!"

Muriel sighed, "I'm sure he is. We just need to figure out how to get the two of you together. Maybe then you will see for yourself. Allison was suddenly excited by the prospect. She gave Muriel a large hug and stated, "I need to be off of my crutches first!" Muriel smiled, "Time for your therapy."

Chapter 15

Gerald's bride kissed him once more before stating, "Thank you darling for making me the happiest woman in the world." He flinched as she ran her fingers through his hair, silently thinking, I don't care if you're the happiest woman in the world, just stay one of the richest, then replied, "If you're happy, I'm happy sweetheart."

Annabelle loved Gerald even though she wasn't too sure why. He was the most self- centered person she had ever known. Her conclusion was, he made her feel young. Since meeting him, she had undergone facial surgery after convincing herself that if the movie stars did it, why not her? She disappeared to Europe for a couple months, choosing not to have the procedure done in the states where her society friends would be more than ready to expose her surgical make-over. When she returned, they suspected but could prove nothing. Her attempt to recapture her youth for Gerald was disappointing. He never mentioned the change. She prayed that he looked upon her as a woman not a mother, even though she spoiled him like a child. Another thing that plagued her was if she was pleasing him sexually. Now at the age of forty-eight and having survived a heart attack, which she never mentioned to him, fearing that he would identify it with being old, she was ready to dedicate the rest of her life to him. She stood and stated, "I'm going to change into something very sheer and sexy for you darling," and kissed him once more before leaving the room.

Gerald gazed down at the gold and diamond band surrounding his finger. Not only did she have money, she liked spending it, especially on him. He sat there dreading her return. It was their honeymoon and he knew he would have to perform. Silently he groaned, "Annabelle, Annabelle, why can't you just disappear and your money stay?" He looked into the mirror and admired the burgundy silk smoking jacket he wore. Yes, he was pleased with himself but not with Annabelle. Oh, how he wished that it was Allison behind the closed door preparing for him. He deserved her, not the old lady behind it.

"Jonathon," Allison cried with delight as he kissed her. It had been a couple of weeks since he came to visit, being he was preoccupied playing tournaments and doing quite well. Soon, he hoped to be playing the circuit. Allison looked at him closely. Her little brother was maturing. He asked, "Has Aaron been to see you?"

"Yes, Allison replied and I'm worried about him, he's changed." Jonathon became concerned and questioned, "In what way?" She felt it might be due to Dorie's diary but remembered Aaron's word's, they were not to tell anyone, not even Jonathon. She replied, "He just seems depressed. If I mention my concern, he just laughs and says I'm imagining it." Jonathon exclaimed, "I'll call him tomorrow and see if he can meet me for lunch. Maybe I can find out what it is."

Jonathon stayed for dinner and noticed Blake's absence. Aaron had mentioned to him that Blake was staying in the guest house during Allison's stay and both agreed that it was unnecessary and were disappointed that Allison hadn't corrected the situation, but knowing Allison's stubborn side, they remained silent.

Aaron lay in the dark on his bed. He couldn't get his mind off of Melissa. She had become even more aggressive in trying to promote a relationship. Dear God, how he wanted her. How long was he going to be strong enough to discourage her? He remembered the hurt look on her face when he informed her that he was too busy to be involved with anyone after she had put her arms around him confessing she wanted to be with him. What else could he have told her? Certainly not "Melissa I can't be with you because I'm a Negro." Not only would he lose her, but his job as well, two things he loved. He lit another cigarette. Tomorrow he was having lunch with Jonathon and was looking forward to it. He prayed that Jonathon would never discover that their father had cheated on Lillian and that he and Allison were the offspring's of that romance. At least Jonathon was free of Negro blood. It still seemed impossible to him that Lillian wasn't their mother too. There were times he almost hated the father he had loved so much, then he would think of Melissa and realize how helpless a man can be, when in love. Yes, he could forgive him.

Jonathon saw the depressed look on Aaron's face that Allison was talking about. They sat across from each other after having consumed Chan's Golden Gate Special. He listened as Aaron talked about world news and the paper. It was obvious to Jonathon he was happy with his job, but what was bothering him? If there were a problem he was keeping it deep inside himself. Jonathon decided to take a chance. "Aaron is something wrong?" The question took Aaron by surprise, leaving him wondering why he would ask such a question. Was it that obvious he had a problem? He replied, "Why do you ask?"

Now Jonathon was feeling uncomfortable with the question. If there was a problem, Aaron obviously didn't want to share it with either he or Allison. He answered, "Your not quite yourself, even Allison noticed it."

Aaron laughed, "Little brother, I am myself, just overworked. Don't waste energy worrying about me, worry about the tournament you're going to be playing next week. Concentrate on that. I expect to see your name on the sports page next week announcing you the winner of the Bayside Club tournament."

"Okay," Jonathon replied, still not convinced a problem didn't exist. "I'll try not to disappoint you Aaron."

Aaron assured him he wouldn't. They discussed Allison and Blake for awhile before departing. Both felt Allison should overcome her spiteful feelings towards the man, a man they both respected.

The visit with Jonathon left Aaron even more distressed. The fact that it was obvious he was troubled disturbed him. Allison even noticed it. He wondered, who he could confess his fears too. Was there anyone he could confide in? Tullah, entered his mind. She had been like a mother to him and she was Negro. Maybe she could help him accept and not fear his bloodline. Melissa's statement regarding the Nigger messenger at the paper haunted him the most. The burning returned to the pit of his stomach. Her southern upbringing cemented the impossibility of their ever having a relationship. He knew he had to continue rejecting her advances and as bad as it would hurt, praying she would find someone else and lose interest in him for both their sakes. He would give some thought into whether or not he should confide in Tullah.

Allison caught herself thinking of Blake, not Gerald. It had been several days since she and Muriel had the conversation regarding him. Her thoughts drifted to the first time she met him, and his image appeared. Now that she could see past Gerald, she realized what a handsome man Blake was. Perhaps, she had matured, making it possible for her realize it. He no longer seemed old to her. She wasn't sure of their age difference, but suddenly didn't care. The flowers he sent once again came to mind and she could almost see the rose, in full bloom surrounded by the hardy wildflowers, and she smiled to herself, then, momentarily found herself angry. How could he have been so sure? Now she started feeling shame for the way she had treated him after all he had done. Aaron was right Blake didn't force their father to sell the Marshall Building. He gave them a fair price for the house, pulled her from the rubble of the quake and opened his home to her and her friend. He really might love her. She pictured him once again as she had done so many times since meeting with him at the guest house, standing there so tall and tanned, bare chested, looking down at her with those deep blue eyes.

"Allison," Muriel's voice disrupted the vision, "It's time to exercise." According to Muriel, the crutches would be a thing of the past by next week. This made her happy as well as sad. That meant it would be time to leave her beloved home once again. Blake had already informed them that the apartment was completed and ready whenever she was recovered enough to return. The possibility Muriel just might be wrong about Blake's feelings towards her was tending to keep her from expressing her new found feelings. If she was to make an attempt, it would have to be with-in the next week.

Aaron let out a cheer. The sports report was on his desk. Jonathon won the tournament. Melissa wasn't sure what had caused the outburst of joy from Aaron but enjoyed the rare smile on his face.

"What is it," she asked.

"Golf, Melissa, golf, and my little brother won the tournament!" Melissa seized the moment, knowing she might jeopardize her job by her continued aggressiveness, but she had to take the chance.

"Well, she stated, "This is something you should go celebrate and perhaps take me with you." Once more Aaron felt the pressure of having to hurt her. He decided he couldn't do it again. It would just be a simple dinner date.

"Well, she asked, Please don't say no."

He was defeated. "Okay, Miss Barnum, would you join me for dinner and help me celebrate my brother's victory?" Melissa held back tears of relief as she answered, "Yes, Thank you Mr. Marshall. I can't think of anything I rather do." Aaron's willpower had been depleted and the gate to their hopeless future had been opened.

Allison, Bea and Muriel were to leave in the morning. Their stay was over. The only sign of Allison's injuries were a slight limp, which she would have the rest her life. A message was sent to the guesthouse inviting Blake to join them for dinner, expressing their wishes to thank him for his generosity. Since her awakening, Allison had only seen him a couple of times from her window, repairing the fencing. She decided she would wear her best dress that evening, one she earned while working at DeLeons.

Blake dressed for the occasion. While straightening his tie, he wondered whose idea it was to invite him. He came to the conclusion, between the three of them it more than likely was Muriel. He put on the dinner jacket and headed to the house. It was a warm, peaceful night. A small breeze brought the scent of the bay to him. He had grown to love this place, as Allison did. Reaching the porch, he complimented himself on a job well done. It was sturdy now. Having to ring the doorbell to his home made him chuckle to himself. It would feel good, to be back in his own bedroom again, he found comfort there. Tullah opened the door and greeted him. She too felt strange with the situation, inviting him into his own house. She never did understand why he was staying in the guesthouse, but it was none of her business. She led him into the parlor where the three women awaited him.

As he entered the room, Allison immediately became uneasy. When she was around him before, she was always so busy being angry or defensive, now, she felt intimidated by her feelings. She wanted to be near him. The thought made her blush.

Muriel stood there smiling as she absorbed his image into her mind with hopes she could retain it forever. This more than likely would be the last time she would see him.

Bea was the one to step forward and greet him. "Mr. Donlan, I can't believe we have been here all this time and seen so little of you."

Blake smiled and replied, "After seeing how lovely you look this evening, I regret my absence." She giggled and thanked him for the compliment. Muriel marveled how suave he was, telling herself, "He has it all." She watched as he turned his attention to Allison. She wore a champagne silk dress that unlike the still popular chemise caressed her curves. Their eyes met and Allison flushed, leaving Muriel envious the way it made her even more attractive. Blake took her hand and gave a slight bow, his eyes admiring the curves as he did so. "Miss Marshall, you look beautiful as always." She smiled and thanked him hoping he didn't feel her pulse quicken as she observed for the first time his scarred hands. Muriel held her breath as he approached her, knowing he couldn't tell her she was beautiful or lovely. He took her hand, "And you Muriel are always a delight." With a hidden sigh, she thanked him. She felt complimented yet spared the embarrassment of being lied to and told she was also beautiful.

They sipped homemade wine Bea obtained with the help of her boyfriend. While waiting dinner, Muriel and Blake discussed the importance of the Red Cross. Bea changed the conversation stating that she heard he and his father had purchased the property next to the cannery. Blake told her she was correct. When asked what his plans were for it, he informed her, none at this point. He noticed a lack of conversation from Allison. It was becoming obvious to him the dinner party had not been her idea, which was of no surprise to him.

Allison hated herself for being so quiet. Maybe her idea to have this party was a mistake. Every time he directed a question toward her she could only reply, yes or no. She was completely tongue-tied, leaving her feeling foolish. Never had she felt this way. She became anxious for the evening to end.

Feeling her anxiety, Blake was eager to complete the evening and relieve Allison of his presence. After dinner, he excused himself and returned to the guesthouse holding onto the image of her in the silk dress.

Allison couldn't believe herself. The evening, at least for her anyway, was a disaster. She had experienced shyness, a feeling unfamiliar to her. Bea even questioned if she felt okay. Tomorrow morning she would be leaving, removing any chances of encountering Blake. She had her chance and failed miserably.

Packing, Allison contemplated her return to DeLeons. Kathryn requested that she return as soon as possible. She was unaware of Blake and Kathryn's relationship or the fact he was responsible for her job. She lovingly surveyed the room. Once again she would leave it, this time, possibly forever. If it was true, and Blake really did love her, she could regain everything she had lost. Why couldn't she admit to him how she felt? For some reason, the thought of admitting it to him, humiliated her.

She walked down the hall to his room, entered and closed the door behind her. She stood there and gazed at the four poster bed and wondered what it would be like to share it with him. Instead of blushing at the thought, her heart raced. Still a virgin, all she could do was imagine. For a moment Gerald came to mind, and how she had fantasized having sex with him. She shook the image from her mind, no longer wanting anyone but Blake to occupy it. He would be back in the room tomorrow. Now she wished that he had been in it these past few months. "Maybe," she told herself, being that close for that amount of time, if he really did love her, he might have had the opportunity to tell her so. Now, she was only to assume he did, because of Muriel's statement. Her heart fell to the pit of her stomach. What if Muriel was wrong? She turned out the light and returned to her room.

Aaron and Melissa ate at her favorite restaurant, The Ebb Tide. It overlooked the bay and served the finest seafood in San Francisco. She stared at Aaron sitting across from her. It was the happiest she had ever seen him and hoped she had something to do with it and not just because his brother had won a tournament.

Aaron was so comfortable with her that he put aside his fears for the time being. Tonight he just wanted to enjoy himself. They finished their dinner and Aaron escorted her back to her apartment. Melissa opened the door and stated, "The night is young and so are we. Do you play cribbage?"

Aaron grinned and replied, "Yes, as a matter of fact, I do and I play it very well." He and Jonathon had spent many hours on the game.

"Good," she said with a smile that exposed the wonderful dimpled cheeks. "I challenge you."

"You're on," he said, accepting the challenge, both knowing it would allow them more time together, as they were not ready for the evening to separate them. It was a small apartment, but cozy. She brought out the cribbage board and after four games, Melissa was able to claim only one victory. Aaron stretched and looked at the mantle clock, stating that it was time for him to leave.

"One more game," she pleaded, stating," If I win, you stay the night." Aaron was shocked by the statement but had to laugh as he replied, "What if I purposely lose?" Melissa put her arms around him and exclaimed, "Then it's obvious we both want the same thing and should forget the game." She shocked herself, never had she been this brazen. The only thing she was sure of was that it was up to her to make the advances. She prayed silently that he wouldn't consider her a hussy as she watched his face, while making his decision. She had only known one man, no, a boy, the next door neighbor. It was the typical teenage crush, they lost their virginity together. She moved to Aaron, pressing herself close. It felt like a high volt electrical charge soaring through his body. He cupped her chin and raised her head so he could look in her eyes, stating, "You don't know anything about me Melissa."

She exclaimed, "All I know is that I fell in love with you the moment I saw you. That's all I need to know, nothing else matters." Tears started to make her eyes glisten. He couldn't hurt her again. He moaned and pulled her close to him, once more defeated.

Melissa led him to her room and they proceeded to undress each other. Aaron gazed longingly at the perfect body that he had so many times tried to vision naked as she moved around the office. She had small but pert breasts, a tiny waist, slender legs supported by a thin ankle and petite foot. His manhood became erect at the sight.

Melissa stood in awe as she stared at the defined chest and washboard stomach. What held her attention most was his erection. Compared to her first sexual encounter this spectacle both excited and concerned her. Aaron picked her up and carried her to the overly feminine bed and set her down.

He had been with enough women to be secure in his ability to please. He questioned, "Are you sure about this Melissa?"

"I've prayed for this moment Aaron."

The lovemaking continued through the night. They would sleep a short time then eagerly join themselves once more. It seemed impossible to ever get enough of each other. Aaron held her to him as they lay in the dark; the fear was returning. Now it was more powerful than before. He couldn't bear to lose her. Melissa felt his heart, skip a beat, and silently wondered what had caused it.

CHAPTER 16

Allison and Bea stood in front of the rebuilt building. Chills ran down Allison's spine, remembering that the one time three-story structure had been on top of her. She remembered the weight of it crushing her and gasped.

"Are you all right with this," Bea asked with concern? Allison reached for her friend's hand and replied, "Yes, I'll be okay. I just can't let myself think about that morning." They entered the apartment, which was now on the top floor. Allison never wanted to occupy a bottom floor again. Everything was fresh and new. The furnishings were as before, very tasteful.

"Isn't it great," Bea exclaimed. No Murphy bed, we have twin beds!" Allison observed the beds and her mind drifted to the four-poster. Bea interrupted the vision asking, "Allison, where are you?" Allison smiled and answered, "I'm sorry. I guess I'm just tired." Of course Bea told herself. It was the first time she had really been up and about for such a long period. She put her arms around Allison and suggested she take a small nap. "We can unpack later." Allison readily agreed.

She napped for about an hour. When she awoke, she walked into the living room. What she saw stunned her. On the table sat a bouquet, a dozen, fully bloomed roses, there were no wildflowers. She stared at it for moment before she picked up the note. It simply read, "The rose has bloomed." Blake.

The bouquet appeared so incomplete without the wildflowers. What did it mean? Wasn't he waiting for her anymore? Tears streamed down her face. Bea came from the kitchen. "Jeez, Allison, what happened?" Allison handed her the card. She read it and only became more confused over her reaction exclaiming, "I don't understand Allison!" For the next hour, Allison explained.

Bea, sighed. "No wonder he doesn't know you have any serious feelings towards him. I never even guessed that you cared. I can't believe that all the time we spent at his place, you never invited him up to the house except for a farewell dinner, and then you hardly spoke to him. You didn't even invite him personally, you sent Tullah with a message that could have been from either Muriel or myself. How was he to know it was your idea? You, my friend need to let him know how you feel."

Allison knew everything Bea said was true, but now it was too late to let him know. That was unless she simply went to him and admitted her feelings. No, she just couldn't do that. She looked back at the bouquet and asked herself, "How can a dozen roses look so lonely?"

Melissa was more confused than ever with Aaron's moods. There were times they had fun and laughed and others when he would become distant. It had been six months since they came together and to her dismay, no proposal of marriage. She knew he loved her, but once, she mentioned marriage, and he fell into one of his deep depressed moods, deeply hurting her. She asked what was wrong and he replied, "You don't know anything about me. She had replied, "I told you all I need to know is, I love you, but if you have something to say, go ahead." He never gave an answer.

Aaron drove up to the Marshall house in his Ford Coupe. Getting out of his car, he noticed Blake painting a fence and walked towards him. "That fence is looking mighty good," he stated. Blake turned and the expression on his face showed that he was glad to see him.

"What brings you here Aaron?"

"I came to talk with Tullah, there's something I need to ask her." Blake removed a western style hat and ran his fingers through his dark, loosely waved hair and stated, "Grange and her went to town, but they should be back by now." The two men conversed for a few minutes. As they spoke, Aaron wondered if Blake would ever admit to him, his love for Allison. He thought that possibly something might happen between them after all the time she had spent there. Unfortunately, it appeared nothing had transpired. Probably just as well, he told himself, wondering if the fact Allison had Negro blood in her would change Blake's feelings towards her. A rush of guilt ran through him. He hadn't seen Allison for sometime and he made a mental note to call her.

Blake exclaimed, "I see by the sports column, Jonathon is doing quite well with his golf!" Aaron answered with a proud smile, "Yes, he's very determined to make it professionally"

Blake stated, "I have a feeling he'll make it. After all he's a Marshall. By the way, how is Allison?"

"I'm assuming she's doing okay. As a matter of fact I was feeling guilty just now for not having seen her for awhile. Blake arched a brow and smiled. "That means you're either overloaded at work or a woman has entered your life."

Aaron smiled back, exclaiming, "Both." A car pulled into the driveway, terminating their conversation. Kathryn waved to Blake and he gave a slight wave in return.

Aaron stated, "I guess if I want time to speak with Tullah, I better get up to the house." He shook Blake's hand and returned up the cobblestone path to the house, meeting the distinguished woman along the way, giving her a nod as they passed.

Kathryn gave Blake a kiss and questioned, "Who was that young man?" Blake answered, Aaron Marshall, Allison's twin brother."

"No wonder he looked familiar," she replied, silently appreciating his good looks. The reason I'm here is to discuss the house warming, are you ready?" He didn't particularly want a house warming but felt he would disappoint Kathryn is he didn't agree to it, knowing how she loved to organize events. He answered, "As ready as I'll ever be."

She ignored his lack of enthusiasm and exclaimed, Good, I'll start making the arrangements and preparing the menu, then all I will need is your approval."

"No, you leave me out of this, he insisted. I have complete faith in your decisions. I'll supply the guest list and expenses, nothing more."

Happy with his response, she announced, "I better get back to the boutique!" She kissed him and departed. During her drive, she was relieved, knowing that Allison was back at the boutique. She had gone through three salesgirls during her rehabilitation. Blake never questioned her in regards to Allison. She didn't know what had occurred in the months that Allison stayed at his house, but Blake had mentioned that he occupied the guesthouse while she and her friend were there. Shaking herself from thought, she decided to concentrate on the party, not on Blake and Allison.

Aaron found Tullah in the kitchen. She was happily surprised to see him asking, "What brings you here?" while giving him a hug. Aaron replied, "I need to talk to you about something. When would be a good time, it could take awhile?"

Tullah became alerted to the fact he didn't seem himself. She wanted to talk right then and there but if it were to be a lengthy conversation, it would have to be that evening. There were still chores to be done. She informed him that seven o'clock would be a good time if that worked for him. Aaron felt instant relief in just knowing that there was someone to confide in, and assured her he would be there. Departing, he hoped his courage would remain with him as he questioned himself. "Are you really going to expose yourself and Allison?" He knew he had to. He had to talk to someone.

Annabelle cheered; Gerald won the tennis match. Sitting there watching him, she was thinking how very fortunate she was to have him. They had been married for five months now and the honeymoon seemed to continue. Slightly disappointed, she knew it wasn't their sex life that created the feeling but Gerald's love of travel. They had toured through Europe and he was now requesting that she consider a trip to Asia. She didn't feel she had the stamina the trip would require but dared not disappoint him. Not wanting to appear too old, she agreed. They would be leaving again in a couple of days. She sighed to herself, wondering, "When will he tire?"

After the match Gerald returned to the group sitting under the umbrella covered table. They were sipping iced tea spiked with liquor, each having their own special flask. Annabelle received her usual peck on the cheek, missing the kiss she once received on the mouth. On the mouth seemed so much more sincere to her. He sat down and removed the silver monogrammed flask she bought him and drank straight from it instead of adding it to the tea as the others had. This upset her. He was drinking too much lately. If she mentioned it, he became belligerent and said things that hurt her. She learned if she didn't want to subject herself to verbal abuse, it was best, not bring up the subject.

Gerald choked slightly as he took another sip. He was looking foreword to the Asian trip. He discovered, while in Europe that Annabelle would become weary and retire early, leaving him alone to sightsee. He smiled to himself as he remembered his last sight seeing trip alone, at the hotel cocktail lounge. How great it was to be in a prohibition free country. He met and had sex with several young Italian and French women. Now he was looking foreword to an Asian beauty. Getting away from San Francisco and Annabelle's group allowed him the freedom he desperately needed. Every now and then Gearld's mind would drift to Allison. It had been quite awhile since he had seen her. The party at the warehouse was when they last met. He still had hopes of one day having her sexually, perhaps then, he could forget her, but in the meantime, he would continue on with his charade marriage to Annabelle.

Allison was helping one of DeLeon's best customers, make a selection when she looked up and saw Blake enter the store. Her heart skipped a beat as she asked herself, "What is he doing here?" The question was answered all too soon. Kathryn greeted him by surrounding him in her arms and kissing him, not on the cheek like a friend but on the mouth. Allison felt she might become ill at the sight. She hadn't realized they knew each other. Of course, she told herself, there were a lot of things about Blake she never bothered to find out. After their greeting, Blake noticed her and approached commenting, "Allison, it's nice to see you again." She replied with a "Thank you," turned and left the room. Blake had become accustomed to her walking away from him with few words. Once more he accepted the fact she rather not be near him.

Allison sat in the dressing room wondering how long Blake and Kathryn had known each other. Had he kissed her, or she him? No, she told herself, they kissed each other, confirming it was a mutual act. For the first time in her life, she experienced jealousy. With Gerald she had experienced hurt and disappointment, never this feeling, not even when he married Annabelle. Her customer Mrs. Rothberg was probably wondering where she went. She had to return to the floor. Hopefully by now Blake had left and she would no longer have to witness his and Kathryn's display of affection towards each other. She returned and thankfully, Blake was gone. Kathryn was standing next to a display case reading a piece of paper. She looked up and exclaimed, "Allison, you were quite rude to Blake. After all he has done for you, I would think you would be more appreciative, is there a problem?" Allison replied, "I'm sorry. I just haven't been myself lately." It was the only excuse she could come up with. Having to satisfy her curiosity, she continued, "Have you and Mr. Donlan known each other long?"

Kathryn smiled coyly before answering, yes, as a matter of fact we have. I was telling him how grateful I was that he recommended you for this job.

"My God, Allison cried to herself, trying to hide her disbelief. He was even responsible for her having a job. Anger overwhelmed her. Since the night of her coming out party, he had taken charge of her life.

"Allison," Kathryn's voice brought her back. "I've been helping Blake with his house warming party." She stopped for a moment and returned her attention to the piece of paper, then stated, "This is the guest list and it appears you and your friends Beatrice and Muriel are invited."

"That's nice," Allison answered dryly. Kathryn didn't miss the sudden coolness in her voice and wondered why Blake would bother inviting her. She was becoming even more confidant that she had a chance with him, since Allison definitely appeared disinterested.

It was dusk when Aaron returned to have his talk with Tullah. He was convinced he could confide in her. Several times along the way he almost turned around but realized he was desperate to talk to someone. He sat in front of the house for a moment, once more deciding whether or not he should divulge his and Allison's secret, then told himself he must do it. He climbed the porch steps and rang the bell. Immediately Tullah opened the large, mahogany, beveled glass door, anticipating his return. She hugged him and suggested they go to the parlor to talk.

Aaron gazed at the parlor door before opening it and entering. He remembered all the secrets the room previously held; his parent's private talks. The personal talks Jonathon, Allison, and he had shared with their parents, and now he prayed it would hold another secret. They entered and set themselves down on the parlor chairs, facing each other.

Tullah noticed the haunted look on his face and became concerned. "Aaron, what is it?"

Aaron took a deep breath and cleared his voice before speaking. "Do you know about Dorie's diary?"

"You mean that little black book she always wrote in? Did you find it?"

"Yes," he answered.

"Heavens sake Aaron, what did it say to upset you so?" He had gone this far and felt there was no turning back. The most difficult part of his confession would be not to offend Tullah while he expressed his concern over having Negro blood in him. He wanted to make sure she knew he wasn't ashamed of it. He would never want to do anything to hurt this woman who had been such a big part of his life. She waited anxiously for his answer.

"Tullah, I found out that Dorie was not just our nanny, according to her book she was Allison's and my grandmother. Tullah sat stunned by what she had just heard. Aaron waited anxiously for her response, feeling his very existence depended on it. Her mind was racing backward through time, to the day the twins arrived. She was told they were orphaned and sent to the Marshall's from France. They looked French to her. The Negro blood was well hidden; it obviously had been lost through generations of racially mixed breeding. Dorie had spoken many times of her daughter Trilly who had died young but never mentioned how she died. She broke the silence and asked, "Did she say your mother's name was Trilly?"

He answered, "Yes, we even found a photo of her. We also found a picture of Dorie when she was young with a white man. It appears to be a wedding photo. He must be our grandfather. He continued, Lillian was not Allison's and my mother, Trilly is. Tullah was beginning to realize the deceit that had been imposed on her dear Mrs. Marshall. Momentarily, she became angry until she remembered how much joy the twins had brought Lillian, causing her to silently forgive both Mr. Marshall and

Dorie. Turning her concern back to Aaron, she could see how it had affected him and questioned, "What upsets you the most about what you have learned?"

Aaron prayed for the right words. "Believe me Tullah, I am not ashamed to have Negro blood in my veins, but you know what it's like to be Negro. If Allison and I were discovered we would be shunned by the white community and rejected by the black community. We are not one or the other, but we were raised in the white world." Her heart wept for him and once more, as she had done so many times in her life, she silently questioned, why color separated people, black or white, they were all human? The twins had been raised in the white world and that is where they belonged. Aaron questioned, "What should we do?" Before answering, she asked, "How is Allison taking this?"

"So far, she's doing fine. I don't think she understands the jeopardy we're in."

Tullah sighed, "Aaron I'm not able to answer your question positively. All I can say is, you've gone this long passing as white, go on with your life, that's all you can do. Worry about discovery only if it happens. Do as Allison has, live in your white world, that's where your father and Dorie wanted you."

Aaron felt immediate relief. She had told him what he needed to hear, "Go on with your life in the world you know." He stood and kissed the woman who had been so dear to him. "Thank you Tullah, I love you and I hope you believe me when I say I'm not ashamed of my heritage. In fact, he smiled, according to Dorie, Allison and I have royal blood in us."

She smiled and caressed his face with her hands, replying, "I believe that Aaron, I feel it when I'm with you. You were raised by three good people and they did a fine job." Aaron corrected her, "No, four good people. You were always there and a big part of Allison, Jonathon and my lives." His words drew tears to her eyes. Then she asked about Jonathon. "Does Jonathon know any of this?" She saw the fear immediately return to his face. "No, we haven't told him. I think its better left untold for all our sakes." Tullah agreed, exclaiming, "Your secret is safe with me."

"I know, he replied, that's why I came to you." He left her, promising himself to continue on as white. After all, he was more white than black. Melissa need never know. He loved her too much to take the chance of telling her the truth and losing her.

Chapter 17

Allison, Bea and Muriel arrived at the house warming party. Walking up the steps Allison remembered the parties her parents had thrown. It was good to see the house lit up again, with music flowing from it. Muriel was ecstatic; she had never attended such a function. In fact, the only invitations she ever received were calls from the Red Cross, inviting her to attend disasters. Allison and Bea had helped prepare her for the evening. They styled her hair, applied make-up and helped her choose a dress. The dress wasn't from DeLeons that would have been much too expensive; instead they went to J.C.Penneys. It was a soft blue crepe that despite the thick glasses she wore brought out the blue in her eyes. A pearl necklace, loaned to her from Allison hung gracefully around her neck and for the first time in her life, she almost felt pretty.

On the way to the party both Bea and Muriel lectured Allison to be attentive towards Blake, exclaiming, "How else is he ever going to know how you feel?" The statement left Allison wondering, just how she would accomplish it with Kathryn around.

The room was beautifully decorated making it apparent that Blake hadn't fought expense. Ivory, lace covered tables held large floral arrangements. They were laden with trays of various cheeses, meats and seafood, combined with a mixture of exotic fruits. which defied the depression. Two single tables held huge crystal punch bowls, laced with alcohol. The devious potion swirled non-stop as guests filled their glasses. Never having been exposed to such a drink, Muriel returned frequently to the wonderful beverage and innocently indulged, going unnoticed by her two friends as they accepted offers to dance. She was enjoying the free spirited feeling she received from the concoction.

Allison and Bea found Muriel at the punch bowl and noticed that she was slightly tipsy. Blake approached commenting, "I had to get a little closer to make sure it was really you Muriel, you look wonderful." Once again grateful that he hadn't used the word beautiful, she thanked him. He was in the process of acknowledging Allison and Bea when Kathryn arrived on the scene. She put her arms around him, kissing him on the cheek before addressing them.

"Allison, so glad you and your friends could make it." Allison tried to put on her best smile as she introduced Muriel and Bea. "So nice to meet you," Kathryn stated in an overly sweet voice, while kissing Blake once more. Allison was relieved to see that he was uncomfortable by the act as he and broke away, asking Muriel to dance. Muriel's eyes doubled through her glasses and her heart quickened as she exclaimed, "I don't know how to dance!"

"Sure you do, he replied taking her hand, you just don't know it, come with me." Muriel followed him to the floor, feeling somewhat faint as he put his arms around her. He instructed, "You followed me out here, now all you have to do is continue to follow me, and listen to the music." She was surprised how easily it came to her, telling herself that he could lead her anywhere and she would follow. Silently, she wished the dance would never end. The music and the feel of Blake Donlan's arms around her were sheer heavenly bliss. Sadly, it did come to an end and he returned her to her friends. By this time Kathryn had wandered off, giving Blake time to acknowledge Allison. He admired the black dress she was wearing and the way it clung to her body, thankful her shape no longer was hidden behind the straight lines of a chemise. The image stimulated him, and he immediately started a conversation to divert his thoughts. "Are you and Bea comfortable in your new apartment?"

Allison replied, "Yes, thank you for asking." She gazed around the room before stating, "Strange, it wasn't that long ago that you were the guest in this house and now, I'm the guest." There didn't seem to be any hostility in her voice, only a tone of incredibility. He wanted to blurt out how much he wanted it to be hers again. Her next statement confused him. "I hope you and Kathryn will be very happy here."

"Kathryn, and me? What was she talking about?" Blake was baffled and exclaimed, I'm not quite sure what you mean, but I'm very happy here." He thought he saw a small tear, which a quick blink of her eyes eliminated. "How is Charmer," she asked?"

"I'm sure she misses you, would you like to ride her?" Allison's face lit up and a smile appeared, warming his heart. "I would love to Mr. Donlan." He wished to hear her call him Blake and informed her there was one condition, and the smile disappeared. He continued, it's a small request, just call me Blake." A grin returned and she promised to try to remember his request. He continued, "You can feel free to ride her anytime you wish."

"Is tomorrow too soon Mr., I mean Blake?" He smiled at the sound of his first name finally coming from her, even if it was uneasy.

"I said whenever Allison and I meant it." Kathryn returned and draped herself around him, shrouding him with her flowing red dress. The sight upset Allison and she excused herself. Kathryn observed the way Blake watched as she walked away from them. Silently angered, she tugged on his arm requesting a dance.

Muriel was back on the dance floor with a man who asked her to join him. He stared at her through a pair of equally thick glasses admiring her blue eyes. "Muriel's your name! That's a nice name, Muriel."

She could never remember feeling this happy. The punch bowl had much to do with it. Suddenly her name did sound nice. Not only that, she was actually in the arms of a man, dancing. She said, "Pinch me." He questioned the request. "Pinch you?"

"Yes," she demanded. Puzzled, he asked, "Where do you want me to pinch you Muriel?"

"Anywhere," she answered with a slight slur. He delicately pinched her on top of the arm.

"Thanks, she said. I really am awake and not dreaming." The man was confused but taken with her. He knew she was intoxicated and felt that if she were not, she more than likely would have refused to dance with him. His name was Chadwick, though people chose to call him Chad. The nickname intimidated him. It was much too masculine and he always felt that Chadwick better suited him. He was slight of build with a pale complexion and had worn the thick glasses most his life. The only asset he felt he had going for him was his accounting skills. Both Blake and Elliott Donlan had employed him for several years. Sadly, accounting was not an asset that attracted women. They were on their second dance when the music sped up and he spun her. After the dramatic spin, Muriel looked at him and announced, "You made me sick." It took a moment, due to his inferiority complex to realize she hadn't said, "You make me sick." He noticed the change in her coloring and quickly led her to the powder room. Concerned, he awaited her return.

Allison became excited. She saw Aaron appear with a date, "That must be Melissa," she exclaimed to Bea. She was anxious to finally meet the woman that stole her brother's heart. They greeted each other and were introduced. Allison instantly liked Melissa and could see as well as almost feel the love they had for each other. Aaron informed her that Jonathon had been invited but had to decline. "He has a tournament tomorrow and doesn't trust himself enough to leave the party early, I admire his discipline." Aaron surveyed the room, "The place looks great, doesn't it Allison?" She agreed.

Melissa also viewed the room and mourned the loss of the magnificent house. She knew the story of how the crash of the stock market had robbed his family of almost everything. She couldn't help but mourn the fact, had the market not crashed and Aaron eventually proposed to her she would have married into a fortune. Sighing, she told herself, Aaron was all she needed.

It was getting late. Allison and Bea were ready to leave. It was Muriel they had to convince it was time to go. As Allison scanned the room looking for her, she spotted Blake and their eyes met. He smiled and gave a slight bow. Her heart leaped and she returned a meek smile, asking herself, "What has he done to me?" Bea caught the exchange and commented with frustration, "I just don't believe this. It seems to me, you should be over there standing next to him, not Kathryn."

Agitated, Allison asked, "What do you suggest I do, walk over there and tell Kathryn, who is my employer, to get lost? After all, they did plan this party together and I don't see Blake looking upset over anything?"

Bea sighed, "True, this is probably not the place or time, but you better do something soon or he's going to end up with her and not you. You better find a way to let him know how you feel."

"I know, Allison replied wearily. I accepted his offer to ride Charmer tomorrow. If I can work up the courage to humble myself, I'll tell him, if I see him."

"I don't understand how you could tell Gerald that you loved him but you can't tell Blake!"

Allison answered, "As far back as I can remember, I thought I loved Gerald, the feeling was always there. What I feel for Blake is new to me and unexpected. Besides, you saw my last bouquet; he has given up on me."

"Well, all I can say, is you better do something before you lose him." Allison knew she was right. "Let's get Muriel and leave," I'm tired she exclaimed.

"Sounds good to me," Bea replied as she witnessed the defeated look on her friend's face. They found Muriel with the unpretentious man and announced that it was time to go.

After being sick, Muriel was becoming herself once more and not liking it. However, the man who had helped care for her during one of her most embarrassing moments was still being very attentive. She agreed to leave, but the man with her interrupted and requested they be alone for a moment. Allison and Bea were delighted with his request and agreed to wait another few minutes.

Chad took Muriel by the arm and led her onto the veranda. Letting go of her arm, he held her hand and stated, "May I see you again Muriel?" He dared not ask such a question in front of the other women, fearing the usual rejection. Muriel experienced a small feeling that the nausea might be returning. Quickly, she appraised the man in front of her and wondered what he saw in her. Chad was becoming concerned with her silence. Finally, she swallowed and replied, "Yes, I would like that Mr?"

"Chadwick Webster he answered, my friends call me Chad." Muriel informed him she worked at the Red Cross and to contact her there. He returned her to her friends stating, "I'll see you soon, Muriel."

Allison and Bea had never seen anyone so excited as Muriel was. On the way home she conquered her nausea and talked about how wonderful the party had been, even though there were a few blurred moments. "I danced all night," she exclaimed as they dropped her off at her apartment. Laughter spilled from her friends as she danced to her door and waved goodnight. Bea, stated, "I hate to think of how she's going to feel in the morning." Allison shuttered, remembering her one time experience after consuming too much alcohol.

Allison awoke early. Most the nights sleep escaped her as she tried to visualize what the next day would hold. Would Blake even be at the stables when she arrived? Would they ride together, it was a weekend, he shouldn't be working? She hated the uncertainty, even though life had taught her that nothing was certain. Pouring her coffee, she contemplated her situation once more. Now, she knew she had fallen in love with Blake and was still surprised by the fact. Yes, she would tell him she loved him. Hopefully, it wasn't too late. She took her shower and put on her riding pants and appraised herself. Remembering, Kathryn last night and how elegant she looked in the red gown, she had to admit that she was a beautiful woman and independently well to do. Geralds words came to her, "You have nothing to offer," which maddened her once again. She was sounding like him by thinking Blake was that shallow. Money still shouldn't predict whether you should love someone or not, Blake had more character.

He wasn't at the stables when she arrived leaving her feeling a deep disappointment. She convinced herself that he was probably with Kathryn again. Jacob, Tullah's uncle saddled Charmer for her.

"She's eager and ready to go Miss Allison, "he exclaimed. Allison thanked him as she pulled herself onto the saddle. "C'mon Charmer, lets go to the beach." The mare required nothing more than the request. Allison felt the strength and speed of her beloved horse as they rode away. The sight pleased Jacob. It was good to see her riding again. He pulled out a well-worn hanky and wiped a tear away, remembering her as a child. He made a silent statement, "Maybe someday Miss Allison, you'll be home for good. I know Mr. Donlan wants you here."

The sea breeze they both loved greeted them. Allison's hair and Charmer's mane flowed behind them as they sped down the sandy beach. It was deserted due to the cold weather other than another horse, tethered to a large piece of driftwood. She recognized it as Aaron's. Her heart did a double beat as she realized Blake must be there. Slowing Charmer's pace they approached the rider less horse. Looking out over the bay, she saw Blake emerging from the slow lapping waves and chilled at the sight. She shrugged off the coldness the bay waters must have imposed upon him.

He wasn't sure what time Allison would choose to take her ride and was pleased to see her. Once again he admired how the horse and rider complimented each other. Both were sleek bodied and free spirited.

As he came closer, Allison's heat beat rapidly at the scene. His bathing suit was wet and clinging to his body, outlining his manhood. She tried to keep her eyes from it but they kept drifting to the sight. Blake noticed and hoped she wouldn't get the impression that was all there was, being it was somewhat diminished due to the coldness of the water. "Are you enjoying your ride Allison," he asked while drying himself off.

"Yes, thank you again for your generosity." She watched as he slipped his pants on over his bathing suit. The hair on his head and chest glistened from the water and Allison caught herself wanting to feel it. His voice interrupted the thought, "Mind if I ride with you?"

Thankful for the request, Allison replied, "Not at all, please join us." He climbed onto the saddle and both were silent as the two horses maintained a slow stride down the beach. Allison cursed herself once again for her lack of conversation. She finally broke the silence, deciding to thank him for the flowers.

"Mr. Donlan, excuse me, Blake, I forgot to thank you for the roses. In fact, for the many bouquets you have sent me." There was an edge in her voice he didn't quite understand but chose to ignore it, having become accustomed to her moods.

"You're welcome Allison," he replied without further comment. This frustrated her and she continued, "I'm assuming there will be no more, by the message that came with the last one. Obviously, you realize, as you put it, "The Rose has bloomed," and you're right, I have. Now you can dedicate yourself to Kathryn."

"What the hell is she talking about," Blake asked himself. This was the second time she had mentioned him and Kathryn. He remembered the party when she stated she hoped they would be happy together. Had Kathryn told her there was more than a platonic relationship between them? Besides that, what difference would it make to Allison? It shouldn't bother her, but she appeared to be jealous? He told himself that was impossible.

Allison continued, "Now you won't be needing to protect me anymore from Gerald Edwards, pulling me out from under toppled buildings, sharing your home with me and getting me a job (her voice broke) with your girlfriend."

"My God, he told himself in disbelief, she is jealous." Allison took his silence as an agreement and dismounted Charmer. With her slight limp she turned and led Charmer in the opposite direction. Blake dismounted and grabbed her. "Allison, tell me what you really mean?"

"I don't know what you're talking about," she replied as tears streamed down her cheeks!"

"Yes you do." He pulled her tight against him and he could feel her heart beating like that of a captured bird. He released her, leaned down and cupped the cameo face he had treasured for so long in his hands and kissed her, softly. Her lips quivered momentarily before joining him in the ecstasy of the moment. Once again his muscular arms enveloped her. The feel of his body pressing her close to him gave her an awareness she had never experienced. His body scent was that of the sea and like the sea his kiss created waves, waves of passion, leaving her breathless. Slowly he removed his lips. She felt his warm breath as he whispered in her ear, "I will be here for you forever, if that's what you want Allison." Still breathless from his kiss, she pressed her head into his chest and replied, "I love you Blake. I'm just sorry it took me so long to realize it. That last bouquet made me discover how much a part of my life you had become. I think roses and wild flowers are a good combination." Blake hid his smile. He had hopes the lack of wild flowers would have an effect on her but admitted, this was much more than he had expected. Unable to contain himself, he picked her up in his arms, exclaiming, "I loved you Allison Marshall, from the first moment I saw you" With a large smile, she looked into his face and wondered how she could ever have been intimidated by it, and repeated, I love you, Blake Donlan, and I want to finish that dance that we never completed." He grinned. "That will be our wedding dance if you will marry me Allison?" She felt her heart would burst as she accepted, and silently thanked Muriel for being so sure.

CHAPTER 18

Gerald and Annabelle returned from the orient both exhausted, Annabelle from the long voyage and Gerald from too much of his so-called, sightseeing. He promised her that he would be content to remain in San Francisco for awhile. Immediately, his thoughts turned to Allison. After all the sexual encounters he had experienced, he still thought about her and was anxious to see her again. It had been over a year. After the way he had treated her, he was reasonably sure she would reject any advances from him but one never knew until they tried. Maybe she wasn't over him yet. He knew Annabelle would need a couple days of rest, which would give him time to look her up. A familiar voice broke his thoughts.

"Gerald, Annabelle cried from the bedroom. I need your help getting me out of my dress." He knew it was a call for sex and shuddered, he hadn't touched her in two weeks. The only appealing thing about her had been her money and now that was his, this left Annabelle being nothing more than a burden. He also knew if she suspected his feelings, he could very well lose another fortune. There was now concern as to whether or not he could even get an erection. Each time it was becoming more difficult. "Gerald," she yelled out again, reminding him of a hen calling a rooster. Begrudgingly, he entered the room where she awaited him, telling himself, he would keep his eyes closed and pretend that it was Allison under him, not Annabelle. That might help.

Gerald entered the room and Annabelle silently sighed. She was tired and really didn't want a sexual encounter, but she mustn't let Gerald know that. After all, a younger woman would be more than willing to take care of his needs. It had been a couple of weeks and that was much too long for him, to go without.

Kathryn mumbled to herself, "I told you nothing would come of it. I told you he loved Allison." All this time she had purposely ignored the warnings. She remembered last night at Macky's when Blake informed her of his engagement to Allison. She couldn't hold back her tears, but felt somewhat better seeing how it stressed him. He told her he didn't mean to hurt her, which she knew. His next words stung. "I want to remain friends." Didn't he know the last thing someone being dumped wanted to hear was, let's be friends? That was not what she wanted, she had enough friends. She shrugged herself from the depressing scene. It was a quiet day at the boutique and Allison agreed to stay on until after the marriage. Kathryn was a smart enough businesswoman to not let her resentment of Allison overshadow the need for her, at least not until she could find a replacement, which she already knew was going to be difficult. Still, the situation left them both uneasy with each other.

Allison tried not to visualize Kathryn and Blake together, being she was quite sure there had been intimate moments between them. The popularity of the boutique left little time for the two women to converse, of which both were thankful.

Elliott Donlan sat in his office contemplating what to do. Blake had informed him that he was in love with Allison Marshall and planned to marry her. He had prayed this time would never come. Now, he was in a position where he had to protect his son and their pure Irish bloodline. He prayed for forgiveness from his friend James, for what he was about to do.

Blake entered the office, curious why he had been summoned. Elliott told him it was something best not discussed on the phone. He felt it might have something to do with his plan to marry Allison, due to the fact he knew that his father, for some reason had something he held against her. He couldn't imagine what it could be. Sitting down in one of the leather chairs, he faced his father and was surprised when Elliott pulled a small flask from the drawer and told him to have a drink from it, stating, "The real stuff, Irish whiskey!" It wasn't like his father to drink at such an early hour. He declined but his father insisted. It was now obvious to Blake he had been drinking before his arrival. He indulged and asked, "Now, tell me what's wrong?"

His father appeared to have lost his voice and it took a moment to find it. Then, he looked Blake straight in the eyes and informed him in his courtroom voice, filled with authority, "You can't marry Allison."

Once again Blake couldn't understand his father's attitude towards Allison. What had she ever done to make him this way? Trying to hold back his anger and remain calm, he asked, "Why?"

"She's a negro." Elliott said it quickly, anxious to get the dreaded sentence over with. Blake sat across from one of the few men he respected and loved, wondering what would posses him to say such a thing. There was a deafening silence and Elliott would not look his son in the face, fearing what he might see. He stared at his note pad awaiting a response.

"What makes you say that," Blake questioned. Still not looking up, Elliott told him the story of the twins, Roosevelt and Hattie. Once more there was a long silence as Blake absorbed what he had just heard. The silence was broken again by his next question. "Do Aaron and Allison know about this?" His father finally faced him and replied, "No." As usual, Blake felt protective of Allison and exclaimed, "You must never repeat this story."

Elliott was shocked and asked in disbelief, "You mean to tell me after what you just heard you still intend to marry her?"

"Of course, Blake replied, with a slight edge in his voice, I love her."

"For God's sake Blake if you marry her and have children it will destroy our pure Irish lineage that we have preserved for generations. Please, give it some thought."

Blake became infuriated and leaped from the chair. Looking down on Elliott with a fury, that, Elliott had never witnessed before in his son, he exclaimed, "To hell with your talk of blood. I'm talking flesh and bones! I love Allison and I love you, don't make me choose between the two of you over something as ridiculous as which kind of blood flows through her veins."

Elliott sat in despair. He was proud of their lineage but did it mean more to him than having his sons love and respect? It was obvious to him that Allison would be the winner if Blake had to choose. Defeated, he told himself, to accept his son's decision. Standing, he held a hand out to Blake, "You have my blessings, son."

Blake took his father's hand, thanked him and then hugged him stating, "It would have been hell to have to choose, I love you." Immediately, Elliott knew he had made the right decision. Blake left his fathers, feeling that Allison or Aaron never need know the story he had just heard.

Aaron and Melissa snuggled closely on the too small couch. "Well, she jested, your sister is getting married, why don't we make it a double wedding? After all, your twins and I read that they always do pretty much the same things at the same time" Aaron chuckled. There was no doubt in his mind that he wanted to marry Melissa, he had proposed to her right after his talk with Tullah. Purposely, he antagonized her for a moment with his silence before replying, "Maybe that would be nice, I'll talk to Allison about it." She squealed in delight. "Mrs. Aaron Marshall. What a fine sounding name!"

Aaron had met her parents and they had accepted him. In fact he was actually feeling like part of the family. There was only one time he felt intimidated. Her father started taking to him about the Nigger's in the South and how they were beginning to think they were equal to whites. For a moment the fear had returned. Melissa started getting playful, interrupting his thoughts. They rolled off the couch and made love. Buried deep with-in her, he held her close, vowing his love to her.

Kathryn observed the arrogant man standing in front of her. It was the young man who had married Annabelle Gilder. She squirmed as his eyes scanned her before questioning if Allison was there? She informed him that it was her day off and asked if she could tell her who was enquiring.

"Just tell her Gerald was here to see her and that I'll return." Kathryn became curious and questioned, "Did you know that Allison is engaged to be married?"

Gerald momentarily lost his composure before questioning, "To whom?"

Kathryn noticed the lack of confidence in his voice that had been there before the announcement. She informed him, "Blake Donlan."

Blake Donlan, the name flashed through his head and it finally came to him, "Blake Donlan is my name, remember it in case you ever try to force yourself on Allison again, because it will be the name you'll take to hell with you." Trying to ignore the chill crawling up his spine, he asked Katherine to give her the message.

Aaron questioned Allison regarding her feelings to a double wedding.

"That's a great idea. I'm so glad Melissa thought of it, Allison exclaimed. Have her call me and we can start working on the arrangements." Aaron hung up the phone thinking how pleased he was that Blake and his sister had finally come together. He caught himself wondering if Allison ever thought about Dorie's diary. If so, she still didn't seem concerned with it. He had done his best to not let it plague him and felt he shouldn't be concerned with it either, but every now and then the fear would strike, reminding him how much he could lose.

Blake listened as Allison explained Melissa and her ideas for the double wedding. It was fine with him; all he was interested in was getting the wedding over with so they could consummate the marriage. Each time he held and kissed her, he fought his desire. He gazed lovingly at his future wife telling himself the wedding was only a month away; he had to hold out.

Gerald sat in the lobby of his mother's hotel that at one time had been the parlor. Vera entered and remarked sarcastically, "Gerald, so nice of you to come and visit. It's only been a year since your sister and I have been honored by your presence. Gerald felt little guilt in the statement. Guilt was something he refused to recognize. The only reason he was there now was in hopes of getting some more information regarding Allison. He assumed being a member of the Women's Club she would have the facts about the upcoming wedding.

Vera was bitter as she witnessed him sitting there in his expensive suit and jewelry. He had wealth now and never once offered her any kind of assistance. He jumped right to the subject. "What do you know about this man Allison is going to marry?"

Vera knew very little. After all, she had been so busy with the hotel she missed more meetings at the club than she had attended, therefore missing out on the gossip that went on at the gathering. Besides that she wondered what it was to him, he was married now. Hoping to disappoint him, as he had done so many times to her, she replied, "I'm sorry Gerald, I can tell you nothing, being that I spend all my time here at the hotel. If you could manage to share a little of that wealth with me, I could attend the meetings. He ignored the statement. After all, Annabelle's money was for him to spend on himself, no one else. He replied, "I've wasted my time here, I'll be on my way." He turned to leave, anxious to escape the hotel that once had been his home. Even though it had been refurbished, he found it lacking a good decorator's touch.

Sensing his attitude, Vera decided to verbally stick the knife in. "I can tell you that Blake Donlan and his father own most the real estate in the bay area. Thank heavens Allison saved herself for him, she will want for nothing. In fact, she'll regain everything she lost, including the Marshall Building and the Marshall home, he owns them both."

He hesitated for a moment and then smiled, replying, "That's good. Perhaps we can eventually co-mingle our newfound fortunes." He walked away, leaving his mother speechless. Her statement appeared to have excited him, rather than depress him, leaving her to wonder what he was up to. The phones ring broke the silence; she sighed and answered, "Cypress Lane Hotel."

Gerald's mind was racing. Could it be possible Allison also married for money, if so, now she would understand why he married Annabelle. He became even more determined to return to DeLeons and see her.

Kathryn informed Allison the minute she walked into the boutique. "There was a man here yesterday looking for you. Allison looked at her curiously and questioned, "Who was it?" Kathryn was anxious to see her reaction, knowing he was also the man she was with that evening at Macky's when Blake left her alone, so he could follow Allison home. "Gerald Edwards," she answered.

Allison's heart jumped and Kathryn could feel her tension. She continued, "He said he would be back." Allison thanked her for the message as she removed her jacket to prepare for work. Kathryn caught herself anxious for Gerald's return. Allison was obviously upset that he had been there looking for her. Why would she be upset unless he meant something to her? She would pay close attention when he did return. If there were something going on between them, she could warn Blake and hopefully prevent the marriage. It appeared to be her last hope.

As usual, Melissa snuggled closer to Aaron on the couch discussing wedding plans. She took a deep breath. There was more than one reason she wanted to get married. After another deep breath, she stated, "There's something you need to know." He looked at her curiously before asking, "What is it?"

"We are going to have a baby," she replied proudly. Aaron immediately became lost in thought and his silence bothered her. The thought of a child had never entered his mind.

"Aaron, Melissa pleaded, say something." He smiled, "I'm sorry, you shocked me. After all, I was just informed that I'm going to be a father."

"Does that make you happy," she questioned?"

"I couldn't be happier, he exclaimed, kissing her. They made the decision to keep the pregnancy a secret until after the wedding.

It had been several days since Gerald had stopped by the boutique, leaving Allison uneasy while awaiting his return. Kathryn also waited eagerly, wanting to see the outcome. She was like a predator, waiting for its victim to show a sign of weakness, a weakness that would hopefully destroy the up-coming marriage.

Allison sorted through the clothes on the rack and jumped every time the bell on the shop door rang alerting them a patron had entered. Fearfully, she would glance towards the door, each time sighing with relief that it wasn't Gerald. She asked herself, "Why did she suddenly fear him?" She was positive she no longer loved him and wondered if she really ever had. Her love for Blake was so much more intense, and why was he suddenly looking for her? She couldn't answer the question.

Gerald had been drinking heavily and Annabelle made the mistake of reprimanding him. Gerald's face contorted as he exclaimed, "it's bad that you look old enough to be my mother, but for God's sake, quit acting like you are."

"Please, Annabelle pleaded, don't talk to me that way, you have no idea how badly it hurts me."

"Hurts you? What about my hurt you pathetic old bitch, hanging on to me, trying to preserve your youth while your draining me of mine?"

Hurt and crying, she replied, "Well now we know why I married you, let's hear why you married me!"

To ask that question now puts you in a new category," he replied nastily. Now you're not only an old bitch, but also a stupid one. All you have is money Annabelle, what other reason could there be?"

Annabelle's immediate reaction was to say, "You self-indulgent little bastard, see if you get any of it," but the pain in her chest prevented the words from ever reaching his ears. It was excruciating. Gerald swayed as he observed her condition. He wasn't sure what was happening, but appreciated her silence. He watched in a drunken stupor as she fell to the floor, telling himself as he left the room, that she must have had more to drink then he had.

The front page of the news announced the death of Socialite, Annabelle Gilder, stating that the millionaire had succumbed to a massive heart attack in her home late last evening. Aaron read the article and wondered how much Gerald was grieving. It was a well-known fact that Annabelle was alone and childless when she married him, so he should inherit everything. He also wondered how Allison would react to the fact that Gerald was now single. Melissa entered the office with his coffee, leaving him deciding that enough time had been spent dwelling on Gerald. There was more editing to do before press time.

Blake read the obituary. Recently, he had purchased several pieces of property from Annabelle and found her to be intelligent and delightful, leaving him to wonder as he had with Allison, what had she seen in Gerald? He also wondered how Allison would react to the news. That night at dinner, they discussed the deceased and Blake was surprised at Allison's request that they attend the funeral, stating that she owed it to Gerald, after all, they had been childhood friends. He silently questioned if she merely wanted to see Gerald again. He tried to black out the thought. Allison felt if she made contact with Gerald at the funeral with Blake, he might not return to the boutique looking for her.

It was a graveside service with surprising attendance. As they approached the site, Allison's heart quickened when she saw Gerald in a dark suit, standing next to a floral blanketed casket. Suddenly, she was regretting she had decided to attend the services. Gerald looked towards them and Blake felt Allison's hand tighten on his.

Gerald couldn't take his eyes off her. In one year she had grown into a woman, one of the most beautiful women he had ever seen. He watched intently as her long slender legs brought her closer. The preacher distracted him, announcing the services were to begin. He stared at the casket, not believing his good luck. He was free of Annabelle. Now, the good life as he had known it would be his once more.

The service was short and afterwards the funeral procession continued on to the country club to celebrate Annabelle's life, while Gerald quietly celebrated her death. There was an abundance of food, which everyone indulged in immediately while listening to a pianist play Annabelle's favorite songs. Gerald drank excessively from his flask anxious to finalize his wives existence and get on with his life. He noticed Allison with Blake across the room, sitting with a small group of people. Memories of Blake's threat went ignored as he approached them in a drunken stupor. "Mr. Donlan, I believe we've met!" Blake nodded his head and felt his pulse quicken and the hair rise on the nape of his neck. The man was drunk. "Poor Annabelle, he thought to himself, she at least deserved a sober goodbye from her husband. He was certain in the short time she had been married to Gerald there had been little peace for her.

"Allison, you look great," he slurred as his eyes slowly and wantonly scanned her body, which didn't go unnoticed by Blake. "Gerald exclaimed, I need to talk to you alone!" Out of respect for Annabelle, Blake contained himself.

Allison questioned, "What do you want to talk to me about that we can't discuss here Gerald?"

"No, no, he muttered as he put a finger to his lips, we need to talk alone." Allison turned to Blake and he unwillingly nodded his approval. She followed Gerald out to the balcony feeling insecure without Blake by her side. With-in seconds, Gerald put his arms around her exclaiming, "I have money now Allison, we can be together. Don't marry that Donlan fellow." She pulled away; fearing someone would see his disgusting behavior at his wife's wake, at the same time thinking how often she ached to hear him say they could be together. The statement meant nothing to her now, Blake was right, the rose had bloomed. All she felt for Gerald now, was pity. He reached for her once more and she pulled away.

Gerald was shocked, "What the hell is going on Allison? You know you want me and always have, so why are you acting this way?" Allison understood why he would be confused, since she had confessed her love for him.

"You once informed me Gerald that you couldn't afford me and now it's true. No matter how much money you have gained, I no longer love you and now realize that I never had. I'm going to marry Blake."

"Well, he replied with a smirk while trying to maintain balance, it appears we both sold ourselves for money. I understand your future husband now owns the Marshall Building as well as the Marshall house, not to mention a third of San Francisco. Shocked, she couldn't believe that at one time she thought she loved him. Once more she blamed the crash of the stock market; he was one of its victims. She had loved the young innocent Gerald. He grabbed for her once more and she exclaimed, "Gerald, I love Blake for richer or poorer and I'm ready to take that vow."

Blake became concerned with Allison's overly long absence and arrived on the balcony just in time to hear her speech. His heart filled with his love for her, as he walked slowly towards them and asked Gerald to excuse he and his bride to be, it was time for them to leave. Allison sighed with relief while Gerald stood speechless and bitter as they walked away.

It was another stormy day in San Francisco as Gerald sat across from Annabelle's attorney anticipating just how much her estate was worth. He observed the gray haired man shuffling through the stack of papers that would decide what he was to receive. Finally in a monotone voice he stated, "Mr. Edwards, Annabelle, God rest her soul, had made it very clear to me that if her marriage didn't survive at least five years and there should be a divorce, she wanted you to receive nothing more than the gifts she bestowed you. Anxiety was overcoming Gerald as he sat there silently watching him continue on to the next sheet of paper.

"This is her will. She meant to revise it after the honeymoon so that you would be sole heir if the marriage still existed after the five-year time period or in the event of her death. Unfortunately, she never got around to changing it due to the fact she was out the country so much of the time. I had left her many messages regarding the fact she needed to up-date the will but she never found the time to take care of it. Therefore Mr. Edwards, I must honor what is in front of me and you are not mentioned, even though you were married at the time of her death, I'm afraid the will stays as is, I'm sorry"

Gerald sat there numb as the reality of what he just heard sank in. He was so busy keeping Annabelle touring, that she neglected her personal affairs. The short amount of time they were home she was tired and resting up for the next trip he had planned. His stomach turned as he began to realize another fortune would be lost. He didn't think he could bear it. "My God, he exclaimed, what can I do?"

"Nothing Mr. Edwards, the man replied.

Gerald questioned, "Who is getting her money?"

"Well, as you know, there are no next of kin so she requested her money be distributed to her favorite charities. Would you like to know which ones they are?"

"No, he answered, I don't give a shit." He removed himself from the chair, slamming the door as he left. The attorney wondered if Annabelle had been happily married, somehow he doubted it and felt the right thing had been done. Thankfully, she hadn't found the time to change the will.

CHAPTER 19

Once more, Muriel felt almost pretty. She was a bridesmaid. As she stared at herself in the full-length mirror, she visualized herself wearing a bridal gown of flowing white satin covered in elegant French lace, a veiled headband covered with seed pearls and white gardenias, like Allison was wearing. Instead, she and the other bridesmaids wore a peach chiffon chemise; replica's of Allison's dress she wore the night of her coming out party. Allison considered that dress special, after all, it was what she was wearing when she first met Blake.

Everyone took their places as they heard the organ start the wedding march. Bea, the maid of honor quickly kissed Allison before leading the maids down the isle. Being it was to be a double wedding, it was agreed Allison would go first.

Elliott Donlan sat close to his wife holding her hand, in deep thought. He admired the bride as she came down the isle, she looked radiant. Yes, she was a beauty, and he prayed silently for his son's happiness.

Jonathon led Allison down the isle; she smiled as she looked down at her wedding bouquet, a fully bloomed rose, surrounded by wildflowers. This same combination decorated the right side of the isle and altar. She looked up and saw Blake awaiting her and looking extremely handsome in his white tuxedo. He smiled as she approached. Already she had to control the urge to cry, leaving her concerned if she would be able to repeat the vows. How could she be this fortunate? She reached Blake and they awaited Melissa's entrance.

Once again the organ repeated the wedding march and Melissa entered the chapel. She was dressed in an ivory, white satin lose fitting gown.

Instead of hugging her waist it hugged her hips, hopefully concealing her now rounded belly. Pale yellow silk roses adorned it. Like Allison, she wore a matching headband. The bridesmaids wore yellow silk. Her choice of flowers, were a combination of yellow roses, babies' breath, and ferns. Lydia Barnum smiled as her daughter passed, feeling pride in her, as well as the man she had chosen to marry.

Aaron was overwhelmed as Melissa's father, Douglas delivered her to him. He felt so much love for her and like Allison; he feared his ability to speak due to the lump that had formed in his throat.

Both couples took turns with their vows. When the ceremonies were complete, the preacher announced, "Now gentleman, you may kiss your brides." Cheers and tears surrounded them as both couples returned back up the isle.

At the reception, the bridesmaids waited eagerly for Allison and Melissa to throw their bouquets. Muriel watched intently as Allison's flew through the air offering the recipient a wedding of their own. She held her breath as she felt it touch her fingertips and start to slip away. Determined not to lose her chance and the promise it held she jumped and retrieved it. Once in her hands, she held it close, inhaling and kissing the blossoms, praying that the promise would hold true. She had been seeing Chad quite regularly and they had made it a point to dine at a restaurant, just down from the Red Cross building at least once a week and then to a movie. She loved sitting there close to him in the darkness of the theater, so close, she could hear his breathing. Granted, Chad was no Blake Donlan but he was perfect for her. Muriel was in love and hopefully now that she had caught the bridal bouquet, there would be a wedding in the near future for her.

Vera Edwards admired the couple, agreeing with Selma, a member of the Women's Club, that Allison and Blake made an outstanding pair. She silently wondered how different things would have been had the market not crashed. Would Allison and Gerald have gotten married? Would their fortunes doubled or even tripled? She snapped out of her daydream, telling herself, the market did crash, taking everything along with it, including leaving her with a hotel instead of a home. Gerald had returned home after Annabell's death and was once more living in the basement. Rather than selling his gin, he was drinking it. She tried to console him over the loss of his expected fortune while trying to convince him that drinking wouldn't cure the problem, only to receive the same verbal abuse Annabelle endured. She had given up, coming to the conclusion to leave him alone in his misery.

Most the evening Allison fought her anxiety, remembering the four poster bed that awaited them. She visualized the soft, sheer negligee she had chosen to wear that night. The anticipation was almost overwhelming. It was time to make love with Blake, and she was more than ready. Blake held her hand and looked at his watch. It had been a half-hour since they had started bidding their guest's goodbye. Aaron grinned at Blake, knowing just what he was thinking. Blake had promised himself to fight his desires until his wedding night, wanting it to be special when he introduced Allison to the wonders of sex. Now, two months had gone by since he made that promise and he was ready to have the lessons begin.

Aaron was equally anxious for the wedding party to end. He and Melissa would be spending the evening in the bridal suite at the Drake Hotel, compliments of Blake and Allison.

Jonathon was the last to leave. With all the guests gone, Blake questioned Allison, "Mrs. Donlan, have I told you how much I love you?" She kissed him lightly and replied, "Only a couple of times in the last five minutes."

"Well, he exclaimed, "since we are already in the house, I can't carry you over the threshold but I can carry you upstairs to our room." She laughed and exclaimed, "That's not necessary." "Yes it is," he replied as he picked her up in his arms. "You've had a long day and I want to save what energy you may have left, for me." Understanding what he meant both thrilled and frightened her. Would she disappoint him? As he carried her up the stairs, Allison remembered thinking at one time what it would be like to share his bed with him, now she was about to find out. She snuggled her head into his neck and inhaled the masculine after-shave he wore. His arms felt strong and protective causing her to feel a momentarily loss when they reached the room and released her.

"This is our room," he announced. She decided not to confess that she had visited it at one time. Scanning the room, she realized something was different, it was the bed. He had removed the heavy dark quilt and replaced it with an ivory satin comforter and matching pillows, leaving her to believe that more than likely, under the comforter there would be satin sheets. He also added a full length, carved mahogany mirror to the room exclaiming as she momentarily viewed herself in it, "I'm guessing that one of these is a must for a woman!" She smiled and thanked him. The fireplace was lit, casting a warm glow throughout the room.

Hopeful that he had pleased her, he questioned, "Well, do you like it? She had visualized herself with him so many times since that day she first entered the room with it the way it was, and now it was so different. She held back a grateful tear, realizing that he had considered her and turned it into their room and answered his question, "Yes, it's a wonderful room."

"Good, he smiled for a moment, than his expression turned to one of desire. He pulled her close to him and whispered in her ear, "I need you

Allison. I've needed you for so long." His tongue nibbled at her ear, leaving her short of breath. Now, he was applying soft kisses up and down the sides of her neck. She tensed when his hands cupped her breasts, not of fear but anticipation, leaving the white filmy negligee she so carefully selected, forgotten. Her body had never experienced such feelings and she wanted him to take her completely. He carried her to the bed, laid her down on the ivory comforter and started removing her clothes. A cloud of ivory fabric fell from the air as her wedding gown landed next to the bed. She moaned as he released her perfectly formed breasts from their confinement and fondled the nipples until they became erect. Then he plied his tongue to them to heighten her senses. Allison felt his erection pressing against her, compelling her to touch it. Blake groaned as her hands started searching his body. After a moment he stood and removed his own clothing. She lay there admiring him, anticipating their union, surprised by her lack of modesty.

He returned to the bed and his eyes absorbed her. "Your so beautiful Allison, I'm going to take you as my wife now." His lips brushed her stomach while his hands played with the vaginal entrance, leaving Allison delirious from the experience. Blake wanted to be as gentle as possible with her, hoping the first time wouldn't be too painful and disappointing. Slowly he entered her and she let out a small moan, her body stiffened with the entrance as she felt his manhood filling her. "Trust me Allison, he said in a raspy voice, it will only hurt for a moment, I promise." She was not his first virgin and if all went according to the others, he was not lying." She replied, "It's a good hurt Blake." Suddenly the small amount of discomfort was replaced with the rapture he had promised. Uncontrollable moans escaped from her as they reached the peak of love making and climaxed together. Afterwards, they lay next to each other blissfully exhausted, thinking of all the days and nights they would share together.

CHAPTER 20

It had been six months since the wedding and Aaron paced the maternity waiting room in the company of Melissa'a parents, Allison and Blake. They had been there several hours, every now and then a nurse would appear, assuring them everything was all right. Aaron detested the helpless feeling he was experiencing after seeing the pain on Melissa's face and unable to do anything about it. Finally the nurse re-entered the room and announced that he had a son, the perplexed look on her face going unnoticed due to the excitement. Aaron asked to see Melissa. She nodded her head and he followed her. As he entered the room, he was shocked to see Melissa's face so blank and tear stained. At first, he attributed it to labor and childbirth until he glanced at the tiny bundle lying next to her. His heart sank as he observed the infant. His son showed all the signs of his Negro blood. He even saw Dorie in him. Fear and nausea ran through him as he realized his and Allison's secret would now be discovered.

Melissa's voice broke his silence, as she sobbed, "I never cheated on you Aaron, how could this be? I was awake through the delivery so I know they didn't give us the wrong baby!" Aaron couldn't face her. He turned his back on her and hit the wall with his fists. This action added even more stress to Melissa. What was happening? Was she having some kind of horrible nightmare?

Aaron turned to her with tears in his own eyes and begged forgiveness for having deceived her. She listened to his confession in horror, telling herself, "I married a Negro. I bore a Negro child." The thought was not only repugnant to her, how would her parents handle this? She couldn't beg him to tell her it wasn't true, the evidence lay next to her. In a slow, overly

Southern drawl, hardly recognizable to Aaron, she asked him to leave the room and have the nurse remove the baby as well.

He looked at his wife and child. What was to be one of the happiest days of their lives had turned out to be the most miserable. All he feared had surfaced. Never once had he considered the fact his child could be born black. After all, he and Allison looked white, and there was Melissa's white bloodline. How could this happen? He left the room as requested and summoned the nurse to remove the child. The parties of awaiting guests were confused as Aaron walked past them and out of the door without comment. He walked several steps and returned long enough to retrieve Allison and ask Blake if he would excuse them for a moment.

Allison followed Aaron, concerned by his stress and the obvious fact that he had cried. Reaching the end of the hallway, he turned her to face him and exclaimed, "Hattie, it's time to face who we really are. The charade is over."

Hattie? She hadn't heard that name since the day they found Dorie's diary. She had put it aside along with the infant gowns and pictures. Now, he was reminding her and she asked, "Why are you calling me Hattie, Aaron?"

"Don't call me Aaron again, I'm Roosevelt. We are both Negro's and so is my son."

Still stunned, Allison was slowly beginning to understand what had happened. He grabbed her and shook her. "My son is black, understand?" He hugged her quickly and rushed away, leaving her speechless. Stunned, she returned to the waiting room fearing what would come next. Now she must face Blake with their secret. Her white world had just ended with the birth of Aaron's son. Would he hate her for not telling him? She tried to imagine what Melissa must have said to cause such a horrible pained look on Aaron's face. When she re-entered the room, Blake informed her that Lydia had gone to see Melissa, and was thankful he hadn't questioned what was wrong with Aaron. After a short time, Lydia returned, crying and whispered something in her husband's ear. Blake silently observed Douglas Barnum's face redden as he turned and glared at Allison with unconcealed horror and rage. Then, without a word, the two of them returned to their daughter's room. At that moment, Allison asked a passing nurse if they could see the baby. The nurse reached into her pocket and handed her a small card that read, Baby Marshall. "Take this to the nursery down the hall and give it to one of the attendants and they will show you the child."

Blake followed her, still not quite sure what was going on. Allison was prepared for what they were going to see, telling herself Aaron lost Melissa that afternoon and she must be ready to lose Blake. The thought terrified her but there was no way out. What some people considered their defect couldn't be changed anymore than they could change the color of their eyes. She remembered Dorie telling her and Aaron in her book, they had royal blood, so she held her head high, holding the card out for the nurse to see and awaited her nephew's arrival at the observation window. Her heart was beating rapidly.

A moment later a stern looking nurse returned with an appalled look that accentuated her homely face. Holding the small bundle, she pulled the blanket aside, exposing the infant. All Allison's fears escaped as she looked at him and marveled. It was Aaron's child, Dorie's grandchild, and her nephew, the little body housed her loved ones and he was the most wonderful, beautiful thing she had ever seen.

Blake observed the child and his heart went out to Aaron. Now there was little doubt as to what had happened. Allison turned to him, the smile on her face disappearing as she awaited his response. He was surprised that she wasn't shocked. She must have known the secret all along, but how? He was sure his father hadn't told her. After a moments silence, he smiled, put his arms around her and exclaimed, "He's great, what's the problem? I see two hands, two feet, ten fingers and toes. His eyes are a little swollen but I'm sure after awhile they'll be okay!" Allison was dumbfounded, couldn't he see? Blake felt the need to spare her anymore anxiety and confessed.

"Allison, I know all about Aaron and you, I have for a long time. You're forgetting that my father was your father's attorney." She remained speechless as she looked at him through tears of love. He had known and still married her. Blake continued, "Do you prefer to be called Hattie or Allison, personally I prefer Allison, only because I'm accustomed to the name?"

"So am I," she replied as she went to him, embracing him. Once again, she felt safety in his arms. Suddenly she felt guilty for being so fortunate, poor Aaron. She asked, "Blake, what can we do about Aaron and the baby? From the way Aaron talked, Melissa wants nothing more to do with him or the child."

Blake answered, hoping he could believe what he was saying, "Melissa is just tired and in a state of shock right now. I'm sure she'll be all right after she's rested and had time to think about it. She loves Aaron; therefore she will love their child. He hoped that her strict Southern upbringing wouldn't defeat her love for Aaron. They returned to the waiting room, hopeful that Aaron had returned. It was empty except for Jonathon, who greeted them anxiously.

"I'm sorry I had to finish the greens before I could leave." Where is everybody? Has the baby arrived?" Through all of this, Allison had forgotten about Jonathon. Now it was his turn to find out the truth. She found it impossible to believe that he would denounce her and Aaron. Blake suggested they go somewhere to talk, leaving Jonathon perplexed by their strange behavior.

The threesome sat quietly in a booth at a cafe across the street from the hospital. Allison didn't know where to start and was relieved when Blake broke the silence. His voice sounded much as his father's had that day in the office when Elliott informed them of their parents will. Jonathon recognized the tone and prepared himself for bad news, assuming something was terribly wrong with the baby. Either it had died or was abnormal.

Blake brought Jonathon back to the twins beginning's. He sat silent and listened intently. Every now and then he would meet Allisons eyes and she could see the disbelief in them. When Blake completed the story, Jonathon exclaimed, "Allison, I can't believe, you and Aaron aren't my mother's children! Dorie was your grandmother! My father, cheated on my mother, did she know it? "No, "Allison replied.

He felt sick as he experienced a dislike for his father, a man he had respected and loved. He wanted to deny everything he had just heard. The only thing he couldn't deny was his love for Allison and Aaron, no matter what. Dorie raised him to respect people of any color, so had his parents. It was quiet for a moment while he dwelled on the history of his brother and sister before exclaiming, "I hope I win that tournament tomorrow Allison, so you and Aaron can be as proud of me as I am of you. Now, may I go back to the hospital and see my nephew?"

Allison reached across the table and held his hand, "Jonathon, I have been proud of you as far back as I can remember." Blake put an arm around Jonathon, before stating, "You're a good man Jonathon, from a good family!"

They returned to the nursery and once again requested to see Baby Marshall. The same disgruntled nurse displayed their tiny nephew to them, enduring their smiles of admiration for the infant. She silently wondered if any of them were really Negro's. She certainly hadn't guessed the father was.

Melissa lay crying. She had heard the word heartbreak and was now experiencing it. She loved Aaron so much. She could have accepted anything about him. If he beat her, she told herself she could accept it. If he were to lose his job, she would provide, and if he turned into an alcoholic she would try everything she could to help him recover, but she could never help him from being Negro. God decided who was to be black and who was to be white and it was sinful to mix the two. She remembered the look of horror on her parent's face as they had gazed in shock at her child. The child held no beauty to either of them, or her. It was as though someone else had produced it. She cried herself to sleep, missing the comfort of Aaron's body next to hers, a feeling she knew she would never experience again.

"I should kill that Nigger for what he's done,' raged Douglas Barnum. If we were back in the South, the Klan would help me hang him!"

Lydia continued to cry as her head bobbed up and down showing she agreed with him. Breaking her sobs, she exclaimed, "He was so nice and looked so white, how possibly, could Melissa have known! What are we going to do when our family finds out? We told them we were becoming grandparents."

Douglas's anger was suddenly replaced with the same fear as his wife's. "My God, what were they going to tell them, "Oh, by the way, we are proud grandparents of a nigger baby?" Once more the urge to kill was overwhelming. "Quit crying" he yelled at Lydia, I can't think." The rest of the ride home remained silent.

It had been a week since the delivery of Aaron's son and tomorrow Allison and her brother would go to the hospital and retrieve Melissa's unwanted child. Allison watched as Grange entered the room with the small crib he removed from the attic. She was not sure whether it had been hers or Aaron's. He set it down and returned to the attic, this time returning with a chest of drawers filled with baby clothing. Sighing, she sorted through the tiny frocks. The clothes in the top drawer were much too small for the baby. She became even more emotional, thinking and seeing how small Aaron and her had been. Opening the second drawer she found the larger sizes. Her heart ached for her brother as she recalled the night he came to her a couple of days after his son's birth. He looked so tired and sad, reeking of stale cigarette smoke, leaving her to wonder if it was the smoke that reddened his eyes, or tears. His clothes were rumpled, proving he had slept in them. The once immaculate Aaron stood before her, appearing almost a stranger, hidden behind an unshaven face. She cried out when she saw him. He reached for her, cradling her in his arms, asking her to forgive him for having not shown any concern for her, while drowning in his own self-pity. Fearing the answer, he asked, "Are you all right and what did Blake say when he found out?"

Tears streaming down her cheeks she replied, "I'm fine Aaron. Blake has known about us for sometime. We both forgot that his father was daddy's attorney. Elliott Donlan made all the arrangements for us to be brought to the Marshall house with Dorie." For the first time in days, Aaron felt relief; Allison was going to be okay.

Bitterly he said, "You've found true love Allison, I wish I could say the same."

She had asked with concern, "Have you talked to Melissa?"

"I saw Melissa just long enough for her to inform me that the child was mine alone. He shuddered, remembering the look of repulsion on her face as she confessed she couldn't accept either of them. He found it so hard to believe it was the same face and eyes that had looked at him with so much love, just a short time ago. He reminded her that he had told her she knew nothing about him and she had stated, "I need to know nothing more than you love me." Her reply was, "I said that to a man I assumed was white, not a Negro pretending to be white." Once more his gut wretched, at the memory.

Allison cried along with him as they held each other. "What are you going to do about the baby," she questioned after a few moments?

Aaron stiffened and replied, "He's my son and I'll do whatever I can for him. Then he questioned, "How can an innocent child like that enter into the world so condemned? Both his mother and grandparents have shunned him, only because he just wasn't the color they wanted him to be. It's like he was an item in a department store that displeased them so they returned it. His words made Allison's heart bleed.

She exclaimed, "Tullah and I can help care for him. Bring him here to this house, where we were both raised. I'm sure Blake won't mind!" It seemed to Aaron that since the first night he met Blake at Macky's, for some reason, he was to become an important part of both he and Allison's life. If Blake agreed, who could be better to help bring up his child than, Tullah and his sister? Suddenly a rush of guilt came over him. It had been almost a week since his son's birth and the child remained nameless. "I've got to name the little guy Allison!"

"Yes, she agreed, you need to choose a name before we pick him up tomorrow. Are you bringing him here?"

"If your sure Blake wouldn't mind, just until I can make some kind of arrangements for him and myself, I would appreciate it."

"Good, she replied, now for heavens sake go home and clean up." Her words impacted him. Yes, it was time to quit grieving over his loss and start celebrating his son.

Grange re-entered the room, bringing her back to the present. She observed the room that had been Dories. This was where the child would stay. Her heart grew heavy, picturing once more as she had done so many times, her little nephew that night at the hospital. She silently stated, "Quite a reception you received my little one, we'll make it up to you, I promise." She put the clothing into a basket and brought it to Tullah for cleaning.

As Tullah tended to the infants garments, she tried to fight the guilt she felt. She had let Aaron down. He came to her that one night and she had told

DYANN WEBB

him to continue on as white. Anger rushed through her once again. White world, Black world, wasn't it everyone's world? She decided that they would never know peace, unless people became color blind. Remembering how terrible he looked that day he came to see Allison broke her heart. She cried inwardly, "My poor Aaron." The air was fresh and clear as she hung the child's clothes on the line to dry. She held one of the small frocks close to her breast, leaving her wondering how Melissa could walk away from her child.

CHAPTER 21

Blake stared out at the Bay, contemplating the child's arrival. He had assured both Allison and Aaron that he was more than happy to have the baby with them as long as need be. He held one fear, his parents. He realized how hard it was for his father to accept his marriage. When he and Allison decide to have children, how would they react should their child bear the signs of its black heritage? If born black it would be living testament of the deterioration of the Donlan bloodlines. Would they reject the child as Melissa's parents had? There was a difficult road ahead for all of them. With the birth of Aaron's son, the twin's secret was going to be the subject of gossip throughout San Francisco.

Elliott Donlan paced the floor of his den puffing frantically on a fine cigar as he remembered his encounter with Sean O'hara at the country club. Sean's chubby face supported an enlarged nose, reddened from years of drinking. The nostrils expanded as he commented. "If that pretty little wife of your sons conceives, there goes your fine Irish line. Is Blake gonna let that happen?".

"None of you're damn business Sean O'Hara," he had replied, even though he knew most of San Francisco would make it their business. "Damn it Blake," he shouted to himself, "What have you done to us?" He could no longer protect the twins or his family. The only thing that would help people accept Blake's union with Allison would be that she did have the Marshall blood in her and Blake was powerful, he now owned almost a third of downtown San Francisco, making him a very wealthy man. His wife, Molly entered the room still oblivious to what was happening. He knew it was time to tell her, preparing her for what she would no doubt hear from her peers. God, how he had hoped the twins would never be exposed, for everyone's sake, the living and the dead. He sat her down and started explaining the whole story to her. She listened without interruption, which Elliott knew was rare. She felt speechless. True, she had raised Blake to respect all people regardless of nationality or religion, being Irish, she knew discrimination and so did her beloved husband. He had worked hard for his position and acceptance in the city of San Francisco, but it took more than his hard work to succeed, it took James Marshall. James introduced him to the cities leading citizens, convincing them if Elliott was good enough to be his attorney, why shouldn't he be theirs. She pictured Allison in her mind and was unable to see any black features. Elliott broke her concentration.

"Don't you have anything to say?"

"Yes, she said quietly. Our son chose to marry Allison knowing the truth. I will honor and stand by his choice. Allison is a lovely girl and the daughter of our good friend, James."

Her answer left him with mixed emotions. Yes, James Marshall was their friend and responsible for a large part of his success, he owed him. He had accepted Allison, assuming her heritage would never be revealed, but now that Aaron's wife had given birth, everything had changed. He had to face the fact that not only was his bloodline being ruined he may lose his clients. After all, he had been a participant in James deceit. He held Molly's hand and exclaimed, "You realize that by now the whole bay area knows about it." A soft "yes", was her reply," We will just have to live with it. Our son is the one who's important, not other people." They both sat silently, wondering what the future held.

Vera Edwards returned hurriedly from the Women's Club. Not only was it good to play Mah Jong once again, it enabled her to get in on the latest gossip. Today's topic had been Aaron and Allison. The twins were not James deceased, sisters after all. They were his mistresses, a Negro. Poor, Lillian. She wondered if her friend had ever suspected. Once home, she immediately went to the basement to inform Gerald of the discovery. She carefully descended the creaky stairs and tried to muffle the odor from the still by applying a hanky over her nose. She hated that smell. It was an odor that clung constantly to Gerald and his clothing. After returning home, he now resided in the basement, since she needed the other rooms for income. It had been six months since the death of his wife and he was a recluse. She scanned the room. Gerald was asleep on a small bed she had provided him. She looked down on him and wondered what he was dreaming about. A small smile appeared on his face. For a moment she saw the child he once was and became saddened. Gently she shook him. His eyelids fluttered, fighting the disturbance. She repeated his name several times, realizing he was in another drunken stupor. Suddenly he sat up, startling her by the sudden move. She let out a small scream, putting her hand next to her heart and exclaimed, "Gerald, for Gods sake, you scared me half to death."

"What are you doing down here," he asked, puzzled by the visit, knowing her dislike of the room.

"I came to share some news with you. Now he was curious. "What news?" Vera told him all she had learned about the twins. A renewed grin spread on his face. The perfect Marshall family wasn't so perfect after all. They had a flaw just like everyone else, a big one at that. He silently remembered how Allison rejected him the day of Annabelle's funeral. She thought that she was too good for him since she had married into a fortune. He wondered how she felt now, and what the mighty Blake Donlan, thought of his Negro wife.

Vera noticed the grin and questioned, "What is funny about this?"

He stated, "Life's funny mother, life's funny." He lay back down and closed his eyes. Vera groaned with frustration as she exited the foul room.

It was the talk of the boutique as women were trying to concentrate on their selections in between the gossip. Kathryn listened intently, wondering what Blake must be thinking and if he was going to continue to accept Allison now that he knew what she really was. One thing she knew for sure, she was ready to try again. San Francisco society would accept her as his wife and she could be beneficial to him, not a burden. A small surge of hope rushed through her. Maybe she didn't have to write Blake off after all.

The news of Aaron and his sister may as well have been put on the headlines, as fast as the story was traveling. Robert Cunningham awaited Aaron's arrival. Aaron had called him that morning after missing two days of work, apologizing for his absence saying he fully understood if he was to be terminated. He wondered if Aaron felt jeopardized due to his absence or because of his Negro blood. True, the only Negro's working for the newspaper was messengers and janitors but Aaron was much too educated and talented for that. "Best damn assistant editor I ever had," he mumbled to himself. Talk was that Aaron hadn't known about his Negro blood anymore than Lillian Marshall had. It must have been a hell of a shock. His thoughts were scattered as his secretary informed him Aaron was here to see him. Still unsure as to how he was going to handle the situation, he told her to send him in.

Observing him as he entered, Cunningham was pleased to see him standing tall and proud, not the broken or humbled man he feared might have replaced the Aaron he knew. He walked across the room to meet him, not knowing how to start the conversation. A decision was made, nothing would be questioned other than his absence. He had no desire to ask him to resign, to hell with the rest of the staff if they didn't like it.

He spoke, "I know you have a good excuse for missing work," he said gruffly, although I remember telling you once, that the newspaper can't stop for the staff's personnel problems. There's that small amount of time after the news has gone to press that we have for ourselves. Now, unless you want to quit your job, get to work." Aaron took a deep sigh of relief and thanked his boss. Cunningham felt himself getting emotional and quickly stated, "I said get to work."

Aaron sat at his desk and tried to visualize Melissa as she was when he first met her. Her dimpled smile, her cute walk, the way she brought him his coffee. His heart felt so heavy and ached with the images. A voice from with-in told him to snap out of it, he had a job to do. The clock on the wall, plus a large stack of papers in front of him reminded him there was a deadline to meet. "Not all is bad," he told himself; I still have a job and tomorrow he and Allison would retrieve his son from the hospital.

Melissa left the hospital with her parents, ignoring the innocent child they were leaving behind. Her eyes were swollen from crying. The tears were not for Aaron or the child but strictly for herself and her lost dreams. She despised herself each time she caught herself missing Aaron, his smile, the warmth of his body next to her and worst of all, God forgive her, his lovemaking. How could he have done this to her? The shame and humiliation was more than she could bear. The three sat quietly in the front seat of the car. Her father stared straight ahead, trance-like, while her mother's arms surrounded her as if protecting her prematurely from family and friends inevitable, distasteful questions.

They arrived home with Lydia instructing her daughter to go to her room, "You need rest, bearing that child has taken its toll on you," Melissa obeyed.

She looked around the room that had been hers before she married, it hadn't changed. "Of course not she thought sadly, you haven't been married long enough to give your parents time to turn it into anything else, like the sewing room her mother always desired. She never missed this room but she was already deeply missing the apartment her and Aaron had so carefully decorated. A slight moaned slipped past her lips as she prepared for bed. All she wanted to do was escape. Sleep allowed her that, except for the one night at the hospital when she had a dream. It was a hot summer night; her and Aaron made love and afterwards, held each other tenderly. Suddenly she felt suffocated by the heat and went to the bathroom. Turning on the faucet she soaked a washrag and applied it to her face, enjoying the coolness. Slowly, she removed it. Opening her eyes she became startled and confused by the image in the mirror, there was a black woman staring at her. At first she didn't recognize who it was, when she did, she became horrified; the image belonged to her. Aaron entered the room holding their baby. He looked at her and smiled lovingly. He appeared not to notice the change in her. She was awakened by her own scream. Once more, she surveyed the room, walked to her vanity table and looked into the mirror. She questioned her reflection. "What if she had turned into a Negro, would there be anything so different about her other than the color of her skin?" She could think of nothing, other than the horror of such a thing happening. Wearily, she crawled into bed. Lying there, she wondered, would she have been able to accept their child had he been born looking as white as Aaron, even if she knew he had Negro blood? That was a question she had asked herself many times since giving birth. Slowly, she drifted off to sleep, hoping for a dreamless night.

It was a sunny day in the bay area. Aaron and Allison were on their way to the hospital to retrieve the child. Allison questioned, "Have you come up with a name for your son yet?" Aaron smiled and replied, "What do you think of the name Trent? He was curious as to whether Allison would remember Dorie's diary, it was their grandfather's name.

Allison's eyes watered, she remembered. "Oh, Aaron, I think it's a fine, strong name, Dorie would be so proud!"

"Good, then Trent, it is."

They waited eagerly for someone to bring Trent to them. Unfortunately, the same, disgruntled nurse that had attended Melissa was the one to arrive with him. As she handed the infant to Aaron, she remarked, "You're going to have a hard time passing this one off as white!" Allison gasped and Aaron's usually easy going mannerisms vanished as he replied, "I have no desire to, although it does seem to me it would be a much easier task than trying to pass you off as a human being, much less a woman. Look in a mirror, you surly will see, the attempt would be futile!" Allison tried to conceal the grin on her face by covering her mouth with her hand. Without another word, the nurse stomped out of the room.

They both stared down at the little bundle that had been handed so abruptly to his father. Trent was asleep, oblivious to all the traumatic events his birth had caused. His lips feigned a sucking motion and their hearts ached, remembering the woman who deserted him, her breasts filled with mother's milk.

"C'mon little fellow, we're going home." He handed Trent to Allison and she held him close, unable to understand how Melissa could turn her back on both her husband and her child. She held back a tear as she wondered whom she felt the most sorry for, Trent, Aaron or Melissa.

Tullah greeted them at the door, just as she had done the first day they had arrived as infants, and again, when Lillian returned from the hospital with Jonathon. It was a welcome sight for Allison and Aaron as they climbed the stairs. Allison noticed the rose garden and could almost see Dorie there, trimming her favorite bush, the one that was two-toned. She often referred to it as her Roosevelt and Hattie bush, which Allison never understood until reading the diary. Tullah reached for the child as Aaron introduced her to Trent. She cuddled him and her heart ached while she admired the sleeping infant whose mother had rejected him. It wasn't going to be an easy life for him, but hopefully, since he was born a Marshall that would be an advantage, plus he had his Uncle. Blake Donlan's wealth and power would help protect him. She became overwhelmed at how they had all come together again as they entered the house that was once again their home.

Muriel knocked on the door, since hearing the gossip she was anxious to assure Allison she was her friend and would always be there for her. Allison answered the door and became buried in the arms of Muriel as she questioned, "Are you all right?"

Allison witnessed the look of concern for her through Muriel's thick glasses that now sat slanted from the embrace. "Yes, of course I am, she answered, come in." Muriel released her and adjusted her glasses. They went into the parlor and Allison rang for Tullah, requesting tea, before stating, "It's obvious that you and Bea have heard all about Aaron and me."

"Yes, Muriel replied, it was a shock for both of us. I can only imagine what it must have been for you."

"At first it was, but now it's becoming easier to accept, after all I loved Dorie. I just wish I could have met my real mother." Muriel watched as Allison went over to a small table and returned with a small silver, framed picture of Trilly. "This is my mother," she exclaimed.

Muriel stared at the picture for a moment and then stated, "She was beautiful. You inherited her beauty." Allison thanked her. Tullah entered the room with the teacart.

Allison insisted that she join them. The three sipped tea and shared biscuits while Muriel told them all about Chad. She was sure a proposal was in the future. She exclaimed, "Honestly, I didn't think anyone would ever fall in love with me. Remember Allison, I told you that, but Chad actually told me he loved me. If it were not for you and Blake, I would never have met him. My whole life would still be revolved around the Red

Cross." Allison was thankful that Chad was able to see past her friend's outward appearance and saw all the good and beauty, tucked inside. Sadly, she thought, too many people base too much on appearance and therefore a lot of fine people remain lonely throughout their lives. She stated, "Chad knows a good woman when he sees one." Muriel hugged and thanked her.

After tea she took Muriel up to the nursery to meet the child whose birth shocked the people of the bay area. She observed him; he was a beautiful child. His hair lay in soft dark waves; tiny brows hovered over surprisingly deep green eyes that showed unusual alertness for an infant. She had never seen such green eyes like that on anyone other than his mother, Melissa.

After they left the nursery, Muriel questioned, "How is Aaron doing?"

She replied, "About as good as could be expected. He loved Melissa very much. Unfortunately, in this case, love was not enough. I try to accept that she was raised with strict Southern upbringing and all this must have been a terrible shock, it was to all of us. I just find it hard to conceive that she could just walk away from Aaron and her child like they never existed." Once again Muriel embraced her exclaiming, "Thank God he has you."

Douglas Barnum stared at the newspaper that lay in front of him. Bitterness overwhelmed him as he remembered how proud he had been that his son-in-law was an editor for San Francisco's largest newspaper. He reached for it and slowly crushed each page one by one, each time feeling it was Aaron's life he was crushing with his bare hands. His eyes were expressionless as Lydia entered the room. Observing his actions, she let out a small cry. She walked to him and put her hand on his, hoping to get his attention and free him from his trance-like state, "Doug, she cried, what are you doing?" He looked at the stack of crumpled paper and replied, "You don't want to know."

Lydia was trying her hardest to deal with all that had happened. She really had become fond of Aaron and was still finding it hard to believe he had Negro blood in him, but the child was living proof and there was Aaron's confession to Melissa. This never would have happened if they had stayed in the South. Now, both her child and husband were on the verge of nervous breakdowns. She pleaded with him, "Doug, can't we go back home, take Melissa away from Aaron and the baby. We would be so much better off. We already informed the family she had a still-born, there will be no embarrassment or shame to face. We can say that Melissa and Aaron were distraught; and decided to separate for awhile. Eventually it could end in divorce."

Douglas's fists slammed on the table, tipping over a small lamp, "No damn Nigger is running me and my family out of town." The action startled as well as frightened Lydia, defeated she left the room and returned to the kitchen where she found Melissa sitting at the table with a cup of coffee. Observing her was difficult. The birth of the child had removed more than just one life from her body. She appeared ghost-like. The once sparkling green eyes held a void stare.

"What was daddy screaming about," she questioned, in a weary tone?

Hesitantly, Lydia replied, "I mentioned that I thought we should return to Montgomery, he didn't care for the suggestion."

"Me neither, I like it here,' Melissa informed her while sipping her coffee. Lydia sighed, "I just thought it would eliminate any possibility of you having to worry about running into Aaron." At the mention of his name, Melissa's heart skipped a beat, especially at the thought of seeing him again.

She replied, "San Francisco is a big city, I'll make it a point not to encounter him." Lydia prayed Douglas would do the same. The thought of him encountering Aaron again sent chills down her spine, especially after the scene she had just witnessed.

Blake stared across the dinner table at Allison, telling himself how fortunate he was to have gained her love.

"Why are you staring at me like that," she questioned in a concerned voice? She wondered if he were trying to detect her Negro blood. Since her and Aaron's identity had been discovered, she had become extremely uncomfortable if anyone stared at her, feeling that they were looking for defects.

Blake answered her question. "I'm looking at what I consider my most beautiful piece of property." He was not prepared for her reaction.

"She exclaimed. Yes, I guess since I'm Negro, I am now considered a piece of property." Horrified, he set down his wineglass and stared at her once more, only this time it was in disbelief at what he just heard. "My God Allison, I can't believe you said that." Tears welled up in her eyes as she ran from the room, leaving Blake completely stunned. He knew there had been a lot for her to have to deal with these last few weeks, especially with a new baby in the house, but the statement involved heredity. Had he misjudged her by assuming she had come to terms with the situation? He sipped his wine and decided he would give her time to calm down before going to her.

Allison lay across the bed making no attempt to stop the tears from flowing; she had held them back too long. Pictures of Dorie and Trilly drifted through her mind. Even though she never met her mother, she now felt close to her, leaving her with renewed guilt over her death. She wondered if Lillian would have accepted her and Aaron had she known the truth, probably not, after all, her husbands black mistress conceived them. How could she even think she might have accepted them? The look on Blake's face when she made that ridiculous statement returned to her. She shouldn't have said such a thing to him, knowing he loved her, despite everything.

"Allison." The deep, smooth, soothing voice came to her, making her ache with love for him as he looked down at her with concern. Suddenly she needed to feel his arms around her. "Blake, I'm sorry for what I said, she stated in a whimpered voice, please hold me." He gazed at the small form lying there appearing so fragile and lay next to her, holding her close. Once more, she started crying.

"What is it Allison? What has happened to cause this? She didn't want to tell him that Aaron told her the newspaper was getting threats for giving a black man a white man's job. Nor did she want to tell him of her trip to DeLeons the other day that ended up with her returning home without the new dress she felt she needed to cheer herself. The stares and whispers drove her away. She overheard someone state, "Blake Donlan's, Negress. Kathryn had feigned a sympathetic smile as she left the boutique empty handed. On the way home she asked herself many questions. Would she ever be able to buy a new dress again? Was she going to be the ruin of Blake? Would anyone ever forget the story of the Marshall twins? She was frightened but refused to admit it, telling Blake that she was just overtired. He pulled from her stating, "No, it's more than that. The statement you made at dinner tells me so." She rolled over and faced him and he went weak, staring into the sad brown eyes. All he wanted was to make her happy. He pleaded, "Please tell me what it is."

"Just hold me and make love to me, I need you now." He forgot everything as their lips met. His hands caressed the perfectly shaped body as he eagerly removed the hindering clothing from her. The silk, warm feel of her flesh next to him and her words of love further excited his more than ready body. He entered her slowly, experiencing total ecstasy as she surrounded him both inwardly and outwardly. Her arms and legs wrapped around him with surprising strength. Never had he felt she needed him as she did now, leaving him fighting to hold back the river of passion that was waiting to be released.

"Blake, Blake, love me forever, promise."

"Yes Allison, forever." He moaned as together they reached the peak of their lovemaking. Satisfied and spent, he lay holding her, pulling a damp curl away from her forehead. She had fallen asleep. Still, she hadn't told him what caused the scene earlier downstairs. He promised to find out for himself. He would question Tullah in the morning. Hopefully she could tell him what was wrong.

Tullah was in the kitchen when Blake entered. The room was filled with the aroma of fresh rising dough and cinnamon. She was taken by surprise, Blake never entered the kitchen unless it was to repair something and nothing needed repairing. She smiled, "Mr. Donlan, what brings you in here?"

"I need to talk to you in regards to Allison."

Tullah became concerned, putting aside the rolls she was in the process of making, and inquired, what's wrong?"

"That's what I hope you can tell me, he replied. He informed her of the conversation at the dinner table. Tullah shook her head sadly while listening. Blake asked, "Can you tell me anything that might have caused her to react that way? Until that outburst, I thought she had accepted everything." Tullah became nervous and explained that she felt she shouldn't mention things that were told to her in confidence from Allison. Understanding her predicament, he merely asked her to think about it and if she decided it was something he should know, would she please come to him. He noticed her sigh of relief, and felt secure that she would do whatever was best for Allison.

Tullah wanted desperately to tell him of Allison's experience at the boutique but felt it wasn't anything terribly jeopardizing at this point, at least, not enough to break Allison's trust.

It had been a month since the birth of Trent. Robert Cunningham sat in his office reading another threatening letter to the newspaper regarding the employment of the nigger, Aaron Marshall. "Get rid of the nigger, or we will burn the building." Disgusted, he threw it, missing the wastebasket while questioning whether someone really would do such a thing. He was a stubborn man and didn't want to be harassed into getting rid of Aaron; but then again he had the other employee's to consider. Aaron entered the room and approached his boss. He noticed the crumpled piece of paper on the floor and retrieved it stating, "Your shot is getting pretty bad these days. Hopefully it's not something I edited," he said jokingly as he went to put it into the basket.

"Read it,' Cunningham instructed, gruffly. Aaron's heart sank to the pit of his stomach realizing it must be another threat. Hesitantly, he smoothed it out and read.

After a moment Cunningham broke the silence, "What the hell am I supposed to do Aaron? Other than me, you're the best damn editor the paper has ever had. I don't know whether to take these threats seriously or not."

Once more the letter was crushed as Aaron put it into his pocket. "Do what you have to do Robert. I just need the word from you that I'm dismissed."

"Shit, Aaron, you know that's the last thing I want. All we can do is call the bluff and hope it really is one. I'm guessing that it's just some bored idiot that has nothing better to do.

Aaron had grown to respect the man before him and stated, "You know how I feel about the newspaper. I love my work but if for one moment you believe that I'm a detriment to it, you must let me go and I will understand."

Robert rose and patted him on the shoulder and replied, "Yes, I know, now get back to work; there's that deadline to meet."

Aaron returned to his office and received the cup of coffee he had requested from his secretary. Susan was an older, plump woman for which he was thankful. She certainly couldn't remind him of Melissa. He thanked her and watched as she left the room with a funny little wobble, her dowdy dress length exposing a pair of thick ankles. He finished up with his work and decided to go see his son. This was that short time in between deadlines that Robert talked about. My son, the sound of it filled him with pride, to be replaced almost immediately by sorrow. Holding Trent would remind him that Melissa would never be there to embrace their child. Trent would never know his mother's arms around him and the softness of her breasts as he snuggled securely next to them. He reminded himself, that neither he nor Allison had ever known their real mother but due to the love they received, neither of them knew the difference. The same would be true for Trent. The love he would receive from Allison, Tullah and himself would be enough. He finished another cup of coffee and headed for the Marshall house.

Chapter 22

The house radiated the warmth from with-in. It was dusk and the lights in the windows cast an amber glow throughout, which reflected the fall season's own amber bursts of color. He loved it here. It was here that he had been innocent and free of discrimination. He was simply, Aaron Marshall, son of Lillian and James, one of San Francisco's elite families. Here, his biggest concern had been what to do since completing college. How could so many changes have taken place in such a short time? A smile spread across his face as he noticed Jonathon's car in the driveway. It had been several weeks since he had seen his brother. Tullah opened the door and reached for him, giving him her usual hug.

"Tullah, you're still the most beautiful woman I know." She gave him a small slap on the chest and replied, "Didn't Dorie and I teach you not to tell lies?" He grinned and gave her a kiss on the cheek before asking where to find everyone.

"They're all in the parlor with your son. She looked into his eyes and exclaimed, he's going to be all right Aaron. There's a lot of love here for him."

He replied, "I know Tullah, thanks."

Jonathon leaped up to greet him as he entered the room. Aaron noticed that he was starting to fill out, no longer looking so lanky, he was becoming a man. As far as he was concerned, Jonathon became a man the day he discovered the truth about Allison and himself, swearing that it made no difference in his love for them or his parent's. They hugged as Jonathon exclaimed, "That nephew of mine can empty a bottle faster than a prohibition officer," the sound of laughter filled the room. Allison was in a chair next to the fire feeding Trent. He went to her and she turned Trent over to him. He sat down in a large leather chair that matched the one Blake sat in.

"How are things going at the newspaper," Blake asked innocently? Both Aaron and Allison's heart's beat quickly. Aaron had no intentions of dragging Blake into anymore of his problems, nor did he want Jonathon to know what was happening. He was already regretful he had mentioned it to Allison, but after hearing of her trip to DeLeons, he felt they needed each other to confide in. He lied as he answered Blake's question.

"Just fine," then changed the subject, "Jonathon, you're making the sports section more and more lately.

Jonathon smiled with pride, "Yes, and now I'm finally getting a percentage of my winnings. I'm getting an apartment next week."

"Good for you, Aaron replied. Got a girlfriend yet?"

"No," I don't seem to have time for women."

Blake spoke, "You'll eventually find the time." Jonathon agreed, but wasn't real sure it would actually happen. Tullah entered the room to retrieve Trent, stating, "It's time for this little fellow to get to bed." Aaron handed him over to her, but not until he gave him a kiss on the forehead, promising to return soon.

"He's such a good baby," Allison exclaimed. Tullah agreed which brought a proud smile on Aaron's face. Jonathon looked at the clock on the mantle and announced it was time for him to leave.

"Me too, Aaron exclaimed, I just wanted to stop by and say hello and hold Trent for a moment. I've been working late and mornings come too soon." They both kissed their sister and shook Blake's hand. Allison watched as her brother's exited. She was proud of them and was sure Dorie, James and Lillian would be pleased also, they were good men. She was concerned for Aaron and wanted to question whether or not there had been any more threats but with Blake and Jonathon in the room there had been no opportunity. She wondered if she was the only one to notice how tired Aaron appeared.

Blake interrupted her thoughts exclaiming, "I sense that something is going on with both you and Aaron. What is it?"

Allison was taken by surprise with the question. She hated lying to him but felt she must, he just didn't need to hear about their problems. He had done enough for them. Besides, there was nothing he could do about it. "Nothing I can think of," she answered. Blake sighed, he had failed once more. Why wouldn't she confide in him? He went to her chair and leaned over her, his eyes piercing hers. "I know something is wrong Allison and don't understand why you won't confide in me. You know how much I love you and therefore need to know what it is that is making you so unhappy." She remained silent. He shook his head in defeat and suggested, "How about we go out tomorrow night and indulge ourselves. It will be good for both of us." Fear swept through Allison. What if people were to stare at her and make comments like they did at the boutique? Blake noticed her hesitation and exclaimed, "I won't take no for an answer, it will be good for us." She shook her head, agreeing. She had no desire to go but Blake had made up his mind. It was a rare occasion, when he left her no choice.

Aaron decided to start looking for another apartment, a place where he and Trent could start fresh. Everything here reminded him of Melissa, the couch that they snuggled together on while listening to their favorite radio program, the curtains they had selected so carefully and the small porcelain figurine she had bought, a Dutch boy and girl kissing. He remembered the day she returned from shopping with it. Excitedly, she removed it from the bag exclaiming, "It's you and me Aaron, just like us, they are inseparable!" Picking up the figurine he threw it against the wall and watched as it shattered into pieces. They hadn't talked since the hospital and he wondered if he was the only one suffering. God, how was he ever going to stop loving her? He entered the bedroom, the worst reminder of his lost love. He tried not to re-live the countless hours they had spent in it making love on the rickety, old bed. He never went to bed until he was so tired and exhausted he would be able to drift off quickly. Putting on his slippers, he returned to the kitchen, poured a glass of homemade wine a customer had gifted him and sat at the small table Melissa had painted an apple green. He picked up yesterday's paper and started to read. His concentration drifted to the threats the newspaper had been receiving. Deep down, he suspected his father-in law. There was no way of proving it but even if there was, he would protect him, after all, he was Melissa's father and for her and Trent's sake he would keep his suspicions to himself.

Blake hummed as he straightened his tie. He was sure this evening out would cheer Allison up. She entered the room in a pale blue silk dress with a matching mid-length jacket. Pale gray fur trimmed both the bottom of the sleeves as well as the lapels. He turned from the mirror to admire her.

"You look beautiful Allison. Is that your new dress?"

"No," she replied, I've had this one for sometime."

"Oh, I thought you told me you were going to get a new dress last week, how come you're not wearing it?" It took her a moment to reply.

"I went looking for one but couldn't find anything I liked."

"Well you look great, but a smile would help." She forced a smile and gave him a kiss, thanking him for the compliment. She observed her image in the full- length mirror. She hadn't changed, people had, and the evening frightened her. Blake took her arm and escorted her to the car unaware of the fear his wife held with-in her.

It was a typical foggy night on the waterfront when they arrived at The Breakwaters. It was a new place for café society to meet. Since the depression, home parties were becoming a thing of the past and considered a blatant show of ones wealth, therefore people socialized at the café's and clubs. There was a line of hopefuls waiting to enter. Blake let out a groan. He had neglected to make reservations. "I'm sorry, he sighed. I promised you a night out."

Allison was relieved, "That's alright, it isn't important."

"Yes it is. I'll take you to Macky's. It's not the Breakwater, but its good food. The name Macky's meant nothing to Allison. The night she went there with Gerald, the establishment's name hadn't been mentioned. Blake parked the car and they walked towards the building. As they neared she began to recognize the place and exclaimed, "Blake, this is a speakeasy."

"You remember, he replied with a small grin, I wasn't sure you would."

Her face reddened, "Yes, I remember but it seems that night was so long ago." They were led to a familiar linen covered table with the usual single rose in a vase and Allison smiled, remembering how it had momentarily upset her the night she was there with Gerald, because it reminded her of Blake. The smile didn't go unnoticed by Blake and he exclaimed, "See, I told you a night out would be good for you!" A waiter appeared and left a menu, leaving with an order for champagne. The music was soothing, not loud like she remembered it and she felt herself relaxing.

After indulging in a lobster dinner, Blake informed her that the dance band was about to start, stating "Macky never has the band play dance music during dinner hours." A few minutes later, people were doing the Charleston and the Macky's she remembered, came to life.

Kathryn sat across the room, going unnoticed by the couple enjoying themselves. Despite all that had happened, Blake looked happier than she had ever seen him and Allison looked radiant, totally unaffected by her discovery.

"Kathryn, her date nudged her, hasn't anyone ever told you it's not nice to stare?" She returned her attention to him and apologized.

"I'm sorry. It's just a couple I haven't seen for sometime."

"Who are they," he asked curiously?

"The Donlan's, Blake Donlan owns most the bay area."

Alex admired the stunning couple. "Well, all I can say is, some have it all, his wife is gorgeous!" Kathryn held back the anger she was experiencing and calmly replied, "Yes, you would never guess she is a Negro."

"What," Alex replied in astonishment? Kathryn proceeded to tell him all about the Marshall twins. Now it was he that was staring, finding the story incredible. He exclaimed, "There was no way anyone would guess it by looking at her." She was one of the most beautiful women he had ever seen.

Blake and Allison remained unaware of Kathryn and Alex's presence until they stopped by their table on the way out.

"Blake, Allison, how nice to see you. Meet my date, Alex Freed." Kathryn clung to him as she had done so many times to Blake. They acknowledged the introduction. Allison's heart stood still at Kathryn's next statement. "Allison, I'm so sorry for the behavior of my customers last week when you arrived." She continued on in an overly sympathetic voice. "Surely, you realize I have no control over their evil, wagging tongues."

"Allison replied, "I understand quite well Kathryn." She knew Kathryn was enjoying her situation, still bitter over the loss of Blake. The man Alex was making her feel more uncomfortable as he stared down at her.

Blake was beginning to understand now, why Allison had been so upset. Anger surged through him. He could only imagine what those society biddies must have said. He sat quietly seething as Kathryn continued.

"Well, you must not let such things bother you my dear. Please come back, I'll give you a private showing. We have some wonderful new styles, shoulder pads are the rage. After all, we must keep up your appearance now that you're the new Mrs. Donlan, right Blake?" He held his anger, calmingly stating, "That might be a difficult task for you Kathryn since I'm taking Allison to Monterey to do her shopping. I hear the boutiques there are superb and I want nothing but the best for her." Now it was Kathryn trying to hold back her anger. Alex grabbed her arm and stated, "Well, I guess we better go, nice meeting you." Kathryn followed without a last word."

"Do you want to tell me about it Allison?" She held back a tear that left her emotional after Blake's statement to Kathryn.

"Not now Blake, you promised me an evening out and I don't want it ruined. She was thankful, for the calming effect the champagne had given her and requested, "Please dance with me." He led her to the floor and held her close. He had one goal and that was Allison's happiness and God help anyone who would hurt her physically or mentally, that included Kathryn DeLeon.

Doug Barnum's threats to the newspaper were proving futile. He needed to do something to punish Aaron for what he had done to his family. Finishing the letter, he sat back in his chair confident everything would be taken care of now. He knew who could help him get revenge, his kin.

Melissa stood across the street and gazed longingly at the little apartment house. She wanted to be back there with Aaron. God, forgive her, she still loved him, but despised what he was and loathed herself for wanting him. Her return there would be short. She just wanted a few of her belongings. She crossed the street and climbed the stairs to the second floor. Aaron would not be there at this hour. Her heart beat rapidly as she turned the key and entered. Now, it fell to the pit of her stomach as she scanned the rooms. They were empty, he had moved. The scene made her feel equally as empty. The apartment they had shared so much love and tenderness in was forever gone. She walked through it, re-living the happiness she once had. Her foot kicked something. She bent over and picked up a small piece of porcelain. Tears welled in her eyes as she recognized the remaining piece of the small figurine she had bought them. Carefully, she wrapped it in her hanky, and put the shattered remains of her marriage into her purse, questioning herself, "Can I survive without him?"

Allison answered the phone, barely recognizing the voice on the other end of the line due to the excited, high pitch. Muriel exclaimed, "Allison, it happened, Chad proposed to me." Noticing her own voice rise with excitement she replied, "Muriel that's wonderful." Suddenly, she heard her crying and questioned if she was okay.

"Yes, I'm just so happy. The wedding will be September sixth. Will you be my maid of honor?" Allison accepted the offer exclaiming, "I'm so glad for you."

"Thank you Allison, you and Blake. I know this sounds awful but that earthquake was the best thing that ever happened to me. It brought me you, and Chad. You just never know what will alter you're life."

"I understand," Allison replied, shuddering at the memory of being buried alive and truly understanding how occurrences can alter ones life. Muriel informed her she had to call Bea and thanked her for everything before hanging up.

Sitting on the window seat, overlooking the gardens, she sipped the tea Tullah had brought her. The roses were gone for the year. She looked forward to their return. It made her feel Dorie was near. Her thoughts drifted to Blake, remembering the look of fury on his face as she finally explained what had taken place at DeLeons that day. He had comprehended most of what happened from Kathryn's conversation, but wanted details, which she now realized was typical of him. What bothered her was he said very little other than, he would take care of it. What was he going to do?

Blake requested his secretary to bring him the lease papers for the building on the corner of 3rd street and Shoreline Drive. A few minutes later, Dorothy returned with the folder. Returning to her desk, she was happy see he was finally getting back to work. She remembered that day, long ago when the Negro lady came to the office to see Mr. Marshall and had been curious about the visit, but eventually forgot it until the story of the twins came up. The thought of Mr. Marshall having a Negro mistress seemed impossible to her. Now poor Mr. Donlan would be the one to suffer because of it. The phone rang bringing her attention back to her work.

Blake thumbed through the documents until he found the lease agreement for DeLeons. "Yes, he told himself, I am right, the lease is due for renewal next month." He set the folder aside, turned around in his chair and looked out the window. The bay was churning, like the blood in his veins. Kathryn Deleon would pay for what she had done.

Kathryn tried to calm herself as she watched Blake approach. He called and asked to talk with her. Though he appeared angry with her the other night at Macky's, was it possible that he had time to think about it and realized the mistake he made by marrying Allison. Why else would he ask to meet with her?

He greeted her, lacking the warmth of a smile, alerting her immediately that something was wrong. She had never seen an expression on his face like this before. Perhaps he discovered something else about the Marshall's. She questioned, "What's wrong Blake?"

He replied, as he took a seat, "What's wrong, is the information I received from Allison regarding her visit to your store last week, which by the way I might never have known except for your pathetic apology the other night at Macky's." The incident disturbs me, Kathryn. It didn't escape me that you seemed to relish the situation she faced, therefore, in my eyes, making you as guilty as your stuffy clientele.

Kathryn couldn't believe what she was hearing and became nervous. By the look on his face, she knew there was more to come. His next words horrified her.

"Your lease at DeLeons is up next month and I'm not renewing it Kathryn." Shocked, she cried out, "Blake, for Gods sake, what was I supposed to do?"

"You might have stepped forward in Allison's defense and degrade the offenders."

Kathryn's face reddened as she exclaimed, "What, and lose my customers?" Blake stared at her coldly and replied, "You know very well those women would not stop shopping at DeLeons." Deep down she knew he was right. All she would have had to do was tactfully shame them for their actions. Unable to defend herself, she exclaimed, "Where the hell am I supposed to go with DeLeons, you own just about every available space in the bay area?"

"True, I guess you'll just have to move to the lower end of town and your clientele will have to mingle with the less fortunate if they want to continue shopping at your boutique.

"I can't survive there, she exclaimed. No one of any status would shop in that area." An expressionless face stared back at her before stating, "How does it feel Kathryn, not having any control over what's happening to you? You will be the same person with the same fine boutique and now be discriminated against by your fine aristocratic customers merely because of something as simple as the location of your business. Now perhaps you will be able to understand and respect Allison's situation." Without another word, he left her sitting alone and stunned.

Blake returned to his office. He didn't like what he had just done to Kathryn, but felt it necessary. Hopefully, there would be no other incidents he would have to settle on Allison's behalf.

The meeting came to order and Dexter Honeycutt stepped up to the podium. He cleared his throat, allowing the deep southern drawl he took pride in, radiate to his audience. "Brother's of the Klan, most of us know mah cousin Douglas Barnum. Well, he may have left the South some years ago, but he has always remained a true Southerner, born and raised one. He maintains Southern standards and a firm belief that there is no place for negra's in awe society. I hold right here in mah hand a letter from awe brother Douglas. He has asked the Klan to swear secrecy to this heah letter, before I read it." There was a wave of murmurs, before a vow of secrecy was decreed. Dexter read the letter. Upon completion, the appalled audience sat stunned.

"Now, Dexter continued, we all know that the North is a nigger lovin, society, and as far as I am concerned, they're goin to be sorry someday for freeing em. Now, they have niggers there passing themselves off as white men. This, my brothers, is very upsetting news, especially so when this deceit was inflicted upon one of our fine Southern women. The audience mumbled amongst themselves for a moment. Dexter continued, I have here, in my hand, two tickets, sent from our brother Douglas, pleading for help in punishing the white negra that betrayed his daughter. I will go, who will take the other ticket and help teach this Northern, white Negro boy a lesson?" Once again murmurs spilled through the crowd before half a dozen Klansmen volunteered.

DYANN WEBB

CHAPTER 23

Allison finished dressing Trent, stating, "You're two months old today my little man and your daddy's coming to get you and take you for a ride." Trent stared at her and a smile formed as if he understood. She carried him downstairs to wait for Aaron. He would be taking Trent to the doctors, for his first exam. Aaron's voice announced his arrival. She met him in the hall, with his son.

"Hey, how's my little boy," Aaron questioned as he reached out for him?"

"He's not so little, Allison replied, he has your appetite." Aaron gave her a rare smile and looked at his watch. "We will be back in about an hour. Thanks for having him ready for me. He gave Allison a kiss and departed.

Dr. Blairs office was about a twenty minute drive from the house. He had been the family doctor as far back as Aaron could remember. By the time he arrived Trent was asleep in the backseat. Gently, he lifted him into his arms and carried him into the clinic. It was actually the doctor's home, a charming white clapboard house, surrounded by a wrought iron fence and gate with carefully maintained gardens decorating the grounds. As he opened the door, a small bell jingled, announcing their entry. He looked around the room. An elderly man was engrossed in a crossword puzzle, and a young mother and daughter were reading movie magazines. The receptionist was busy writing in a large ledger, her white cap concealing all but a little of her red hair as it bobbed in rhythm with the pen she was using. He approached the desk and waited for a brief moment before she raised her head to greet him. Shock shot through his body with electrical force. My

God, it was Melissa. He pulled Trent close and protectively against him, hoping the hard beating of his heart wouldn't disturb him.

Melissa froze, unable to believe what she was seeing and unable to take her eyes off of the handsome man standing in front of her grasping a small bundle to his chest. "How could this be," she asked herself?" She had only been working for Dr. Blair for two days. Of all places, she would never have guessed she would run into Aaron here. The silence between them seemed to last forever, going unnoticed by the other clients.

Aaron was the first to speak. He stared coldly at her. "My son has an eleven o'clock appointment." Melissa's hand shook as she turned the pages of the appointment book.

"Trent Marshall, nice name" she stated in a trembling voice, without looking up.

"Yes, I think so, he replied, it was my grandfather's name." When she did look up, he witnessed the green eyes of his son facing him. "I'll tell the doctor you're here." He went and sat down on the hard oak chair next to the others and waited.

Melissa informed the doctor, "Mr. Marshall is here for his son's exam."

"Are you alright Melissa?" He was concerned by her sudden state. She had become pale and obviously upset.

"Yes, I'll be okay in a minute. I just don't know what came over me."

"Well, if you're not feeling better soon, let me know." She forced a smile and agreed to his request. With a worried look on his face he stated, "Send Aaron in."

The familiarity in his voice made her realize that he obviously knew Aaron, leaving her to wonder if he had seen the child before, so she asked if this was Trent Marshall's first visit.

"Yes it is he answered, quite a sad story, I'll tell you about it later." Knowing what the story would be, she silently agreed to herself, yes, it is a sad story. Returning to the waiting room, she informed Aaron he could take Trent in.

Aaron glared at her as he passed by with their child. Melissa felt his closeness as he brushed past her, leaving a faint aromatic trace of the wonderful after-shave he always wore. "Aaron, Aaron," she cried inwardly to herself.

The exam took approximately, fifteen minutes. Aaron exited the examination room holding his son, still covered under the soft blanket so she need not see him. She watched as they silently walked out of her life for good.

Still shaking, she removed the tear stained hanky from her pocket, dabbing her eyes, hoping the two awaiting patients hadn't noticed.

Lunch was spent in the kitchen of the old house with the doctor usually discussing the clinic and its patients. Today, she was eager to hear what he had to say.

He sat at the table eating a sandwich and drinking a large glass of milk when she entered.

"Melissa, you still look ill." He set his sandwich down and went to her, placing his hand on her forehead. "You don't feel like you have a fever but its best I take your temperature."

"No, she replied, it's really not necessary. I just have a headache, perhaps just an aspirin." He went to the cabinet and returned with the requested pill. She thanked him as she swallowed it with a glass of water, before eagerly asking, "Now, tell me, did the Marshall baby pass his exam?" She felt her heart stop as she awaited the answer.

"Yes, he's a strong, healthy fellow." She waited for more information but nothing else was said.

"You mentioned there was a sad story involved with him, what is it?" He took a drink of milk and with a sigh and a sad shake of the head began telling her the story of Roosevelt and Hattie. He finished the story, telling her that unfortunately Aaron had married a young woman from the South. He and his wife were shocked when the child was born black. It's what we call, a throw back. From what I understand, the mother, being of strict Southern upbringing was appalled that she had a Negro child. She turned her back on them, leaving Aaron to raise the child alone. No one, including myself knew of his or his sister's true identity. He was quiet for a moment before questioning, "You're from the South Miss Barnum, how do you think you would handle such a situation?" In a meek voice, hoping he wouldn't detect her guilt, she replied, "I don't know doctor, but it really is a very sad story."

On the drive home, after a day that seemed to last forever, Melissa pictured Aaron, standing so tall and handsome in front of her clutching the outcome of their lovemaking. Oh, how she wished she could run to him and ask him to hold her once more. She had wanted to go into the exam room and just take a peek at Trent but knew better. She deserted her baby by choice and still felt deeply against mothering a Negro child, yet her motherly instincts had kicked in. She had fought the urge to ask to embrace the tiny bundle that Aaron held so close and protectively to him. She remembered how badly her breasts ached in the hospital when she refused to nurse him. It was days of misery before the milk eventually dried up. Both the child and Aaron haunted her. She said a silent prayer, asking God to give her the strength she needed, to forget them.

Depression overwhelmed Aaron as he returned home. The renewed image of Melissa still lingered in his mind.. He questioned himself, "How could he love and dislike someone so much?" The shock of seeing her was still clinging to him. A cars horn honked, urging him to move on through a green light. Due to the tension, by the time he arrived back at the house, he felt as though someone had beaten him. His muscles started to relax as he entered the house and witnessed Tullah approaching him to retrieve Trent. Little Marshall toddled along behind her.

"Well, is our boy Trent as perfect as we all think he is, she asked?"

"Absolutely," he replied with a smile. She sensed there was something wrong and questioned, "Are you alright Aaron?"

"Yes, I'm fine. Please tell Allison the exam went well and I'm sorry I couldn't stay but I have to get back to work. Tell her I will see her later." She watched uneasy, as he walked away, slumped shouldered, like a defeated man. Her heart ached to see him this way, leaving her to wonder what could have happened to cause it.

Douglas Barnum watched as the piece of paper burned in the wastebasket. It wouldn't be much longer now before he would have his revenge on Aaron. The Klan agreed to support him with his ordeal. He was instructed to be out in public on the designated evening and be seen. He must have proof as to where he was at the time of the white nigger's punishment. His heart raced at the thought of what was about to happen. He had participated several times while in the South, punishing uppity nigger's. Usually a good beating and a few horrific threats scared them enough to put them in place. Hopefully, between the threats to the newspaper and a beating, Aaron would leave town and take his nigger baby with him. The thought brought a lost smile back on Doug's face.

Cunningham was pleased with the way things were going. The threats to the newspaper had ceased. He put on his hat and coat, turned off his desk light and stopped at Aaron's office to inform him it was time to go home. He stood in front of Aaron's desk, casting a shadow

"I told you there's that short period of time that we have for ourselves. I suggest you take advantage of it." Aaron looked up from the stack of papers in front of him and Cunningham became concerned, he appeared exhausted. "Go home Aaron, you look like hell. You'll be of no use to the paper if you don't take care of yourself."

"Thanks for the compliment Robert. You're right, I'm just finishing up a couple of more things and then I'll go home."

"I trust you to do that. You're a hard worker Aaron and your father would have been proud of you, goodnight."

"Goodnight, Aaron echoed back to him, see you tomorrow." He watched as the overweight man with whom he had become so fond of, waddled down the hall and disappeared into the elevator.

Dexter and his companion handed the wedding photo back and forth to each other several times. Both were amazed at the lack of Negro characteristics in the groom. After studying it carefully they both agreed they could detect a few. "Sure is hard to tell though," Dexter exclaimed. His partner agreed, "I sure can see how that poor little girl got deceived." The train ride had been a long one and both men were eager to get the job done and return home. Sighs of relief escaped them when the conductor informed the passengers they had arrived in San Francisco.

Aaron decided to take his bosses advice, and go home. He was tired and hadn't slept well since his visit to the doctor's office and his encounter with Melissa. Due to the fog, it was a slow drive, causing him to remember the night that claimed his father, Lillian and Dorie. He wondered to himself, which was worse. Losing someone to death, or having someone chose to leave you? He made the decision that it was harder to lose someone who had a choice. While in deep thought, Aaron didn't notice the car that followed him closely. Pulling into his usual parking spot across from his new apartment, he removed the keys to the car and entered into the foggy evening. A voice startled him.

"Where are you goin nigger boy?" He turned in the darkness trying to determine who had made the disgusting comment. He questioned the shadowed figure, "What the hell did you just say?" A second voice replied, "He said, where, are you goin nigger." Aaron could barely distinguish who the offenders were but he detected a Southern drawl from both and knew he was in trouble. Instinctively, he smashed the second voice in the face. He felt and heard the crunch of the man's jaw under his knuckles. Suddenly there was another sound of bone being attacked, his own, it was his skull. He felt it crack as a blunt object made contact. Afterwards, all he could remember was the pain before he lost consciousness. When he awoke, he was on the sand at the beach. Both his hands and legs were tied behind him and a rag was stuffed in his mouth. He felt warm blood streaming down his face from the wound on his head. It was in his eyes, preventing him from identifying his attackers. A slow drawling voice whispered in his ear.

"Aren't you ashamed of yourself, trying to pass yourself off as a white man? We're here tonight to make sure your no kind of man at all. Know what I mean Nigger, you're not goin to have no more white nigra babies."

Aaron's stomach leaped as he realized what they were implying. He tried to wriggle free, as they unzipped his pants. Helpless, he could only lay there as they continued with their sadistic deed. A flash of unbearable hot, searing pain shot through him. With-in seconds he had been castrated, his scream remaining silent under the rag that had been placed in his mouth.

"Well, nigger, our job is done. I'm goin to take these here ropes off before we leave. You may want to get help for yourself before you bleed to death."

Aaron felt the pressure of the ropes releasing his hands and feet. Through blurry eyes, he watched as the car sped away. He lay there listening to the sound of the waves, splashing in the bay. "No, he told himself, I won't get help." Even the thought of Trent could not supply him with the will to live as he questioned, "Was it Douglas Barnum that had done this to him? He lay there on the beach quietly waiting for his life to slip away. Closing his eyes for the final time, he saw Melissa. He was back at their apartment, lying on the warm couch beside her, not the cold, damp sand. He smiled as once more, she confessed her love for him.

Allison screamed, awakening Blake. He reached for her and held her to him.

"What is it Allison, what's wrong?" Crying hysterically, she answered.

"I don't know. It was like my life was slipping away. I felt so cold and damp. It was so real!" Blake tried to soothe her, telling her she just had a bad dream. After a few minutes she settled down. He continued to hold her through the night, though neither one of them slept well.

The phone rang at Robert Cunningham's. Still half asleep, he rolled over in bed and answered it, eliminating the aggravating sound and demanded, "Who's calling me at this hour?"

"It's me, Sam," the voice on the other end of the line replied.

"Sam, why the hell are you calling me at this hour, it better be good?" Robert knew Sam tended to get overly excited when it came time to print the news.

"It's Aaron Marshall. They discovered his body on the beach early this morning. He was beaten and mutilated." Robert's heart sank as he asked Sam to repeat what he had just said and then questioned, "How was he mutilated?" He listened as Sam told him the grim details. As the reality sank in, he dropped the phone, ran to the bathroom and became ill. When he was through, he yelled to the unknown assailants, "Why the hell, couldn't you have just burned the newspaper, you sick bastard, whoever you are?"

Blake looked at the clock. It was five in the morning and someone was knocking on the door. The sound also woke Allison and once again a feeling of panic surrounded her. She knew something terrible had happened and she knew it involved Aaron. After awakening the first time, she remembered all the times her and Aaron shared experiences, especially the ones that occurred while they were separated. One in particular she remembered was when she was at finishing school writing an essay. Her arm started aching so badly, she had to put the pen down. Later on she found out that Aaron had entered an arm wrestling contest and suffered a badly sprained shoulder that same day. Aaron once mentioned to her about the time he was feeling feverish, but his temperature was normal, according to the school nurse, later to find out Allison, at that time had contacted Scarlet Fever.

The knocking continued as her and Blake put on their robes and went to the door. The sight of the two officers standing there weakened her knees. They stood there with grim faces, allowing her no time for hope.

"It's my brother she screamed, what has happened to him?" Blake was taken by her outburst, questioning why should she presume such a thing? In a low, sympathetic voice an officer replied, "I'm afraid I have to inform you Mrs. Donlan that your brother is dead."

Allison let out a mournful groan and Blake caught her before she hit the floor. Tullah and Grange entered the room just in time to witness her faint. Tullah cried, "What's happening, what's wrong with Allison. Her heart stood still, awaiting an answer.

Blake instructed Grange, "Call Dr. Blair immediately, were going to need him." Grange rushed to make the call and Tullah followed close behind Blake as he carried Allison upstairs to their room. He laid her on the bed and turned to Tullah. Knowing she had been like a mother to Aaron, he asked her to sit down. She sat on the bed next to Allison, frightened by the unanswered question, "What was wrong?"

Blake held her small hand in his, "Tullah, the officers downstairs just informed us that Aaron is dead." She felt her heart stop. The weight of it suddenly felt like a brick. She pulled her hand from his to muffle the mournful scream with-in her calling Aaron's name. Blake observed the large tears flowing from the look of disbelief in her eyes. He hugged her gently, telling her he would go back downstairs and speak with the officers. He needed to get the details, then requested, "In the meantime Tullah, I need you to stay with Allison. She will need you when she regains consciousness. Hopefully Dr. Blair will get here soon and sedate her." He left the two devastated women and went to speak with the police.

They were pacing the floor when he entered the room. Blake apologized for his absence and requested they give him details of the accident.

The eldest of the two officers stepped foreword and exclaimed, "It wasn't an accident Mr. Donlan, Aaron Marshall was murdered. His body was discovered on the beach this morning, beaten and mutilated." The words, beaten and mutilated surged through Blake's mind and he questioned with dread, "Mutilated in what way?" The officer had a difficult time getting the words out. "He... was... castrated." Blake felt as though someone had just punched him in the gut, knocking the wind out of him, leaving him unable to respond verbally. The officer questioned, "Can you think of anyone that would do something like this to him?" His mind screamed Douglas Barnum, but surely the man wouldn't resort to such a horrific act. The officer repeated the question. Struggling to regain his voice, it took another moment for him to answer. "I know that Aaron's father-in-law resented him, but I can't imagine him capable of such a horrendous thing!" The officer knew the story of Aaron and Melissa Marshall, who didn't? He replied, "We plan on talking to Mr. Barnum." He tipped his hat to Blake, stating, "We don't want to keep you from your wife Mr. Donlan, we'll be going. Once again, we regret our mission here." Blake thanked the two men, stating, "Please find whoever did this to Aaron, he was a fine man." With a silent nod, they left the room.

Anger and disbelief welled through Blake as he questioned, how much more could Allison take? Could all his love for her be enough to carry her through this? His thoughts drifted to the child Trent. If Douglas did kill Aaron, one day Trent would find out that his grandfather killed his father, merely because it was discovered after he was born there was black blood in the family. They wouldn't be able to protect him from the truth. If Douglas Barnum were responsible for this tragedy, he will have destroyed more than one life.

Douglas hadn't slept that night. As planned, he took Lydia and Melissa out to dinner. They went to The Breakwaters. To make sure he would be remembered, he over-tipped the waiter after purposely causing him to spill a tray of drinks. Lydia and Melissa questioned him on what the occasion was and he had told them, "I just think it's time for us to start living again and try to forget the past." He looked at the clock on the bedside table and decided to get up and have a cup of coffee. Putting on his blue striped flannel robe, he went to the kitchen. He gave life to the stove with a match. The gas flame flickered as he set the percolator on it and waited for his anticipated cup of coffee.

A knock on the door startled him. He saw the officer's uniforms through the small window and froze, asking himself if Aaron had accused him of the beating? That was the whole reason for an evening out, an alibi, just in case he did. He went to the door and opened it.

"Mr. Barnum?" He nodded his head. "We apologize for disturbing you so early in the morning but we need to talk to you in regards to Aaron Marshall."

"Aaron, he questioned, trying to act concerned. What about him?"

"May we come in, then, we can give you the details." Douglas stepped aside, hoping they wouldn't detect the nerves that were vibrating in his body. He set them at the kitchen table and offered coffee, they declined. Officer Mitchell was the first to speak "Aaron Marshall is dead Mr. Barnum. He was found on the beach this morning beaten and mutilated." Douglas no longer had to act. Shock waves rushed through him as he silently wondered what went wrong and why Dexter had killed him. He was only supposed to give him a small beating and a few threats to scare him into leaving town. The officers were surprised by the stunned reaction. They had felt the man was more than likely guilty, but by the look on his face they suddenly doubted it. "Are you all right Mr. Barnum?"

"Yes, I'm sorry, I just can't believe it."

"We understand there was a conflict between you and your son-in-law. Is that true?" Doug's heart raced as he exclaimed, "Yes, it's true, but for Gods sake, I wouldn't kill the man."

"Where were you last night Mr. Barnum?" Douglas informed them that he was at The Breakwaters with his wife and daughter having dinner. Afterwards, they returned home and went directly to bed. Officer Mitchell handed him a card and stated, "If there's anything you think you might have forgotten to tell me, please let me know." Douglas walked them to the door, assuring them that he would. He watched as they drove away and then returned to the kitchen. He wondered if Lydia and Melissa would suspect him when they heard the news. Damn, what a mess. He heard the newspaper hit the porch. Opening the door, he picked it up, hoping there hadn't been time to print the story yet. There it was, on the front page.

AARON MARSHALL FOUND MURDERED

The body of Aaron Marshall was discovered early this morning on the beach by Pelican Landing. He had been beaten and mutilated. Aaron was the assistant editor at The Bayside News, as well as our friend. The newspaper is offering a thousand-dollar reward for any information leading to an arrest. This inexcusable crime must not go unpunished. Our hearts go out to Aaron's survivors.

Robert Cunningham, Editor

He folded the paper, dreading the thought of Lydia and Melissa reading it. He looked up at the wall clock, if they were on schedule, they would be down shortly. He decided to prolong the inevitable as long as he could and took the paper out to the trash, once more cursing his cousin. He had made the agreement with Dexter that after the mission was accomplished, they would not make contact for a least one year. He wanted to call him and ask what the hell went wrong, but didn't dare. "Damn, he told himself, it's going to be a long year."

Lydia and Melissa entered the kitchen with-in minutes of each other. Melissa poured a cup of coffee and grabbed a piece of toast from the blue floral plate that had been in the family as far back as she could remember. She scanned the table searching for the morning paper. Reading the news, secretly made her feel closer to Aaron. "Where is the paper, She asked?"

Douglas replied "We didn't receive one this morning. I guess we must have another new paperboy." He was sure she would eventually read the paper at work, but had no desire to see her reaction when she did. It disgusted him, but he knew she still had feelings for Aaron. She finished her breakfast and grabbed her lunch. Her father was not a morning person and rarely carried a conversation at the table so his silence never forewarned her for what she was to learn later on that day. Lydia wished her a good day as she walked out the door. After she left, Douglas decided he should tell Lydia of Aaron's death.

He watched as the shocked look spread over Lydia's face. Her voice was strained as she questioned, "Do they know who did it?" Douglas squirmed as he answered, "No, not yet." The squirm did not go unnoticed by Lydia and she wondered if he was guilty. "No," she told herself he couldn't be responsible for it, they were together last night having dinner at The Breakwaters. Although the way Aaron had died left silent doubts. Her stomach turned as she pictured Aaron lying cold and bloody on the beach. She remembered how fond of him she had been at one time. Her thoughts drifted to her daughter and she became frightened, thinking what effect it would have on her. Just because Melissa couldn't accept Aaron, didn't necessarily mean she wasn't still in love with him.

Doctor Blair sedated both Allison and Tullah, despite their protests. As Blake led him to the door, he stated, "I'm sorry about Aaron, he was a fine young man. Hopefully they will find out who did it. Are you going to continue to care for the child?"

"Of course, Blake replied, he's part of our family." The doctor patted him on the shoulder, "You're a good man." He put on his hat and coat, leaving instructions regarding the two women. Just as they reached the door, Jonathon appeared with reddened and swollen eyes. He saw the doctor and grabbed Blake, "Is Allison alright?" He knew the twins capability of experiencing each other's pain and sorrow every since they were children, and wondered if Allison had felt Aaron's pain. Both Blake and the doctor assured him she would be all right. Blake put his arm around Jonathon and stated, "The doctor has sedated her. "He cried, "My God, who could do such a thing to Aaron?

That's a question we are all asking Jonathon.

"Do you think Douglas Barnum had anything to do with it?" Blake sighed, "Let's hope not, for everyone's sake."

"Barnum, Dr. Blair questioned?

"Yes, Jonathon replied, he was Aaron's father-in-law." The doctor was silent for a moment and then questioned, "Is Melissa Barnum his daughter?" Both of them nodded their heads. Now, he understood why she had looked so distraught the day Aaron brought Trent in for an exam. "Well, I'll be, he exclaimed, remembering their conversation. Blake questioned him. "Do you know, Melissa?"

"Yes, she's my receptionist. She's been with me just a few weeks, and was there when Aaron brought Trent in for his check-up. Now I know why she was so distraught. He didn't mention the conversation they shared at lunch. "I better get back to the clinic. Allison and Tullah should sleep for a couple of hours, we can't keep sedating them. Sooner or later they're going to have to face Aaron's death, but the initial shock is over." He expressed his sympathy once more before departing.

Jonathon turned to Blake. "Did Aaron say anything about meeting Melissa to you or Allison?" "Not to me, but maybe to Allison. We can question her on it later." Blake then suggested that Jonathon go to her room. "If she awakens, she will want to be with you." He readily agreed, and ran up the stairs to be with her.

When Allison did awake, both Jonathon and Blake were at her bedside. Tears welled up in her deep brown eyes as she questioned them, "What am I going to do without Aaron?" Blake held her hand. "You're going to do what he would want you to do, you will go on living, and raise his son for him. Aaron's left part of himself to us, and for Trent's sake, you will be strong." Jonathon turned away, trying to conceal his misery. Allison asked Blake, "Please bring Trent to me." He nodded and left the room, thankful that she was not asking the details of Aaron's death and dreading the time that she would.

Jonathon," she cried. I knew he was hurt and dying, I felt it. I felt the damp sand and the coldness of his body as his life slipped away." He held her hand firmly, stating he believed her and knew how horrible it must have been for her, while silently wishing she was able to tell them who it was, responsible for Aaron's death.

Blake arrived with Trent and placed him next to Allison. He was awake and appeared to be quite pleased with all the attention. She held him close to her and looked at him. Yes, he did resemble Aaron, except for the green eyes that were his mothers. The threesome stared at him, each silently vowing to protect and care for him.

Tullah sat staring blankly. Her eyes burned and she was sickened at the thought that she might be responsible for Aaron's death. Once again she reminded herself that she was the one he had confided in and she told him to continue living as white. She knew it had been what he wanted to hear, and that he feared admitting he was black. She also knew what being black was like, and had wanted to spare him. She cried out loud, "Lord in heaven, my poor baby." She put her arms around herself and rocked. Grange sat silently across from her, knowing she needed this time, she had lost a child.

Melissa opened the clinic, wondering where the doctor was. She looked through the appointment book, the schedule was small for which she was thankful. She turned the pages back to the date of Trent's appointment and stared at his name. She wondered if he looked like his father. For the short time she was with him, she had observed nothing but his coloring. She remembered how well Aaron looked, standing there in front of her desk, so tall and handsome in a dark grey cashmere overcoat, holding the small bundle protectively against him. Had he transferred his love for her over to the child? She took a deep breath, remembering his shaving lotion and wishing the scent were still lingering in the room. Trying to shake the depression she was suddenly feeling, she looked at her watch. The first appointment wasn't for another half hour. She went to the kitchen and was pleased to see the morning paper and a pot of coffee simmering on the stove. Pouring a cup, she went to the table and sat down, anxious to read the news. The bold headline jumped out at her.

Aaron Marshall Murdered.
Aaron Marshall, found dead, beaten and mutilated.

She read it over several times, unable to comprehend the words. When they did sink in, she became numb all over, and realized it was a feeling that would be with her forever. She too was now dead, a living dead. "Aaaaaron," she screamed his name as if trying to call him back to her, but it was too late, he was gone. She left the clinic in a zombie like trance, passing a client on the way out. He had heard the horrible scream and was baffled by what had caused it. He yelled after her, "Do you need help?" There was no reply as he silently watched her speed away.

The ride home was a blank. All she knew was that in some way or another, her father was involved with Aaron's death and suddenly she hated him. Hated him for all that he had taught her to believe, especially that white was superior. The only thing Aaron had been guilty of was being in love with her, and she took that love and turned it into a sin. Arriving home, she went directly to her room, but not before giving her father a hateful, silent look that told him she knew. Douglas was sure she held him responsible. He also knew Lydia was suspicious.

Lydia was pretty sure of her husband's involvement with Aaron's death in one way or another, even though they had been together all evening. Looking back on that night at The Breakwater, he was extremely tense. He even knocked a tray of drinks out of the waiter's hands. She had asked him outright if he was involved in any way and he denied knowing anything or having any connection to his death. She heard Melissa's arrival and assumed that she had discovered Aaron's death. She went to her room to find her sitting in the bedside chair staring into space, her eyes swollen, un-wiped tears flowed freely down her cheeks, staining the collar of her uniform. "Melissa, "I'm so sorry. I heard the news." In a lifeless voice Melissa replied, "Go away. I need to be alone." Lydia obeyed and returned downstairs.

It was getting late when Lydia decided to bring Melissa up the dinner she had refused earlier. She dished up a small bowl of the evening's stew. Slowly she climbed the stairs that were a constant reminder of just how bad her rheumatism had become. A light knock on the door left her without an answer. Balancing the tray she entered the darkened room and whispered, "Melissa honey, are you awake?" Again there was no answer. Suddenly the dark and stillness created a fear in her as she reached for light and it didn't work. There was a lamp next to the bed. She turned it on. Her scream shot through the house and Douglas as he ran up the stairs, apprehensive as to what he would encounter.

Lydia was on her knees with the spilled tray of food. He followed her horrified stare, to find his daughter hanging from the ceiling fixture. It had broken away, but not enough to prevent her from strangling herself. "Oh, God, no" he cried as he quickly reached for her and removed the long, knotted wool scarf from around her neck. He laid her on the bed, confused. Surely she couldn't have loved Aaron that much, he was a nigger. Unable to revive her, he cried openly. Through his tears, he saw Lydia trying to hand him a note, he reached up and took it. She stood in shock staring at her daughter's lifeless body as he silently read.

Mother and father, you brought me up to believe that God chooses who will be black and who will be white, this is true, but God also chooses who you fall in love with, he is not prejudice I didn't go looking for Aaron, God sent him to me. I took that gift, a sweet, pure love and turned it into something wrong and evil. After receiving still another gift, our child, I refused it also. I pray God will forgive me for my ignorance and let me join Aaron once more. We leave behind a son named Trent, who is now the only living proof of our love. The Donlan's are good people and I know they will take care of him. Please forgive me and may God also forgive you both, for your ignorance.

Love, Melissa

Douglas had mixed feelings as he read. Years of bigotry allowed little, if no room for understanding his daughter's accusations. She was wrong and he was angered. It is a sin for black and whites to mix and God did chose to make whites supreme. Still, the loss of her weighed heavily upon him. He noticed that she had put her wedding ring back on and her hand was clenched. He unfolded it, exposing a small piece of a figurine.

Lydia called Allison, ignoring her husband's objections. She requested that Melissa be buried next to Aaron, stating that "Douglas and I prevented them from being together in life; the least we can do is let them be together in death."

Allison wanted to refuse Lydia, knowing how miserable they had made her brother, but couldn't, knowing Aaron would have wanted Melissa laying next him. He told her many times how difficult it was to sleep without her, now he would sleep peacefully. She had no desire to ever forgive the Barnum's for their bigotry. She felt nothing but disgust for them. Tears filled her eyes once again as she thought of how such a short time ago there had been a double wedding and now there would be a double funeral. Tomorrow, they would bury Aaron and Melissa together.

The procession was one of the largest the area had seen. Allison was thankful for a sunny day. Her parent's funeral had been dark, wet and gloomy. She remembered how everything was so cold, the dampness chilled her and the trees looked bare and lifeless. It was as if everything had died. Today the trees were covered in the colors of autumn and the suns rays filtered through the heavily laden branches, warming her.

Blake stood staring at the two coffins and then glanced over at the expressionless Douglas Barnum, feeling that if he were responsible for Aaron's death, he had paid for it with his daughter's life.

Jonathon bowed his head trying to fight the rage he felt, hoping the preacher's words would console him. After a moment he realized they were of no help. He would be angry until Jonathon's killer was found. He looked up at the caskets and found it so hard to believe that his brother and Melissa were lying cold and lifeless inside, when they both had been so full of love and life at one time.

Douglas and Lydia's eyes never met Allison's or her families. Douglas just wanted it to be over with. He felt the tension and was still upset with Lydia for insisting his daughter be buried next to the Nigger.

Lydia remembered Doug's statement when she suggested Aaron and Melissa should be buried side by side. "Are you supporting her marriage to a nigger? Why the hell don't you just have them buried on top of each other in a single coffin?" The comment sickened her. True, she had been raised in the South, but she could remember her Negro nanny that she loved more than her own mother. It was something she would never admit to, and being a Southerner she had always acted out her part, belief in white supremacy, never truly believing it. That would be a secret she would have to keep forever. She wondered about the grandson she would never hold. In fact, the only grandchild she would ever have, and she cried inwardly. After the services, they quietly departed without and exchange of words.

Back at the house, Allison held Trent close as the town's people expressed their sympathy. She gazed lovingly at him and whispered in his tiny ear, "Blake's right, there's still apart of your father here, in you, I love you." Suddenly, there was a soft whisper in her ear, "I love you." She looked up expecting to see Blake but he wasn't there, he was across the room talking with his father. A warm feeling engulfed her and she smiled. Just as she had felt Aaron's death, she now felt his presence. After all, twins are, inseparable.

Hattie Part 2

CHAPTER 1

Blake smiled with pride as Allison entered the room to join him for breakfast. She was starting to show the signs of her pregnancy. The child growing with-in her seemed to have given her new life. It had been over a year since the deaths of Aaron and Melissa and he was thankful she had their child to look forward to after her devastating loss. The first few months after Aaron's funeral, she became a recluse. Her only activity consisted of daily rides on Charmer, which lasted for hours. She seemed quite content to be only with those close to her, Tullah, Grange, Marshall, Trent, Jonathon and himself. Not that he minded. He just knew it wasn't healthy. She needed to be around others again, especially her two friends Muriel and Bea, who had both tried to talk her out of her self-imposed confinement.

Allison gave Blake a morning kiss before setting herself across from him at the old mahogany table, just as Lillian had done so many times with James.

"How are you this morning?" Blake questioned, knowing that at times morning sickness occurred.

"I feel wonderful, she replied, I felt the baby move this morning for the first time. I think it's going to be a boy."

Blake grinned, "A boy would be a good playmate for Marshall and Trent."

"Yes, but then again, I think we need more women in the house, Tullah and I are out numbered."

"You can say that again," Tullah stated as she entered the room holding Trent. Hopefully you're carrying a sweet little girl child."

"I honestly don't care if it's a boy or a girl," Allison replied. Blake smiled at her and agreed.

"Well, I do, Tullah said, there's enough men in this house." She sat Trent into the highchair next to Allison. He was a year and a half old now and innocently accepted Blake and Allison as his parents. He was a healthy, happy child and resembled Aaron except for his dark coloring and the shocking green eyes of his mother. He received a kiss on the cheek from Allison before receiving a piece of toast.,

Allison exclaimed, "I've decided to go to Berkshires this afternoon and shop for the baby!" The announcement pleased Blake.

"I think that's a great idea. Have Grange drive you, I don't want you driving in your condition, and take Tullah with you, I rather you not be alone." Allison knew better than to argue with Blake in regards to her so-called condition. She learned a long time ago that Blake was dedicated to being her protector. She remembered when he informed her that he refused to re-new the lease to DeLeons because of the way she had been treated. She was shocked and had to plead with him to reconsider. Not that she had any feelings for Kathryn; she just felt it was unjust, knowing her actions mainly stemmed from the loss of Blake. Most the clientele from DeLeons that day had attended the funeral and appeared remorseful, even Kathryn. Her thoughts were broken as Blake stood and announced his departure, stating, "I'll tell Grange to have the car ready for you. When do you want to leave?"

"Give me an hour," she replied as he kissed her goodbye. She watched him exit the room, silently thankful for her blessings. She was happy now, but the loss of Aaron continued to haunt her, part of her was missing, and not even the growth of the child with-in her could eliminate the void. There were moments when he entered her mind and she could feel his presence, which was consoling. Frustration started to consume her as it always did at the thought the murderer had not been found. Blake offered a substantial reward along with the newspapers, but no one claimed it. The police were baffled and finally gave up on Douglas Barnum, he had a solid alibi. There were no other suspects, leaving the unanswered question that plagued her, "Who could have done such a thing to Aaron?" Her thoughts were interrupted as little Marshall came running into the dining room with Tullah close behind, demanding, "You give that roll back to your mama right now." Marshall threw himself on Allison, seeking protection as Trent watched, wide-eyed from his highchair. Allison smiled as she gazed at the angelic face of the two-year old. In his hand was the sweet roll his mother was demanding he return.

"Marshall, Allison said softly, you're mama doesn't want you to have that and I bet it's because you haven't eaten your breakfast."

"That's right," Tullah exclaimed as she tugged the roll from his tiny hand. "He hasn't touched his oatmeal. I swear I love him Allison but he plain wears me out. Surly a girl would be much easier."

"We will find out in a few months," Allison replied as she hugged Marshall, reassuring him that his mama would return the sweet roll to him once he finished his breakfast. Disappointed, he followed his mother back into the kitchen, while listening to her lecture on the importance of the dreaded oatmeal.

"Allison, Allison, her name echoed through Berkshires, it was Vera Edwards. As she approached, Allison noticed a smile on her face, something which hadn't appeared much since the market had crashed. Vera's pale face scanned her before questioning, "My dear, since you're in the maternity department, should I assume you're pregnant?"

"Yes," Allison confirmed the statement. Tullah stepped aside. She, like Dorie, didn't care for the woman, and the small insignificant glance she received from her reinforced the feeling.

"Well, my dear, congratulations, when is the baby due?" While asking the question, Vera silently wondered if the child would be born black, like Aarons was, even though having Negro blood mixed into his own was obviously not a matter of concern to Blake Donlan.

"March," Allison replied, then changed the subject. "I hear the hotel is doing quite well."

"Yes, as a matter of fact, she stated proudly, it's full right now." Allison hesitated a moment before asking how Gerald was. Vera wished she could say he was well, but she could not, Gerald had become a drunken recluse, that's all there was to it. "Let me put it this way Allison, Gerald has never overcome the loss of his wife. He stays pretty much alone these days."

"I'm sorry to hear that," Allison replied, surprised that Gerald would be mourning, especially after his actions at Annabelle's funeral. Vera placed a small peck on Allison's cheek, "I must be running. I'm on way to the Women's Club for a game of Mah Jong, but had to stop here first, to replace some linen's for the hotel. Do take care Allison, and so nice to see you." She watched Vera walk away, still dwelling on what she had said about Gerald.

Tullah shook her lightly stating they had best get their shopping completed, "Marshall and Trent are going to be crying for us pretty soon." Allison smiled and replied, "Your right and that reminds me, Blake wants me to start looking for a nanny. He feels I'll need help. Would you be interested in giving up your position as head servant to become the children's nanny?" Tullah's eyes lit up for a moment before having to state,

"I can't think of anything else I rather do but I don't think Grange would be happy with having to sleep alone. I would have to be next to the nursery."

"I'm sorry Tullah, I hadn't thought about that." After a moment, Allison excitedly exclaimed, "I know what we can do. We can turn Dorie's room into the nursery. It will be small but will do for some time, and you, Grange and Marshall can have my old room, it's about the size of the one your in now. How does that sound?"

"Sound good to me," Tullah exclaimed. The thought of putting her energy into the raising of the children pleased her. Dorie flashed through her mind. She had learned much from her through the years while raising the twins and Jonathon, leaving her with a secure feeling that she was qualified for the job. They continued on with their shopping and after purchasing several new maternity dresses and miscellaneous baby supplies, the twosome headed home.

Vera climbed the steps to the hotel, enjoying the sign that read, No Vacancy. Even though her patrons were not of the upper class, she was thankful at this point for the few people that had the couple of dollars she requested for a nights stay. She always tried to convince herself that it would one day become her home again. She still damned Edward for his stupidity and shuddered each time she saw him behind the teller's cage at the bank. He seemed to be content, which she found impossible to understand. The words, pathetic and fool, slipped from her as she entered the lobby. She went to the desk to see if there were any massages.

Gerald entered the room, reeking of gin and rubbing his eyes. She looked at the clock. It was three o'clock in the afternoon and obvious that he was just waking up from another one of his drunken sleeps.

"Gerald, what do you want and why are you here in the lobby?" His head swayed as he observed his surroundings.

"Oh, is this what it's supposed to be? Well all I can say is, I've seen a hell of a lot better lobby's in my day. Did you know, Annabelle, God rest her damn soul, always made sure we stayed at the best hotels?" Vera observed her son with disgust, repelled by his odor.

"Yes, Gerald, you have told me that many times over, but that was yesterday and this is now. I plead with you, get yourself together. There still must be some older, rich,

women that would be interested in you!" Gerald looked at her through blurred eyes. He didn't want another old lady, even if she were rich. He wanted a rich, young one and Allison was now, both. He didn't even care if she did have Negro blood in her as long as she had the money. Slurring through a gin, numbed tongue, he informed his mother he had a plan. Shocked, that he was ever sober enough to plan anything she questioned,

"Oh and what might that be?"

"Allison, I'm going to have Allison," he replied, with an arrogant look appearing on his face. Vera held back a sarcastic laugh before replying, "Have you forgotten, that Allison is now a married woman and I just found out this afternoon, she's pregnant." She seems very happy without you, Gerald. Why should she be interested in you? What do you have to offer her that Blake Donlan can't give her?"

"Me, he replied, I know she still desires me, after all, she's married to a man almost ten years older than herself, I know how that goes." Vera wondered if Gerald had looked in a mirror lately. Sadly, she told herself, alcohol had deteriorated the once handsome man. She remarked, "Forget it Gerald, both you and your father are losers."

He tried to compose himself on wobbly legs before replying, "True, possibly father, but not me. He lost his money but I haven't lost my looks. That alone, can get me anything I want." Unable to contain herself any longer, Vera screamed, "For Gods sake Gerald, sober up and look in a mirror." He stood there trying to comprehend what it was she met as she walked away. He returned to his room, wondering why he had left it in the first place. He poured himself a drink and walked over to the mirror hanging over the small, neglected sink. He blinked several times, finding it hard to distinguish the image staring back at him. Looking closer, he faced the sheer horror of realizing the bloated, puffy eyed stranger was himself. He turned on the faucet and washed his face, hoping it would erase the terrible image. No, it was still there. Not only had he lost two fortunes, now his looks had vanished. He wasn't even sure how long the transition had taken, he'd lost track of time. He threw the glass of gin at the depressing image. The glass shattered but the mirror did not. Picking up a piece of broken glass, he considered swiping it across his wrist. It would be easy, just two quick slashes. He took a deep breath and raised the shattered piece and let it ride across the first wrist, releasing the pressure as it hit. "No, he told himself, don't do it. You can get both your looks and money back." He set down the piece of blood tainted shard of glass and vowed, "I will regain both."

The months passed quickly for Allison. Blake remodeled the nursery, allowing room for several children as well as spacious, connecting living quarters for Tullah and her family. The first pain alerted her as she sat in the parlor reading a long awaited book by Fitzgerald. After another few minutes, another pain gripped her. Before informing Tullah, she went to the mantle and picked up the silver framed picture of Trilly. She held it in her hand and prayed that she would be with her at this time. She pictured Dorie trying desperately to help Trilly deliver her and Aaron into the world without the help of a physician. She corrected herself, Roosevelt and Hattie. A tear dropped onto the photo as once more she realized that they had robbed Trilly of her young life. She wiped the tear away and called for Tullah.

The delivery went well and Allison, much to her surprise, delivered a daughter. She had been so sure it would be a boy. She smiled, knowing how happy Tullah would be. Blake, his parent's and Jonathon had taken turns pacing the waiting room floor. Elliott Donlan was silently praying the baby would be born concealing its Negro blood. He convinced himself that he would accept his grandchild whatever color it might be, smiling at the possibility he just might be teaching a black child, Gaelic and Irish history. A nurse entered the room and announced Allison had delivered a healthy baby girl. Elliott looked her in the face, hoping to tell if she was trying to conceal anything about the baby, it didn't appear so. He sighed, a breath of relief, feeling she surly would have shown some signs of shock if the infant were black. He threw his arms around Blake. "Congratulations son." Jonathon shook his hand. "Hurry up and go in there so we can have our turn, there's two grandparents and an uncle here anxious to meet her"

Blake grinned and followed the nurse eagerly to Allison's room. His heart sank when he saw her. She looked so weak and pale. The nurse, noticing his concern assured him she was all right, just tired.

Allison held the newborn close to her as he approached. He leaned down and admired her as Allison stated, "Meet our daughter." He touched the tiny colored hand before remarking, "I didn't know if we were going to have a black or white child, it appears we got a red one." Allison laughed outwardly. "Yes, we did. I promise you Blake, the red will go away. He held both their hands and replied, I guess I have another rose to watch bloom. I would like to call her Rose, if you agree."

Allison repeated the name, "Rose Donlan," "Yes, I think it's a perfect name for her."

Jonathon, Elliott and Molly stood at the observation window, staring at the child. She was perfect and as white as her mother, much to the viewer's relief. Jonathon gazed at her, comparing the difference between her and Trents births. His heart went out to his nephew, who had come into the world rejected by both his mother and grandparents. He was also aware of how the two children's lives would differ, because of color. That was unless the world changed drastically in the next few years, which he sorrowfully doubted.

Tullah anxiously awaited for Blake to hand her Rose. He stated with a grin, "I hope you're happy now with three females in the house."

"You bet I am Mr. Donlan, thank you." She looked at Rose snuggled asleep in the pink blanket she had knitted while insisting that Allison would have a girl. Like everyone else, for the child's sake, she was thankful Rose had fair skin even though she realized as long as she had black blood in her, she would always be considered Negro by the outsiders who knew. The years ahead held many fears for Tullah, not for herself, but for her wards and her son. She prayed for guidance as she brought Rose up to the nursery.

Blake took Allison to their room, instructing her to rest. Before leaving, he kissed her and confessed, "To carry this much love inside of me is almost overwhelming. I love you so much Allison and now you've given me Rose, I pray, I'm deserving of this!"

She returned the kiss and smiled, while holding a scarred hand in hers, a lump began to swell in her throat and she replied, "Believe me Blake, like everything else you do, you earned it."

Trent and Rose slept comfortably in the cribs that Roosevelt and Hattie once occupied. Tullah arranged the blankets around them securely and then checked to make sure the fire would make it through the night. The winter seemed to be lasting longer than usual and she was anxious for the new radiator, steam heating system that Mr. Donlan had promised to install.

"Come to bed Tullah, the babies are just fine and you need your sleep," Grange demanded from the adjoining room. She sighed, it had been a long day, not just a long day but a long few months, waiting for Roses birth. She could sleep easier now. Her eyes rested on Trent. She was thankful for his infant innocence and dreaded the day; he would eventually have to enter the world he really belonged in. Returning to her room she checked Marshall, who was asleep on the small bed next to hers. She looked lovingly at the cherub face and small hand that appeared to still be clenching a sweet roll. Tucking him in, she started humming, "Hush little baby, don't you cry." As she did so, it left her wondering how many tears he would shed in his lifetime. The death of Aaron had changed her. She knew now, more than ever, being black in the white world was dangerous. She questioned, whether her and Grange should leave the Donlan's, and return to the black community for her baby's sake, and take Trent with them? She didn't want to, this was their home. Wearily, she crawled into bed next to Grange, thankful for the warmth of his body. Before drifting off to sleep, she decided time would let her know when and if they would have to leave.

It was a warm and humid night, just as Lydia had remembered it. They sat in their wicker rockers on the wrap around porch, back in Montgomery. Douglas had finally received the job transfer he requested. Both had been eager to escape San Francisco, hoping it would help erase the tragic memories. Very few words were spoken as they rocked; each lost in their own thoughts.

Douglas re-lived his long awaited meeting with his cousin Dexter. He had yelled, "You stupid son-of-a-bitch, why did you kill him?"

"We didn't kill him, Dexter yelled back. We untied him and told him to get help before he bled to death. The nigger was just too stupid to do it." Douglas let loose of his cousin's collar and apologized. As of yet, the police hadn't discovered who was responsible and he felt free and clear of any suspicion they might have had about him. He also had to compliment Dexter and his accomplice on the fact, they went completely unnoticed. Even the offer of a reward from both the paper and Blake brought no one forward.

Lydia still doubted her husband's innocence regarding the death of Aaron. As she rocked, her mind drifted back to San Francisco and the grandchild she would never hold. She would never share with him the calming effects the rocking chair provided. Closing her eyes, she tried to feel the warmth of him snuggled against her. She no longer cared what color he was, she just wanted her grandson, but knew it was forbidden and that her arms would remain forever empty.

CHAPTER 2

Blake witnessed the two boys playing with Rose tagging along behind. They were growing fast and he knew the time was getting near to start making decisions regarding their education. At the dinner table that night he informed Allison he had made a decision, the boys would not attend school in the black community. He was obtaining a tutor and eventually Rose would be included in the classes. The children would not be separated until it was absolutely necessary. Both Allison and Tullah were pleased with the decision, as Blake exclaimed, "I think it will be in their best interests until they reach high school age. I've hired a Mr. Milton, he will be their tutor."

Avery Milton arrived at the Donlan household eager to teach. He was thankful for the opportunity to concentrate on just two students instead of a filled classroom. The door opened and a servant led him to the parlor, there he met with Allison. He had already met and had an interview with Mr. Donlan at the office before being hired. He admired her beauty as she stood to greet him.

"Mr. Milton, I can't tell you how glad we are to have you with us. The boy's are anxious to meet you." He expressed his eagerness to meet them as well, and begin their classes. Tullah entered the room with the boys and Allison went to them. "Mr. Milton, this is Marshall and Trent." He stood speechless, staring at them. Allison realized his shock and questioned, "Didn't my husband tell you?"

"No, he didn't. Walking over to the boys, he shook their hands and informed them that he promised to make his classes fun and interesting. Their smiles and enthusiasm returned his eagerness to teach. As Tullah led them from the room, he apologized to Allison. "I wasn't prepared, I didn't know they were Negro, but I want you to understand all I want is to teach children, color makes no difference."

Allison replied, "No, Mr. Milton, you don't owe an apology. My husband tends to forget the boys are colored. It is so typical of him not to mention it. The oldest is Marshall, Tullah's son. She's the children's nanny and considered family. The youngest boy, Trent, is my nephew. It's obvious, your one of the few people in the Bay area that hasn't heard the story of the Marshall twins." He hadn't and admitted to himself, he would like to know it. Allison continued, "We have a daughter, Rose, eventually, in a couple of years, you will be teaching her also." A servant entered with the teacart, and poured them each a cup of tea. They discussed classes and when he should start. After the hour was up, it was decided the sooner the better, tomorrow his teaching would begin.

"Is that man going to teach us how to read and write mama," Marshall asked as he and Trent ate their lunches."

"He is, but you have to be good students to learn how. Especially you Marshall, you're going to have to sit still for once." She sighed and watched as he squirmed in his chair. "Lord, child, I wonder if that's possible!"

Avery was delighted with the boys, tutoring them was sheer joy. In their eagerness to learn, he moved them along more quickly than normal. Both were well he mannered and required little discipline for their ages. The only problem he had was Marshall's habit of tapping his fingers constantly. It was extremely distracting. Often, Trent would beg, "Marshall, don't do that, I can't think." He came to the conclusion that a piano would help teach Marshall to sit and relax as well as conquer the finger tapping habit. It worked, as soon as the Donlan's brought a piano into the house Marshall settled down. All it took was an hour's worth of piano lessons daily, before class. He had a natural talent for music, often attempting to create his own. Avery was an accomplished pianist himself and marveled at Marshall's gift. After several weeks of music lessons, he left him on his own.

Trent was always inquisitive. He excelled in history and was especially fascinated with slavery. He would dwell on it and eventually Avery would have to push him into the next lesson, assuming the six year old would be more than happy to dedicate all his time to just that subject.

Every now and then, the four- year old child Rose would visit the classroom with her mother. Trent would continue on with his studies, but to Marshall, she was an immediate distraction. Allison felt Rose needed exposure to the classroom to prepare her for when she would eventually attend schooling. Next year, she would be five and sitting in permanently.

Both Blake and Allison were pleased with the way Avery Milton handled the children. He was a gifted teacher and his dedication to the children would remain continuos throughout their school years.

The car moved slowly along the crowded street. Grange, with permission, was taking Marshall and Trent on an excursion to the black community, all agreed that they needed the exposure. The boys were fascinated seeing so many people with skin the color of theirs. They were also shocked to see how they lived. Marshall became concerned and questioned as he looked out the car's window, "We're like them papa, shouldn't we be living here too?"

Grange pulled the car to the curb and parked it before grabbing his son by the shoulders. He looked him straight in the face, and replied in a stern but soft voice, "No son, we shouldn't be living here and either should they. No one should live like this but they have no choice, we do. Not only do these people have to face the depression just like everyone else, jobs are limited for them in even in the best of times. Even if they had lots of money, they're not allowed in the white community and there is nowhere else for them to go."

Trent, questioned, "Why don't the white people want to share with them like Uncle Blake and Aunt Allison do with us?" Aunt Allison always tells us it's nice to share."

Grange's large hands cupped Trent's face; and a pair of jade green eyes awaited his answer. What could he say to him? He finally replied, "Someday, maybe, the whites will learn to share." He sighed with relief when the boy accepted his statement without further questioning. Marshall sat quietly, still contemplating the fact that they should probably be there instead of at the Donlan's.

Grange exclaimed, "Lets go home, I smelled a batch of cookies baking when we left." He drove away knowing it was only the first trip to the black community, there would be many more. He knew the day was coming when he and Tullah would have to return with their son and more than likely bring Trent with them.

On their return home, Tullah met them and frantically took Grange aside.

"Allison is in the stables. Charmer is down, go see if you can help." Grange rushed down the path leading to the stables. Allison was trying to persuade Charmer to get up. She pleaded, "C'mon girl, you can do it." All she received was a slight whining from her horse, as it struggled to raise its head. Jake knew the horse would never stand again and the scene broke his heart. He prayed silently, that the vet would get there soon and put the poor horse out of its misery." Grange entered the stall and tried to comfort Allison.

Moments later, to their relief, Blake rushed into the stable. Allison threw herself into his arms, seeking protection from the inevitable, exclaiming, "Blake, I don't want Charmer to suffer but I can't bear the thought of being without her. What can we do?"

He held her close, not wanting to discourage her before the vet's diagnosis, replying, "Wait and see what Dr. Kleary has to say, then we will decide what to do." She pulled away from him and returned to Charmer. Once more, she stroked the long silk neck, trying to give her horse what comfort she could.

After what seemed forever, Dr. Kleary entered the stable, missing his characteristic smile. He was a small middle aged man with dark hair and blue eyes that now lacked the usual Irish twinkle, verifying the fact he had missed sleep.

"Sorry for my delay, he stated, my car had a flat tire on the way, how long has she been down?"

Jake replied, "I'm not sure, I found her this way when I came into the stable this morning, she was fine when I left last night. I tried to get her up but she refused." Kleary opened his satchel and began examining the beautiful mare. The threesome watched intently, awaiting a diagnosis. Another small whine was heard from Charmer. It was as though she was trying to explain something to the doctor as she tried raising her head. Her large, dark eyes were filled with pain.

Dr. Kleary rose and exclaimed, "I'm sorry Allison, but Charmer has to be put down, she's suffering and there's nothing I can do, she has a twisted gut." Both Jake and Grange had guessed the situation but held out hopes they might be wrong. They watched sadly as Allison threw herself over her horse, sobbing and declaring her love.

After a few moments, Blake reached down to her exclaiming, "Allison, I'm so sorry but you mustn't let Charmer suffer any longer, come back up to the house with me." In a daze, she followed him, knowing there would never be another ride along the bay with her best friend. They returned to the house, and a few minutes later, Allison heard the shot that relieved her beloved mare of its pain. Once again, she had lost a loved one. Quietly, she said, "Goodbye my Charmer."

Business was thriving at DeLeons and Kathryn was grateful Blake had changed his mind and renewed her lease, but not without informing her first, that it was only because Allison requested he do it. She had learned a lesson, Blake proved to her what a helpless feeling it was when you lose control over situations regarding your future. Total fear had engulfed her at the thought of losing her business if she could no longer reside at the prestigious location, and would have to move the lower class section of town. That was four years ago and Allison still had yet to return to DeLeons. Word was she would go on a shopping spree several times a year in Monterey. These trips made her wardrobe the talk of the town. Kathryn had seen her out with Blake several times and admired her appearance. She marveled that Allison managed to maintain a youthful figure after her pregnancy. Kathryn walked over to one of the full length-mirrors to assure herself she too had remained shapely. Pleased with the image, she wondered why she was still unwed. Surly someone should have replaced Blake for her by this time. A shrill voiced customer requesting a dress one size larger, distracted the image of him in her mind, and she silently cursed the woman.

Chapter 3

    From the terrace, Allison observed the children playing in the gardens. They appeared to be having a tea party. Rose, now nine was being indulged by the boys. Both Marshall and Trent were responsible for spoiling her, especially Marshall, he was totally dedicated to her. She remembered the time Rose had wandered off into the stables when she was only three. Marshall was grooming one of the mares when he noticed her. She was behind the horse, preparing to pull its tail. He yelled at her and pushed her aside just before the spooked horse bucked, hitting him in the back. He lay on the ground with the wind knocked out of him, gasping for breath. Rose cried, waiting for him to get up. A few minutes later he pulled himself up and walked her back to the house. He told his mother what had happened, only because a painful tear had left a stain mark on his face, leaving her to question him. A doctor was called and he was diagnosed to have a couple broken ribs, aside from being badly bruised.

    Only for Rose's sake, Marshall sipped the dreadful tasting tea, thankful there was a small cookie to help him swallow the brew. He would do anything for her. He loved her as far back as he could remember. At thirteen, he dreamed that someday she would grow to love him as much. "I'll wait no matter how long it takes," he told himself as he watched the elegant young lady pour Trent his tea.

    Trent adored his cousin and like Marshall, he too drank from the dainty cup she handed him. There were times he questioned their relationship due to the difference in their coloring. He remembered what his Aunt Allison told him when he asked about it. "It's hereditary, you inherited your great grandmother Dorie's coloring and your mother's green eyes, just as Rose inherited my brown eyes and coloring." It still confused him, this heredity thing. Why wasn't he white like his parent's picture on the mantle? Another thing that had left him curious was the death of his parents. He was told they were taken away tragically, that's all they would say. Once he looked up the word tragic in the dictionary and even more confusing words stared at him from the page, catastrophe, suffering, tribulation. The words were frightening, leaving him sure he wasn't ready to hear the whole story. Someday when Aunt Allison felt he was ready he knew he would be told.

"Want some more tea Trent," Rose asked hopefully. He replied, no thanks, but I'll take another cookie."

Tullah rounded up the children, announcing it was time to return to Mr. Milton in the library and continue their lessons. She chuckled to herself as Rose moaned a protest over the interruption of the tea party, while the two boys sighed with relief. She knew the time was getting close for her and Grange to return back to the black community with the two boys. The Donlan's had secured one of the finest houses available there and improved on it, plus there would be a generous monthly income for them. Even so, she dreaded their return. She would once again have to leave what she considered home, but it was time for Marshall and Trent to enroll in the black school, even Mr. Milton agreed. He would still teach Rose, until it was time for her to go to finishing school.

Allison returned her attention back to her needlework. The last few years had been good to her. They had been peaceful ones, watching the children grow. Her only regret was the miscarriage she suffered, preventing her from having more children. Now, the world was in turmoil. The Japanese had bombed Pearl Harbor. A twinge a fear swept over her. Jonathon had been drafted. As of yet, he was still in the states but it was questionable, for how long. She sighed as she watched the black thread follow the needle back and forth through the white fabric as she monogrammed the cuffs of Blake's shirt.

Just as James Marshall had done so many years ago, Blake sat at his desk reminiscing. He had added three more floors to the building which now put his office high atop the fifth floor, providing an exceptional view of the bay. He realized that it wasn't the bay this time causing his restless mood, but its occupants, it was filled with battleships. The draft had been executed and men ages twenty-one through thirty-six were being called upon for service. He was beyond draft age but could no longer endure the view from his window. He made the decision to volunteer.

"No, how could you even think of doing this to us," Allison shouted in disbelief at Blake. He looked at the hurt on her face and replied in a soft but determined voice.

DYANN WEBB

"I can't explain it other than I feel the need to join. Everyday, I look out at the bay and see all those ships with those men on them, going to fight for our country and ask "How can I just sit here and watch? He held her close hoping that she would understand what he had said. In a child-like frightened voice, she finally replied, "There is nothing I can do to make you change your mind is there?"

"No," he answered, holding her even closer. She cried, "Oh Blake, I love you so much. What would I do if you never came back to me?"

"We can't live, fearing the words, what if? Think, of all the things we wouldn't have accomplished if we feared those two words. I love you and Rose and I can only promise you that I will do everything in my power to return, the rest will be up to God."

Her heart quickened. She believed that God had nothing to do with her losses, everything was destiny, leaving her fearing, was she forever destined to lose her loved ones?

Gerald couldn't believe his luck. He was exempt from the draft for having, of all things, flat feet. As far as he was concerned, he was long overdue in the luck department. For the last few years he felt he had already been through combat, fighting his alcoholism. Rumor was that Blake Donlan had volunteered for duty, which pleased Gerald. Blake had two pieces of property he wanted, the land on cannery row and Allison. With him out of the picture, he just might be able to obtain both. He looked into the mirror with pride. Not only had he not had a drink for several years, he had completely renovated his mother's house, turning it into one of the bay areas finest hotels. The gifts he received from Annabelle, the polo pony, diamond rings and his car were all cashed in and spent on turning the Mediterranean style house into a hotel much like the ones he had experienced while in Spain. The basics were all there. The tiled roof, stucco exterior and acreage. Most the work he had done himself, except for the wrought iron verandas that allowed the guests to enjoy the view from their second and third story rooms. The bank happily agreed to lend his mother the money to add a third floor, after seeing how successful the hotel had become. Prestigious clients and profits were now steady. He raised the comb to his hair and was pleased the way his biceps enlarged as he bent his arm. His body was muscular and firmer than it had ever been. The labor that had gone into landscaping was responsible for the transition. It took him over two years to complete the grounds and gardens. There were times he ached so bad and was so tired his instincts were to have a drink to kill the pain, but he didn't. Now, he was ready to build his next hotel and hopefully it would be on the cannery row property.

Allison tried to curb her depression. It was time for Marshall and Trent to leave the safe confinement of their home and attend school. They were ready to meet the challenges the school would offer them, thanks to Avery Milton. Rose would continue her lessons with him until she turned thirteen, then she would be sent to Blessed Sacrament. The time was coming for the children to meet the real world and she feared for them but knew they couldn't be protected forever. She turned her attention back to the letter on her lap and read once again how much Blake loved and missed her and Rose. He expressed how he longed for the comfort of home and the warmth of her body next to his at night. He stated that the evenings, when they were not in combat were the worst. It allowed too much time to think while sitting in the cold, dark trenches. She noticed that never once had he mentioned regretting his decision. She still resented the fact he had enlisted but at the same time felt proud of him.

"Allison," Muriel's voice filled the air and she set the letter aside once more. Muriel gave her a hug and noticed the military stationary and questioned, "How is he doing?"

"As well as can be expected," Allison replied.

"I've been thinking Allison, the Red Cross could really use some help, especially at the canteen. Why don't you come and serve coffee and donuts to the boys?" The request left her silent.

"C'mon Allison, Muriel begged, it will be good for you." She awaited an answer. After a moments thought, Allison replied, I guess it would feel good to do something to participate, in some way during this war."

"Good, then it's settled, Muriel exclaimed with delight. Meet me at the canteen tomorrow morning."

"Tomorrow, that soon," Allison questioned?

"Yes, that soon. We need to spoil these boys as much and as long as possible before they get shipped out." A surge of excitement filled Allison as she agreed to be there.

Allison arrived at the navel base as scheduled. The guard at the gate questioned her. "Do you have a pass?" Taken by surprise, she replied, "I'm a Red Cross volunteer!" The statement didn't sway him. "I'm sorry lady, without a pass I can't let you in." Allison suggested that he call the canteen and ask for Muriel. He did as requested and returned with a smile, informing her to proceed and thanking her for volunteering.

He watched as she drove away, telling himself, he would definitely go to the canteen when off duty.

Muriel greeted her with a smile. "I'm sorry Allison, I should have left your name at the gate, but I forgot." You'll understand why I forgot once you start helping out, there's so much to do." Allison assured her she understood.

"Well, Muriel stated, put this apron on and start pouring coffee, but let me warn you, you'll get all kinds of propositions, don't take them personally. These boys are going off to war and become panicky, thinking that you're possibly the last female they will ever see again."

Allison put on the crisp, white apron and picked up the coffeepot. She was nervous at first and her hand shook slightly as she poured the first cup for a young man. He was oblivious to her shaking as he wrote a letter. She took a quick glance as she poured and realized that it was a love letter. The next young man smiled and thanked her. Before long, she was chatting with the soldiers and truly enjoying herself, but Muriel's words hung heavily over her, "We have to spoil them as much as possible before they get shipped out." A lump formed in her throat as she poured a redheaded young man with freckles, another cup of coffee, wondering if he would survive the war. He grinned and thanked her, then asked if she was going to attend the dance Friday. The question took her by surprise as she observed the anxious look on his face, waiting for a reply. She asked, "What dance?"

"Aren't you with the Red Cross?"

"Yes, she answered, but this is my first day."

"Oh, he said, the Red Cross puts on a dance for the servicemen every Friday night. I hope you will be there, I'd sure like a dance with you" Allison hesitated before answering then surprising herself by stating she would be there. A large grin covered his face, and he requested, "Be sure and save a dance for me. She promised him she would. The day went by fast and Allison hadn't realized how tired she was until she arrived home. She took a long, hot bath and relived the day's experience. Muriel was pleased when she told her she would attend the dance Friday, exclaiming, "Good for you Allison, the more time you can volunteer the better." Refreshed, she sat down at her desk to write Blake.

Muriel was elated that Allison was involved with the canteen. She adjusted her thick glasses as she went over the list of the wounded and dead that the Red Cross received daily. Once again, she prayed Blake Donlan's name wouldn't appear. She always found it hard to breathe until she got past the D- list. More than often the Red Cross would receive the news before the next of kin. Exhaling, she silently thanked God once more, that Blake Donlan was not listed.

The picture on her desk smiled back at her, Chad and their two children, Daniel and Patricia. Never in a million years could she have ever guessed she would be so blessed. As far as she was concerned, if not for the

Donlan's, none of this happiness would have been hers. She shuddered at the thought of her once dreary life. A moan from down the hospital corridor pulled her from her thoughts and she rushed down the hall to attend a young soldier who had returned to the states, minus a leg.

It was the night of the dance. Allison stood in front of the mirror critiquing one of the many dresses she had tried on. She wanted to look nice, not too conservative, and be careful not to appear seductive and provoke a young mans lust. In just the few days she had spent at the canteen she found the men had one thing on their minds as, Muriel had warned, and it wasn't the war. She removed the deep green dress, feeling it was to form fitting. The previous dress showed too much cleavage, leaving her to finally settle on the navy blue one. It had a rounded collar-less neckline. She added an ornamental gold pin to the shoulder, shoulder pads were popular and the pin helped accentuate the fashion statement. After piling her hair on top her head, she added a pair matching gold earrings. Silk stockings were no longer available so she had painted her legs with the newfound pancake make-up, choosing to eliminate the false seam some women would draw down the backs of their legs. Putting on her ankle strap heels, she took a final glimpse in the mirror and decided she was perfectly dressed for the occasion.

On her arrival, she felt awkward, out of place. She never attended an event that was strictly for dancing. Always, it had been dining and dancing, with someone accompanying her. The band was playing Glenn Miller and cigarette smoke filled the room, a smell she had become adjusted too from working the canteen. She glanced around anxiously, searching for Muriel, she was nowhere in sight and neither was Bea. Muriel had said they both would be there. The young soldier with the freckles appeared and his smile calmed her. "I'm glad you made it, he exclaimed, may I have this dance?" Allison accepted and followed him onto the floor. He put his arms around her and for a moment she became very uncomfortable at being held so close, leaving her to wonder just how much longer it would be before she would be in her husbands arms again, if ever. She spotted, Bea and Muriel, they both were dancing. By the time the song ended another soldier was eagerly waiting for a turn.

After half a dozen dances Allison finally met up with Muriel. They watched Bea dancing with an officer. "She's in love," Muriel exclaimed, she met him at the last dance and he's being shipped out tomorrow." Allison felt a combination of joy and sadness for her friend. The dance ended and Bea brought the officer to them.

"Muriel, you already know Mitchell, now Allison, I want you to meet him." He stepped forward in a military manor, extending his hand to her, stating, "Bea has talked so much about you, I already feel we have met." Allison wondered just how much she had told him as she accepted his hand. He was tall and extremely handsome. Bea hugged both her and Muriel, and stated excitedly, "Were getting married in the morning. Will you please be there, it will be in the small chapel, on base?"

Allison and Muriel looked at each other and then back at Bea. "Of course we will," they agreed in unison.

By the end of the evening, Allison's feet were aching as she listened to Muriel suggest that she give herself a foot -bath when she got home. The drive home left Allison deep in thought. They were to meet Bea and Mitchell at the base church in the morning at ten o'clock. After the ceremony, the newly weds would only have a couple of hours together. She worried for her friend, questioning if Bea really had time to fall in love with this man. Was she just feeling the pressure of having to make a quick decision because of the war, fearing the possibility that he wouldn't return, after all, they had only known each other for a week. She questioned herself, could people really fall in love that fast? She remembered how long it took her to recognize her love for Blake. Remembering upset her, realizing the time she could have had with him as well as the time she was now losing. Her heart fell, once more she had to convince herself that he would return and they would have the rest of their lives together. She pulled into the driveway, anxious for the suggested foot- bath, Muriel had recommended.

The next morning Allison and Muriel witnessed Bea and Mitchell exchange wedding vows. With such short preparation, Bea had chosen to wear her favorite floral dress. There were no flowers other than a corsage. She looked so small standing next to the six foot two Mitchell, in his dress whites. Once again Allison concerned herself wondering if all this was too fast, even though Muriel had brought to her attention that Bea was pushing thirty and had expressed her desire to be wed for several years and had turned down a couple offers of marriage. She observed the look on Bea's face as she said, "I, do." It was the true look of love. Allison held back a tear, praying for their happiness and his safe return. After the ceremony the newly weds departed immediately, desiring to be alone for the short time they're allowed.

Gerald put on his best attire. This was the day he would attempt to see Allison and hopefully get her to convince Blake to sell him the cannery row property he needed for his new hotel. Five years had been lost in a sea of booze and the next few were spent on renovating his mother's hotel. He hadn't seen Allison personally for almost ten years, purposely staying away until he felt he was presentable and successful enough to approach her. Nearing the familiar Marshall house, anxiety struck him as he remembered the things he had said to Allison, when she declared her love, and wondered if she still loved him. He understood the way she treated him at Annabelle's funeral, after all he had been drunk.

"Mrs. Donlan, there's a Mr. Gerald Edwards here to see you." Allison's heart quickened as she asked herself, "Gerald, what would possibly bring him to her after all these years?" The maid stood silent, awaiting a reply.

"Send him to the den please and tell him I will join him in a few minutes." She left with the message, silently wondering why the den and not the parlor.

Allison paced a few moments. She purposely wanted Gerald in the den, hoping he would feel Blake's presence. She inspected herself in the mirror over the mantle, took a deep breath and went to meet with him.

Gerald observed his surroundings. A large hand carved desk stood in front of the leaded window. A dark leather chair sat empty behind it. He opened a cigar box to find several Cuban cigars, leaving him to wonder if they were saved for special occasions, such as a new real estate purchase. A map of the area hung on the wall, red highlights indicated what Gerald assumed were Donlan properties. Envy flooded through him. Observing it closer, he spotted the land at cannery row.

"Gerald," the soft voice reached his ears. He turned to face her and his heart quickened, she had grown even more beautiful, which he hadn't thought possible. She was no longer a girl but a woman. He cleared his throat, hoping the words would come out.

"Allison, so much time has gone by and you have only improved. I can't tell you how nervous I've been, contemplating this meeting."

The statement confused Allison and she questioned, "Why would you ever be nervous meeting with me Gerald?" He stammered, "Because of things I once said to you."

Allison exclaimed, "You need not worry about things that were said when we were so young. I put those words aside a long time ago. I just hope you have overcome the bitterness you obtained after the market crashed." Gerald considered her statement for a moment. No, he would always be bitter, the crash not only robbed him as heir to a fortune it robbed him of his youth. He broke his silence with a lie, "Like you Allison, I've buried the past." He silently laughed, telling himself, the only thing he actually buried was Annabelle.

Allison accepted the lie and replied, "I'm glad to hear that Gerald. Now, what brings you here after all this time"? Once more he cleared his throat.

"I've come to see about purchasing the property on cannery row, I want to build a hotel on it."

Allison remained silent for a moment before stating, "Gerald, I have nothing to do with Blake's properties, you'll have to deal with his father Elliott. I'm impressed with what you have done with your mother's hotel, as most people are. You've turned it into a landmark." Gerald relished in her praise exclaiming, "Thank you Allison, but I know I can build one even bigger and better, I just need the right property, could you put in a word for me to Elliott?"

"I don't really know how much good it will do, but I'll be more than happy to mention your interest in the land." Gerald smiled and her heart did a sudden flip, as she momentarily saw the Gerald from their youth.

"I won't take anymore of your time Allison and I just want you to know, I've missed you." Shaken, she said, "That's nice to know Gerald." She told him she would talk with her father-in-law about his idea for a hotel on the property. He gave her a gentle kiss on the cheek before leaving.

The kiss lingered as Allison watched from the window. He got into his car and drove away. She was surprised. She had expected him to look much older, due to his known use of alcohol, instead, he looked extremely handsome and mature. She couldn't help but notice how his body had filled out. His hair was blonder than she remembered, probably from exposure to the sun, based on his tanned skin. He had truly come along way and she would do the best she could to help him. The property he wanted was now all Blakes, Elliott had given his half to them as a wedding gift. She went to the phone and called her father-in-law.

Elliott dropped everything as he always did whenever Allison called or needed him in any way. He listened as she explained her visit from Gerald.

"So, he's interested in buying that piece of property, is he? Well, I don't think Blake has ever intended to sell it. I assume this Gerald fellow will be getting in contact with me fairly soon."

"Yes, I'm sure he will," Allison replied.

Dropping the subject he questioned, "How's our little Rose?" Rose was his pride and joy. He loved lavishing her with gifts. Nothing was too good for his granddaughter.

"She's just fine, and asking when you and her grandmother coming to see her? "Tell her we will be there this week-end." "I'll tell her and thank you for considering Gerald's request." She hung up the phone, relieved that she had done as promised. Now, hopefully Gerald would have no need for a return visit.

It had been several days since Gerald visited Allison and he hoped by now she had contacted Elliott Donlan. Knowing the bank was behind him he was getting impatient to start building his hotel, all he needed was that perfect piece of property. He called Elliott's office and was pleasantly surprised when the secretary informed him that Mr. Donlan had been expecting him. He asked if he could meet with him that afternoon. There was a moment of silence before she questioned if two o'clock would be okay. He agreed to the time. Hanging up the phone, he suffered anxiety, wondering what the outcome might be.

Elliott looked at his watch, Gerald Thomas was prompt it was exactly two o'clock. He stood to greet him and shake hands. It was an unpleasant shake; the hand was callused and seemed to have lost the strength that had caused calluses. Through the years, Elliott had learned a handshake told a lot about a man. He instructed him "Please, sit down Mr. Thomas."

As he sat, Gerald noticed a stack of papers on the desk and silently wondered if they concerned the sale of the property.

Elliott returned to his chair and clasped his hands together, then stated, "Mr. Thomas, I understand that you are interested in purchasing the property at cannery row with visions of building a hotel there, is that correct?"

Gerald hated himself for stammering. "Yes, that's, that's correct, I intend to build the largest hotel on the West Coast. I've already created one of the finest and this will be both, the largest and finest." Elliott knew the story behind Gerald's success and couldn't help but appreciate his ability to do as he said, even though he disrespected the man. He shook his head and exclaimed, "Mr. Thomas, the property is not for sale." The statement made Gerald's stomach turn. Trying to hold back his fury he questioned, why not?"

Elliott answered, "Blake has always said he would rent the property, not sell it. In fact, I believe my son hasn't sold a piece of land since the beginning of the depression. He just borrows against one piece to purchase another. I know he wouldn't want to sell. If you would be interested in a lease, that's possible. I have a long- term lease agreement written up that might be appealing to you, contingent of course that you do build the hotel. He handed Gerald the stack of papers in front of him stating, "Please take time to read these and then get back to me."

Gerald accepted the papers. Leaving the office he silently cursed both Blake Donlan and his father, telling himself bitterly, "They won't be happy until they own all of the bay area." That lot was the only one big enough left to accommodate a hotel the size he envisioned.

He spent the evening reading the agreement. The Donlan's were smart businessmen. The only way he could have his hotel was to let Blake Donlan finance the construction instead of the bank. Even though the interest rate was the same as the banks, it upset him knowing that Blake would be collecting the interest. The lease was for twenty-five years, with a twenty-five year option. Gerald realized he would eventually own the hotel, but never the property it sat on, damn how he hated Blake Donlan. The next day he begrudgingly signed the lease, refusing a handshake from Elliott.

Elliott hoped he hadn't made a mistake. He wasn't concerned with Gerald's ability to build a fine hotel. He was simply concerned about his character. The lease was long term and it would connect Blake to him for many years, unless Gerald did something to terminate the contract. Hopefully Blake wouldn't be upset, after all, he had left the decision-making up to him during his absence and had even given him power of attorney. Instead of placing several buildings on that piece of land, he had invested a large amount of Blake's money on just one building. Once again he went over his figures. Gerald's monthly payments, considering the long term lease, as well as interest on the loan, the investment should quickly be returned to his account. He shrugged his doubts, secure that the hotel would be successful. San Francisco was ready for such a building.

Chapter 4

She asked herself, how could it be possible that war was still going on? Allison applied a stamp to the letter she had completed to Blake, leaving her to wonder just how many she had written. She told herself that if she really wanted to know all she would have to do was count the ones she had saved from Blake and double it, since she received a letter for every other one she wrote. Now she was also writing Jonathon. He'd been drafted and her worries were doubled.

There had been a lot of changes. Tullah and Grange returned to the black community with Trent and Marshall, leaving Rose terribly upset. It had been difficult explaining to her that it was time for the boys to go to school elsewhere. She would continue to be tutored by Mr. Milton for another year before attending Blessed Sacrament Catholic Girls School. Allison could still see the look of confusion and anger on her daughter's face as she informed her that Trent and Marshall had to attend a black school, instead of the local school that would have enabled them to remain home. The boys seemed to understand the situation, thanks to Grange's many trips with them to the black community, in fact they appeared anxious. Poor Rose, she missed her father and now Trent and Marshall were leaving her. Oh, how she wished Blake was there to help her through this trying time. For a swift moment, anger surged through her, as she felt deserted. Then her eyes drifted to the newspaper on the table, sitting next to her coffee cup. The horrors and atrocities of the war blazed the headlines, and her anger was once again replaced with admiration for her husband.

A picture of Gerald passed through her mind. The hotel was to be completed with-in the next three months and all of San Francisco awaited its opening. She remembered the day Gerald returned to thank her for putting in a word for him to Elliott and insisting he take her to dinner. She tried to decline but he was insistent. When she did agree it left her feeling guilty, as though she were cheating on Blake, even though it was nothing more to her than dinner with a friend. The evening went well and Gerald was completely charming, she had enjoyed herself and it felt good to go somewhere other than the canteen. Since then, they had shared a couple of dinners together while she listened to Gerald discuss his hotel. He remained a gentleman, putting her at ease and leaving her happy for him. The bitterness the depression had left on him appeared to be over with. The letter to Blake was heavier than usual, a photo was included. She looked at her watch and realized the postman was due. Hurriedly, she brought it to the mailbox.

Blake felt the weight of his back pack. They had been marching for hours. He closed his eyes for a moment and visualized himself giving Rose one of her much enjoyed piggy-back rides, that helped ease the weight. He smiled to himself as he pictured her sweet face, so much like her mothers. Reaching into his pocket, he removed a photo that Allison had sent him. Allison appeared radiant as ever, Rose stood next to Marshall with his arm protectively around her and Trent stood looking ever so serious. Tullah and Grange were in the background waving, God how he missed them, but he told himself, not anymore than the men in front of him or the ones behind him missed their loved ones. He quickly returned the photo to his jacket pocket when the sound of a bullet whisked past his helmet, bringing him to the present. His only thought now, was to survive another attack. He felt his eardrums would explode from the noise as the bombs fell. Chunks of metal and dirt attacked him as he advanced towards the enemy with the rest of his troop. For the first time, Blake felt he might not survive this battle. He concentrated on the enemy, feeling lost in hell and time. Sometimes while in battle, what seemed like minutes were hours and other times what seemed like hours were only minutes. This one felt as though it was lasting an eternity. Suddenly, there he was in front of him, the enemy. This wasn't Blake's first hand to hand combat but experience didn't matter since each encounter was different. Once again he looked into another mans face filled with the same determination to live as he, two soldiers with adrenaline running through them, providing the strength needed for a life or death struggle. The force of their bodies met leaving both hoping the impact would take the other off balance, allowing time to use their bayonet. Both swayed but held their balance. Blake saw the tip of the soldier's bayonet glisten as it came towards him. He ducked, missing the blade. This time it threw the soldier off balance and Blake took the advantage, plunging his bayonet through him. The next thing he remembered was a hot, searing pain shoot through his shoulder. Another soldier had attacked him from behind. He felt the knife being pulled out, and turned around trying to protect himself from a final attack. The enemy screamed and lunged towards him for the kill. Suddenly to his surprise the man tripped and fell to the ground allowing Blake the moment needed to perform his deadly task. He stood in shock as he stared down at the dead soldier, realizing what had caused the man to fall. It was the body of the first man he encountered. The first soldier he killed had unwillingly saved his life.

Gerald shouted at the workmen, anxious to get the hotel completed. It was getting close to the scheduled grand opening and he doubted if he was going to be ready. He admired the dark green awning as it was being placed over the elaborate front entry. The large polished brass letters that hung over the revolving glass door read, The Grandview Hotel. It had been half a year, and in his attempt to complete the hotel he hadn't found the time he needed to pursue Allison, although, when his thoughts were not on the building, they were on her. He was probably the only person in the world that didn't want the war to end. If Blake should survive, his return could upset his plans. He needed time to hopefully regain Allison's love, feeling he could accomplish it now that he was successful.

The young nurse admired the handsome soldier she was tending to. As she changed the dressing on his shoulder she couldn't help but notice the scars on his hands and wondered silently what had caused them. Blake was anxious to return home, feeling secure that he had done his share in the war. There was another reason he was eager to return, Gerald Thomas. Elliott had written and explained the plans for the hotel and Blake agreed that it was a good investment but was left concerned that Gerald had entered back into Allison's life. Her letters should have left him with little to worry about. She always expressed her love, but the fact she had gone to his father in support of Gerald left him wondering if she still had feelings for him. Blake told himself that he had been out of control of his life for so long, perhaps he had become paranoid. The nurse finished her duty, leaving him alone with his thoughts.

Muriel started shaking as she read Blake's name on the register of soldiers wounded in action. The list never mentioned how severely. She set it down on the desk and put on her coat, wanting to reach Allison before she received the letter stating he had been wounded. Letters from the military were apologetic, but cold. First she had to find out exactly how badly he was injured and then what hospital he was in. After a couple of hours going through proper channels she had all the details the Red Cross and military could provide. The information was a relief to her as she hurriedly drove to the canteen to inform Allison.

Allison was busily preparing sandwiches when Muriel arrived. The smile Allison directed towards her faded upon noticing the serious look on her friends face.

"Muriel, what is it, what has happened?" Muriel was sorry that she couldn't hide her concern. She took Allison's hand in hers and exclaimed, "Allison, please trust me when I say there is no need to panic, Blake has been wounded." Allison felt herself becoming weak-kneed as Muriel continued. "It's a shoulder wound and he's going to be alright. The good news is, they're going to release him from the hospital next week and send him home, the war is over for Blake." Muriel watched anxiously, as Allison tried to comprehend all that she had just heard. A moment later she started crying uncontrollably and Muriel led her to a chair. The thought of Blake being hurt was unbearable. They were mixed tears, tears of relief and tears of happiness. She couldn't stop crying as she released almost two years of worry and fear hidden deep from with-in her, the fear she would never see him again. Several soldiers who had become fond of Allison became concerned and were relieved to discover her tears were not because she had lost her husband. A soldier whose name she now knew to be Arnold, kneeled down in front of her and took her hand in his and exclaimed, "I'm so happy the war is over for you and your husband Allison. He has a wonderful woman to return home too and you have a man to be proud of. I ship out tomorrow and I hope when I return you'll be waiting for me also, and pour me another cup of the infamous, canteen coffee." Allison wiped away a tear and stated, "I'll be here Arnold, waiting for your return. The coffee will be just as you like it, with cream and two lumps of sugar." She gave him a gentle kiss on the forehead, "I'll miss you Arnold. Take care of yourself." Now, Muriel wiped a tear while trying to remain optimistic as she remembered the list she read daily.

Blake looked out the small window of the military plane as it flew over San Francisco. Nothing appeared to have changed much in the time he had been gone, other than the large structure that now stood below taking up almost a city block, Gerald's hotel. The landing was smooth and Blake was eager to get off of the plane and set his feet on California soil once again, he loved San Francisco. The sun was shining and the bay was as beautiful as he remembered it. He had informed Allison he would be home today, but not when, explaining he couldn't picture their reunion at a cold military base, besides, there was something he wanted to do.

Allison peered out the window once more. This time her heart leaped as she saw the cab approach. The thought of it actually being Blake suddenly made her feel shy and nervous, much like that time he was invited to dinner. With the curtain aside, she witnessed the handsome man in uniform exit the car, paying the cabby. He turned towards the window and smiled at her. Suddenly she abandoned her shyness and cried to herself, "Blake." She ran to the door to greet him as he stood there gazing at her from behind a bouquet of wildflowers. In the middle were two roses, one had bloomed and the other just a bud. The sight brought tears to her eyes.

Blake fought to hold back his own tears as he opened his arms and engulfed her in them. He delighted in the feel of her and breathed in the aroma of her perfume that he knew so well, my God, had he really survived the war and was actually home? He hadn't been this elated since the day on the beach when Allison confessed her love for him.

"Daddy," a voice came from behind, drawing their attention. Allison stepped aside and Blake stared in amazement at his daughter. Pictures had done her little justice. She was as beautiful as her mother, and the last year and half had changed her from a little girl to a little lady. He had lost that time with her, but still remained steadfast that he had to join the war. "Rose," he held his arms and she ran to him. The exuberant embrace caused his wound to ache and Allison noticed a wince from him. Concerned, she stated, "Let's go into the house, you need to sit down Blake." He handed her the flowers and entered the home he had missed so badly, proud that the porch he had repaired still showed the signs of a job well done.

That evening Blake's parents came over to welcome him back home. He was glad to see them but his thoughts remained on Allison and bedtime. As they questioned how he received his wound, he merely stated a bayonet, leaving them to understand he had little desire to go into detail and relive the episode. Not even talk of the hotel could pull his thoughts from the large bed awaiting upstairs, it had been way too long. He ached to hold his wife intimately again and bury himself deep with-in her.

Finally they were alone and once more Allison had to fight shyness, even though her body longed to be with him. It had been so long since they had been together. Entering the bedroom, they both stood silently for a moment staring at the bed. Blake broke the silence exclaiming, "There's nothing I would rather do than pick you up Allison, and carry you over to that bed and remove your clothes, but unfortunately, right now my shoulder won't allow it." His statement overcame her nervousness and she exclaimed, "Blake, hopefully you won't consider me a harlot for saying this but there is nothing I rather do than lead you to the bed and help you remove your clothes."

Blake grinned and replied, "You know I could never refuse you anything." With a lustful smile Allison led him to the bed. Slowly she started unbuttoning his uniform jacket and set it aside. Blake started to remove his tie and she swatted his hand exclaiming, "I said I wanted to undress you." He stood speechless as she removed the tie and started on his shirt buttons, which upon opening, began to expose the hair on his chest. Allison's breath shortened as she observed the molded muscles underneath the naturally tan skin. Removing his shirt, she stopped momentarily, noticing the scar left from his wound. She touched it softly and then started kissing it. Blake wondered how much more of this he could take, she was driving him wild. Allison instructed him to sit on the bed while she removed his shoes and socks. Once that task was done, she had him stand while she removed his belt and trousers. A moan slipped from him as his hardened manhood was released from the garments that had restricted it. Witnessing this, Allison experienced a renewed aching between her thighs, and longed for the emptiness with-in her to be filled. Blake fought to restrain himself. Allison started to remove her own clothing and he watched as her body became exposed to him. He devoured her with his eyes and then pulled her on the bed next to him ignoring the pain in his shoulder, concentrating on an even greater pain elsewhere. Allison felt his hardness on her abdomen as he kissed her and ran his fingers through her hair. His tongue teased her ear for a moment before returning to her lips, while his fingers teased the most sensitive place between her legs, preparing her for his entry. Unable to restrain himself any longer, he entered her, and in the ecstasy of their lovemaking, they became one again.

Afterwards Blake held her close to him, stating, "Allison, The only regret I have for joining the service is the time I missed with you and Rose. This I promise you, I will never leave you again of my own free will." She held back a tear, thankful for his safe return and replied, "I won't forget this promise." Content, they fell to sleep.

The next morning, Blake was anxious to return to his office, as well as inspect the new hotel Gerald had built. He was more than ready to regain control of his life again and neglected to question Allison in regards to her concern for Gerald. Their lovemaking last night left him feeling secure. He pulled up to the curb and gazed at the building that a large percent of his fortune was invested in. He was impressed, telling himself, "Yes," Gerald Thomas had a talent for building hotels. Like his father, he knew it was a good investment and hopefully Gerald would be as good at managing hotels as he was at creating them. Anxious to get to his office, he decided not to go into The Grandview. He would wait for the grand opening, scheduled next week.

The office was as he left it, except for Dorothy. She decided to retire when he volunteered for service. The ships were still anchored in the bay, but now he looked at them guilt free, knowing he had done his time and could only hope that the war would end soon. It was a clear, warm day and Blake promised himself a swim in the bay, knowing it would be good therapy for his injured shoulder. There were many times he had sat in a foxhole trying to envision the bay and feel its cool water surrounding him. He decided his first job of the day would be calling the paper and placing an ad for a new secretary. Afterwards, his thoughts were directed towards Rose. Allison had informed him in letters that Rose was having a hard time understanding the separation from Trent and Marshall. Her outburst at breakfast that morning saddened him. After a lengthy discussion, he and Allison decided that it would be best for her to attend a private school, being the story of Roosevelt and Hattie, still lingered on the lips of the townspeople. In a private school, she would be more protected. Blake knew that money for tuition plus a very generous contribution to the school would allow her entrance, without questions. When they informed her it was time to let Mr. Milton go, and that she would have to attend a private school, she pleaded, "Please, I want to go to the school Trent and Marshall go to." I don't care what you say, she had cried, color shouldn't have anything to do with it. I can't help being white!" Blake sighed, color was the issue, as senseless as it seemed, and hopefully Rose would eventually come to terms with it. A picture of her young, innocent face flashed before him and he slammed his fist on the desk, grabbing his shoulder as a pain shot through it, silently questioning, "Damn, will all this nonsense ever end over race and color, Germans, Jews, blacks and whites? God help us." He remembered the Jews that were being annihilated simply because of their race. How could he answer Rose's question when he didn't understand himself, why color or nationality should decide a person's worth. He certainly couldn't tell her someday she would understand if he didn't.

Rose sat pouting in her room. She had hopes that when her father returned, he would be able to change things. Instead, all he did was confirm everything that her mother had told her, whites were not allowed at the black schools. For the first time in her life, she couldn't get what she wanted. She stared into the mirror and wished she were black.

Allison was jubilant that morning reliving having Blake beside her once more, she felt complete again. After their lovemaking, she had laid her head on his chest, enjoying the soft sound of his snoring. The words "I'll never leave you again" ran through her mind, completing her newfound happiness. She regretted he had to witness Rose's outburst that morning and wished she could have come to his aid but what could she say that she hadn't already discussed with her daughter? Each time the subject of race came up it reopened wounds in her over the loss of Aaron, wounds that would never completely heal. Her thoughts turned to Jonathon. His last letter informed her that he was in France and not to worry, he would return to her, and golf. She prayed silently, "Dear God let his words be true."

Marshall and Trent were doing well in school, at least as far as their grades were concerned. In the beginning, it seemed to Marshall that he was always breaking up a fight involving Trent. He understood the taunting Trent suffered over his jade green eyes, were usually the reason for the conflicts. "Hey nigger boy, where did you get those green eyes? Who messed with a whitey, your mama or your papa?" Trent had a quick temper and after a short time the green eyes were soon ignored.

Marshall looked forward to the weekends when they would go and visit the Donlan's. He especially missed Rose. The last time they visited he played and sang a song he wrote for her. Smiling, he remembered the delighted look on her face as she listened. The piano was his best friend, he confided in it through music. All his feelings flowed from under his fingertips onto the ivory keys, happiness, sorrow, and love. Once again he was grateful to the Donlan's, for having sent the piano with him when they moved.

The visits were also important to Tullah, after all Allison was like her daughter. They would sit and have tea and she would brief Allison as to what the boys were up to. Rose was everyone's concern. It was time for her to be in the company of other young women, and Blessed Sacrament seemed the answer. They realized that other than Muriel's children and the boys, Rose had little contact with her peers, having been tutored at home. Tullah was thankful that Blake was home, Allison needed him there now more than ever. She looked at the wall clock as Marshall and Grange entered the kitchen, it was dinnertime.

"Where's Trent," she questioned?" There was a moment's silence before Marshall answered, knowing his mother would find out sooner or later. "He had to stay after school again."

Tullah sighed, "What did he do this time?"

Marshall took a gulp of milk and replied, "The usual."

Now both Grange and Tullah moaned, "Another fight?"

Marshall shook his head, "Yes, but he was right. He was defending Negro rights and became frustrated when Buford Jackson said nigger's had no rights and never would."

"And what might those rights be," Tullah questioned?

"The right to live outside Nigger Town," Marshall replied.

Grange remembered his lecture to the boys on their first trip to the black community, telling the boys that none of the inhabitants were there by choice. He never imagined Trent would have taken it as seriously as he had, after all he was only a boy. Now, he was thirteen and adamant that blacks had rights, and that included, living where they pleased. Grange had many talks with him explaining that fighting amongst his own was not the way, but Trent had little, if no patience, with anyone who appeared to be defeated and accepting the situation.

Tullah was silent as she put the food on the table. Once more, a plate would be set aside for Trent, combined with a lecture to refrain from fighting. The three of them shared mixed emotions regarding Trent's obsession with black rights. Tullah was especially fearful, wondering had her and Grange misguided him, as she had done with his father. Grange feared for Trent, wondering just how long his obsession with equality was going to last. He hoped it would pass, fearing for his safety if it should continue on into his manhood. As for Marshall's feelings, he admired Trent for standing up for what he believed in.

Vera Thomas and her daughter scurried, preparing themselves for the opening of the Grandview Hotel. She swelled with pride. Her son was a success after all. The only thing putting a damper on the occasion was she had smelled liquor on Gerald's breath. Dear God, was he going to blow everything he had struggled for? She hoped this was just a rare drink, due to the excitement of the evening.

Gerald finished his bow tie and took another drink, convincing himself it was just for the calming effect it gave him and after tonight, there would be no more. He questioned himself, why was he so nervous? The hotel was magnificent in every respect, right down to the best chefs on the West Coast. The rooms were already booked up for two months, so what was there to worry about? He came to the conclusion that it wasn't worry that was eating at him, it was resentment and jealousy. He hated the fact that in reality, Blake owned the hotel, until it was paid off, and even then the property would never be his. The Grandview, his creation belonged to Blake Donlan. He cursed that Blake had returned from the war, and instead of being killed, he received the Purple Heart. A picture of Allison came to him. He hadn't the time needed to try and win her back, leaving Blake with everything. Damn, how he hated that man. He had been his nemesis every since that night he had tried to seduce Allison in the car. Tonight, they would both be attending the grand opening. Fighting his tension, he had one more drink.

Blake admired his wife, as she stood before him in a long, simple black sheath that clung to her body. The wedding pearls he had given her hung gracefully between her long neck and feminine bare shoulders. He placed a white fur stole around her and requested, "May I have the pleasure of escorting you, Mrs. Donlan, to an evening at the Grandview Hotel?"

He kissed her neck gently making her giggle, "I would be honored Mr. Donlan."

The hotel glowed in the dark as they pulled up and admired its grandeur. Blake handed over his car keys to a young man dressed in a uniform of hunter green, fastened with shiny brass buttons and gold braid on the shoulders. A doorman greeted them as they entered the lobby. Just as the guests before them had done, they gasped at the elegance before them. Now Blake understood why the expenses had been so great. European influence filled the room. They gazed at marbled floors and dark mahogany woodwork. Half a dozen crystal chandeliers lit the room, casting a warm glow over its occupants. Gigantic marbled and brass urns overflowed with the largest ferns Allison had ever seen. Tapestries decorated the walls and elaborate velvet drapes hung from the oversized windows. The lobby was crowded with people drinking cocktails while awaiting their turn in the dining room.

From across the room, Gerald gazed at Allison, telling himself she was as beautiful and elegant as the surroundings. He winced as Blake put his arm around her and gave her an affectionate kiss on the cheek. Forcing a smile, he approached them. "Allison, Blake, welcome the Grandview Hotel."

Blake didn't particularly like the way Gerald's voice lingered on Allison's name or the way his eyes seemed to devour her. Etiquette forced him to hold a hand out to Gerald and state, "Congratulations, the hotel is quite an achievement." Blake couldn't ignore the limp handshake or the lack of eye contact as Gerald responded with little enthusiasm, while still appraising Allison. Gerald's attention was solely on Allison as he stated, "Allison, I apologize for not taking you out at least once more for lunch or dinner before Blake's return but as you can see, the project kept me from it." Allison became flustered. She hadn't mentioned to Blake that she had gone out with him. Gerald, was pleased with Blake's reaction, he appeared stunned. After a moments silence Allison replied, "Dinner with a good friend is always enjoyable Gerald but I realize that you were busy and the hotel proves your dedication, it's beautiful." He thanked her and exclaimed, "Your approval is very important to me." Blake had to restrain himself. The man was pushing him to the point of no return. He grabbed Allison by the arm and led her away without any further acknowledgment to the detestable Gerald Thomas. The rest of the evening was very quiet for Allison as they ate a delicious prime rib dinner. Blake offered little conversation and she could see he was in deep thought. They only danced once and she could feel the tension in his body, causing her to regret any contact she had with Gerald. Their return home was silent.

Blake tried to convince himself that Allison's words were true, "Dinner with a friend." If that were true, why hadn't she mentioned it? Was there something to hide?

Allison cursed herself all evening for not having told Blake, she should have known that Gerald would mention the fact they had dinner together. Now, she knew Blake was waiting for answers.

Arriving home, Blake went to the den and poured a drink. Allison followed, wanting to discuss the situation before bedtime. She spoke, "Blake, I want to apologize for not mentioning to you that I had gone to dinner with Gerald, it meant nothing. He said it was just his way of thanking me for putting in a word for him with your father."

Blake replied gruffly, "It sounds to me he thanked you more than once!"

"We had several dinners together and he was a perfect gentleman." Blake sneered, "Gerald Thomas will never be a perfect gentleman. He's not capable of it."

Allison sighed, "I know you don't like him and once more, I apologize. You must, by now realize how much I love you." She approached him. "The young girl, that thought she was in love with Gerald, grew up a long time ago." He pulled her close, trying to discard the picture he had in his mind, of her and Gerald. He had to believe her, what else could he do? With a kiss he sealed his trust in her.

Gerald woke up in the room at the hotel that was permanently reserved for him. A young woman he vaguely remembered from the evening was in bed with him. She was draped around him and her voice hurt his throbbing head when she spoke. It was the most obnoxious sound her had ever heard. She was asking him that since he had taken her so quickly last night, would he care to try once more. All he wanted to do was escape the voice. He couldn't tell if the rank smell of the liquor was heavier on her or him. As she reached for him, he noticed that the mascara she wore had drifted off her lashes forming small, black half moons under her eyes. He leaped from the bed, leaving her grasping for him.

"Where are you going, she asked with a disappointed pout?" Gerald questioned what her name was. "Barbra," she replied.

"Well, Barbra, I have to go to work, I have a hotel to run." Once more, the voice grated on him as she questioned when they would be together again. Abruptly he answered, "Never Barbra, you're just not my type." A verbal lashing followed him into the bathroom as he showered. He was successful now and he deserved a lady, a lady like Allison, and he wasn't about to give up his obsession to have her and the property. Damn, why couldn't Blake have been a war casualty, everything would have been so much easier. When he returned, the irritating, Barbra was gone. A business card lay on the bed. He picked it up. It read Barbra Hennison. The throbbing in his head returned and his uneasy stomach climbed closer to his throat. Barbra Hennison, he recognized the name, she was heiress to the Hennison Oil Company. Under her name was a hand written note, turn over. He turned the card over; "You're not my type either. I've had more fun making love to myself, thanks for nothing." He laughed uncontrollably telling himself, this woman was capable of buying the Grandview a hundred times over, and he blew it.

The war was over and Allison once more awaited the return of a soldier. Blake, Rose, Tullah, Grange, the boys and her, all stood on the porch anxiously waiting for Jonathon to emerge from the cab. She held back tears as he came towards her. He was a man now, and the weary look on his face showed the signs of battle fatigue, which Blake immediately recognized. They all embraced and entered the house. When the initial excitement of his safe return calmed down, Allison prompted Blake, "Bring it to him now." Blake exited the room and re-entered with a new set of golf clubs, exclaiming, "It's your time now, Jonathon. You helped conquer the Germans, now its time to conquer the golf circuit." Jonathon choked up as he wrapped his hand around the shaft of a club, knowing that they were the best money could buy. He exclaimed, "I hope I still have what it takes." They all reassured him that he would play as professionally as he had before. He thanked all of them, silently hoping that he wouldn't disappoint them. Allison sat quietly, observing Jonathon and Blake, and thanking God for returning both of them to her. She had regained her belief in him, not destiny.

CHAPTER 5

Marshall played his music soft and slow. He enjoyed the weekday evenings at the bar. It allowed him time to play his own music, unlike the weekends when he had to work with the band. His thoughts drifted to Rose as he played another song dedicated to her. She was eighteen now and what he considered an American Beauty Rose. She was beautiful to observe but watch out for the thorns. He wasn't sure whom she inherited her wild ways from. Every since she graduated from the finishing school, she had become defiant. The sound of a quarter being dropped into his tip cup interrupted his thoughts. A familiar voice exclaimed, "Hey, Marshall, play something that will bring back the dead." Marshall smiled as he stared into a pair of jade green eyes.

"Trent, he replied, sometimes people like to play dead so they can escape life's reality for awhile." Trent smiled for a moment and then became serious.

"Well not me, I'm going to confront reality. I've been reading about some Southerners that are fighting for equal rights. Remember when your father told us that none of us belong here? Well, he was right. The only thing is, he never did anything about it. These Southerners are."

"Settle down Trent, good things come in time."

"Yes and now is the time." Marshall knew he could say nothing that would squelch Trent's enthusiasm, so with a grin, he hit the keys and Trent pulled a young girl to the dance floor. He loved Trent and remained frightened for him on his quest for equal rights. He also remembered the day Trent discovered the truth regarding his parent's deaths. He was fifteen and asking too many questions, so his Aunt Allison gave him his great grandmother's diary to read. Afterwards she explained the consequences of his parent's love for each other. Till this day his father's killer had never been discovered or brought to justice, leaving bitterness, eating away at him, especially towards his Southern grandparents. Marshall admired Trent as he danced. He was extremely graceful for a man that stood six foot three. He especially admired Trent's hair. It lay in soft waves unlike his tight curls and had a slight hint of red in it. Women loved him, referring to him affectionately as the "Green eyed devil," leaving Marshall wondering if there ever would be just one woman in Trent's life. He doubted it.

Rose was ecstatic. Her schooling was over and it was the end of having to wear the ugly navy and white uniform she detested. No more nuns and long sermons threatening her and her classmates with hell and damnation for merely doing things that seemed perfectly normal to her. What was wrong with partying and wanting to be with boys? It was finally time to live and she intended to do just that. Unlike her mother, she wouldn't be having a so-called coming out party, just a graduation party and this evening, the celebration was to take place. Smiling, she appraised herself in the full-length mirror deciding that she would wear the red dress, not the yellow one. Rose was almost a replica of her mother except for being slightly taller and having her father's deep blue eyes. She was pleased with the image in the mirror and especially liked the way the red dress showed off her newly developed curves, proud of the fact that both boys as well as men were showing interest in her. Satisfied, she left the room.

Blake and Allison observed their daughter as she entered the parlor. Blake swelled with pride that she had turned into such a beautiful young, woman. He was anxious to present her with their graduation gift, a new car, but Allison had persuaded him to wait until all the guests had arrived.

Allison was worried over the fact that Rose hadn't requested they invite any of her classmates. Her only concern had been if Trent and Marshall would be there. Dances were popular at the school she had attended, which allowed the girls to meet equally influential young men, but she never expressed interest in any of them. Knowing her love for Trent and Marshall, led Allison to believe that Rose would more than likely to fall in love with a black man. Either way, she knew, would be disastrous. If she fell in love with a white man, would he be as compassionate as Blake had been, once he discovered she had Negro blood? If she fell in love with a black man, would his peers shun her for having fair skin? Allison carried a deep hidden guilt concerning her daughter. She questioned if she had wronged her, for bringing her into a world filled with bigotry. Observing Blake, her heart ached with love for him and his lack of prejudice, which left her wondering if he also had the same hidden fears for Rose, if so, it hadn't been discussed.

   Blake embraced his daughter, giving her a kiss on the cheek before questioning the red dress. "You look beautiful sweetheart, but don't you think that dress is a little too revealing?" Rolling her eyes, she stated, "Daddy, I'm no longer going to be your little girl in the navy and white uniform. You must let me be a woman now." Blake sighed, stating that he would try. Allison smiled, remembering telling those words to Dorie the night of her coming out party, and also remembered her reply, "You may be a woman to all those men down there but you'll always be my baby." Yes, Rose also, would always be their baby.

   The guests arrived, Muriel and Chad with their children, Tullah, Grange, Trent and Marshall. Jonathon was on tour and unable to make it. Her grandparents arrived shortly there after. With everyone accounted for Allison finally gave Blake the okay to give Rose, her gift. The guests were instructed to follow them to the garage, where the car had been concealed. The door to the garage opened and Blake grinned, handing her the keys, pointing to a white Jaguar. Rose squealed with disbelief. "Is it mine?" Blake and Allison put their arms around her and replied, "Yes, then Allison stated, "We felt you earned it for having to attend Blessed Sacrament, and even though you almost got expelled a couple of times, you did finish." The guests laughed and then applauded her. "Can I take it for a drive," she asked excitedly. "No, Blake replied, not until you have a license. I'll take you down to get it tomorrow." Slightly disappointed for not being able to drive it that night, Rose kissed and thanked her parents and they returned to the house.

   She stood next to the piano listening to another a song that Marshall had composed for the occasion. Rose observed the way his long, lean fingers drifted across the keys with such ease, each one knowing its purpose. His voice was smooth. Romantic words drifted from his mouth as he gazed at the young woman standing before him. For the first time, the occupants in the room began to realize these were the words, of a man in love, leaving Trent the only one who knew Marshall had been in love with Rose since he was twelve.

   With the sudden realization that possibly her son was in love with Rose, Tullah's heart fell. She screamed to herself, No, this can't be. It was no longer pretend tea parties, they were in two different worlds, and society was still unable to accept such a relationship, the black community or the white. Rose was raised in the white world and that was where she belonged, with a white man, like her mother and grandmother. Tullah cried inwardly, would she have to suffer another loss like Aaron, if Rose loved Marshall in return? Would some racist kill Marshall not realizing that Allison was Negro?

Trent observed Tullah and knew what she was thinking. He remembered the story of his parents and the horror of their deaths merely for being in love. He was thankful that his Aunt Allison had found Blake. Once more bitterness overwhelmed Trent as he thought of the grandparents that had rejected him and his father for being the wrong color. He was determined to end the insanity of it all, racial discrimination had to end.

Allison took Blake's hand in hers as they watched the scene before them. She too, was beginning to realize that Rose could be in love with Marshall, or at least think she was. Quietly, she prayed it wasn't so, for everyone's sake.

Later into the party, Rose requested that Marshall be allowed to take her for a drive in her new car. Blake handed him the keys stating, "Don't hit the accelerator too hard!" Marshall smiled, "I promise not to test its power. I know what a Jag is capable of. Let's just hope Rose doesn't push the pedal too hard once she starts driving it. You know how wild she is!" Rose swatted at him, "Don't tell daddy that. I'm not wild." Blake tended to forget his daughter's temperament, and was suddenly beginning to wonder if he should have gifted her with such a car. With a heavy sigh, he watched as they pulled out of the driveway.

The drive was silent for the first mile then Rose questioned, "Like my new car?" He smiled and shook his head, "It's a dream. But I was serious when I mentioned to your father that I hope you don't use all the power this cars capable of. I know you, and it worries me." With a coy smile she questioned, "Do you worry about me a lot Marshall?" He glanced over, trying to ignore her now developed breasts and replied, "Yes."

Rose wanted to tell him she would be pleased if he would just stop the car and take her into his arms and tell her that he loved her. What she needed to know was if he loved her as a sister, or a woman. Was she reading things into the songs he had written? She continued the questioning. "If you worry about me that means you love me, right?"

Her questioning was starting to make him nervous. Once more, he answered, "Yes, of course." Before she could continue, he looked at his watch and exclaimed, "I have to get you back to the party. I play at the club tonight." Rose tried to hide her disappointment that he had dropped the subject so abruptly. Arriving home, he questioned, "Are you pleased with your car?" A simple yes, was her reply. He got out and opened the door for her. She exited and his heart skipped a beat, as the red dress slipped up to her thighs. Rose caught his quick glimpse and felt satisfaction. He congratulated her once more, followed by his usual kiss on the cheek.

Shocking him, she pulled his face down to hers, kissing him softly on the mouth, and stated, "There, that's what really pleases me." She returned into the house, leaving him speechless. Marshall ran his tongue over his lips and tasted the trace of her lipstick, then questioned if she was just having fun with him. Rose was well known for liking to shock people. Shrugging, he got into his car and drove to the club.

Tullah gazed at her son as he ate his beloved honey bun, accompanied now with a cup of coffee instead of a glass of milk. He was deeply engrossed in the newspaper. Since the night of Rose's graduation party she had felt a need to talk with him regarding Rose. Now would be a good time she decided, since both Trent and Grange were gone. She approached him asking if he would like more coffee. Glancing up from the paper he smiled and replied, "Thanks mama, I would." As she poured, she asked, "Can we talk for a moment?" He looked up again after hearing the concern in her voice. "Sure mama." She sat down across from him.

"Marshall, I noticed something the other night at Rose's graduation party that concerns me deeply." Marshall's body tensed. "What is it" he asked, feeling he already knew the answer? It had been almost impossible to conceal his true feelings for Rose the last couple of years. His mother looked directly at him. "You know how much we all love Rose. I always knew you loved her, but there's a big difference in loving her and being in love with her. If you have serious feelings for Rose you must curb them for both your sakes. As much as I hate seeing you hurt, I pray she doesn't love you in return."

Marshall stared back sadly at his mother before questioning in a sad voice, "How do you curb such a feeling mama? Tell me, I would happily do it if I could. Don't you think I know how hopeless my love for her is?" Tullah sat silent, hoping for an answer as he continued. "I have loved her as far back as I can remember and I can't tell you how many times I looked at her and wished her skin was as dark as mine or mine as white as hers, so there would be some hope. Rose is in my heart, my soul and even in my music."

Tullah's fears were confirmed and her mind drifted back to the night Aaron had come to her for advise, and how she had failed him. Marshall waited for a response. She reached across the table and held his hand in hers. "Son, I wish I had the answer. I know you just can't shut down your emotions, but you must never pursue your love for her. Rose is in the white mans world and that is where she must stay and you can't go there."

Marshall's hand tightened over his mothers and he exclaimed, "I know, and I have already made the decision to stay away from her as much as possible. It's difficult just to be in the same room as her. He stood and kissed his mother's cheek and left the room. Moments later, Tullah heard the piano. The song he played was a melancholy tune she had never heard before, but she was sure it had Rose's name in it somewhere and her heart ached for him.

Gerald Thomas walked his usual path through the hotel. It had been five years and yes, it was a great success. He had been able to make all the payments to Blake and still created a very prosperous living for himself. In another few years he figured the hotel would be his and he would be debt free. The only draw back was the never- ending bitterness that the property would never be his. He didn't care if it was a long- term lease with a renewal, he wanted the whole package and it was a constant thorn in his side knowing it would never be his completely, God, how he hated Blake Donlan. The fact that Blake was also prospering from the hotel, constantly ate at him. He watched over the years with continued envy as Blake devoured even more of San Francisco's prime land for himself. Resentment welled up inside him as he entered the bar and ordered a whiskey. He gazed at the amber fluid and was thankful for the relief it offered him. He had fallen into drinking again. The only difference was that when he was with Annabelle he had no goals other than waiting to inherit her money, so drinking until he was oblivious wasn't threatening. Now, he had a goal and only drank enough to keep calm and be able to concentrate on the immediate problem, Blake. With his success came an unending stream of beautiful women but none were able to give him the satisfaction he needed, Allison's image always interfered. She had been his at one time, but the collapse of the stock market and the depression had robbed him of both his family inheritance and her. He laughed to himself before downing another shot remembering his youthful arrogance, years before. He had been so sure all he needed to do when he was through trying the available women in town, was to go to Allison and propose, then the Marshall and Thomas fortunes would be combined and he would have had it all. "The Great Depression, they called it. "What the hell was so great about it?" he mumbled before slamming the glass on the counter startling the lone drinker next to him.

CHAPTER 6

The gloved hand set a small bouquet on the already floral crowded gravesites. The air was crisp as Lydia Barnum wrapped her coat closer to her. She stared at the tombstones, once more reliving the tragedy of Aaron and her daughter's deaths. Both were so young, and so in love. The tears flowed freely now, no longer to be hidden. Douglas had been dead for almost a year and if he had anything to do with Aaron's death, it went to the grave with him. Only once, shortly after the murder he mumbled something in his sleep saying he hadn't told them to do that. She knew better than to question it. The decision to return to San Francisco and look up her grandson had been an easy one, now that Douglas was gone. Through the years of his illness it had been her intent to do so at the first opportunity. She returned to the waiting cab. Tomorrow, she would go see Allison and hopefully, meet her grandson.

Allison and Rose were both enjoying a novel when Allison was informed that there was a Mrs. Barnum to see her. Rose watched concerned as the color drained from her mother's face and her hands started trembling, causing her to set the book on her lap.

"What is it mother? Who is Mrs. Barnum?" Allison was silent for a moment before instructing Rose to leave the room, exclaiming that she would tell her later. Rose did as she was told, disturbed at being excluded from the stranger's visit. As she made her exit, Rose passed the elderly woman and wondered what possibly she could have done to create such an effect on her mother.

Lydia entered the room and marveled how well Allison had retained her beauty through the years. As for herself, she knew the years had been cruel to her appearance. Sorrow was permanently etched on her pale face and her hair had grayed shortly after Aaron and Melissa's deaths. The years of care she had given to her ailing husband left her thin and shapeless.

Allison was the first to speak. "What brings you back to San Francisco Lydia?" She waited for the pathetic figure standing in front of her to reply. "I've come to see my grandson."

Allison couldn't believe what she had just heard and it took her a moment to state, "You surely can't be serious Lydia, it's been twenty years, and may I add, nothing has changed, he is still a Negro." The words stabbed at Lydia as she fought to hold back tears. Bitterly Allison continued, "Have you and Douglas grown senile in your old age and forgotten?"

Lydia spoke, her voice quivered as she choked out her words. "Douglas died last year and unfortunately, he was a bigot to the end. I myself have prayed everyday since the deaths of Aaron and Melissa to be forgiven for my actions. I know my request to meet my grandson must seem incredible to you, and I understand, but I pray you'll believe me when I tell you I have wanted to seek him out for years, but my marriage to Douglas prevented it. I shamefully admit that I wasn't brave enough to leave him. I was also to blame for what happened, but I beg you to try and understand, I was just an innocent, brainwashed Southerner. Please don't hold that against me. I couldn't help it anymore than Aaron could help what color he was, it was my breeding."

Allison grasped Lydia's last words and suddenly shocking her self, she felt pity for the emaciated woman standing in front of her. She replied in a much softer voice, "Trent doesn't live here with us. He lives in the black community. If you want to see him Lydia, you'll have to go there."

Lydia sighed with relief. It appeared Allison was going to help her. "His name is Trent," she questioned"? Allison informed her that it was his grandfather's name. Lydia asked, "Does he know the cause of his parent's deaths?"

"Yes, we told him." The fact that Lydia hadn't questioned if Aaron's killer had ever been caught, reaffirmed Allison's belief that Douglas Barnum was responsible, one way or another. She had to ask, feeling now that Douglas was dead Lydia might confess his involvement. "Did your husband have anything to do with Aaron's death Lydia?"

With tired eyes, Lydia stated, "I honestly don't know, but it's possible." Allison believed the woman was speaking the truth. Lydia watched as Allison went to her desk and jotted something on a piece of stationary.

She handed her the paper, "This is Trent's address. I could give you his phone number, but you have a better chance of seeing him if you just go to where he lives, at least he can't hang up on you. Be prepared, he's very bitter towards you."

Lydia accepted the paper, expressing her gratitude. Allison watched the pathetic woman as she exited the room, and caught herself silently wishing her luck.

Rose returned to the room immediately after the woman's departure, anxious to find out about the mysterious stranger. "Who is she mother?"

Allison instructed her to sit down, deciding it was time for Rose to read Dories diary. Thus far, Rose only knew she had Negro blood in her from the photos on the mantle, but had never been told the whole story. She handed Rose the little book and stated, "I will tell you who Lydia Barnum is after your done reading." Allison left the room, leaving her daughter alone to discover Roosevelt and Hattie.

She turned the pages slowly, reading the fine penmanship of her great grandmother. Completing the book she tried to absorb all that she had read, being more intrigued than shocked by the diary. Lillian Marshall had never guessed the truth about the twins.

Allison returned, sat down and exclaimed "Now I'll tell you the rest of the story. Rose listened with fascination as her mother talked. That was until she got to the part where Trent was born and how Lydia Barnum fitted in. The fascination turned into horror. She interrupted her mother asking if Trent knew how his parent's had died. "Yes, Allison replied, causing Rose to shriek, "I don't understand how you could even consider letting that woman re-enter into his life!"

Allison sighed, "She's his grandmother, and he knows the story. It's up to him to shut her out if he wants to, not me."

"Well, I hope he tells her to go to hell," Rose declared as she stomped out of the room. Silently, Allison thought, that's more than likely, is what will happen. She went to the phone to forewarn Tullah that Lydia Barnum would be arriving.

Rose lay on her bed, her thoughts on Trent. No one, including him had ever wanted to talk about what had happened to his parents. She had only questioned it once and quickly realized it was not a topic to be discussed. Now she knew, and the horror of it weighed heavily on her. She observed the framed photo of her Trent and Marshall that had been taken last year. Now, the contrast in their coloring jumped out, as it had never done before. Her mind drifted to Marshall. There were no longer any songs written to her. She wondered if the kiss she gave him at her graduation party was what had distanced them. Then again, maybe he was frightened at the thought of loving her because she appeared to be white. Especially, after what had happened to Trent's parents. She let out a moan, once more regretting her fair skin.

Lydia repeated the address to the cab driver once more. He questioned, "That's nigger Town, are you sure you want to go there, lady?"

"Yes, I'm sure," Lydia stated, quietly thinking to herself, that Southerners were not the only racists. The ride seemed to last forever, and she was becoming uneasy wondering if her grandson would treat her cruelly and send her away. She wouldn't blame him if he did but she had to take the chance. Observing her surroundings as they drove created concern in her for Trent. The blacks here lived a little nicer than the Southern blacks but not much. Her heart raced when the cabby informed her they had arrived. Lydia observed the neatly painted and well kept home in front of her as she exited the cab and was pleased. She informed the driver to wait for her. Tension and arthritis caused her body to ache as she climbed the steps and knocked on the door.

Tullah answered, still unable to believe that the woman had the gall to show up looking for Trent after all these years.

"Is there a Trent Marshall living here?"

"Yes, Tullah replied coldly, but he's not here right now." Lydia couldn't hide her disappointment and questioned, "When will he be home?"

"Tullah replied, I expect him anytime now." Lydia sensed the woman didn't like her and excused herself, informing her that she would wait a short time in the cab.

An hour later, Tullah looked out the window and she was still there waiting. The cab driver appeared to be taking a nap. She shook her head at the thought of the fare. The sound of the back door slamming told her that Trent was home.

He entered the room and knew something was wrong by the expression on Tullah's face and questioned, "What has happened?" She looked at him and then returned her attention back out the window. Going to the window he followed her stare. "Who is it?" Tullah faced him and replied with a whispered voice, "Your grandmother." It was as though the wind had been knocked out of him as he gasped, "What is she doing here?" "She's come to see you."

The old lady noticed the two of them peering from the window and pulled herself from the cab. Once more she experienced pain as she climbed the stairs. Tullah answered the door, leaving Trent standing stunned in the living room. With-in a few moments they entered the room and Trent observed the tiny structured woman. This was his grandmother? He momentarily wondered where his grandfather might be and why she came alone.

Remaining speechless, Lydia walked towards him and let out a small gasp as she got closer and observed his jade green eyes. "You inherited your mother's eyes," she exclaimed!"

"Yes, I did, he replied and I also inherited my grandmother's black skin. He then demanded, "What do you want?"

The gruffness in his voice startled her. "I'm your grandmother and I want to get to know you."

Trent snarled, "It's too late old lady, go away." She flinched at his words as he and Tullah left the room. She stood there alone for a moment and then returned to the cab, telling herself that she would try once more.

Tullah was not surprised by Trent's reaction to his grandmother and listened as he stated, "I just can't believe that she would just try to walk into my life after twenty years like nothing had ever happened and suddenly my being a Negro doesn't bother her. What the hell did she think I would do, say I think its okay that you and my grandfather's bigotry destroyed my parents and robbed me of them? God, she must be crazy!" After a moments silence he mentioned, "The old man wasn't here with her, he must still have his wits!"

Tullah broke her silence "Douglas Barnum died last year according to Allison."

"Good, Trent replied coldly, I hope he suffered."

Tullah was not used to seeing her sweet Trent, act in such a manor even though she understood. "Your Aunt Allison also told me what made her decide to tell Lydia where you lived." Silently, he waited to hear what it possibly could have been. Tullah continued, Lydia told Allison that she was born a Southerner and raised as one. Racism was something she was taught from the cradle. She claims she had no more control over her breeding than you did with yours. If you think about it Trent, both of you are innocent victims."

Trent sat quietly, dwelling on Tullah's words, making him even more determined to fight for equal rights. Not only did blacks need to be free from racial extremists, the extremists needed freedom from their bigotry. The insanity of it all had to end. Still, he couldn't find it in his heart to forgive his grandparents for what they had done. Hopefully, the old lady would go away and forget him just as she had done twenty years ago.

"Come on Jeffrey, please." He watched as Rose finished off another drink. They were returning from a wedding and both had been celebrating since noon and it was now eight o'clock in the evening. Another please came from her.

"Rose, you must be crazy. I'm not taking you to Nigger Town. Why would you want to go there anyway?"

She smiled and exclaimed, "I have some very special people that live there and one of them is a piano player in the band. Let's go listen to his music and dance."

Jeffrey tried to resist as Rose pushed herself against him and nibbled on his ear, purring, please. The thought of relinquishing his evening with her while she was in such a seductive mood prompted him to finally agree, despite warnings from with-in.

It was a busy evening at the Jack of Spades. The band was playing loudly to the boisterous crowd. Marshall's fingers skimmed across the keyboard while Elmira, the bands lead singer stood next to the piano admiring his ability to bring so much life to the ivories. Marshall always appeared happy to her when he was at the piano but when he walked away from it he seemed to leave that happiness dormant on the keyboard until his return. Something was hidden deep with-in him and she wanted to know what it was. Even though they had been intimate, he remained a stranger. It was time to give the crowd a slow dance and she began singing one of Marshall's songs.

Marshall smiled at her. Oh, how she could sing his music. Her voice was sultry and the words of love floated smoothly from her, wrapping themselves around all that listened. She returned his smile leaving him wondering why he couldn't fall in love with her, she was a beautiful woman. As usual, the only answer was Rose.

"There it is" Rose exclaimed. Once more Jeffrey tried to convince her it wasn't a good idea. Already they were receiving suspicious looks from the town's inhabitants but now Rose was extremely drunk and out of control.

"If you don't come in with me Jeffrey, I'll go all by myself. I want to surprise Marshall." Reluctantly, he parked the car, took a large drink from the bottle and escorted her into the loud, crowded, smoke filled bar. Rose was oblivious to the attention they had created. Unable to see Marshall through the throng of people, she decided to dance. By now, Jeffrey was as inebriated as Rose, both ignoring the intimidating looks from the crowd. Especially from the women, who found themselves losing the attention of their men.

Rose had on a dress that clung to her like a perfectly wrapped gift, leaving all the males wondering what it would be like to remove the wrap and discover what surprises lay inside the package. Rose gyrated to the music, lost in its rhythm. Suddenly, Jeffrey felt ill and left her unaware of his departure. A large man approached her and exclaimed, "Seems your partner has left little white lady, may I have the rest of this dance?" Rose was confused as to where Jeffrey had gone and consented to dance with him. They continued on to the next dance, a slow one and Rose recognized the music. "My friend wrote that song," she announced. The man was suddenly holding her much too close and she could feel the hardness of his manhood against her causing her to become somewhat sober and frightened. Suddenly another man interrupted the dance, asking for a turn. The large man ignored the request, and a fight broke out. The disturbance caused the band to stop playing and the dance floor became deserted except for Rose and the two men. Marshall couldn't believe his eyes telling himself that perhaps all the smoke in the room was playing games with him. He blinked several times hoping, that was it. No, it really was Rose in the middle of the disturbance. "What the hell was she doing there?" He ran to her just as the larger of the two men won the battle. He put his arms around her and she cried out his name. The man grabbed Marshall and pushed him to the floor, returning his attention to Rose. Marshall measured the man. He was probably about three inches taller than he and carried an easy fifty pounds more weight. A quick decision was made to try and talk him down. He stood and confronted him, "Hey brother, this is a friend of mine and she's not only drunk, she's just a kid. Why don't we all just get back to having a good time?"

The man exclaimed, "I plan on having a good time. She doesn't look like a kid to me. She must have come here looking for some black meat and I have a lot to give her."

There was an instant reflex as Marshall smashed the man in the face. He felt his knuckles split as they made contact. His victim stood dazed for a moment and then grabbed him, punching him in the stomach, knocking the wind out of him. For a moment, Marshall's thought drifted back to the stables that one day when he had protected Rose from the horse. He heard her scream and he looked up. She was kicking the man and he gave her a shove, sending her to the floor. Before landing, she hit her head on the corner of a table leaving her unconscious. The sight enraged Marshall and he started to rise.

"Okay, okay, break it up." It was the owner, Jack. He called the large man by name and instructed him to sit down or get out. He leaned down to help Marshall up. Elmira tended to Rose.

Jeffrey returned asking, "What happened?" Marshall grabbed him by the collar and shoved his face into his before asking, "Why the hell did you bring her to this place?" Jeffrey, coming out of his drunken state answered, "Because she begged me to. She said she had a friend here that played piano and wanted to surprise him."

Marshall loosened his grip and demanded, "Get out of here now."

"He questioned, "What about Rose? I can't go without her."

"I'm the friend she wanted to surprise and she succeeded, I'll bring her home." Jeffrey appeared relieved and quickly made an exit. Marshall returned his attention to Rose. She was still unconscious. Jack instructed him to carry her to his office above the bar. Gently Marshall picked up his burden and carried her up the stairs. His concern didn't go unnoticed by Elmira. Now she was beginning to understand the reason for Marshall's unhappiness, he was in love with a white woman.

Marshall laid her on the bed and ran his swollen fingers through her hair searching for the results of her fall. A sigh of relief escaped him, as he discovered no abrasions, just a large lump.

"Rose, Rose," he shook her gently knowing he had to awaken her, fearing a concussion. He watched anxiously as her eyelids began to flutter. She murmured something before instinctively reaching for the lump on her head. Then she focused on Marshall and tried to sit up. He pushed her back down.

"Stay put for awhile Rose, you had a fall, and hit your head on the corner of a table. He wanted to reprimand her for her actions but looking down at her lying there left him speechless.

Rose noticed Marshall's bleeding and swollen hand. Panic overwhelmed her as she cried to him, "Your hand Marshall, your piano hand, it's my fault. I just wanted to come here and surprise you and listen to you play with the band. I didn't know it would turn out like this."

In his concern for Rose, he had forgotten about his injury. He looked at the damaged hand and tried to reassure her that it would be okay, even though he had a little doubt. She reached up and pulled his hand to her mouth and started kissing it gently. Her tears stung as they fell into the wounds and she begged, "Please forgive me, I'm so sorry."

Marshall knew she was innocent of her actions, after all, between himself, Trent and his mother and father, she was raised with a mostly black family, which left her little reason to fear the black community. What she didn't realize was that a white woman, especially one like her amongst black men inevitably would create a problem. She was much too tempting in that dress. Marshall understood the large mans desire as he pulled her head away from his hand and wiped her tears gently with the unharmed hand.

"I love you so much Marshall, Rose said in a whimper of a voice, much like a secret that must not be heard. Their eyes locked and after a moment, he lost all restraint. He leaned over and kissed her long and passionately and became surprised at her fast response. Almost immediately he felt the pressure of his manhood begging for satisfaction. Everything he ever imagined about her was correct. He became lost in passion as he explored her warm body, the perfect breasts with the taunt nipples, the curves and the warmth between her thighs. Suddenly his mother's words rang in his ears, "She belongs in the white mans world." He pulled away, resenting the interference, but knew the voice was right, she could never be his, not if he loved her, and he did. Trying to regain his composure, he prayed to God for the strength he needed.

Rose was left breathless as Marshall retreated from his intimate assault on her. He had just awakened all sexual feelings that had been hidden deep with-in her, leaving her anxious to surrender her virginity. She had been with many young men for her age but until now just enjoyed the game of teasing, not delivering. No one aroused her as Marshall had just done. She reached for him trying to get him to continue, not wanting to relinquish the moment.

"No Rose, this can't happen. The only love I am allowed for you is that of a sister, not a woman. Your white and I'm black, together there is no place for us."

Rose cried, "I don't care about the rest of the world, I just care about us and I don't want you to look at me as a little girl or sister anymore, I love you and I'm a woman now."

Marshall let out a small bitter laugh, "Yes Rose, I know you're a woman now and for years I convinced myself that when you grew up we would be together, it was a young boys dream. We can't live in a dream world Rose. We have to live in this one. He stood and exclaimed, I need to take you home, your parent's will be worried.

Rose became defiant, "Yes, Marshall, take me home. Obviously you don't love me enough to say to hell with everyone."

Marshall stared directly into her eyes and exclaimed, "If it were easy as saying, to hell with everyone I would do it Rose but that's not reality, we have to share the world with others, were not alone. For God's sake, look what happened to your great grandmother Dorie, your grandmother Trilly and your Uncle Aaron. Nothing has changed."

Rose silently admitted to herself that all three relationships had ended in tragedy. She also knew the day Marshall and Trent were sent away to school had been her first realization that there were two separate worlds.

Suddenly the door opened and Jack entered the room asking if Rose was all right.

"Yes, Marshall replied, I'm taking her home." Jack looked at Rose and stated, "Don't come back here again, it's no place for a white woman."

Rose stiffened at his statement and exclaimed, "It appears that whites are not the only ones with racial problems."

Jack was silent for a moment before replying, "Don't get on your high horse with me young lady. Many a black man has been either tortured or executed because he merely looked at a white woman. We may not be in the South but there's a pact. White and blacks don't mix." Rose challenged him, "What would you say if I told you I have Negro blood in me?"

Jack scanned her before replying, "I would say it's damn well hidden, so keep it that way, you're better off." He turned to Marshall and stated, "I hope you're smart enough to know what you have to do." Noticing his hand he exclaimed, "It appears the band will be without a piano player for awhile. You better get that taken care of." He left the room leaving the two of them alone with their plight.

Marshall respected Jack and was regretful for what had taken place. He also knew Jack was upset not only because of the disturbance, Elmira was his daughter and she had never tried to hide the fact that she was in love with him. He instructed Rose it was time to leave.

Allison paced the floor as Blake watched. Where was their daughter? It was three o'clock in the morning. Silently, Blake was happy that they had only produced one child. Rose was enough. It seemed to him that he had been telling her to slow down every since she got home from school. There were times he wished her Irish blood hadn't been so domineering. A car pulled up and they both rushed to the door. Relief and anger surged through them as they observed Marshall leading her to the door. They rushed to meet them.

Blake questioned, "For God's sake, what's going on? We were just about to call the police." Rose remained silent as Marshall spoke.

"Rose decided to surprise me with a visit to the bar last night. A little trouble broke out but she's okay. I'm sorry, I should have called you." Blake and Allison looked angrily at their daughter. Blake stated, "Since it appears you have nothing to say for yourself, go to bed, it's late."

She broke into tears exclaiming, "I have a lot to say but I learned this evening that nothing I say changes anything, so why bother?" She fled the room leaving the three of them momentarily silent from her outburst.

Marshall stated, "She's had a long night and realizes that she made a mistake by coming to the black district."

Blake patted him on the shoulder, "Thanks for taking care of her." Allison hugged him stating how he always seemed to be there for Rose. Guilt surged through him as he wondered how she would feel if she knew his true feelings towards Rose. He bid them goodnight and drove back to where he belonged, there was only one place for Negro's.

Thankful for their daughter's safe return and both weary, Blake and Allison returned to their room hoping to finally get some sleep. That didn't come easy for Allison as she lay there wondering what really had happened that evening. The fact that Rose had gone to the bar to see Marshall pretty much convinced her that the two of them were in love. Rose's statement, "I have lots to say," left her wondering just what it was. She would talk with her later on. She snuggled up next to Blake and appreciated the warmth of his body and the secure feeling she felt, grateful that she was able to be with the man she loved. Sadly, she knew that Rose would be robbed of that privilege. A silent prayer fell from her lips for her daughter and Marshall. "Please don't let this happen. I love them both so much, spare them the suffering."

Rose, lay in her room, reliving her encounter with Marshall, if she ever questioned what she felt for him might have been brotherly love, disappeared that evening. What she had experienced was a woman's love for a man. She touched her lips and remembered the searing paths his had left them. Her heart skipped a beat as she closed her eyes, recalling the way he touched her. A small cry escaped her as she realized the helplessness of her situation. How could she live a life knowing she could never be with the one man she loved? Her thoughts drifted to Melissa Barnum and her Uncle Aaron, telling herself, "Their love never had a chance and either will mine." Exhausted, she finally drifted off to sleep.

Marshall drove home slowly as he relived the moment he had been hoping for every since he had become aware of his male emotions for Rose. His body ached at the thought of if he had taken her completely. Still, he took pride in the fact that he restrained himself. Had he pursued and satisfied his desire for her, he would have betrayed the Donlans, to which he owed so much. Suddenly pain shot through his hand. Through the ordeal he once again had ignored his injury. He looked at the swollen knuckles as they lay on the steering wheel and wondered how long it would be until he could play again.

Tullah heard her son's late arrival. Trent had stopped by the bar after the incident and Elmira informed him of Marshall's ordeal, of which he passed onto her. She felt the ache in her heart for her son and she too prayed. She prayed that Rose didn't love Marshall, that way only one person she loved would be hurt. Now that he was home, she rolled over hoping to get some sleep.

It had been over a week since Lydia attempted to see her grandson. She had no desire to live in San Francisco but was determined to remain until Trent made peace with her, even if it took the rest of her lifetime. Once more she climbed into the cab, having to convince the driver she wanted to go to the black community. On her arrival Grange was the one to inform her that Trent was not there. She insisted he tell her where he could be found. Grange sighed, "He's down at the pool hall on Second Street." She returned to the cab, instructing him to deliver her to the hall.

The cabby watched with curiosity as the elderly woman entered the building, asking him self, "What the hell could she possibly want in there?"

Murmurs drifted through the room at her entrance, leaving the patrons wondering the same thing as the cabby. The room was dark after entering from the bright sunny day out side and it took her a moment to adjust to the change. Scanning the room, she was finally able to focus her attention on Trent. He stared at her in disbelief as she approached him at the pool table. He demanded, "What do you want old lady?"

"My grandson," she replied. The murmurs in the room silenced as the occupants witnessed the confrontation.

Trent exclaimed, "It must be difficult for you having to stand here in a room full of Nigger's looking for a grandson! Let me spare you, he's not here, go away." When she didn't respond, he set down his cue stick and left her standing alone once again. All watched with quiet curiosity as she slowly left the room and entered the waiting cab.

Trent stood in the men's room and slammed his fists on the counter top. The vision of her standing there was lodged into his brain. She looked so pitiful and lost. Why did she have to show up after all these years? Accepting her into his life would be impossible. She was still a Southerner, therefore bigotry was deeply seeded. Hopefully, he told him self, this would be their last encounter.

Wearily, Lydia instructed the driver to return her to her hotel. She sat back in the seat and decided she would try approaching Trent again in a few days.

Allison smiled as she hung up the phone. She had been talking with Jonathon. He called to inform her he had just won the Atlanta Tournament. He also informed her that he was about to be married. "I fell in love with the editor's daughter of Sport News Magazine, she was covering the golf tournaments." Rose entered the room and raised a brow, much like her father did before asking a question. "What are those?"

Allison held several tiny baby frocks on her lap. She held one up and replied, "These were made by your great grandmother Dorie, for Roosevelt and Hattie!" She enjoyed the rare opportunity to use the names.

Rose reached for one of the garments and marveled at the tiny handmade stitches, causing her to realize the act of love that had created it. She questioned, "Why are you looking at them?"

"They remind me how much Dorie sacrificed because of her love for us. She was willing to go through life not claiming her grandchildren. Instead she took on the role of our nanny. It was her act of love, safeguarding us from our Negro blood. Unfortunately, even though many years have passed, we still need that safeguarding. I guess what I'm trying to say is, if you love Marshall, you will sacrifice that love for both your sakes." Allison waited for a response.

Rose felt her Irish temper rising and answered defiantly, "No, no more sacrifices because of color. I'm both black and white and I should have rights to both worlds because of it, not just one."

"Then you do love Marshall."

"Yes, mother, I do and I refuse to be intimidated."

"It's not that I want to intimidate you Rose, I am merely stating the facts. Neither one of you can be in each others world, I'm sorry; it's just the way it is."

"You sound just like Marshall."

Allison was relieved to hear that Marshall understood the situation but she also knew her daughter's determination and hoped he was strong enough to sacrifice his love for Rose and reject her. Deciding the conversation was over Rose stomped out of the room, leaving her mother discouraged.

CHAPTER 7

The beach was deserted this time of year, which Blake preferred. Through the past few years of swimming, his shoulder appeared to be back to normal. He was now able to swim as far as a quarter of a mile from shore and back. He took a deep breath before throwing his body into the cold, brisk waters of the bay. As he reached the point of return his attention was drawn to the sound of a motor boat. To his disbelief, it appeared to be speeding directly towards him. Still disbelieving, he continued to watch. Horrified, he realized it was directed at him and whoever was driving had no intentions of changing its path, reminding him much like a torpedo zeroed in on its target. With-in moments, the craft was nearly on top of him. He dove, ducking the motor's blade. He came up for air, only to find the boat was just a short distance away. He watched for a moment, until once again it headed towards him. He started swimming to the shore with hopes of making it to shallow waters for protection. The noise of the boat's motor drew nearer and now he was sure that someone for some reason was trying to kill him. As it neared, he filled his lungs and dove for safety.

"Damn him," Gerald cursed. He couldn't let him get away. He had planned this for the last few months, watching what time Blake went for swims and on what days he pursued his habit. He even had to purchase a boat and he hated being on the water. In fact he didn't even know how to swim, but he needed to get rid of Blake Donlan once and for all. He cursed again and scolded himself for not taking more time to learn how to maneuver the boat. He needed to surround him in a tight circle, hoping to tire him until he drowned. Gerald was proud of his scheme and sure that Blake's death would be considered accidental. Silently, he thanked

Blake for swimming in the remotest part of the bay. He took another drink from the bottle of whiskey as the boat sped towards its victim, convincing himself that with Blake out of the way Allison would return to him and then he would have it all, the hotels, the property, and her.

Gerald's theory was working. Blake was tiring and knew if he didn't get to shallow waters soon the unknown assailant would win, he would drown. The shore was still a distance away and again the boat's motor roared in his ears. Blake realized a cry for help would never be heard. This time he dove instantly, hoping the driver would lose track of him. He watched, as the boat's propeller passed by, then something caught his attention, it was a piece of driftwood. He swam towards it. The knurled piece of wood was much larger than he had hoped for. Had it been ashore, it would have been impossible to move. The water gave it the buoyancy he needed to hopefully maneuver it the last minute into the speeding boat's path. He waited for his attacker to return. His weight caused the piece of wood to sink, just below the water's surface, hiding it from view. Blake figured that at the rate of speed the boat was traveling, if he dove the last second, whoever was maneuvering the craft would not have time to swerve from the hopefully destructive path. Blake tensed as he relied on his combat skills to face the enemy. The boat and driver were approaching him once again at high speed. With self-discipline he waited until it was almost on top of him, then dove, shoving the driftwood into its path. A chunk of wood grazed his head as he watched the boat flip and the unknown assailant fall into the water. Now he used what little strength he had left to swim to the safety, to exhausted to even make an attempt to save whomever it was that had tried to kill him. As he lay on the deserted beach, struggling to rebuild his strength Blake wondered who it was that attacked him and why?

It happened so fast, Gerald didn't have a chance to prepare himself. Suddenly, he was in the murky water and there was no air. An attempt to scream for help was of no avail as the water rushed in and filled his lungs. Fighting for the breath of life, the last thing he witnessed was Blake's image, blurred by the water, swimming away. His final memories were just as he had heard of people drowning. His life passed before him, the carefree years, the Great Depression, Annabelle and another fortune lost, the Grandview Hotel and Allison. As the shadow of death surrounded him, he wondered if it held anything for him, surely, there must be more.

Blake tried to answer the coastguard's questions. The best he could do was to try and explain the attack to them. There was one witness, a beachcomber that had come to aid Blake as he lay on the beach.

"Yes, I saw it," the shabby, toothless man exclaimed excitedly. The driver of the boat was trying to kill this man. It looked like he was attempting to hit him but it appeared he was having a difficult time maneuvering the boat."

A policeman that arrived on the scene instructed Blake to get into the patrol car and he would take him to the hospital, exclaiming, "You need medical attention." He chose not to call Allison from the hospital. Arriving home, she was waiting for him as usual in the living room reading a novel. As he entered, observing his condition, her smile turned into concern and confusion. Running to him she cried, "Blake, what has happened?"

"I'm alright," he exclaimed, I'm still not sure why, but someone tried to kill me while I was swimming." He continued his story. Allison gasped. Like Blake, she had no idea who would attempt such a thing or why. Suddenly panic overcame her, as she feared that whoever killed Aaron was trying to do the same to her husband. The phone rang. Blake answered it and remained silent for several moments. Allison suffered with anxiety as she waited for the call to end. Finally, he hung up after thanking whoever it was and turned to her exclaiming, "They have identified my assailant!"

"Who was it," she asked? The suspense was agonizing as she awaited his slow answer.

Blake looked her in the eye and announced, "It was "Gerald Edwards." He watched as the impact of what she had just heard sunk in. Allison couldn't believe it, not Gerald. "No, she cried, stating, Gerald has been bitter every since the depression, but I don't believe he would do such a thing, why would he? He has his hotel and is successful. Everything that was lost, he regained and then some."

"Everything but you Allison," Blake replied.

Allison dwelled on his statement before asking "Is he dead?" Blake nodded yes, and awaited her reaction. She went numb. She no longer loved Gerald but he had been a very large part of her life. She realized how badly the depression had changed him and had mentioned how much he cared for her but she felt it impossible that he would go to such extremes to get her back. No tears were shed as she exclaimed, "I don't understand why he would want to kill you, surely he couldn't have believed that I would ever be his, our relationship ended over twenty years ago!"

Blake replied, "Perhaps his ego encouraged him. I can only guess that maybe he felt if I were out of the way, you might fall in love with him again. After a moment of thought, he continued, also with me out of the way, he may have had hopes of not just gaining you but the fortune you would inherit." It suddenly started making sense to Allison. That sounded more like Gerald than he was just driven by love for her. He might have succeeded in killing Blake. The thought made her tremor. Blake put his arms around her and exclaimed, "I put up a good fight. Remember, I told you I would never leave you again!" Chills ran down his spine as he quietly envisioned the confrontation with Gerald.

Allison pulled away from him and questioned, "Do you think he had anything to do with Aaron's death?" The thought had never occurred to Blake. He contemplated for a moment and replied, "I doubt it, there was nothing to gain, but then again, what was there to gain for anyone, with Aaron's death? I just don't know Allison?"

Vera Edwards shed dry tears for her son. The autopsy report declared Gerald had been intoxicated during his attack on Blake. She had been aware of Gerald's hatred and resentment toward him over the hotel but never would have guessed he would have gone to such an extreme. Alcohol had destroyed her son's brain. She sighed, tomorrow she would bury her son and then talk with Elliott and Blake Donlan regarding The Grandview Hotel.

Vera observed the two men sharing the room with her and marveled at their resemblance. The years had been good to both the father and the son. Elliott Donlan spoke. "You've come to discuss the hotel, correct?" Vera knew what she was about to say would turn Gerald over in his grave, but she was too old to take on the burden of a hotel the size of The Grandview. One hotel was all she needed.

"As you know, I have inherited The Grandview and I intend to sell it. I'm assuming that you, her eyes turning to Blake, will want to make the purchase. If so, let's discuss a selling price and if not, I'll put it on the market tomorrow." The offer came as no surprise to the two men, knowing how difficult it would be for her to maintain the business.

Blake questioned, what price, have you come up with Mrs. Edwards?"

She replied "You still carry a small loan on it and you know how much it cost to build. Here are the profit and loss statements, look them over and then make me an offer. I trust it will be a good one Mr. Donlan." She handed him the papers. Accepting them, he promised to let her know with-in twenty-four hours, both already knowing his answer, he would purchase The Grandview.

Elmira stated, "It's good to hear your music again." It had been almost a month since the incident with Rose at the bar and Marshall had done a lot of thinking. He would join Elmira and the band and go to Los Angeles. They had received an offer from a scout to record one of his songs, Elmira would be the vocalist. The timing couldn't have been better. He needed to escape his hopeless situation with Rose.

Elmira began to sing as he exercised his fingers on the keyboard. Her arms and voice gave him comfort as she stood behind him, feeling the warmth of her body against his back. He silently wondered how Rose was going to take the fact that he would be leaving. Hopefully she would understand.

"I can't believe your doing this!" Rose cried, over the phone. I thought you loved me."

"I do love you Rose and that's why I'm going. Please try to understand, it's for the best." She heard Elmira's voice in the background and questioned, "Are you taking her with you?"

He was quiet for a moment before answering, "Yes, she's an important part of the band and sings my songs."

She pleaded, "Please don't leave me Marshall, I love you and need you. You've always been there for me."

His heart felt as though it would burst as he replied, "I'm sorry Rose, I have to do this. Just remember, I'll always love you." Before she could reply and weaken his decision, he hung up.

Rose stared at the voiceless phone. Anger surged through her as she resented his weakness. Unlike him, she had been willing to sacrifice and fight for their right to be in love. It hadn't occurred to her that he had just sacrificed himself. Allison entered the room and questioned her obviously disturbed daughter. "What has happened?" Rose informed her of Marshall's decision. Silently, Allison thanked her dear, sweet Marshall for knowing what was best for Rose. Once more he had unselfishly protected her.

Lydia climbed the stairs to the church. She had been informed that Trent was there for an equal rights meeting. The church was crowded but she managed to find a seat. Trent was at the podium speaking. She swelled with pride as she watched the audience grasp his words and cheer him on.

Trent stared in disbelief as he spoke. The old lady stood out in the crowd, with her white skin and hair, a shocking contrast next to the other occupants in the room. She caught his glance, smiled and sent him a timid wave. Ignoring the jester, he returned his attention back to the congregation and completed his speech. Several other men spoke, but none as well as Trent, Lydia proudly concluded. When the meeting ended, she sat there alone, hoping that he would come to her. The room emptied and she continued to wait. After several minutes she decided that once more she had been denied. Walking towards the door, a voice demanded an answer from her, "What do you want from me?" She froze and her heart performed a flip. Without turning, she replied, "My grandson and a chance to help him with his cause and his destiny."

"Destiny, what is my destiny, old lady?"

She turned and faced him. "To fight for everything you spoke about this evening. Equal rights"

"He questioned, "And just how can you help me with that?"

"Come back to the south with me. Segregation in the south is what you need to help conquer first, then the north. I have enough money for you to attend college at Tuskegee. It's full of young men and women like you, getting educated and ready to fight for integration. There's power in numbers Trent, join them, come with me." I know nothing I can do, will right the wrong your grandfather and I did to you and your parents. I'm not asking for forgiveness, just a chance to help you in your cause, a cause I also believe in. Racism robbed me of my daughter and grandson. Trent suddenly found himself feeling something towards the elderly lady standing there before him, seemingly honest in her newfound belief's. He had to admit he admired the determination in her pursuit of him. He weakened, smiled and clapped his hands; "If I had of known you were going to give such a speech I would have sent you to the podium." His smile warmed Lydia even though she wasn't sure if the remark had been sarcastic. Trent walked towards her and held out his hand and marveled when hers met his. It was so small and white compared to his. Incredulous as it seemed to him, this was his grandmother. "Let's talk," he said, motioning her to sit.

She exclaimed, "Perhaps I should tell the cab driver to go on. I can call him back later."

"I'll take care of it, he replied, now sit down, I'll be right back." Lydia waited his return. The church gave her a feeling of calmness and she gave a quiet prayer of thanks. Trent returned and suggested they go somewhere and have a talk over a cup of coffee.

"If you don't mind I prefer tea!"

"Then tea it is," Trent replied. They walked a couple of blocks and entered the restaurant. Curious eyes followed the unusual twosome as they seated themselves. The hefty waitress asked for their order, "What's it going to be?"

Trent stated, "I will have a cup of coffee and my grandmother wants tea." Hearing the request, she looked at Lydia, so pale, and then at him. She rolled her eyes and replied, "Yeah, sure, your grandmother wants tea." She walked away leaving them looking at each other with silent grins. Despite the grin, Lydia had to brush away a tear, he had called her grandmother.

They talked for sometime, discussing the advantages of moving south with her. Neither brought up the subject of his parents, he felt that he already knew enough, what more could be said? He observed her excitement at the thought of participating in his cause, and believed in her sincerity. She reached across the table and placed her hand on his. "Trent, please come with me. I can't change the past but hopefully I can help towards changing the future! He rested his hand on hers, and her heart skipped a beat as the eyes, so much her daughters, looked directly at her and stated, "I promise you, I will give it thought." She squeezed his hand, "That's a start, and what I hoped you would say, thank you." Trent looked at his watch and exclaimed, "I better take you home now. I have work in the morning!" Lydia objected, "No, call a cab for me." Trent replied, "You found me, now you're going to have to deal with me. Once my mind is made up, don't try and change it, I'm taking you back to the hotel, your not taking a cab." She remembered his father and the first time they met. She had been so impressed with his demeanor. Now, here she was with his son, so much like him. Oh, God, she cried inwardly, how could I have been so misled? Once again, she silently mourned the wasted lives of her daughter and Aaron.

On the ride to the hotel, Lydia questioned, "Where do you work?" The question automatically made Trent ease up on the gas as he replied, I work for the newspaper."

"Which one, she questioned?"

"The same one my father worked for, The Bayside News. I run the printing press." Lydia stated, "I remember your father speaking highly of the editor, Mr, she hesitated, oh, I can't remember his name"

"Cunningham," Trent replied.

"Yes, Mr. Cunningham."

Trent. Sighed before announcing, "He was a good man, died last year. He was always after me to pursue journalism."

"He was right, Lydia exclaimed, especially if you want to help establish equal rights. You've heard the statement, "The power of the press. That's what you should major in." He pulled up in front of the hotel, stopped the car and replied, "You've given me something else to think about." He got out of the car and opened the door for her.

"Please call me Trent, here's my number. I'm not returning home until I hear from you." He noticed her hand shaking and took a hold of it. "I promised you I would let you know, and I keep promises." She thanked him and stood on her tip toes, kissing his cheek and stated, "Even though we have been apart all these years, never a day went by that I didn't think of you. You were always in my heart. Hopefully with what few years I have left, you will let me spend them with you." She turned and walked slowly into the hotel.

Tullah and Grange listened intently as Trent told them of his encounter with his grandmother at the church and her offer. Grange spoke first. "Trent, there's a big difference between the South and San Francisco. I have feared for you here. There, white supremacy is extreme and rules. The southerners are not going to give it up easily. They have the KKK. What you are trying to achieve is very dangerous, even if you have several hundred of our brothers with you." Tullah, shook her head in agreement. Trent observed the two people he loved and exclaimed, "I know it's dangerous, but I feel the need to follow my goals, and Lydia is giving me the opportunity to pursue them. Besides that, all of you have been after me to go on to college, and in the south is the only place I could attend, just another reason to fight for the cause. They both sighed simultaneously and agreed to support him in any decision he made.

Now it was Allison listening as Trent told her of Lydia's proposition. What she heard made sense and she always did want Trent to go to college, but until now he showed little interest in having to leave San Francisco to attend a black university. She was sure Lydia was sincere with her remorse over her upbringing, and she had suffered the penalty for it with the loss of her child. Fighting to overcome guilt for letting a Barnum back into their lives, she stated, "Trent, Lydia has made the long trip here to regain the grandson she gave up years ago. I feel she's suffered through those years for turning her back on you and unable to do anything about it until the death of Douglas. If you can forgive her, so can I."

Trent embraced her, "Thank you aunt Allison. I'll go with her because I believe she's right. I can accomplish more in the south right now than I can here. Allison quietly marveled. She would have never guessed that it would be Lydia Barnum that would inspire Trent and convince him to continue his education. She also was concerned for his safety, but kept it quietly with-in herself.

Rose felt as though her world had come to an end. First Marshall left her and now Trent was leaving. She couldn't believe that he would go with his grandmother after what she had done. She remembered the expression on his face when she brought the subject of his parents up. It was heartbreaking. He stated that was the past and nothing he could do would change it, but he could have some impact on the future.

It had been almost a year since the incident with Marshall, at the bar. He wrote letters to her parents, keeping them updated, although Tullah did the job quite well. She gazed at a favorite photo of Trent, Marshall, and her as children, eating ice cream cones. "Oh, she cried to herself, we were so young and blissfully innocent of the real world." For the last year she dated many times and had come to the conclusion that no one could replace her love for Marshall. Her parents offered her a European trip, which she turned down, in fear that Marshall would change his mind and return. If that should happen, she would need to be there for him. The holidays were nearing and her heart skipped a beat as she conspired a way to see

Marshall once more. Her Uncle Jonathon and Aunt Peggy resided in Los Angeles. They could go spend Christmas with them. She knew Grange and Tullah would be welcome as well. Yes, then Marshall would surely join the festivities. Anxious to make her suggestion, she set the photo aside and went downstairs.

Allison laid down her needlework when Rose entered. She knew her daughter had been suffering terribly the last year and felt completely helpless in the situation. They had been able to give her anything she wanted, but the one thing she wanted the most, carried too high of a price tag. She listened as Rose talked excitedly at the prospect of going to Los Angeles for the holidays. It was obvious to Allison that she was hoping to see Marshall, not wanting to destroy the little bit of excitement Rose had shown in months, she replied,

"Let's discuss this with your father tonight at dinner. It sounds like a good idea." Rose left the room in good spirits, leaving Allison, with the silent conclusion that it might be good for Rose to see Marshall once more. Maybe if she saw that he was content, she could let go.

That evening they approached Blake with the idea.

"Why not, he exclaimed, the holidays will seem awfully empty without the boys here. We need to be with family and my parent's will be in Ireland this year for Christmas, there couldn't be a better time to go. Besides that, we haven't seen Jonathon, Peggy and the kids in a long time." A smile crossed his face as he observed the two of them already in deep discussion, preparing for the trip.

Marshall sat at the piano, reading Jonathon's request that he attend the festivities. Elmira questioned, "Who's the card from?"

"It's from Jonathon. He wants us to come to his place for Christmas. My family will be there."

"That sounds great," she liked Jonathon and Peggy. They had come to the nightclub several times to listen to her and Marshall's music. She was also anxious to meet his parents. Her smile suddenly disappeared when he mentioned that the Donlan's would also be there, because that meant Rose. She remembered the hell she had been through with him this last year watching him try to conquer his love for her. She had been willing to accept the fact she was a second choice but wasn't prepared to spend an evening watching him suffer all over again. "I'm not going," she exclaimed!

Marshall understood her reaction and replied, "I hope you'll change your mind. I don't want to go alone, but I have to go. My parents will be there and the Donlan's are just like family. I lived in their home and was given the same privileges as Rose and Trent. They helped provide for me as a child, as well as buying me my first piano. Not only do I owe them, I love them."

"You don't have to tell me how much you love them, Elmira shouted. I know your love for Rose." Marshall remained silent and after a moment she calmed down and went to him.

"Baby, if that's what you want, I'll go. I'm sorry. I just don't want to see you hurt again. Just remember, I love you, the way you love her, so you should understand how I feel." He reached for her and pulled her close, resting his head on her stomach.

"Believe me Elmira, I do love you." He couldn't control a smile as he felt his child move with-in her.

"I know you do baby, she said softly, now let's practice that new song of yours."

The house was festively decorated for Christmas when the Donlan's arrived from San Francisco. The only thing missing to make it post card perfect was the lack of snow, which was very unlikely to happen in Los Angeles. Jonathon and Peggy greeted them, while their three children smiled in the background. The inside of the house was decorated with the warmth of the season. An ornamented tree stood proudly in the window; decorated packages lying beneath it, garlands of fir and holly draped the rooms, while vases of Poinsettia's were scattered throughout the house. Fresh baked cookies filled the air with a spicy aroma.

Jonathon questioned, "Where are Tullah and Grange?"

Blake replied, "They should be here shortly. He smiled. There was a lack of room in the Cadillac once all the Christmas packages and luggage were packed, so they followed in their own car."

With-in minutes, Tullah and Grange arrived and the greetings were repeated, leaving Jonathon especially pleased with the reunion. It had been too long since they all had been together. Between his successful golfing career and Peggy's job with her father's magazine, which she refused to give up, plus three children, they had been unable to get away. Tomorrow would be Christmas Day and Marshall would be joining them. Other than Trent's absence, this would be a special holiday.

After dinner, Christmas Eve was spent indulging in hot eggnogs laced with brandy, as they discussed the events in their lives. Rose listened carefully, and for the first time realized what they really had gone through. She held back a tear, knowing her fathers love for her mother and wondered if she would ever find that kind of love?

As they drove up, Elmira admired the house. "It's so festive," she exclaimed, while admiring the tree in the window. Marshall agreed, as he opened the car door for her. He was nervous with the reunion. Jonathon and Peggy knew of his and Elmira's relationship, but not his parents or the Donlan's. He knocked on the door and with-in moments Jonathon opened it and greeted them. "Everyone is here" he exclaimed as he led them towards the living room. Marshall became tense as they entered the room. His mother squealed with delight as she ran to embrace him. The rest of the party took turns greeting him. Rose remained across the room, devouring him with her eyes. He looked wonderful, and her heart raced as she anticipated being alone with him. That was until she noticed Elmira, now visible through the crowd. Her heart froze in her throat like a huge cube of ice, leaving speech impossible. Marshall glanced across the room and acknowledged her. He felt weak, as his feelings for her surged through him. Now was the time, he told himself, it had to be done. Oh God, he didn't want to hurt her. He preferred to keep all the pain to himself. He helped Elmira off with her coat, thankful that her pregnancy was not yet visible and announced, "Everyone, This is Elmira, her and I were married yesterday!" The room was momentarily soundless. Jonathon and Peggy were the first to break the silence and congratulate them. Tullah knew that due to their music, Marshall was close to Elmira, but he had spoken very little about her. It all seemed so sudden. Still, she was pleased. She approached Elmira, and put her arms around her exclaiming, "What a Christmas present, it appears that Grange and I now have a daughter." Grange smiled and congratulated them.

Allison and Blake watched their daughter with concern as she and Marshall gazed painfully at each other. Rose wanted to leave the room but her legs wouldn't take her away from the scene. Allison tried to conceal a sympathetic tear, as she went to her daughter, and led her away, hoping that she knew they were as shocked as she was.

She sat next to Rose on the bed, handing her a hanky, giving her a moment before speaking. "None of us knew Rose. It was a surprise to all of us." Silence was the only response she received. She continued.

"Rose, we all know how much Marshall loves you. I believe even Elmira does, but you must let go, as Marshall has done and get on with your life. The most you can do for each other is pray that you both find happiness. Someday, hopefully, with people like Trent fighting for integration, black and whites will be able to live freely amongst each other in a color blind world. All we have is hope. If integration succeeds in the South, we will do everything we can to make it as successful in the North. We can help pave the way so that something as wonderfully simple and pure as love, can survive, despite color. Rose remained silent for a moment contemplating her mother's words. Yes, she knew Marshall would always love her and she him, knowing that was going to have to be enough for her, but not the next generation. Hurt turned into anger. Too many of her ancestors, including herself had suffered lost loves. Like Trent, she now had a goal. Wiping the tears from her eyes, she put her arms around her mother and thanked her.

Allison wiped away her own tears and replied, "Lets go downstairs, the house is filled with loved ones and it's Christmas."

Elmira watched as Marshall took Roses hand and led her out the door. He had told her that he needed to talk with Rose. A rush of jealousy surged through her momentarily until she observed the ring on her finger and put her hand on her belly. The jealousy was quickly replaced with sorrow for the beautiful, young woman.

Once they exited the house, Marshall released Roses hand. The feel of it in his was too intense. The loss of the closeness tore at Roses heart. His hand in hers gave her such a complete feeling, a feeling she now bitterly accepted with his withdrawal, as a hopeless dream. He was a married man. Marshall turned and faced her. "Rose, you have to believe that I love you and always will. If people would allow us our love, I would never leave you, but that's not the way it is. Elmira is a fine woman. She's carrying my child. Unlike poor Trent, it will be welcomed into the world because it's what people accept, a black child from a black couple."

Rose stared at him through tear bleared eyes as the realization sunk in. Defeated, she replied. "We could have had such a beautiful child, you and me." He put his arms around her. "There's no doubt in my mind that we could have." Silently, they returned to the house, both now bitterly accepting the fact that their love would exist, but without each other.

Returning home the next day a package awaited Allison. It was addressed to Allison (Hattie) Donlan. Eagerly, she opened the festive box. The contents consisted of newsletters and articles from Trent. A note read, "Grandmother discovered a check made out to Douglas's cousin, Dexter Honeycutt, a member of the Klan. She's suspicious and has hired a detective to research Dexter's activities at the time of my father's death. I'm hopeful that his killer will finally be discovered. The note renewed in Allison how much she still missed her brother and she whispered his name, Aaron (Roosevelt) Marshall. A news clipping caught her attention. She smiled. It was a large group of blacks, holding protest banners and in the middle of it all was a small, white, gray haired lady with a determined look on her face. Her banner read, abolish racism. Allison carefully folded the note and clippings, before lovingly tucking it into Dorie's diary, which was no longer hidden away. It now had a place of honor on the library table, next to her chair.

ABOUT THE AUTHOR

Dyann Marie Webb was born to be a writer. That desire has always been in her heart and soul. When she writes, it's as if she is actually there living amongst her characters. She spends much time and research making sure her novels are accurate to the times and places in which they occur. Once you start reading Roosevelt and Hattie you will find it nearly impossible to put aside.

Her life has never been an easy one. After her father passed away in 1954, her homelife became unbearable. Her mother, loving but alcoholic, moved from one abusive relationship to another. Barely fourteen years of age, Dyann left home and began supporting herself as a waitress, making enough money to rent a small apartment.

She married, gave birth to three sons, and later divorced. Dyann worked many jobs, including ownership of a custom framing shop, while supporting her family.

Now in her mid sixties, Dyann lives in Sumner, Washington and works as a sales clerk for a major department store. She hopes to someday retire so she can continue her real passion, writing.

Dyann has written two other fine novels, soon to be published.

CPSIA information can be obtained
at www.ICGtesting.com
Printed in the USA
JSHW031155250423
40806JS00005B/250

It's the turn of the century, and wealthy industrialist James Marshall brings home to his wife Lillian twin infants. The children are accepted as his deceased sister's offspring, when in fact they are his own, conceived with his Negro mistress Tilly, who died giving birth.

Three generations of mixed blood make it possible to believe they are descendants of an English mother and French father. The twin's natural grandmother Dorie accompanies them as their nanny…and begins her diary.

Lillian Marshall immediately changes their names from Roosevelt and Hattie to Aaron and Allison, names more acceptable in their white community. Within a year Lillian, thought to be infertile, gives birth to Jonathan and the three siblings are nurtured in the wealth of the Twenties.

The fall of the stock market October 28, 1929, changes their lives forever, creating a family struggle to survive.

On a foggy night the lives of Marshall, Lillian and Dorie are lost in an automobile accident. With very little left of the Marshall estate, Aaron, Allison and Jonathan are forced to sell most of their possessions. In the process of gathering Dorie's belongings, her diary is found-and the true secret of Roosevelt and Hattie is revealed.